Shojo Beat

love★com

Story & Art by
Aya Nakahara

love★com

contents 6

The Story So Far...

Risa and Ôtani are their class's lopsided comedy duo...except that now, Risa's fallen in love with Ôtani! With the support of their friends, Risa screws up the courage to tell him how she feels...only to be turned down. Even so, she decides not to give up on him just yet...

But then, Ôtani's ex-girlfriend Mayu (very cute) suddenly shows up and wants to see him! Funny Girl Risa thinks it's all over for her...but for some reason, Ôtani tells Mayu he can't get together with her. A faint flicker of hope lights up again in Risa's heart...

So when Valentine's Day rolls around, Risa plans to give Ôtani a "for real" valentine—but thanks to Haruka bursting into their classroom and causing a scene, now everybody knows he turned her down before. This makes Ôtani feel he can't accept a "true love" valentine from Risa, and he rejects her homemade chocolate offering for the second year in a row! Risa, however, says Ôtani did nothing wrong, and forces him to take it...

♥ To really get all the details, check out *Lovely Complex* vols. 1-5, available at bookstores everywhere!!

Shojo Beat

love★com

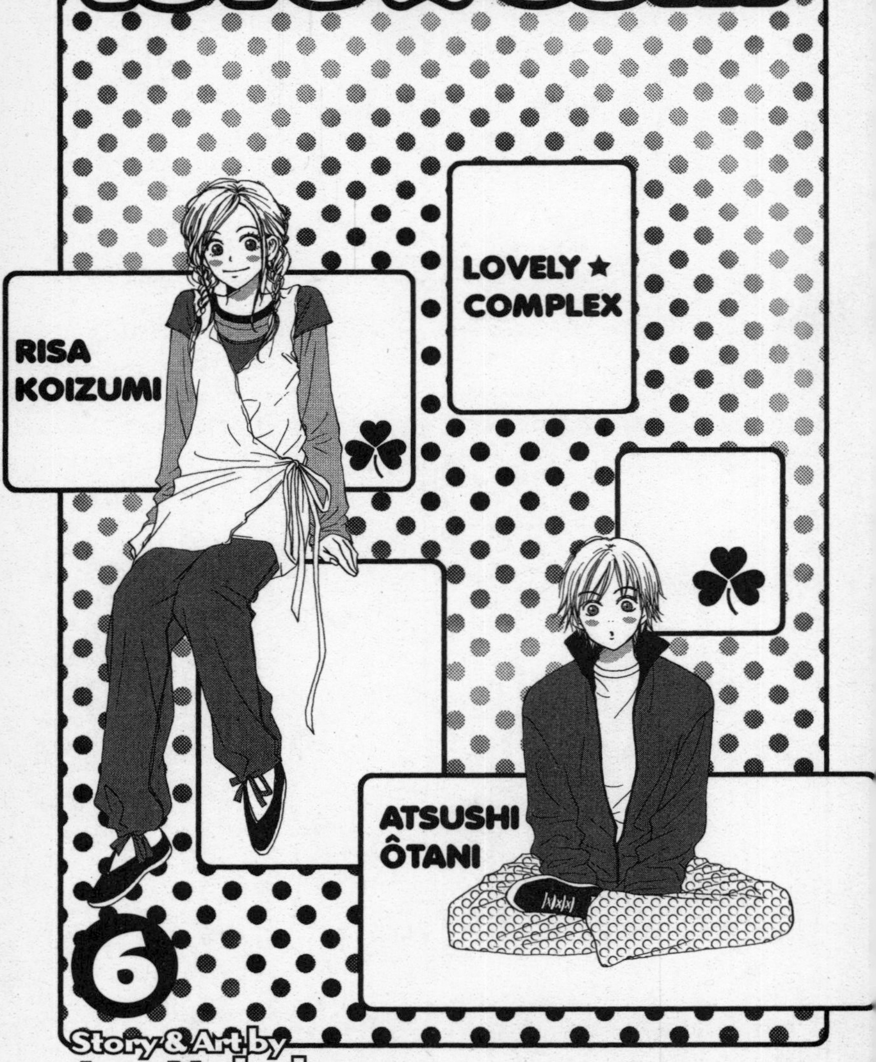
LOVELY★
COMPLEX
RISA
KOIZUMI
ATSUSHI
ÔTANI
6

Story & Art by
Aya Nakahara

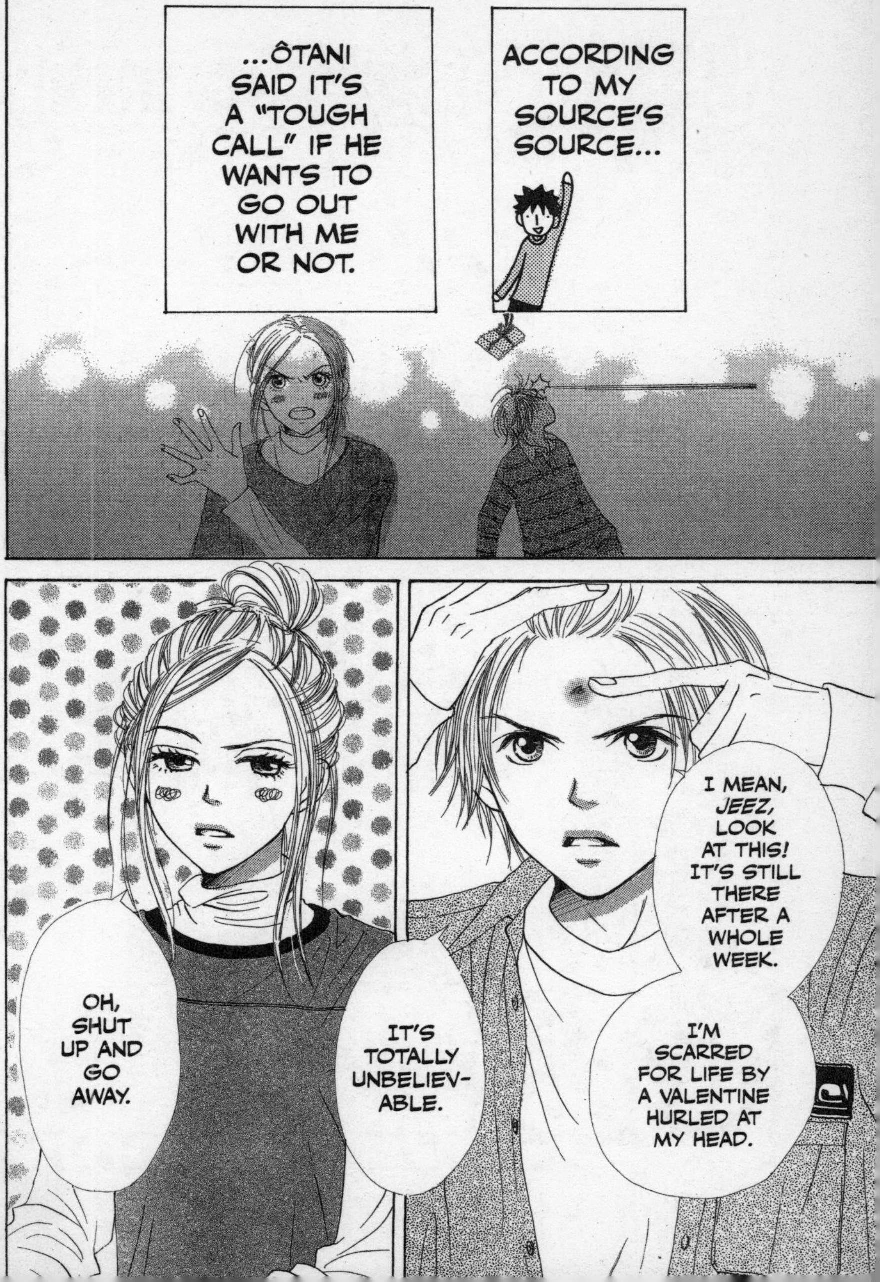
ACCORDING TO MY SOURCE'S SOURCE...
...ÔTANI SAID IT'S A "TOUGH CALL" IF HE WANTS TO GO OUT WITH ME OR NOT.
I MEAN, *JEEZ,* LOOK AT THIS! IT'S STILL THERE AFTER A WHOLE WEEK.
I'M SCARRED FOR LIFE BY A VALENTINE HURLED AT MY HEAD.
IT'S TOTALLY UNBELIEV-ABLE.
OH, SHUT UP AND GO AWAY.

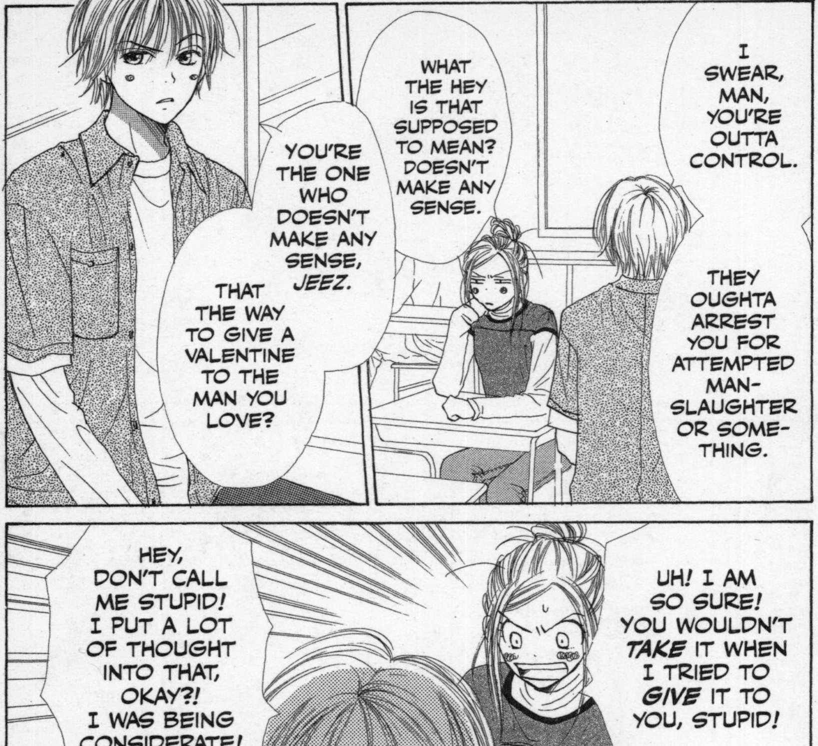
I SWEAR, MAN, YOU'RE OUTTA CONTROL.
THEY OUGHTA ARREST YOU FOR ATTEMPTED MAN-SLAUGHTER OR SOME-THING.
WHAT THE HEY IS THAT SUPPOSED TO MEAN? DOESN'T MAKE ANY SENSE.
YOU'RE THE ONE WHO DOESN'T MAKE ANY SENSE, *JEEZ*.
THAT THE WAY TO GIVE A VALENTINE TO THE MAN YOU LOVE?
UH! I AM SO SURE! YOU WOULDN'T *TAKE* IT WHEN I TRIED TO *GIVE* IT TO YOU, STUPID!
HEY, DON'T CALL ME STUPID! I PUT A LOT OF THOUGHT INTO THAT, OKAY?! I WAS BEING CONSIDERATE!

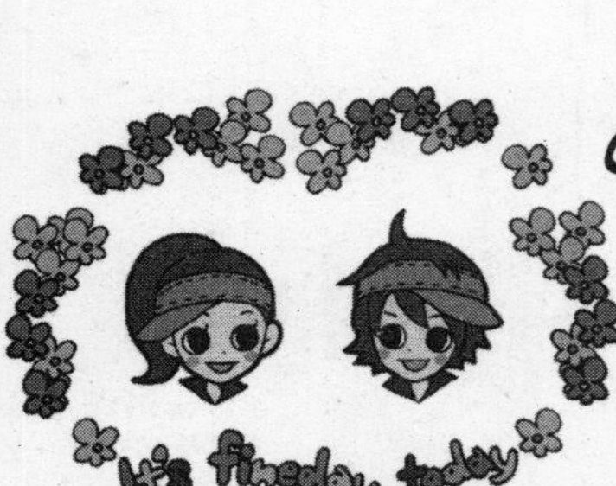
It's fineday today

CHAPTER 21

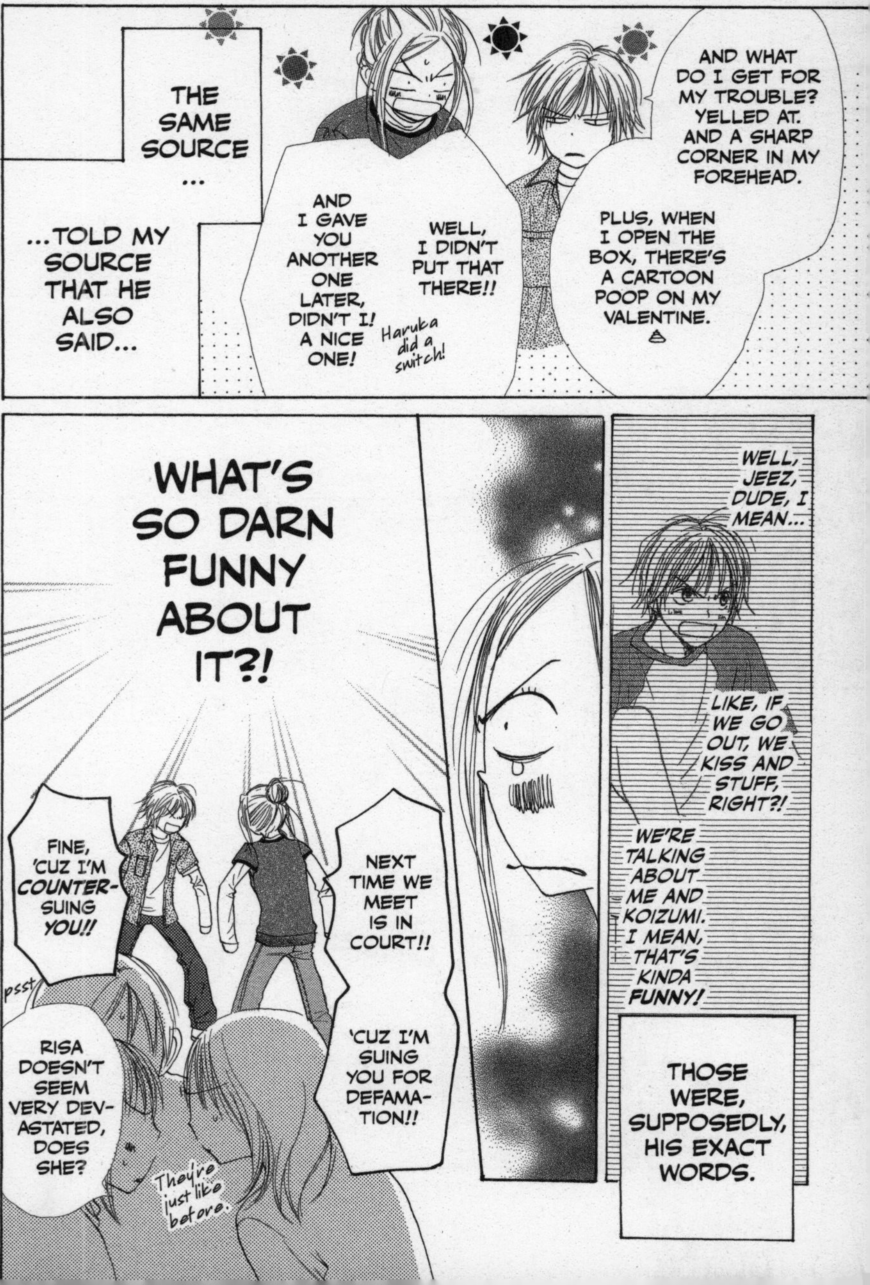
AND WHAT DO I GET FOR MY TROUBLE? YELLED AT. AND A SHARP CORNER IN MY FOREHEAD.
PLUS, WHEN I OPEN THE BOX, THERE'S A CARTOON POOP ON MY VALENTINE.
WELL, I DIDN'T PUT THAT THERE!!
Haruka did a switch!
AND I GAVE YOU ANOTHER ONE LATER, DIDN'T I! A NICE ONE!
THE SAME SOURCE ...
...TOLD MY SOURCE THAT HE ALSO SAID...
WELL, JEEZ, DUDE, I MEAN...
LIKE, IF WE GO OUT, WE KISS AND STUFF, RIGHT?!
WE'RE TALKING ABOUT ME AND KOIZUMI. I MEAN, THAT'S KINDA FUNNY!
THOSE WERE, SUPPOSEDLY, HIS EXACT WORDS.
WHAT'S SO DARN FUNNY ABOUT IT?!
NEXT TIME WE MEET IS IN COURT!!
FINE, 'CUZ I'M COUNTER-SUING YOU!!
'CUZ I'M SUING YOU FOR DEFAMATION!!
psst
RISA DOESN'T SEEM VERY DEVASTATED, DOES SHE?
They're just like before.

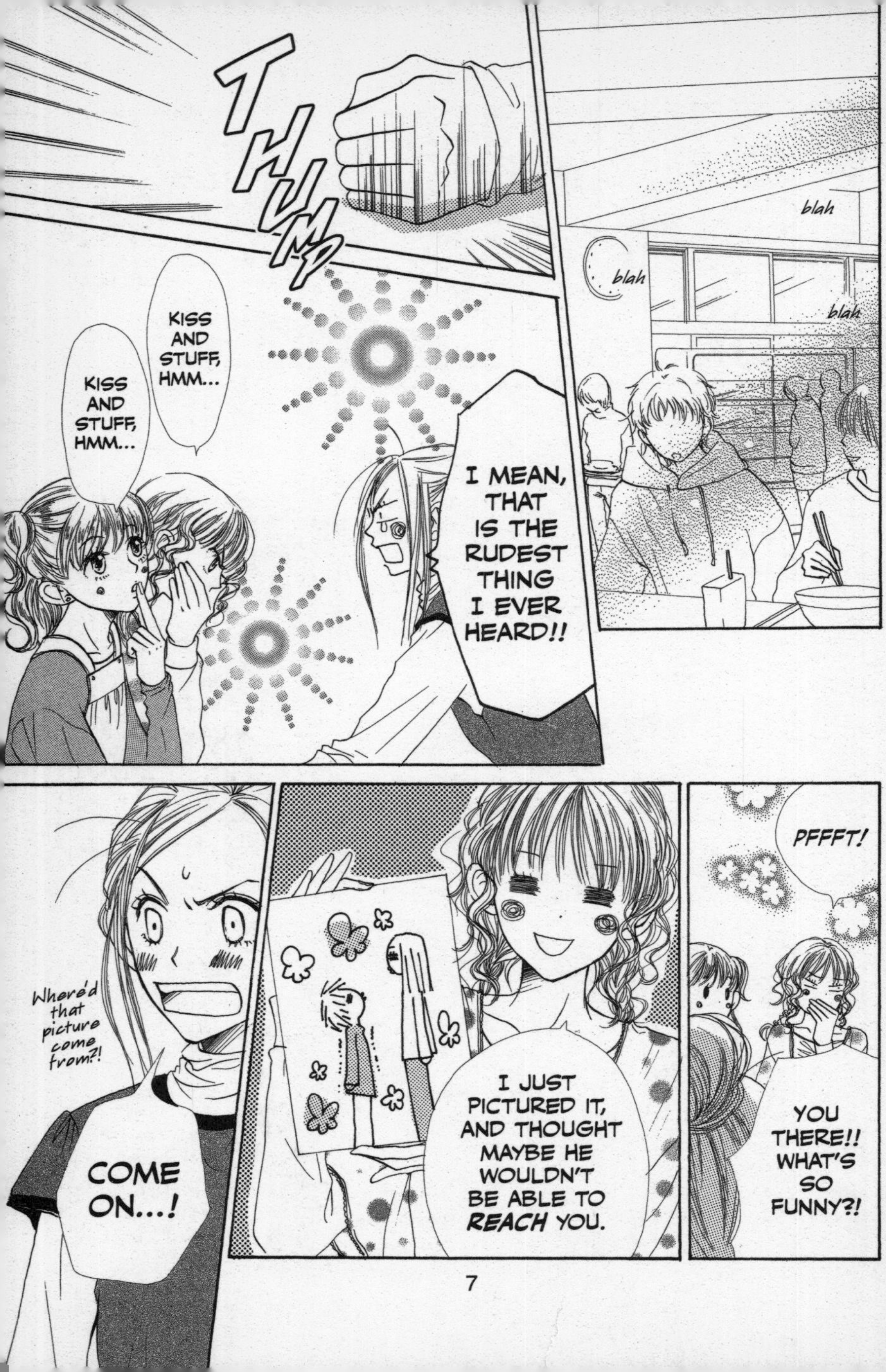
blah
blah
blah
THUMP
I MEAN, THAT IS THE RUDEST THING I EVER HEARD!!
KISS AND STUFF, HMM...
KISS AND STUFF, HMM...
PFFFT!
YOU THERE!! WHAT'S SO FUNNY?!
I JUST PICTURED IT, AND THOUGHT MAYBE HE WOULDN'T BE ABLE TO *REACH* YOU.
COME ON...!
Where'd that picture come from?!

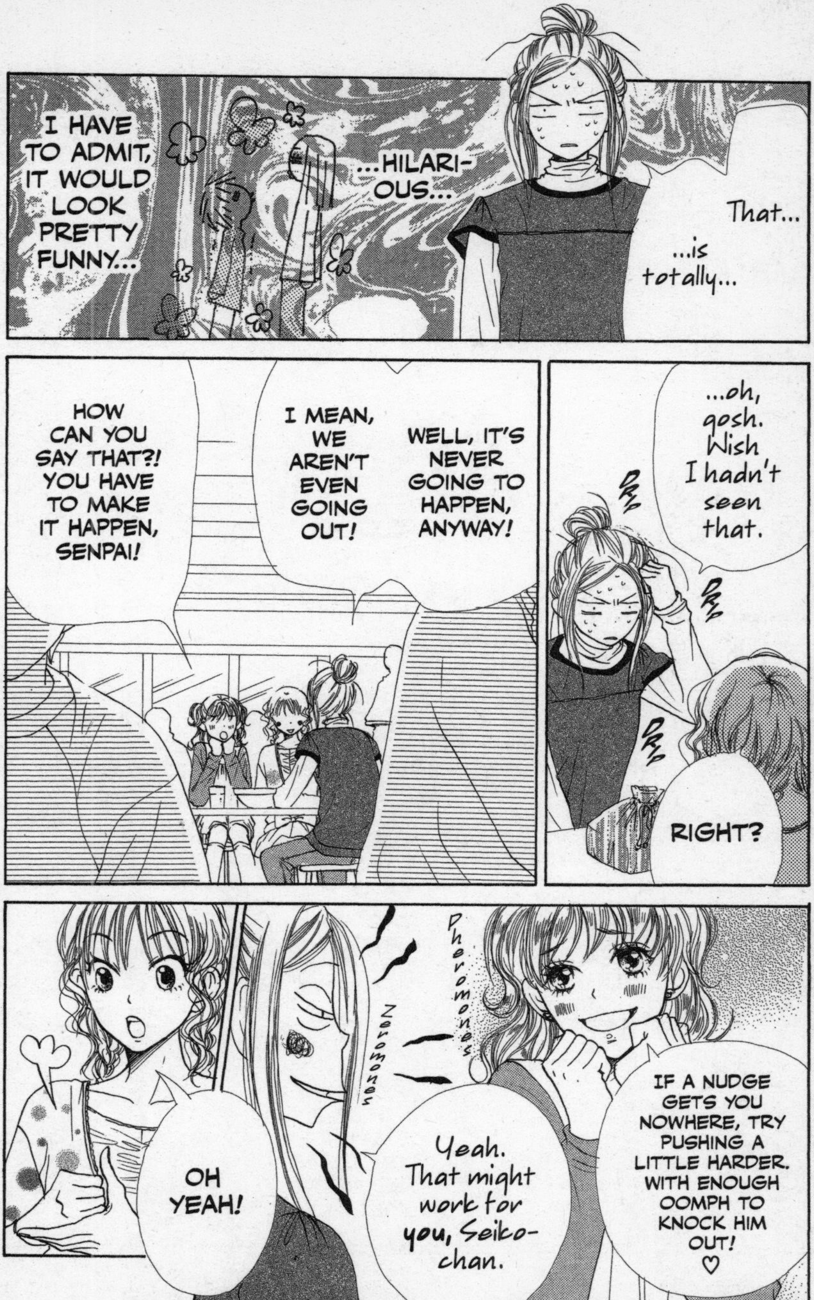
That...
...is totally...
...HILARI-OUS...
I HAVE TO ADMIT, IT WOULD LOOK PRETTY FUNNY...
...oh, gosh. Wish I hadn't seen that.
RIGHT?
WELL, IT'S NEVER GOING TO HAPPEN, ANYWAY!
I MEAN, WE AREN'T EVEN GOING OUT!
HOW CAN YOU SAY THAT?! YOU HAVE TO MAKE IT HAPPEN, SENPAI!
IF A NUDGE GETS YOU NOWHERE, TRY PUSHING A LITTLE HARDER. WITH ENOUGH OOMPH TO KNOCK HIM OUT! ♡
Pheromones
Yeah. That might work for you, Seiko-chan.
Zeromones
OH YEAH!

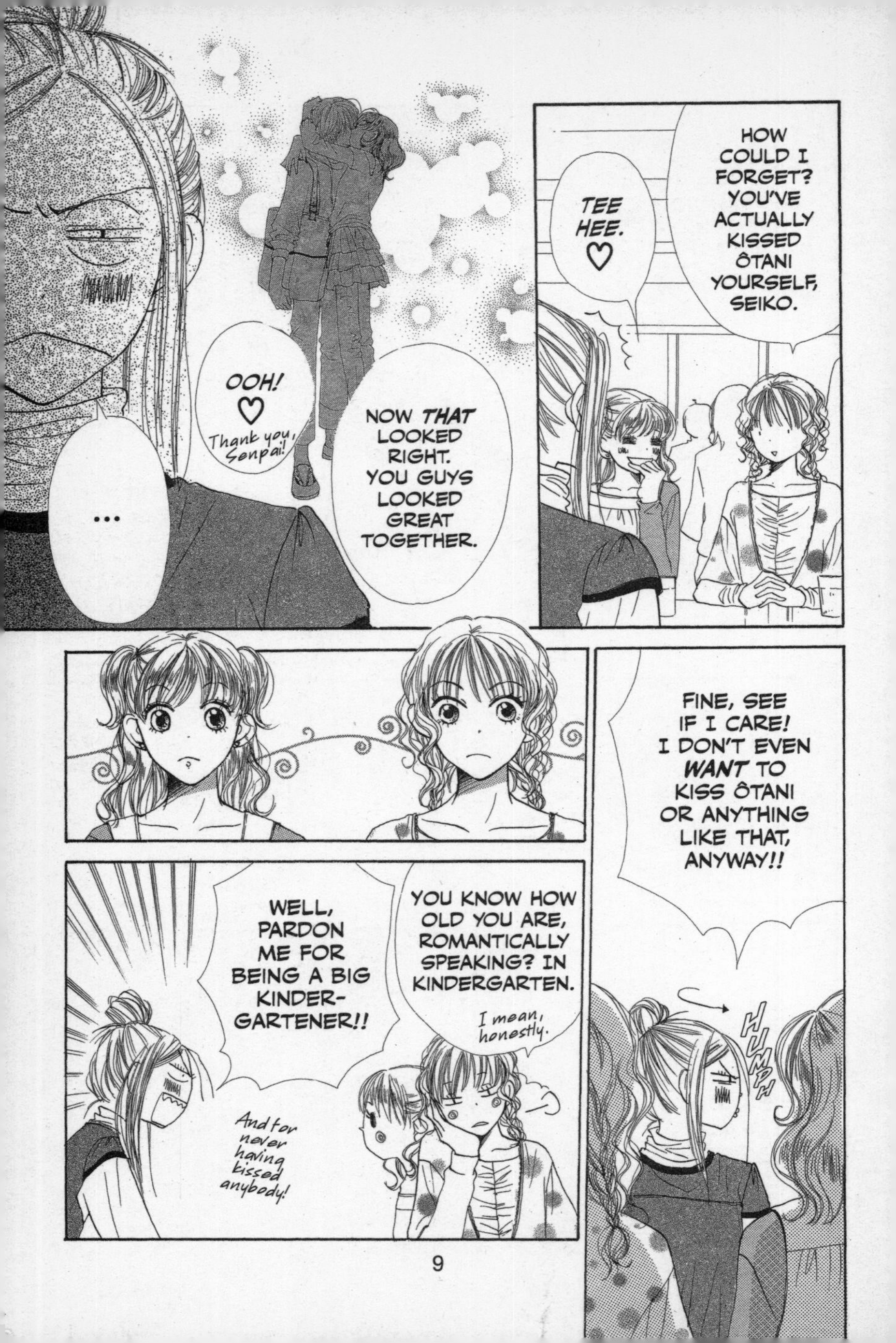
HOW COULD I FORGET? YOU'VE ACTUALLY KISSED ÔTANI YOURSELF, SEIKO.
TEE HEE. ♡
NOW *THAT* LOOKED RIGHT. YOU GUYS LOOKED GREAT TOGETHER.
OOH! ♡
Thank you, Senpai!
...
FINE, SEE IF I CARE! I DON'T EVEN *WANT* TO KISS ÔTANI OR ANYTHING LIKE THAT, ANYWAY!!
HUMPH
YOU KNOW HOW OLD YOU ARE, ROMANTICALLY SPEAKING? IN KINDERGARTEN.
I mean, honestly.
WELL, PARDON ME FOR BEING A BIG KINDER-GARTENER!!
And for never having kissed anybody!

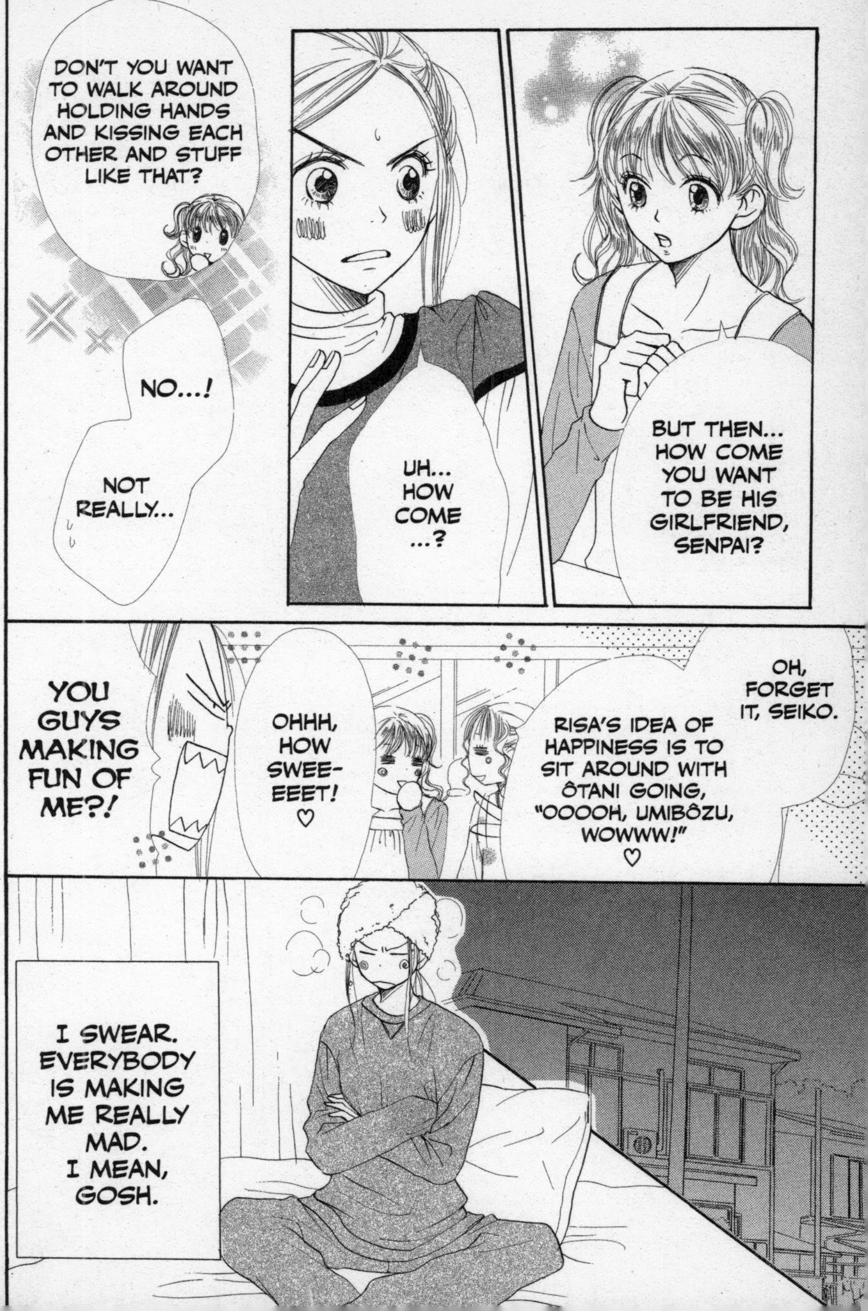
BUT THEN... HOW COME YOU WANT TO BE HIS GIRLFRIEND, SENPAI?
UH... HOW COME ...?
DON'T YOU WANT TO WALK AROUND HOLDING HANDS AND KISSING EACH OTHER AND STUFF LIKE THAT?
NO...!
NOT REALLY...
OH, FORGET IT, SEIKO.
RISA'S IDEA OF HAPPINESS IS TO SIT AROUND WITH ÔTANI GOING, "OOOOH, UMIBÔZU, WOWWW!" ♡
OHHH, HOW SWEE-EEET! ♡
YOU GUYS MAKING FUN OF ME?!
I SWEAR. EVERYBODY IS MAKING ME REALLY MAD. I MEAN, GOSH.

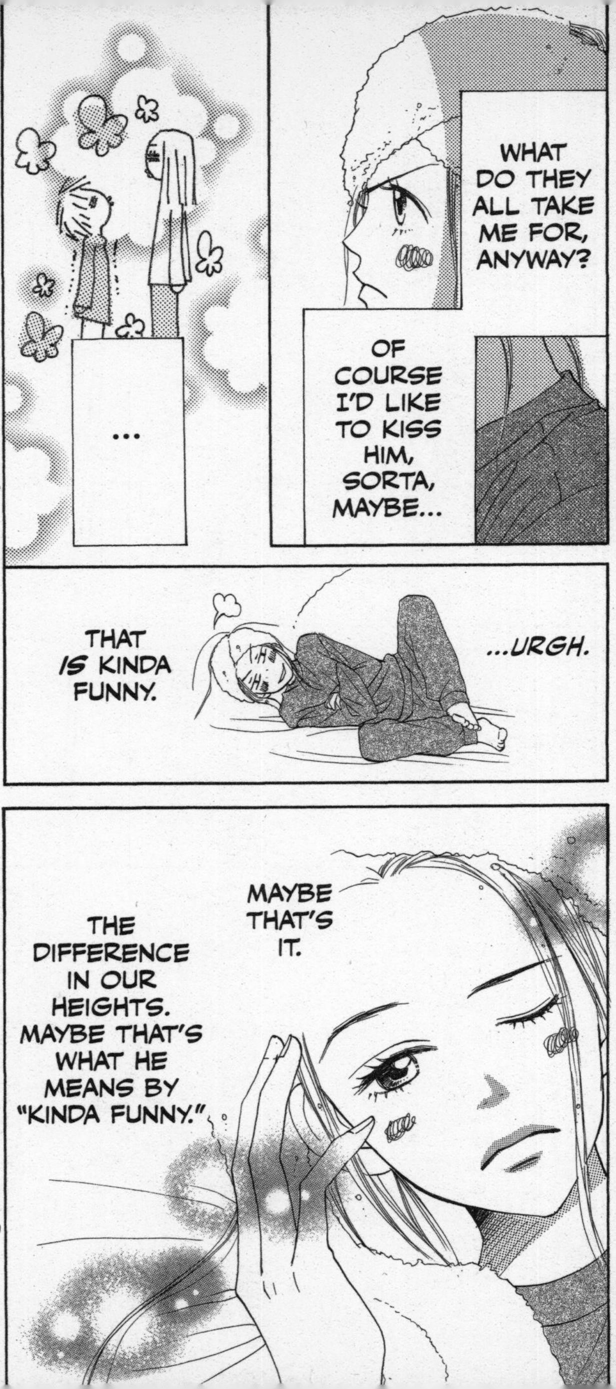
WHAT DO THEY ALL TAKE ME FOR, ANYWAY?
OF COURSE I'D LIKE TO KISS HIM, SORTA, MAYBE...
...
...URGH.
THAT *IS* KINDA FUNNY.
MAYBE THAT'S IT.
THE DIFFERENCE IN OUR HEIGHTS. MAYBE THAT'S WHAT HE MEANS BY "KINDA FUNNY."

1

Hello! Nakahara here. We're up to Volume 6. Wow. This is turning into a very long series...

So far, my series have always been like the Hanshin Tigers, running out of steam very fast indeed, but this time, I seem to be going after my first league title ever. hahahahaha

I hope that, like true Hanshin Tiger fans, you'll continue to give me your steadfast, lukewarm support.

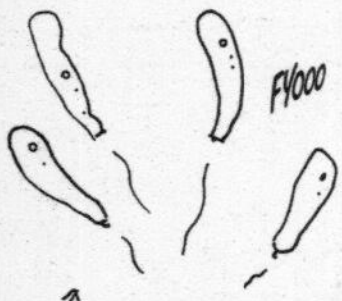
FYOOO

↑Balloons

Who would ever believe a professional manga artist drew these balloons?!

A friend of mine managed to score super-premium tickets to a Hanshin-Kyojin game when the Tigers were on the verge of winning the pennant. I was invited to go, but couldn't because of work. Bummer... I'm not a big baseball fan at all, but like all people from Kansai, I'm always rooting for those Tigers.

Tiger ....

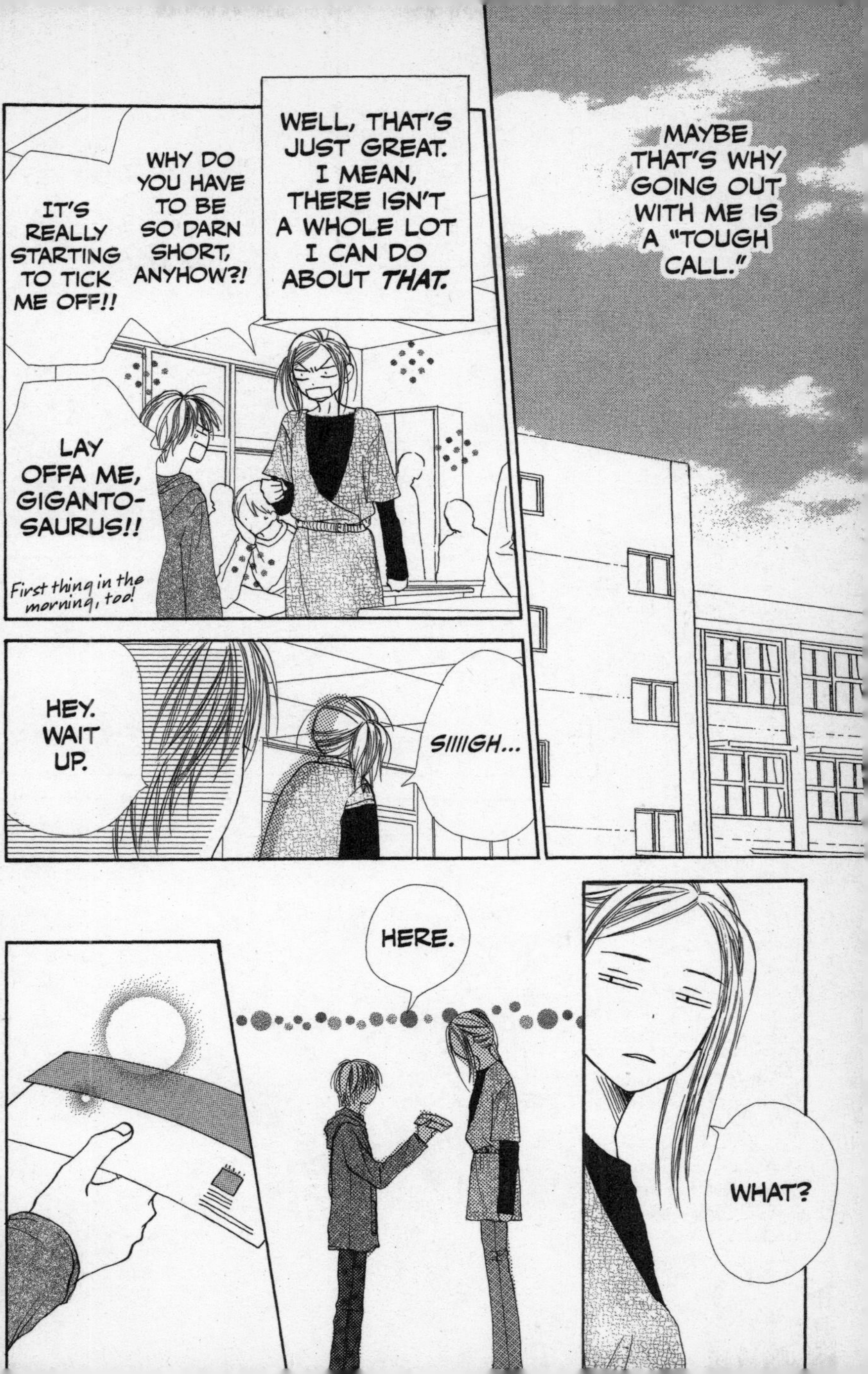
MAYBE THAT'S WHY GOING OUT WITH ME IS A "TOUGH CALL."
WELL, THAT'S JUST GREAT. I MEAN, THERE ISN'T A WHOLE LOT I CAN DO ABOUT THAT.
WHY DO YOU HAVE TO BE SO DARN SHORT, ANYHOW?!
IT'S REALLY STARTING TO TICK ME OFF!!
LAY OFFA ME, GIGANTO-SAURUS!!
First thing in the morning, too!
SIIIGH...
HEY. WAIT UP.
WHAT?
HERE.

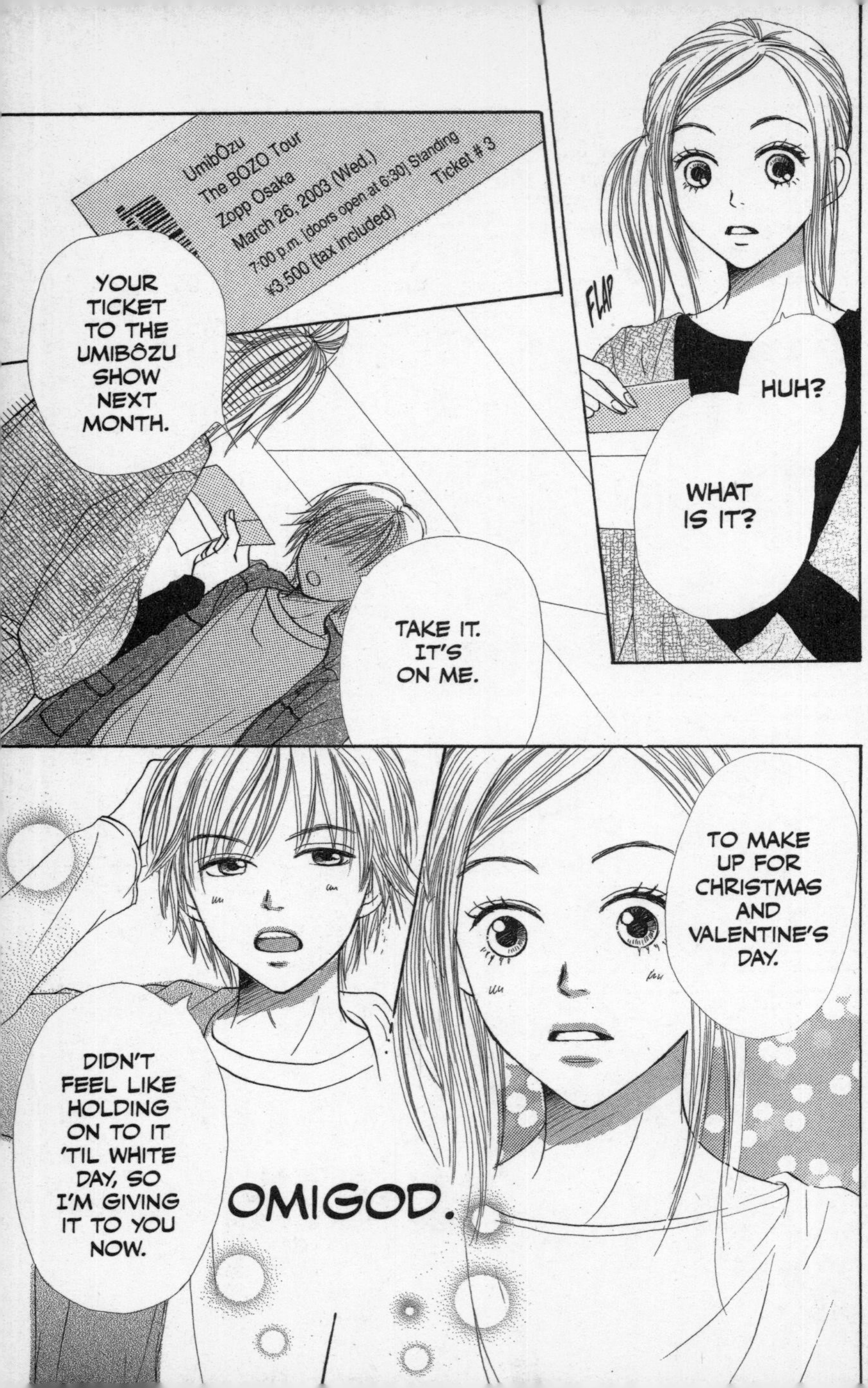
FLAP
HUH?
WHAT IS IT?
UmibÔzu
The BOZO Tour
Zopp Osaka
March 26, 2003 (Wed.)
7:00 p.m. (doors open at 6:30) Standing
¥3.500 (tax included)
Ticket # 3
YOUR TICKET TO THE UMIBÔZU SHOW NEXT MONTH.
TAKE IT. IT'S ON ME.
TO MAKE UP FOR CHRISTMAS AND VALENTINE'S DAY.
DIDN'T FEEL LIKE HOLDING ON TO IT 'TIL WHITE DAY, SO I'M GIVING IT TO YOU NOW.
OMIGOD.

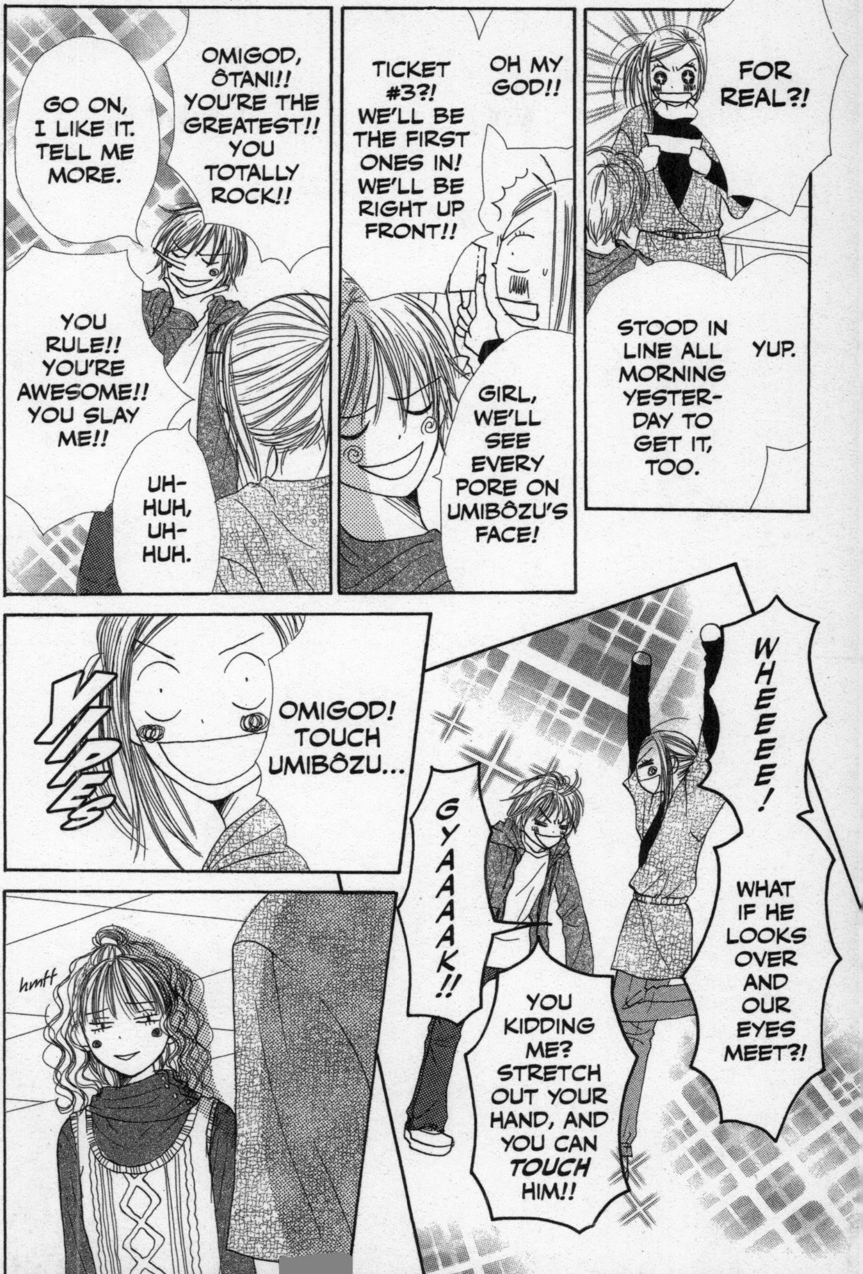
FOR REAL?!
YUP.
STOOD IN LINE ALL MORNING YESTER-DAY TO GET IT, TOO.
OH MY GOD!!
TICKET #3?! WE'LL BE THE FIRST ONES IN! WE'LL BE RIGHT UP FRONT!!
GIRL, WE'LL SEE EVERY PORE ON UMIBÔZU'S FACE!
OMIGOD, ÔTANI!! YOU'RE THE GREATEST!! YOU TOTALLY ROCK!!
GO ON, I LIKE IT. TELL ME MORE.
YOU RULE!! YOU'RE AWESOME!! YOU SLAY ME!!
UH-HUH, UH-HUH.
WHEEEE!
WHAT IF HE LOOKS OVER AND OUR EYES MEET?!
GYAAAAK!!
YOU KIDDING ME? STRETCH OUT YOUR HAND, AND YOU CAN TOUCH HIM!!
OMIGOD! TOUCH UMIBÔZU...
YIPES
hmff

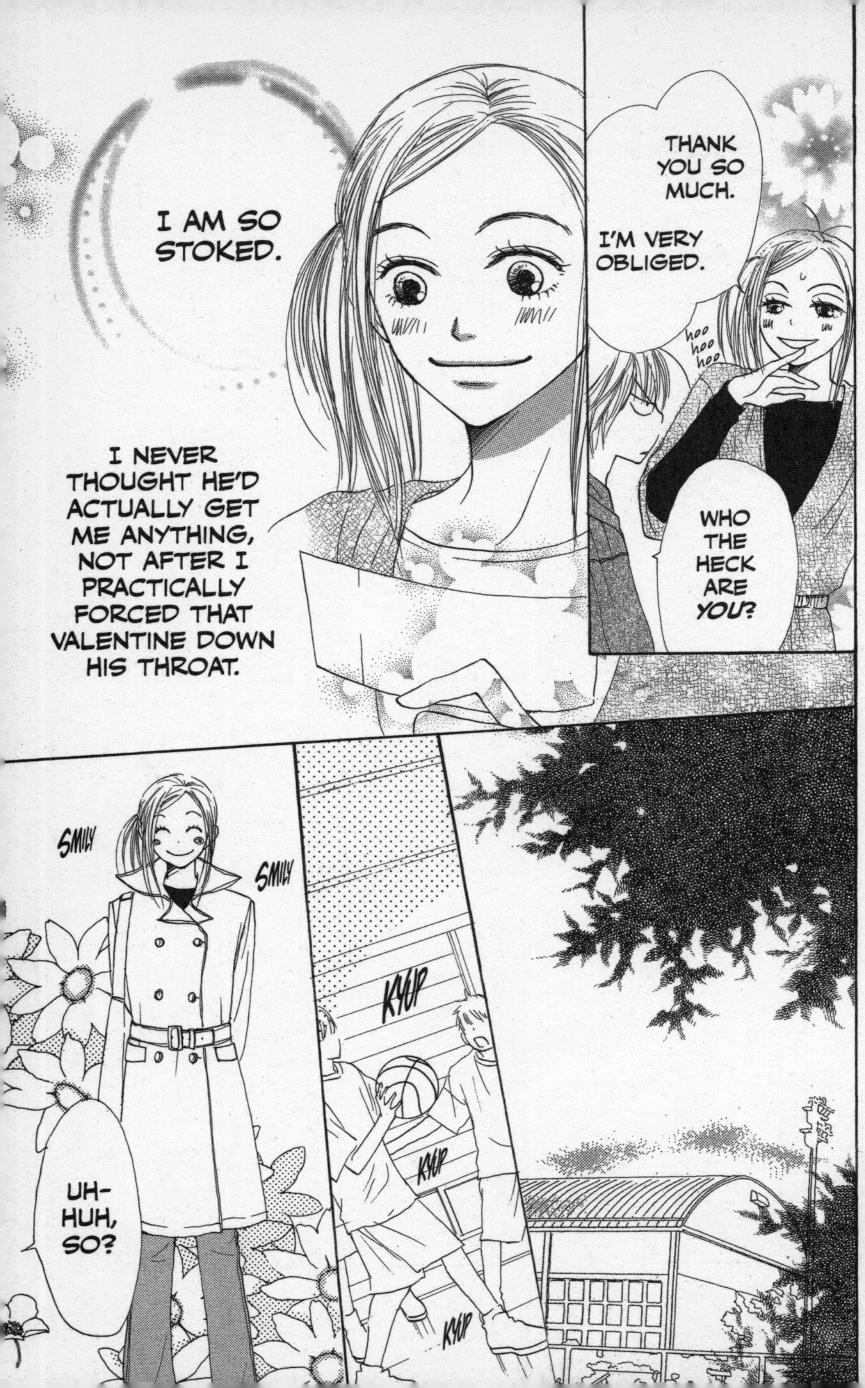

THANK YOU SO MUCH.
I'M VERY OBLIGED.
hoo hoo hoo
WHO THE HECK ARE YOU?
I AM SO STOKED.
I NEVER THOUGHT HE'D ACTUALLY GET ME ANYTHING, NOT AFTER I PRACTICALLY FORCED THAT VALENTINE DOWN HIS THROAT.
KYUP
KYUP
KYUP
SMILY
SMILY
UH-HUH, SO?

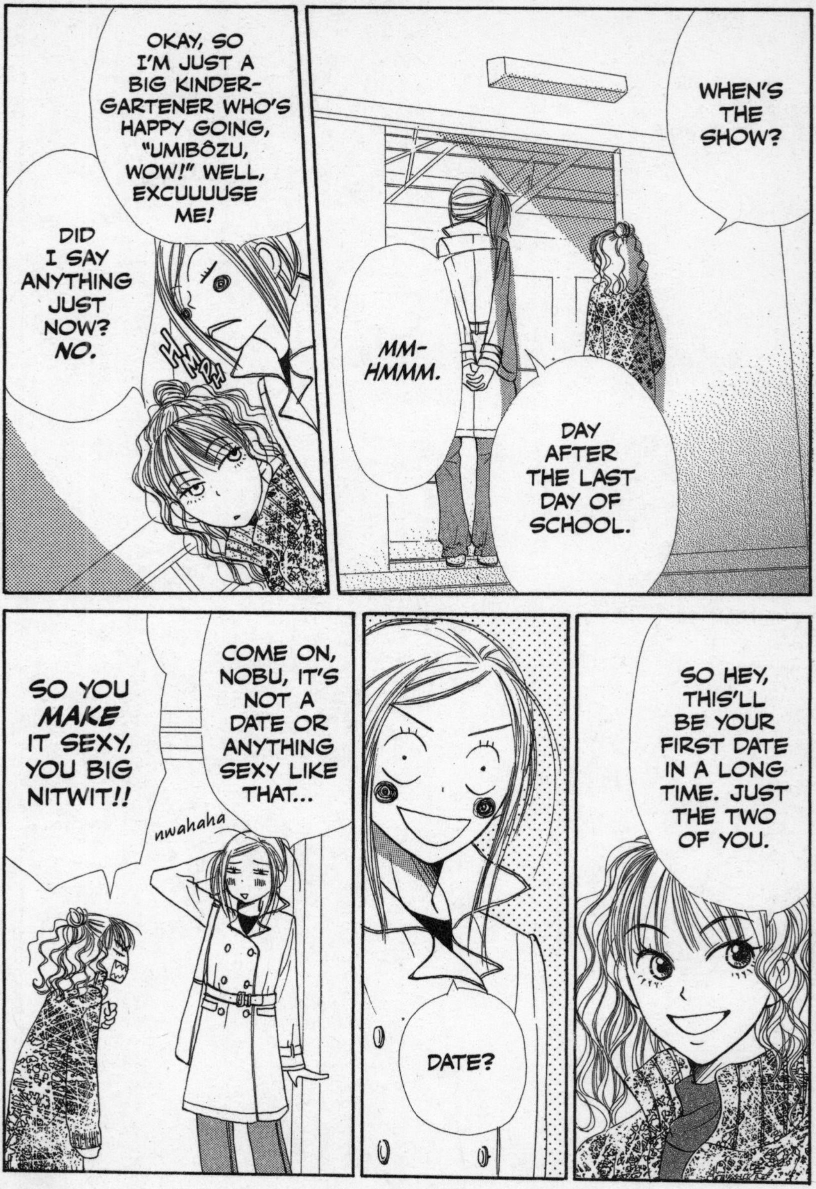
WHEN'S THE SHOW?
DAY AFTER THE LAST DAY OF SCHOOL.
MM-HMMM.
OKAY, SO I'M JUST A BIG KINDER-GARTENER WHO'S HAPPY GOING, "UMIBÔZU, WOW!" WELL, EXCUUUUSE ME!
DID I SAY ANYTHING JUST NOW? *NO.*
SO HEY, THIS'LL BE YOUR FIRST DATE IN A LONG TIME. JUST THE TWO OF YOU.
DATE?
COME ON, NOBU, IT'S NOT A DATE OR ANYTHING SEXY LIKE THAT...
nwahaha
SO YOU *MAKE* IT SEXY, YOU BIG NITWIT!!

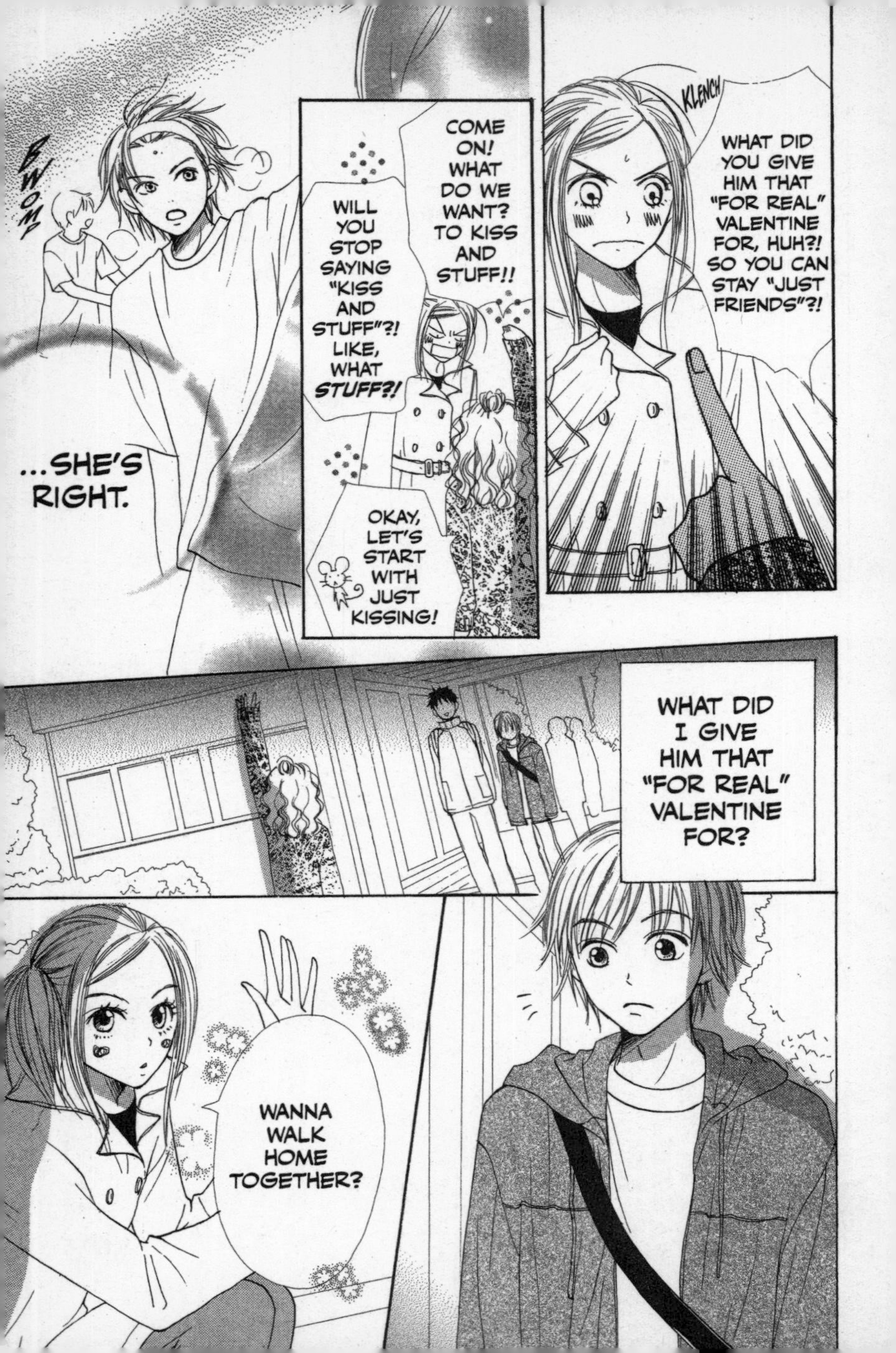
KLENCH
WHAT DID YOU GIVE HIM THAT "FOR REAL" VALENTINE FOR, HUH?! SO YOU CAN STAY "JUST FRIENDS"?!
COME ON! WHAT DO WE WANT? TO KISS AND STUFF!!
WILL YOU STOP SAYING "KISS AND STUFF"?! LIKE, WHAT *STUFF?!*
OKAY, LET'S START WITH JUST KISSING!
BWOMP
...SHE'S RIGHT.
WHAT DID I GIVE HIM THAT "FOR REAL" VALENTINE FOR?
WANNA WALK HOME TOGETHER?

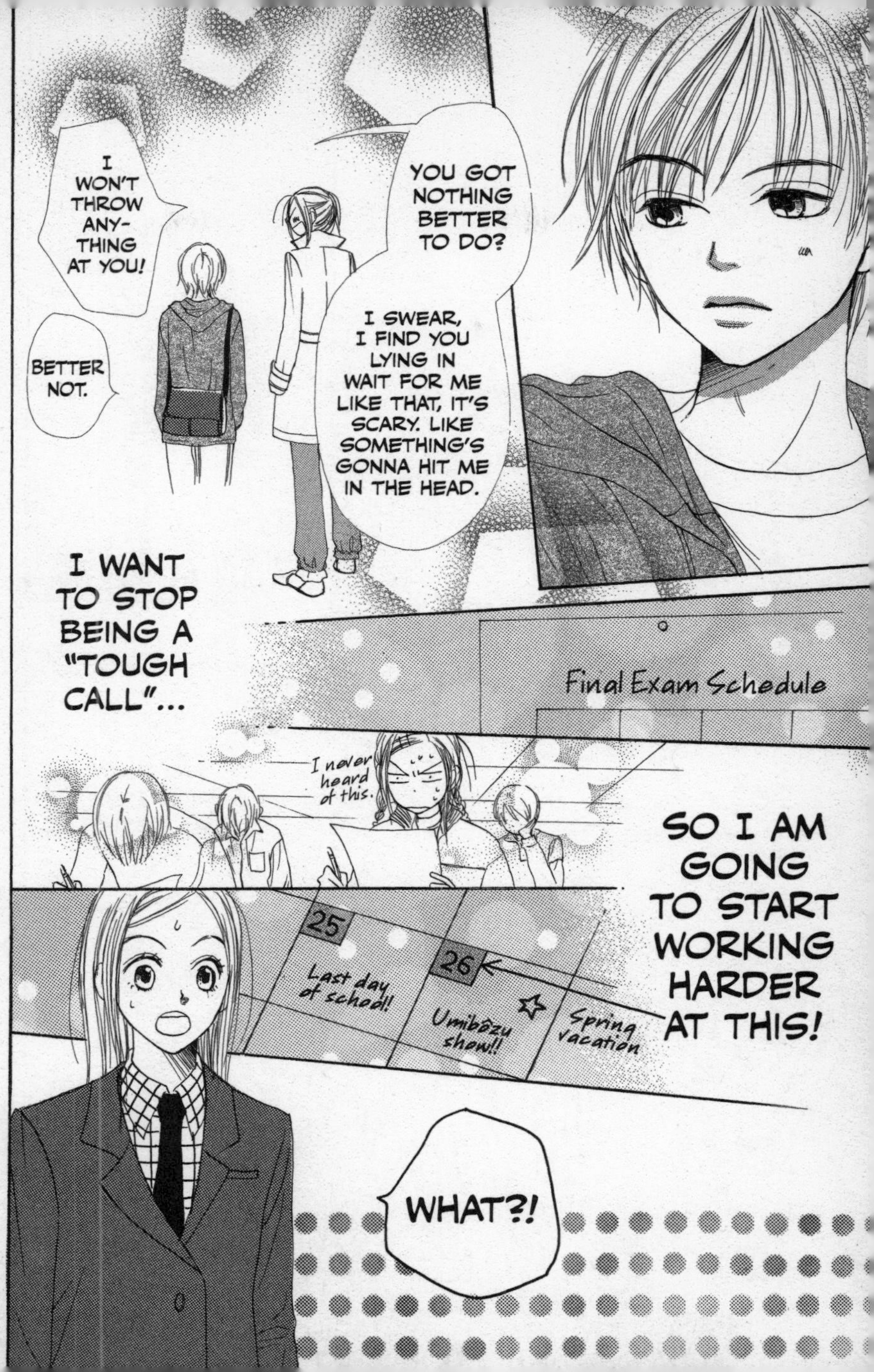
YOU GOT NOTHING BETTER TO DO?
I SWEAR, I FIND YOU LYING IN WAIT FOR ME LIKE THAT, IT'S SCARY. LIKE SOMETHING'S GONNA HIT ME IN THE HEAD.
I WON'T THROW ANY-THING AT YOU!
BETTER NOT.
I WANT TO STOP BEING A "TOUGH CALL"...
Final Exam Schedule
I never heard of this.
SO I AM GOING TO START WORKING HARDER AT THIS!
25
Last day of school!
26
Umibôzu show!!
Spring vacation
WHAT?!

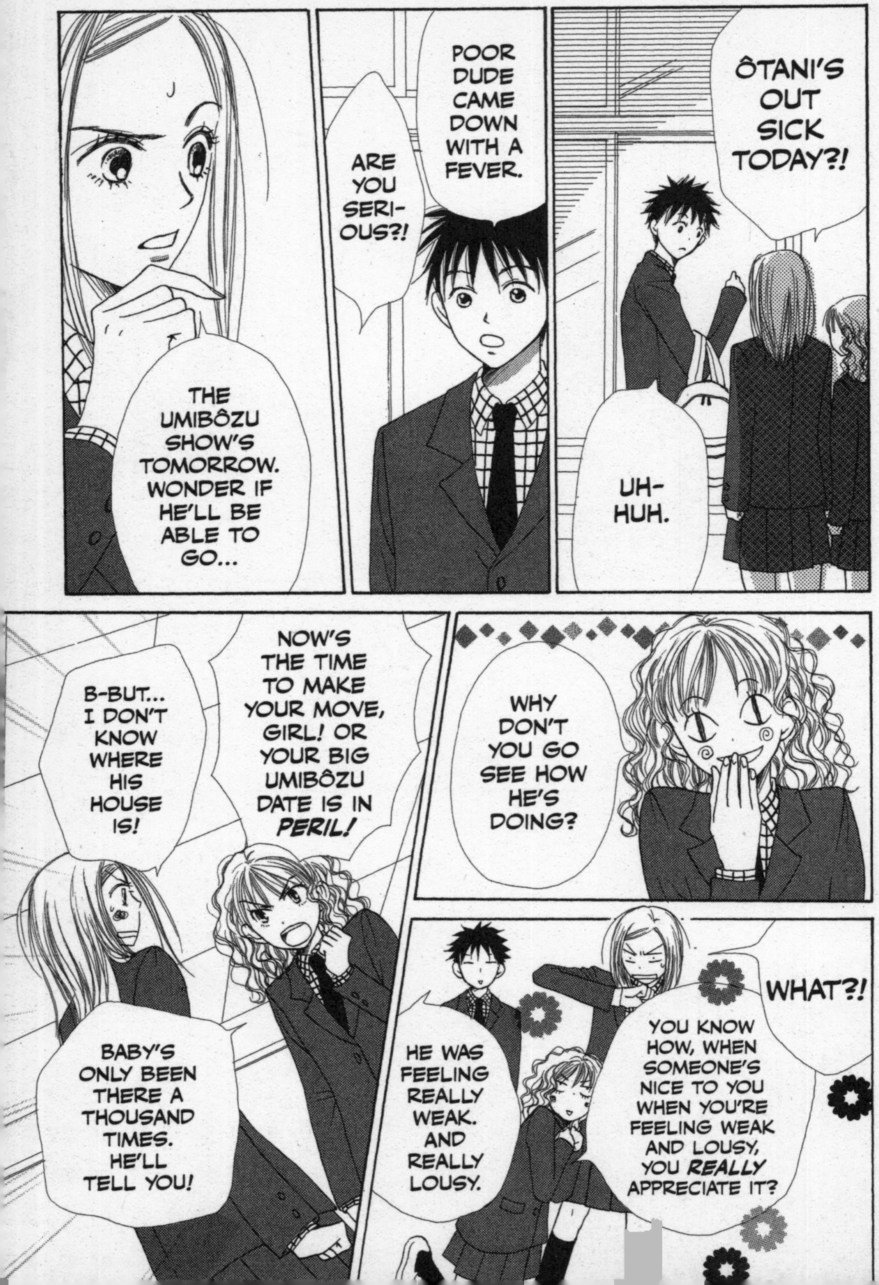
ÔTANI'S OUT SICK TODAY?!
UH-HUH.
POOR DUDE CAME DOWN WITH A FEVER.
ARE YOU SERI-OUS?!
THE UMIBÔZU SHOW'S TOMORROW. WONDER IF HE'LL BE ABLE TO GO...
WHY DON'T YOU GO SEE HOW HE'S DOING?
WHAT?!
YOU KNOW HOW, WHEN SOMEONE'S NICE TO YOU WHEN YOU'RE FEELING WEAK AND LOUSY, YOU *REALLY* APPRECIATE IT?
HE WAS FEELING REALLY WEAK. AND REALLY LOUSY.
NOW'S THE TIME TO MAKE YOUR MOVE, GIRL! OR YOUR BIG UMIBÔZU DATE IS IN *PERIL!*
B-BUT... I DON'T KNOW WHERE HIS HOUSE IS!
BABY'S ONLY BEEN THERE A THOUSAND TIMES. HE'LL TELL YOU!

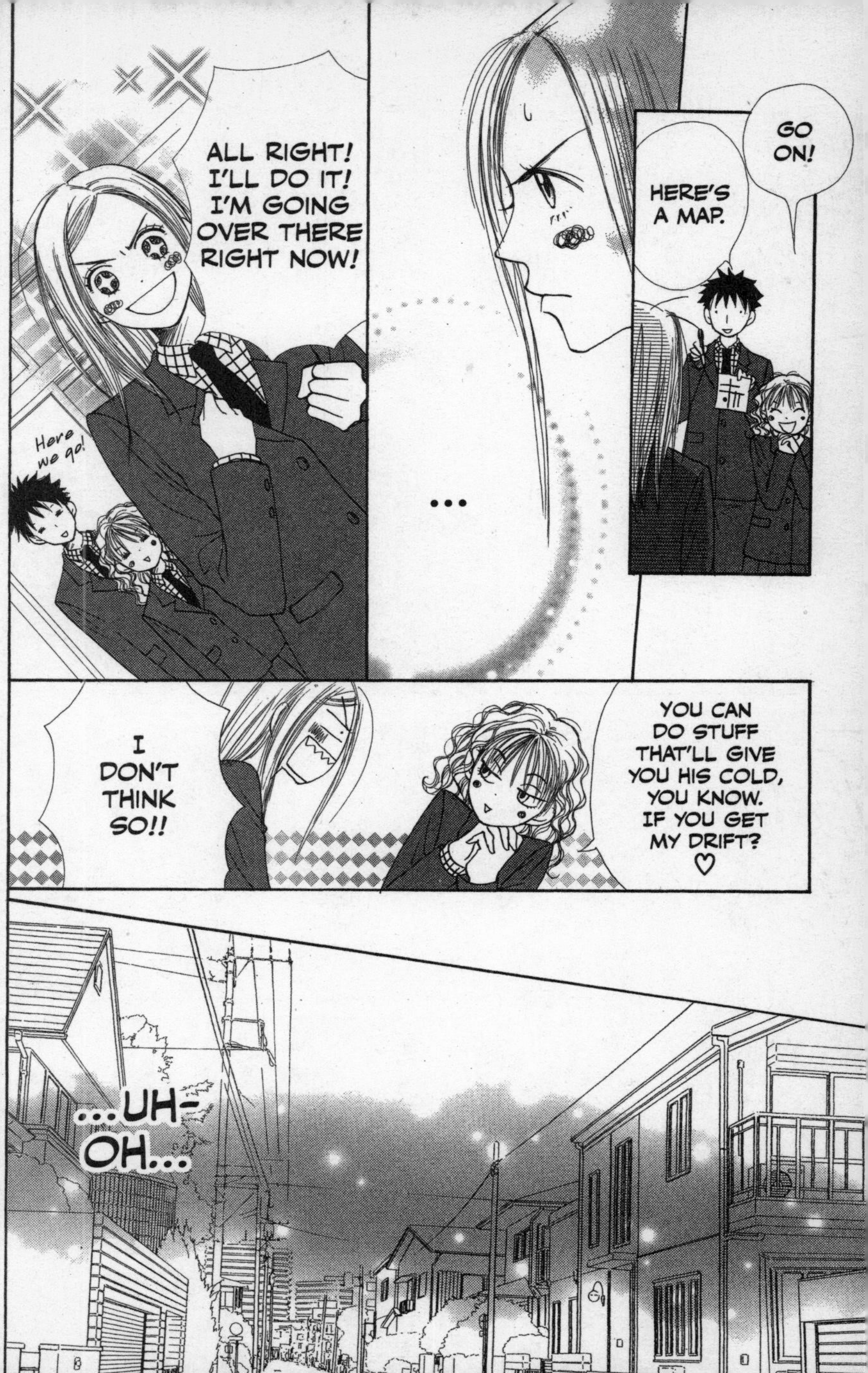
GO ON!
HERE'S A MAP.
...
ALL RIGHT! I'LL DO IT! I'M GOING OVER THERE RIGHT NOW!
Here we go!
YOU CAN DO STUFF THAT'LL GIVE YOU HIS COLD, YOU KNOW. IF YOU GET MY DRIFT? ♡
I DON'T THINK SO!!
...UH-OH...

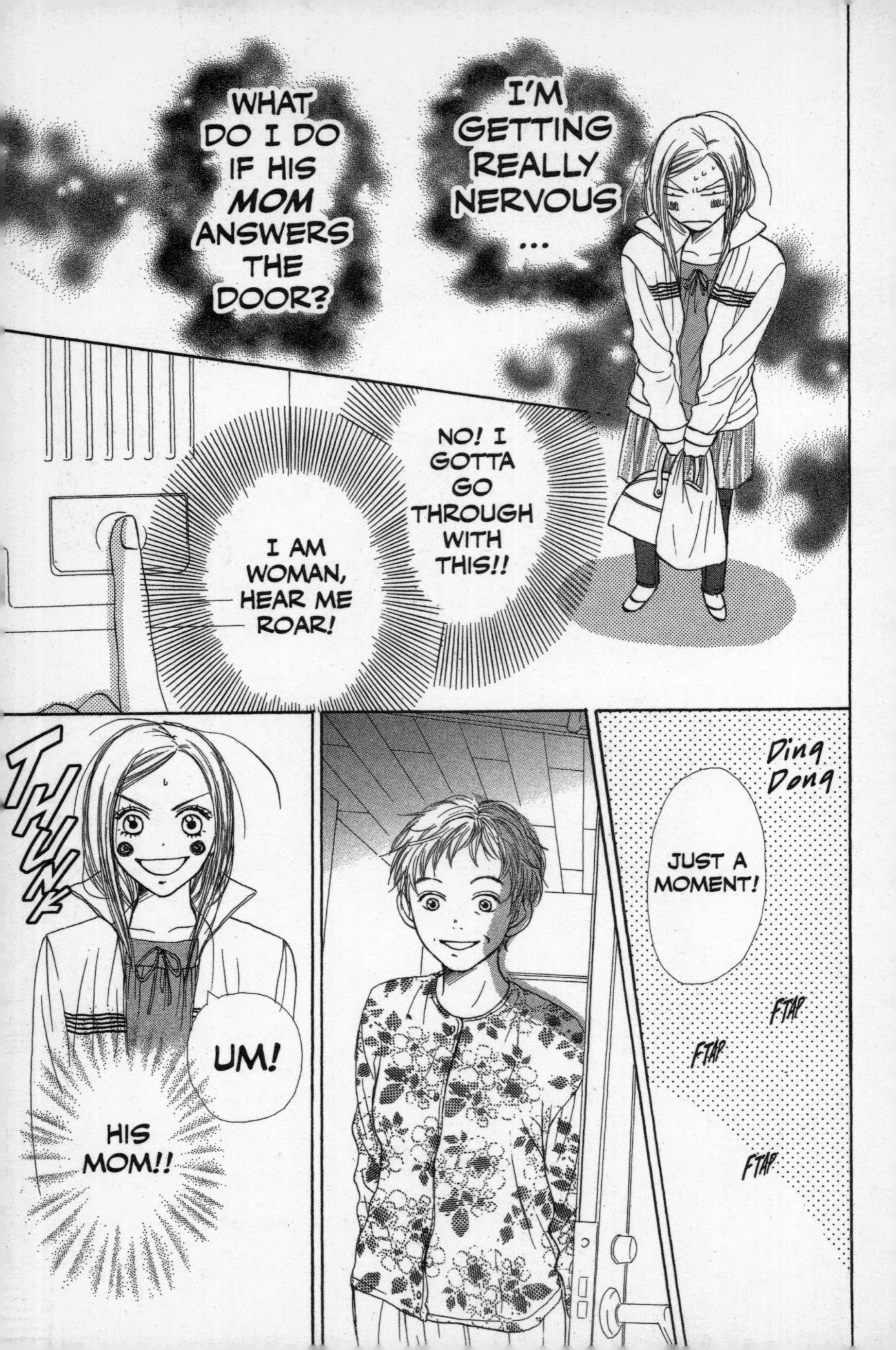
I'M GETTING REALLY NERVOUS...
WHAT DO I DO IF HIS MOM ANSWERS THE DOOR?
NO! I GOTTA GO THROUGH WITH THIS!!
I AM WOMAN, HEAR ME ROAR!
Ding Dong
JUST A MOMENT!
FTAP
FTAP
FTAP
THUNK
UM!
HIS MOM!!

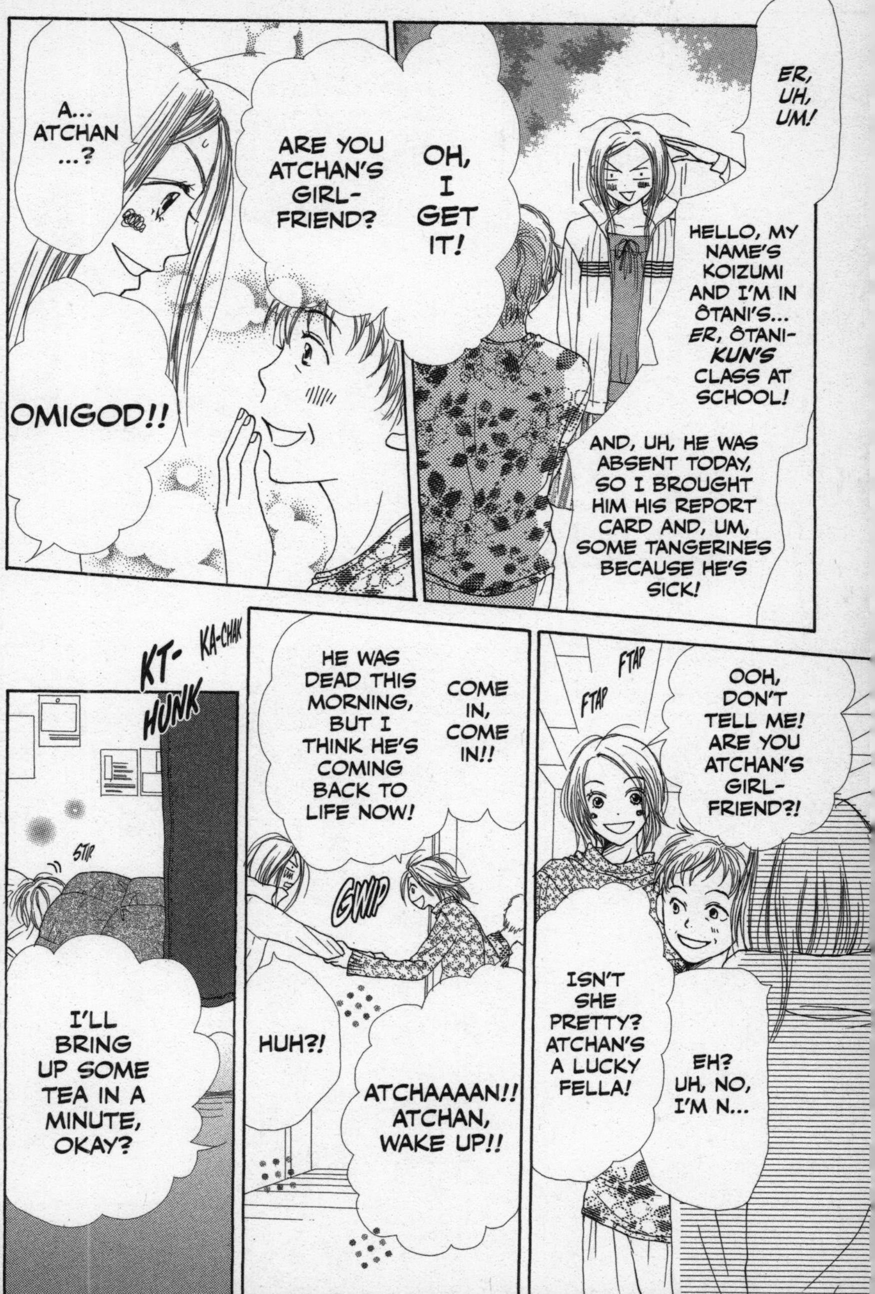
ER, UH, UM!
HELLO, MY NAME'S KOIZUMI AND I'M IN ŌTANI'S... ER, ŌTANI-KUN'S CLASS AT SCHOOL!
AND, UH, HE WAS ABSENT TODAY, SO I BROUGHT HIM HIS REPORT CARD AND, UM, SOME TANGERINES BECAUSE HE'S SICK!
OH, I GET IT!
ARE YOU ATCHAN'S GIRL-FRIEND?
A... ATCHAN ...?
OMIGOD!!
FTAP
FTAP
OOH, DON'T TELL ME! ARE YOU ATCHAN'S GIRL-FRIEND?!
EH? UH, NO, I'M N...
ISN'T SHE PRETTY? ATCHAN'S A LUCKY FELLA!
COME IN, COME IN!!
HE WAS DEAD THIS MORNING, BUT I THINK HE'S COMING BACK TO LIFE NOW!
GWIP
HUH?!
ATCHAAAAN!! ATCHAN, WAKE UP!!
KA-CHAK
KT-HUNK
STIP
I'LL BRING UP SOME TEA IN A MINUTE, OKAY?

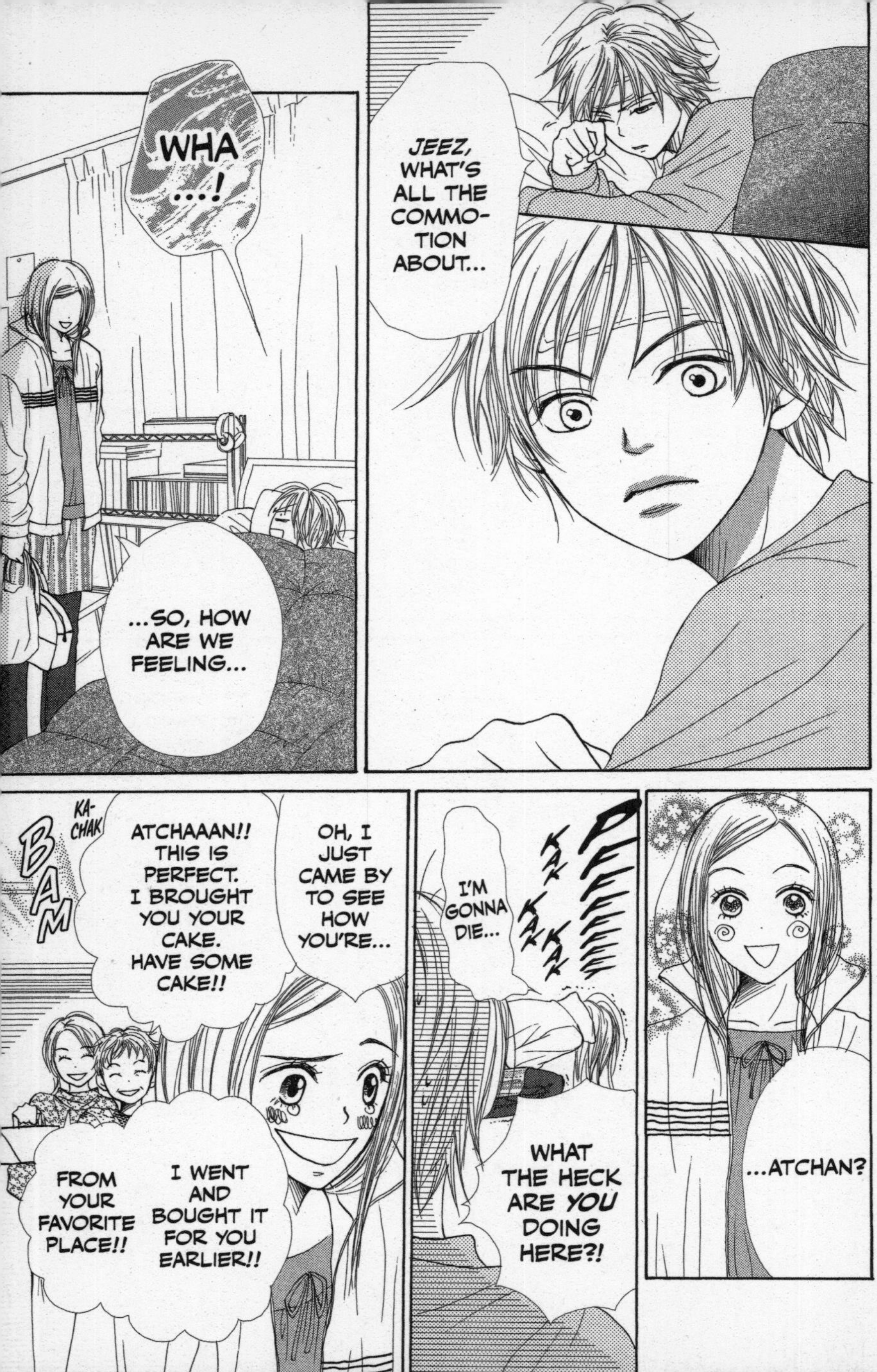
JEEZ, WHAT'S ALL THE COMMOTION ABOUT...
WHA ...!
...SO, HOW ARE WE FEELING...
...ATCHAN?
PFEEEEEE
KAK KAK KAK KAK
I'M GONNA DIE...
WHAT THE HECK ARE YOU DOING HERE?!
OH, I JUST CAME BY TO SEE HOW YOU'RE...
KA-CHAK
BAM
ATCHAAAN!! THIS IS PERFECT. I BROUGHT YOU YOUR CAKE. HAVE SOME CAKE!!
I WENT AND BOUGHT IT FOR YOU EARLIER!!
FROM YOUR FAVORITE PLACE!!

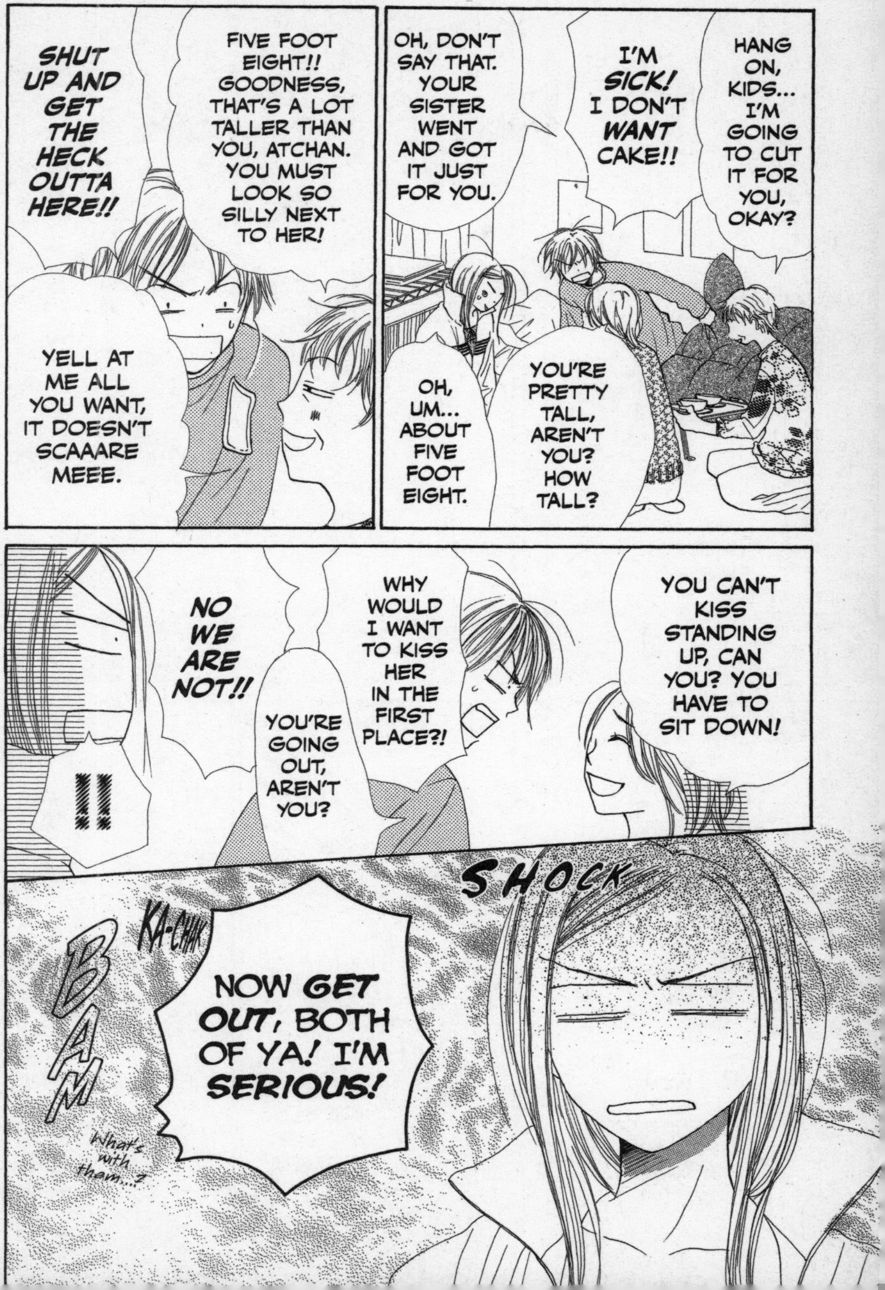
HANG ON, KIDS... I'M GOING TO CUT IT FOR YOU, OKAY?
I'M SICK! I DON'T WANT CAKE!!
OH, DON'T SAY THAT. YOUR SISTER WENT AND GOT IT JUST FOR YOU.
YOU'RE PRETTY TALL, AREN'T YOU? HOW TALL?
OH, UM... ABOUT FIVE FOOT EIGHT.
FIVE FOOT EIGHT!! GOODNESS, THAT'S A LOT TALLER THAN YOU, ATCHAN. YOU MUST LOOK SO SILLY NEXT TO HER!
SHUT UP AND GET THE HECK OUTTA HERE!!
YELL AT ME ALL YOU WANT, IT DOESN'T SCAAARE MEEE.
YOU CAN'T KISS STANDING UP, CAN YOU? YOU HAVE TO SIT DOWN!
WHY WOULD I WANT TO KISS HER IN THE FIRST PLACE?!
YOU'RE GOING OUT, AREN'T YOU?
NO WE ARE NOT!!
!!
SHOCK
NOW GET OUT, BOTH OF YA! I'M SERIOUS!
KA-CHAK
BAM
What's with them...?

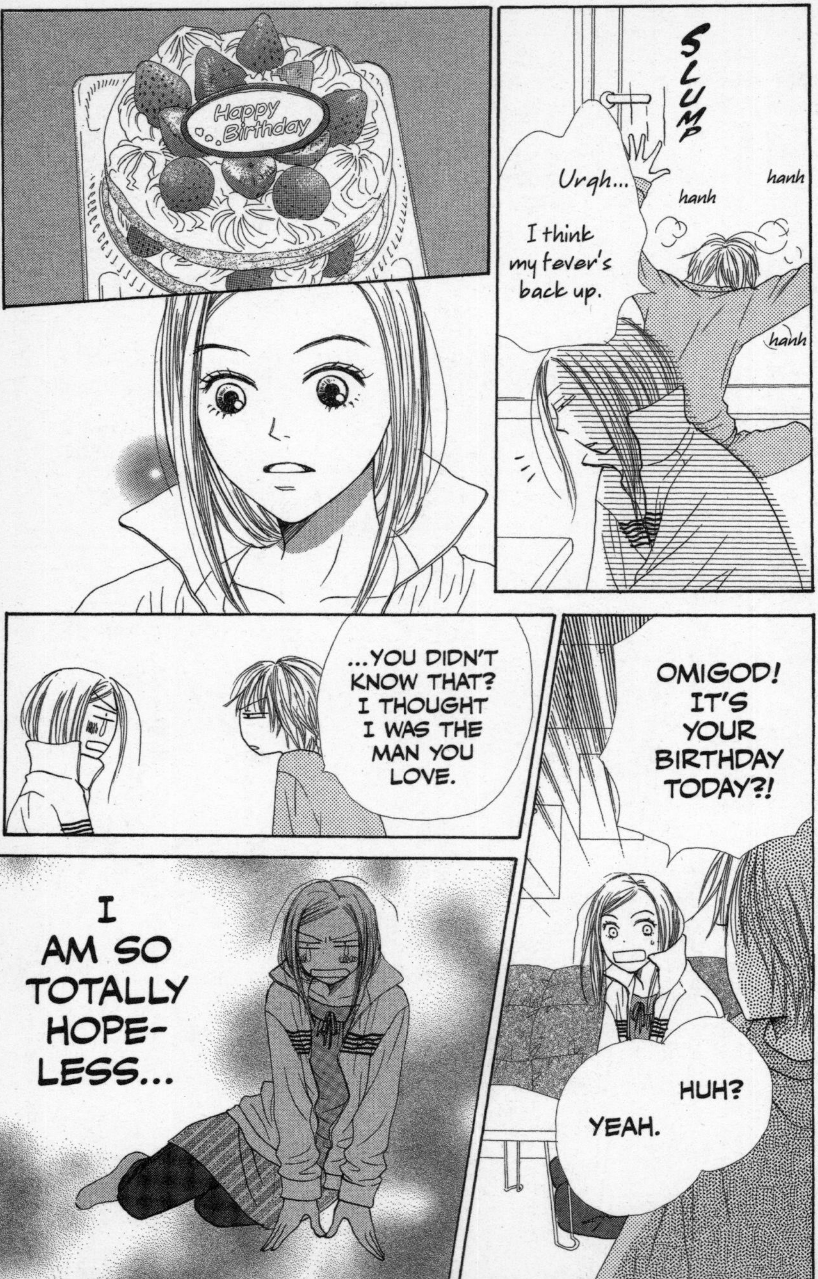
SLUMP
Urgh...
hanh
hanh
I think my fever's back up.
hanh
Happy Birthday
OMIGOD! IT'S YOUR BIRTHDAY TODAY?!
HUH?
YEAH.
...YOU DIDN'T KNOW THAT? I THOUGHT I WAS THE MAN YOU LOVE.
I AM SO TOTALLY HOPE-LESS...

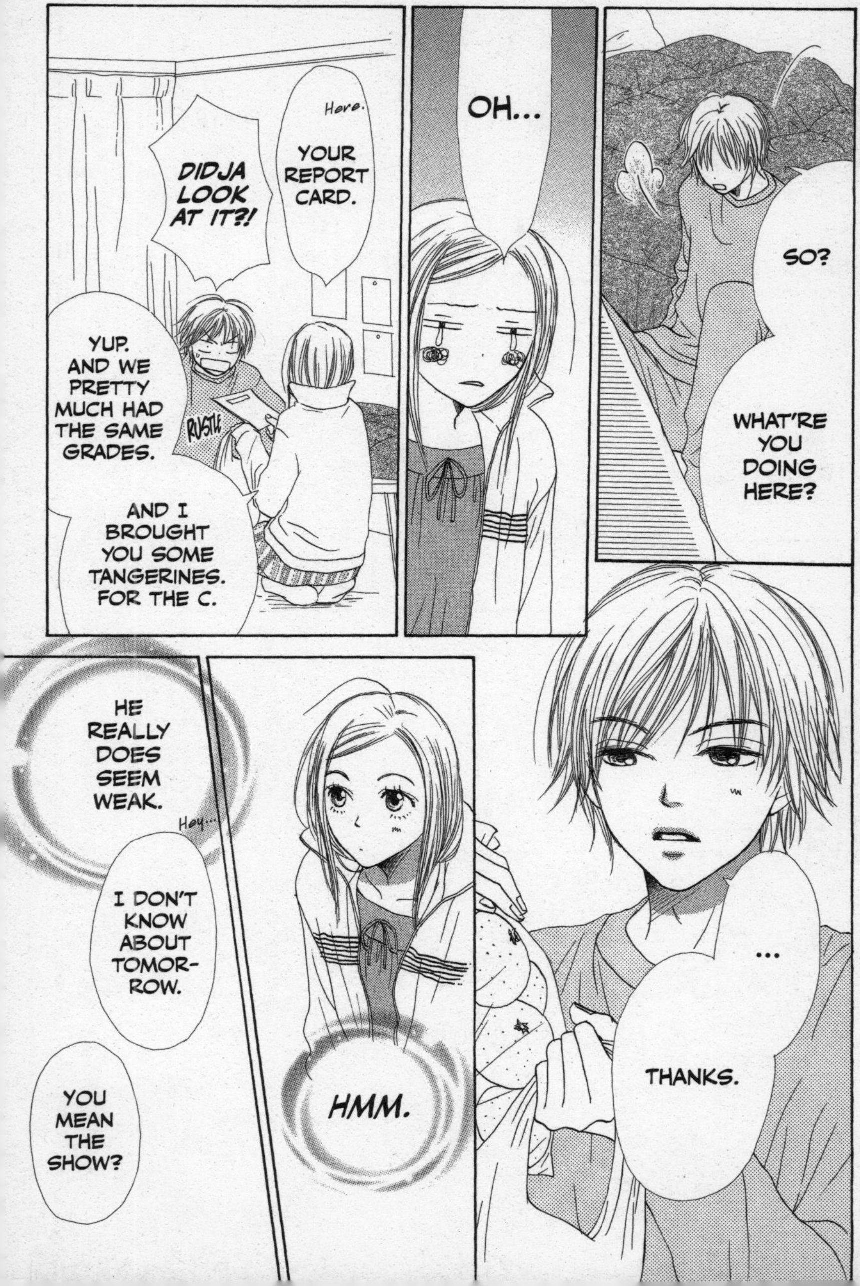
SO?
WHAT'RE YOU DOING HERE?
OH...
Here.
YOUR REPORT CARD.
DIDJA LOOK AT IT?!
YUP. AND WE PRETTY MUCH HAD THE SAME GRADES.
RUSTLE
AND I BROUGHT YOU SOME TANGERINES. FOR THE C.
...
THANKS.
HMM.
HE REALLY DOES SEEM WEAK.
Hey...
I DON'T KNOW ABOUT TOMOR-ROW.
YOU MEAN THE SHOW?

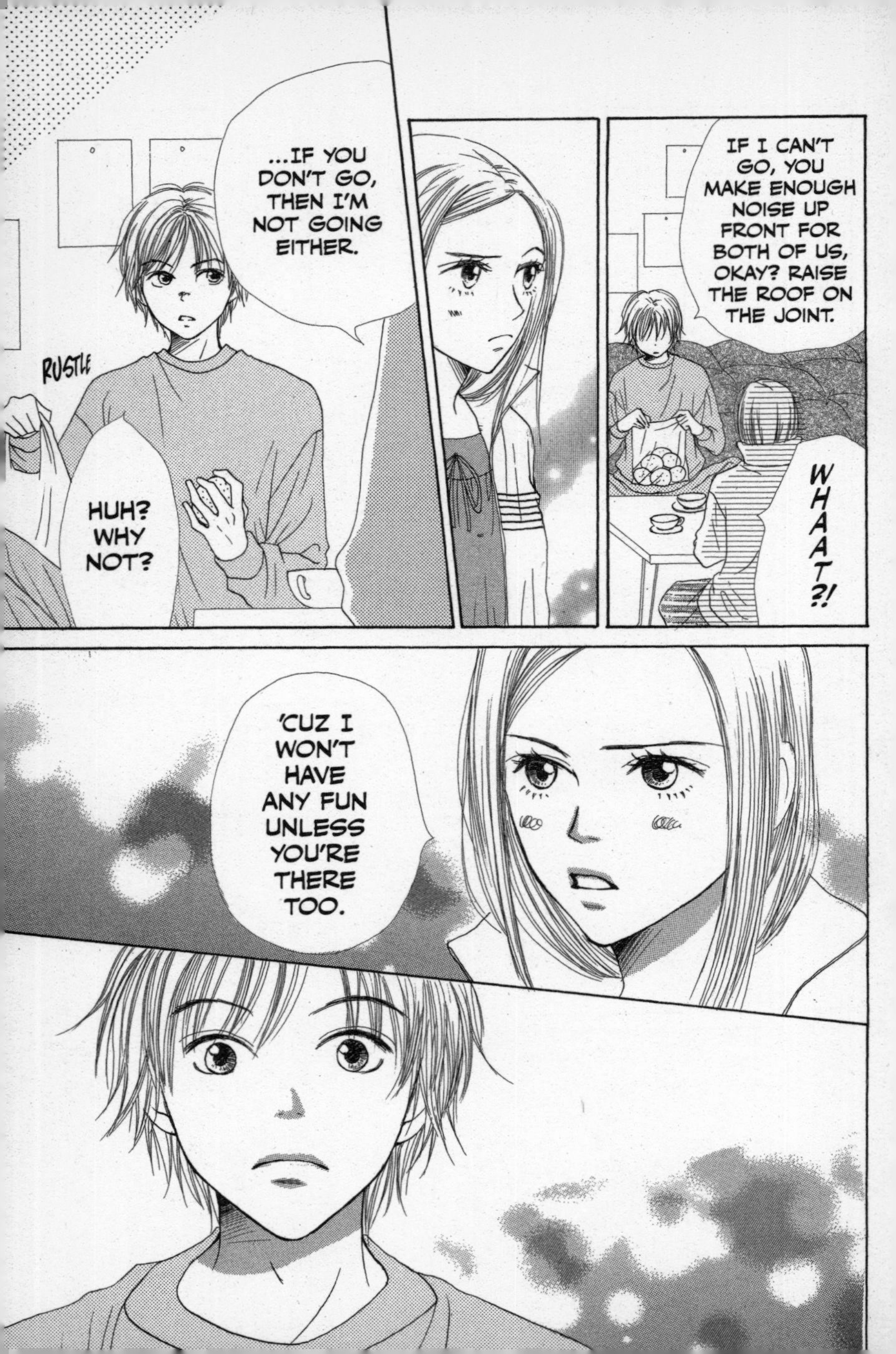
IF I CAN'T GO, YOU MAKE ENOUGH NOISE UP FRONT FOR BOTH OF US, OKAY? RAISE THE ROOF ON THE JOINT.
WHAAAT?!
...IF YOU DON'T GO, THEN I'M NOT GOING EITHER.
RUSTLE
HUH? WHY NOT?
'CUZ I WON'T HAVE ANY FUN UNLESS YOU'RE THERE TOO.

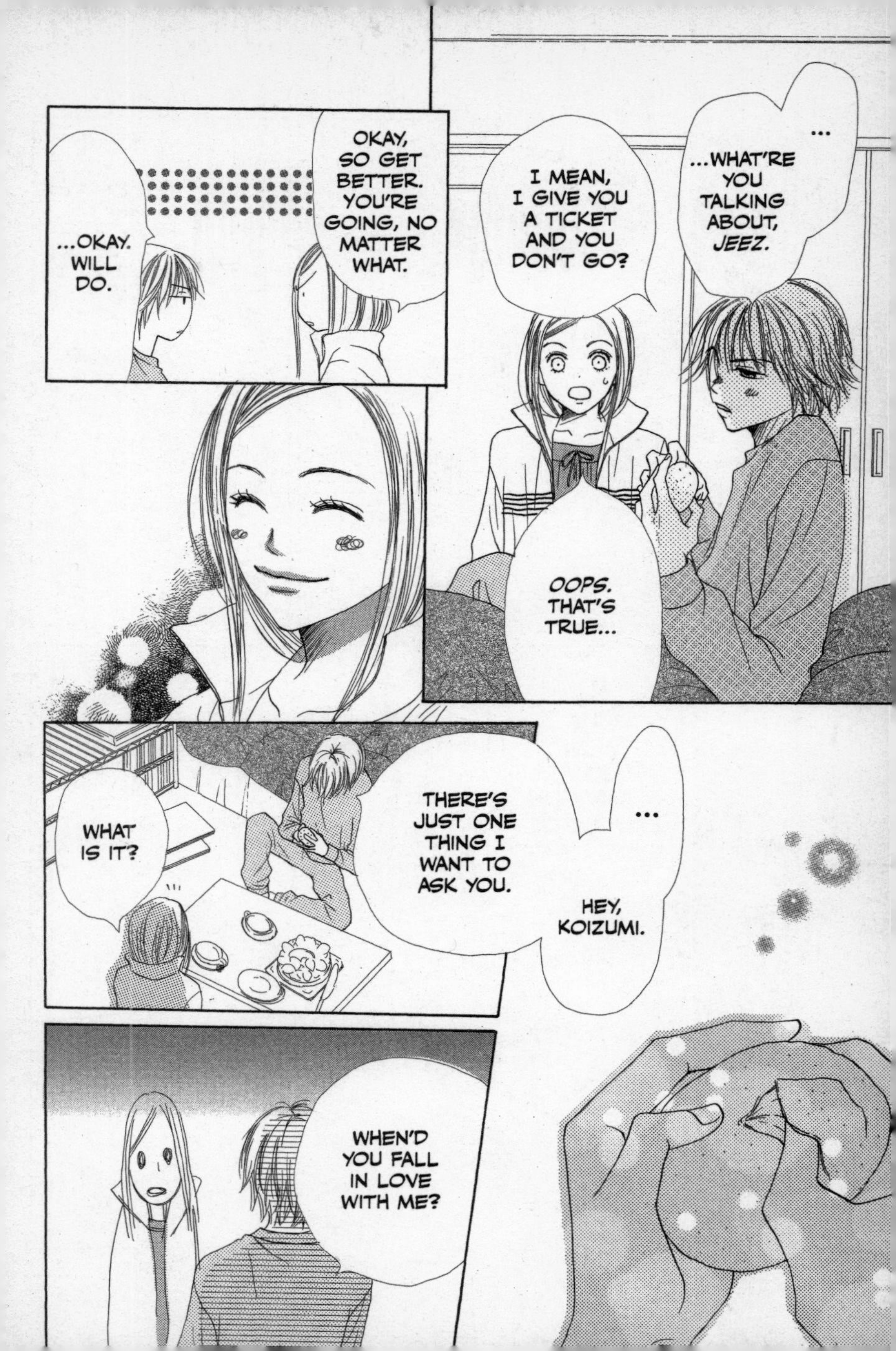
...
...WHAT'RE YOU TALKING ABOUT, *JEEZ.*
I MEAN, I GIVE YOU A TICKET AND YOU DON'T GO?
OOPS. THAT'S TRUE...
OKAY, SO GET BETTER. YOU'RE GOING, NO MATTER WHAT.
...OKAY. WILL DO.
...
HEY, KOIZUMI.
THERE'S JUST ONE THING I WANT TO ASK YOU.
WHAT IS IT?
WHEN'D YOU FALL IN LOVE WITH ME?

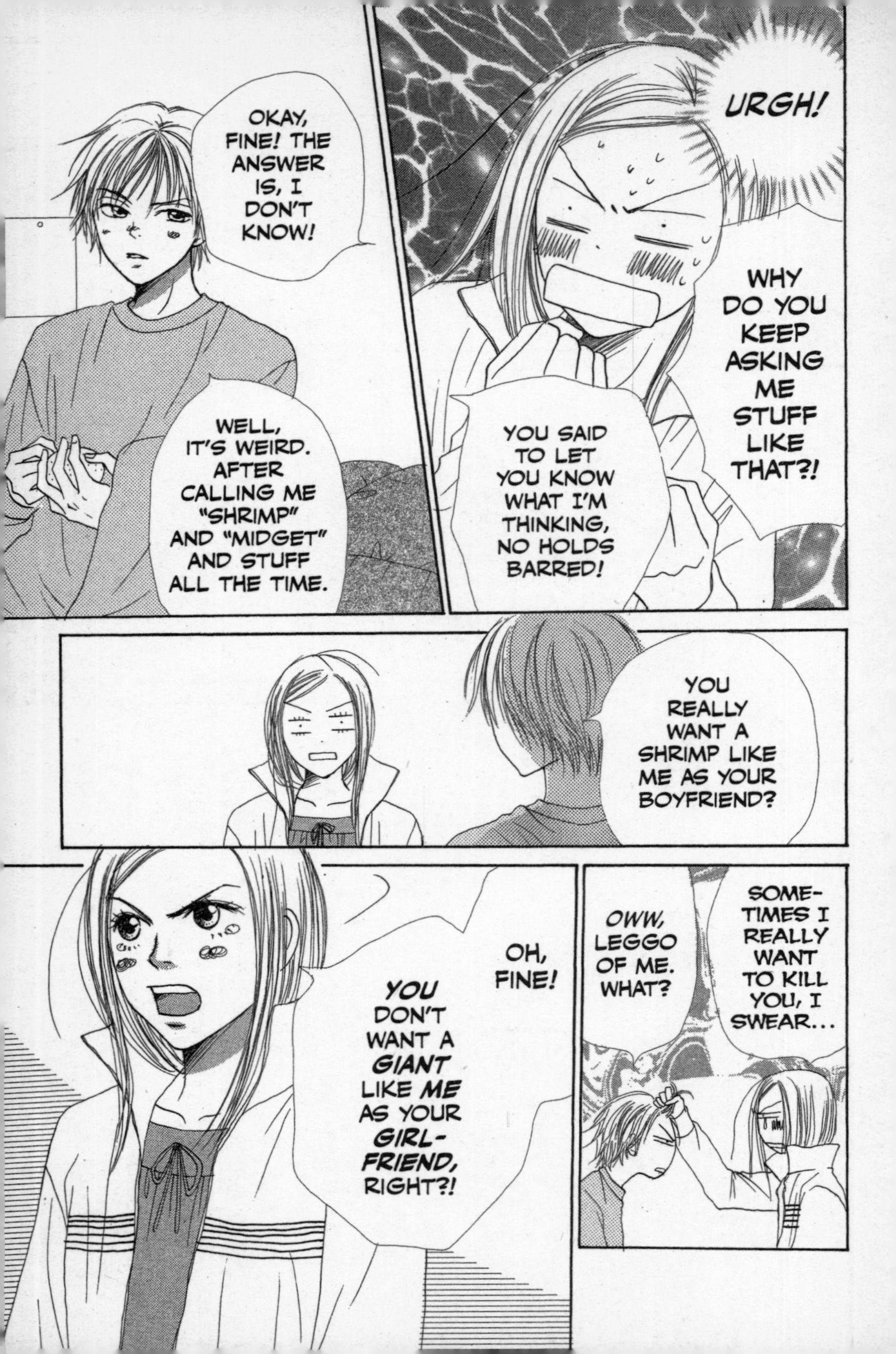
URGH!
WHY DO YOU KEEP ASKING ME STUFF LIKE THAT?!
YOU SAID TO LET YOU KNOW WHAT I'M THINKING, NO HOLDS BARRED!
OKAY, FINE! THE ANSWER IS, I DON'T KNOW!
WELL, IT'S WEIRD. AFTER CALLING ME "SHRIMP" AND "MIDGET" AND STUFF ALL THE TIME.
YOU REALLY WANT A SHRIMP LIKE ME AS YOUR BOYFRIEND?
SOME-TIMES I REALLY WANT TO KILL YOU, I SWEAR...
OWW, LEGGO OF ME. WHAT?
OH, FINE!
YOU DON'T WANT A *GIANT* LIKE *ME* AS YOUR *GIRL-FRIEND,* RIGHT?!

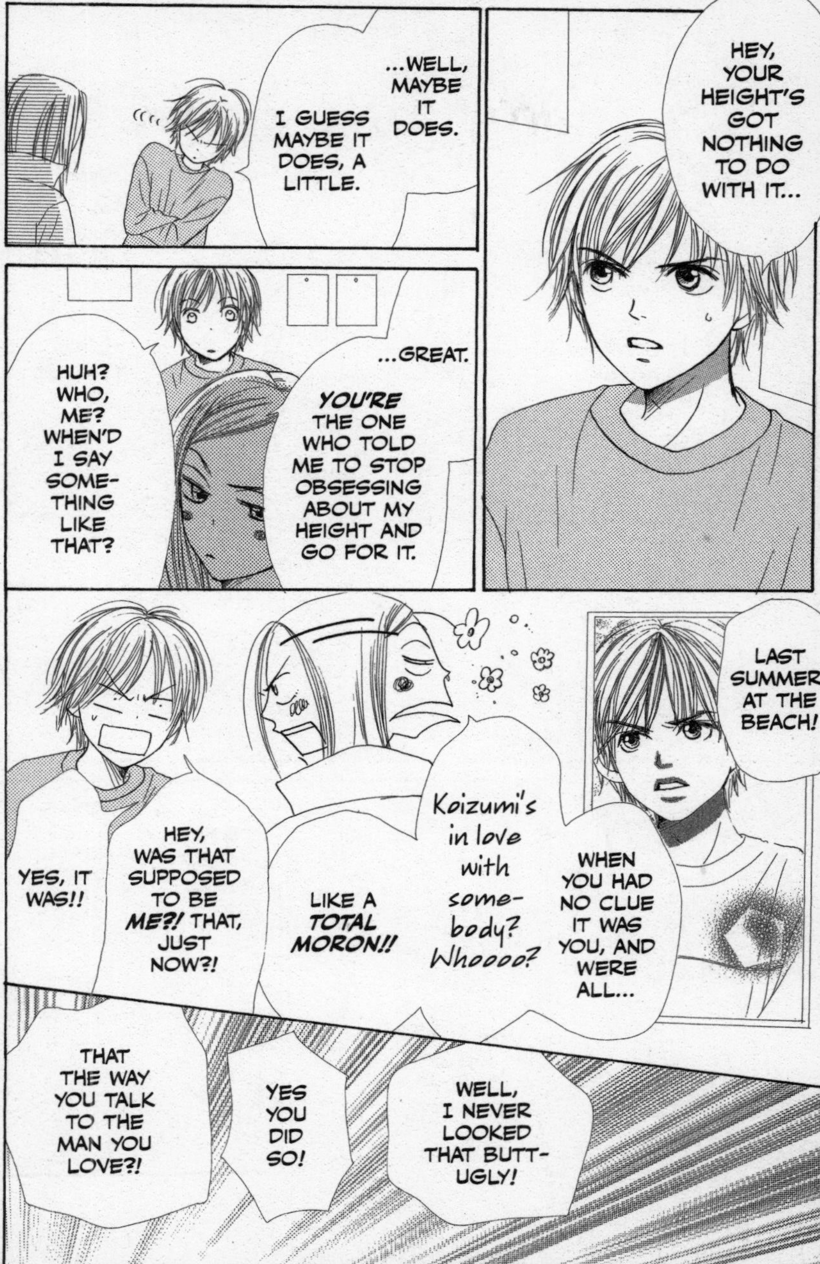
HEY, YOUR HEIGHT'S GOT NOTHING TO DO WITH IT...
...WELL, MAYBE IT DOES.
I GUESS MAYBE IT DOES, A LITTLE.
...GREAT.
YOU'RE THE ONE WHO TOLD ME TO STOP OBSESSING ABOUT MY HEIGHT AND GO FOR IT.
HUH? WHO, ME? WHEN'D I SAY SOME-THING LIKE THAT?
LAST SUMMER! AT THE BEACH!
WHEN YOU HAD NO CLUE IT WAS YOU, AND WERE ALL...
Koizumi's in love with some-body? Whoooo?
LIKE A ***TOTAL MORON!!***
HEY, WAS THAT SUPPOSED TO BE ***ME?!*** THAT, JUST NOW?!
YES, IT WAS!!
WELL, I NEVER LOOKED THAT BUTT-UGLY!
YES YOU DID SO!
THAT THE WAY YOU TALK TO THE MAN YOU LOVE?!

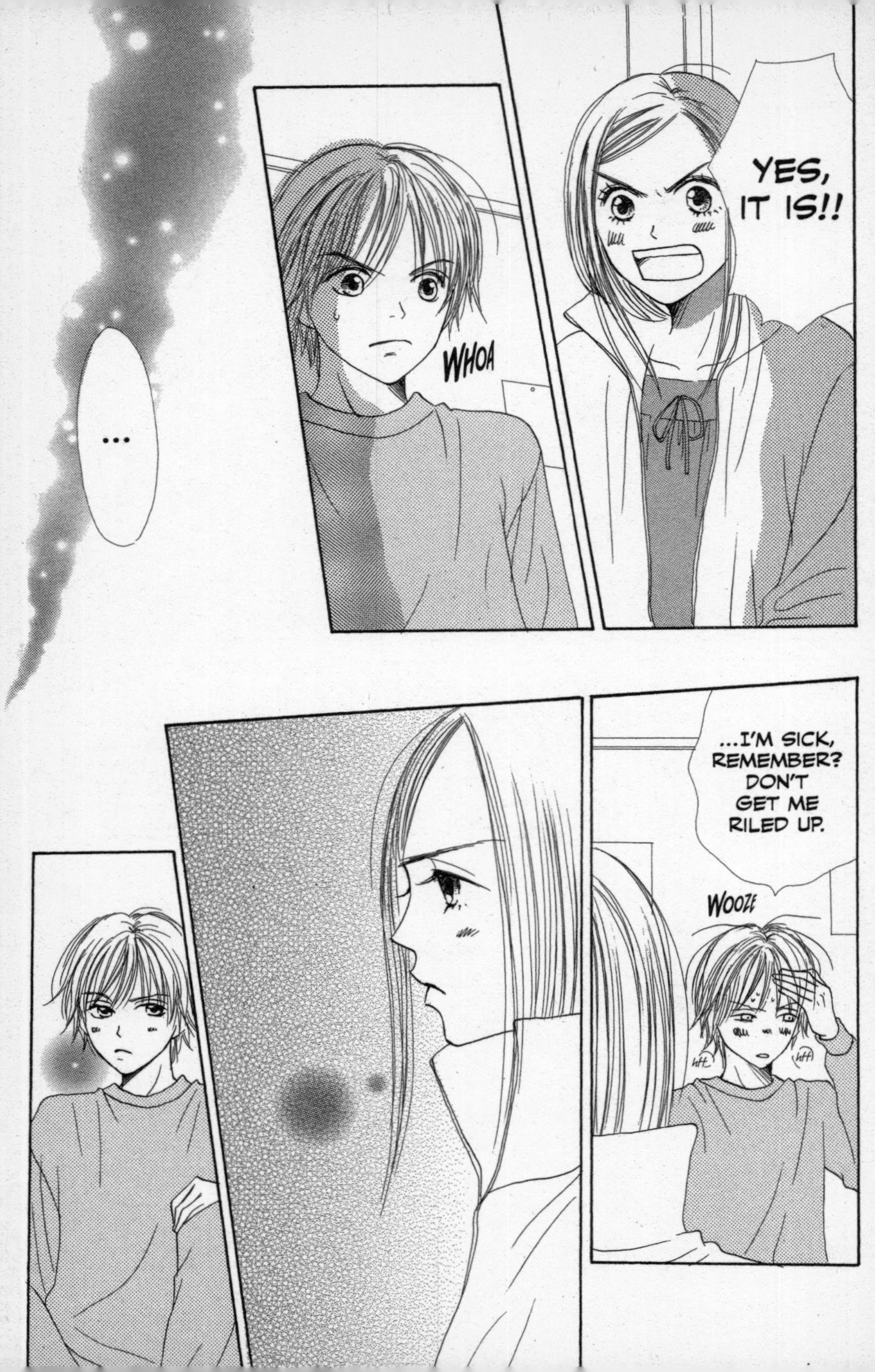
YES, IT IS!!
WHOA
...
...I'M SICK, REMEMBER? DON'T GET ME RILED UP.
WOOZE

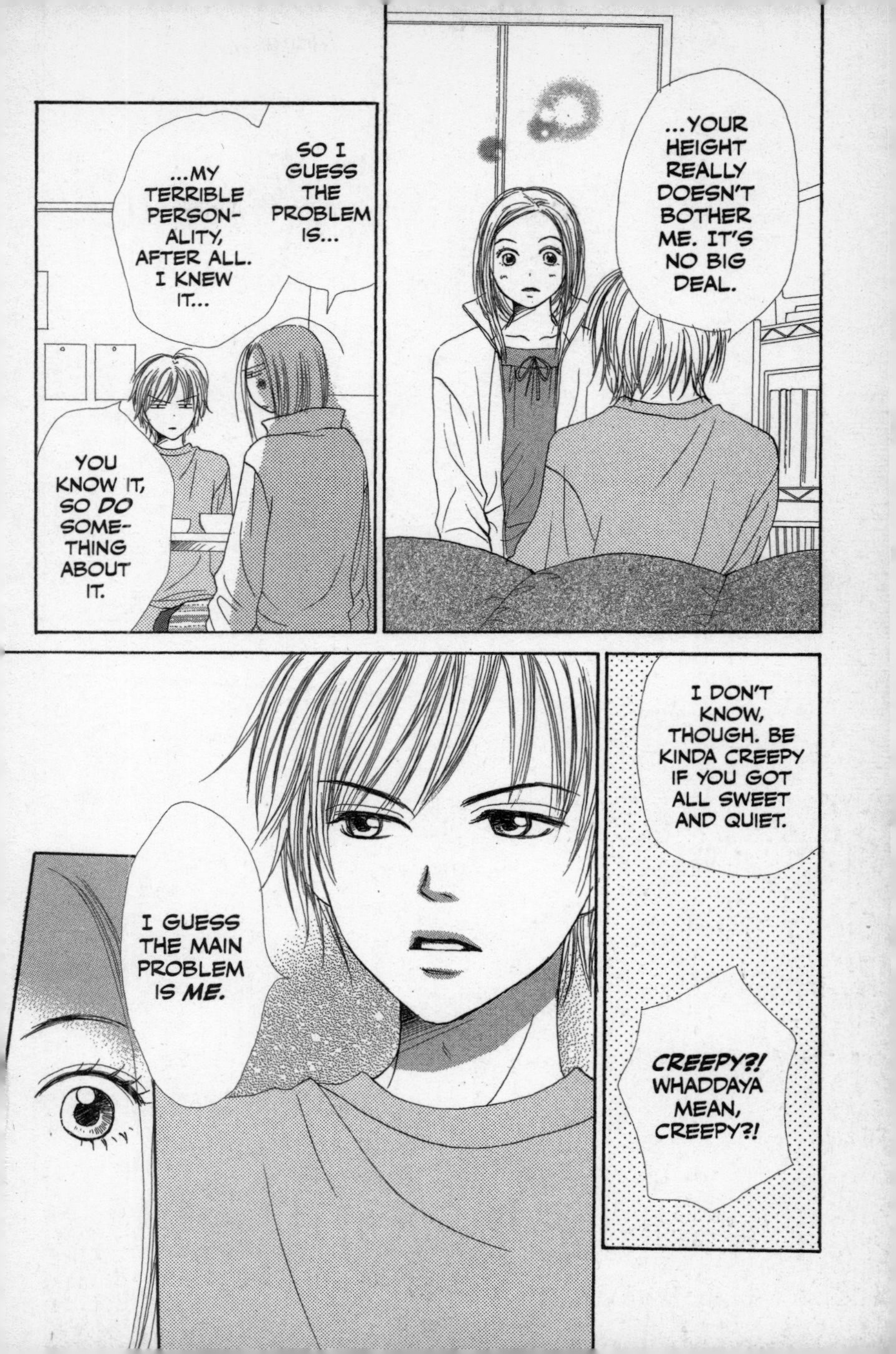
...YOUR HEIGHT REALLY DOESN'T BOTHER ME. IT'S NO BIG DEAL.
SO I GUESS THE PROBLEM IS...
...MY TERRIBLE PERSON-ALITY, AFTER ALL. I KNEW IT...
YOU KNOW IT, SO *DO* SOME-THING ABOUT IT.
I DON'T KNOW, THOUGH. BE KINDA CREEPY IF YOU GOT ALL SWEET AND QUIET.
CREEPY?! WHADDAYA MEAN, CREEPY?!
I GUESS THE MAIN PROBLEM IS *ME.*

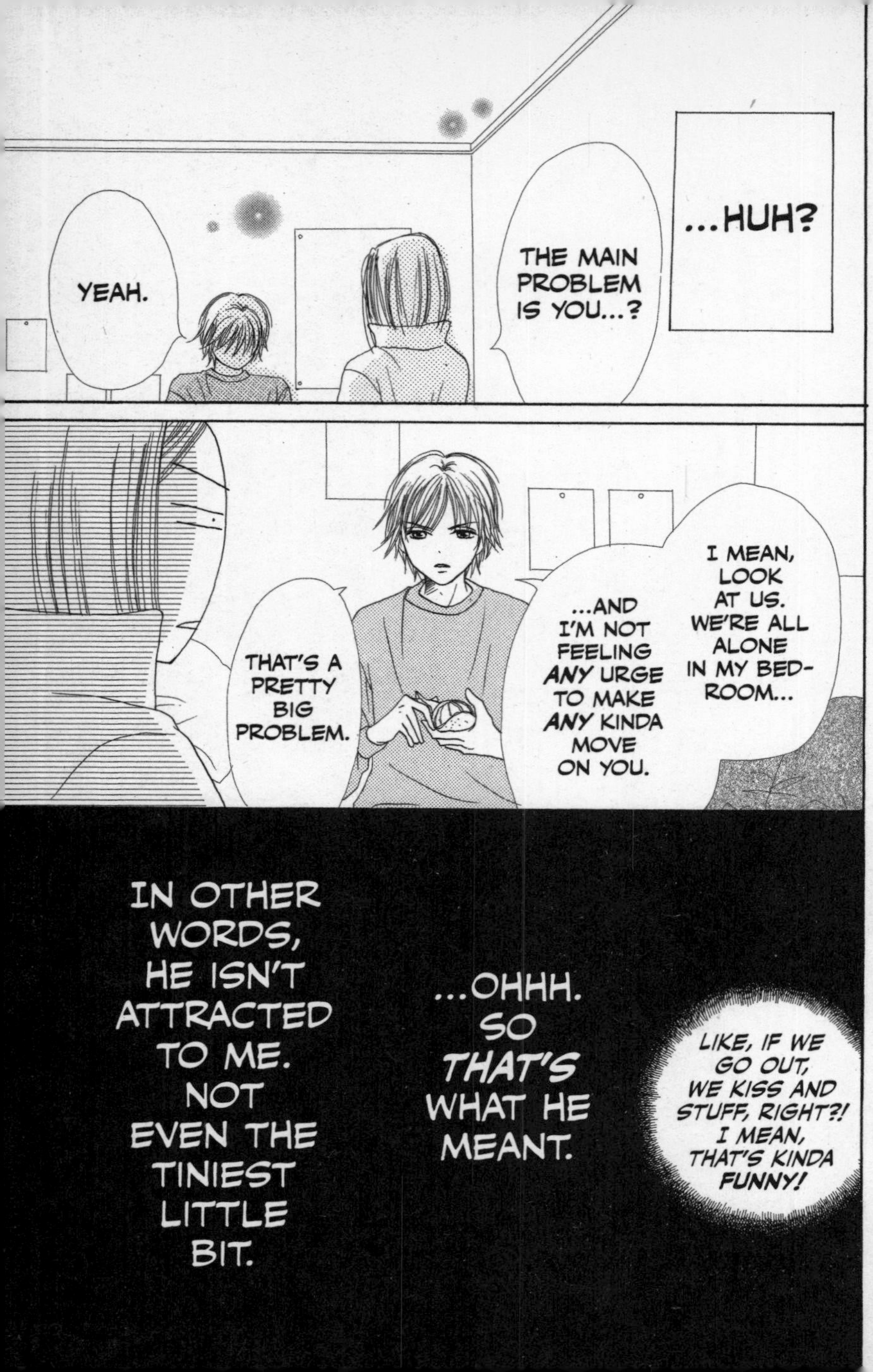
...HUH?
THE MAIN PROBLEM IS YOU...?
YEAH.
I MEAN, LOOK AT US. WE'RE ALL ALONE IN MY BED-ROOM...
...AND I'M NOT FEELING *ANY* URGE TO MAKE *ANY* KINDA MOVE ON YOU.
THAT'S A PRETTY BIG PROBLEM.
LIKE, IF WE GO OUT, WE KISS AND STUFF, RIGHT?! I MEAN, THAT'S KINDA FUNNY!
...OHHH. SO *THAT'S* WHAT HE MEANT.
IN OTHER WORDS, HE ISN'T ATTRACTED TO ME. NOT EVEN THE TINIEST LITTLE BIT.

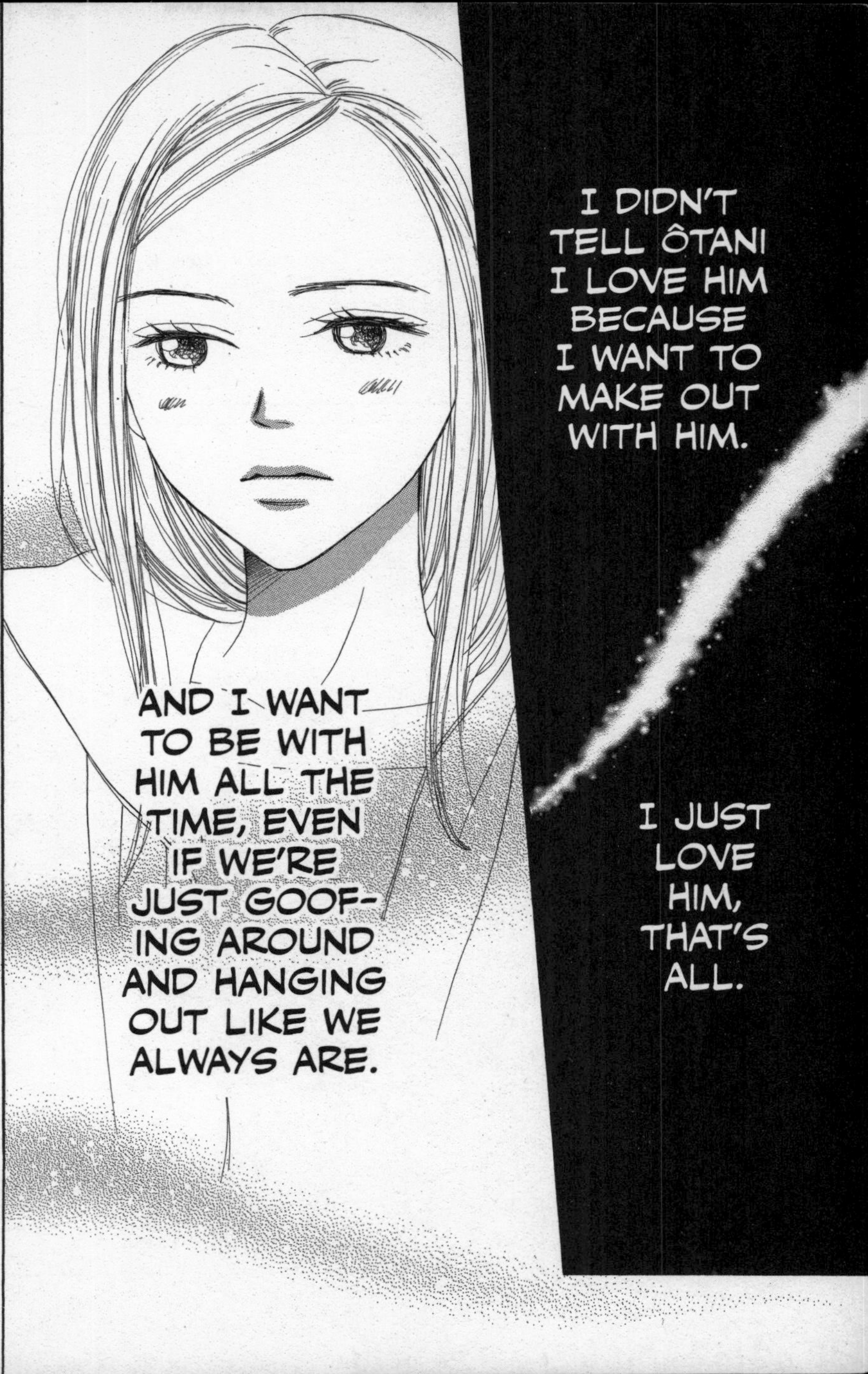
I DIDN'T TELL ÔTANI I LOVE HIM BECAUSE I WANT TO MAKE OUT WITH HIM.
AND I WANT TO BE WITH HIM ALL THE TIME, EVEN IF WE'RE JUST GOOFING AROUND AND HANGING OUT LIKE WE ALWAYS ARE.
I JUST LOVE HIM, THAT'S ALL.

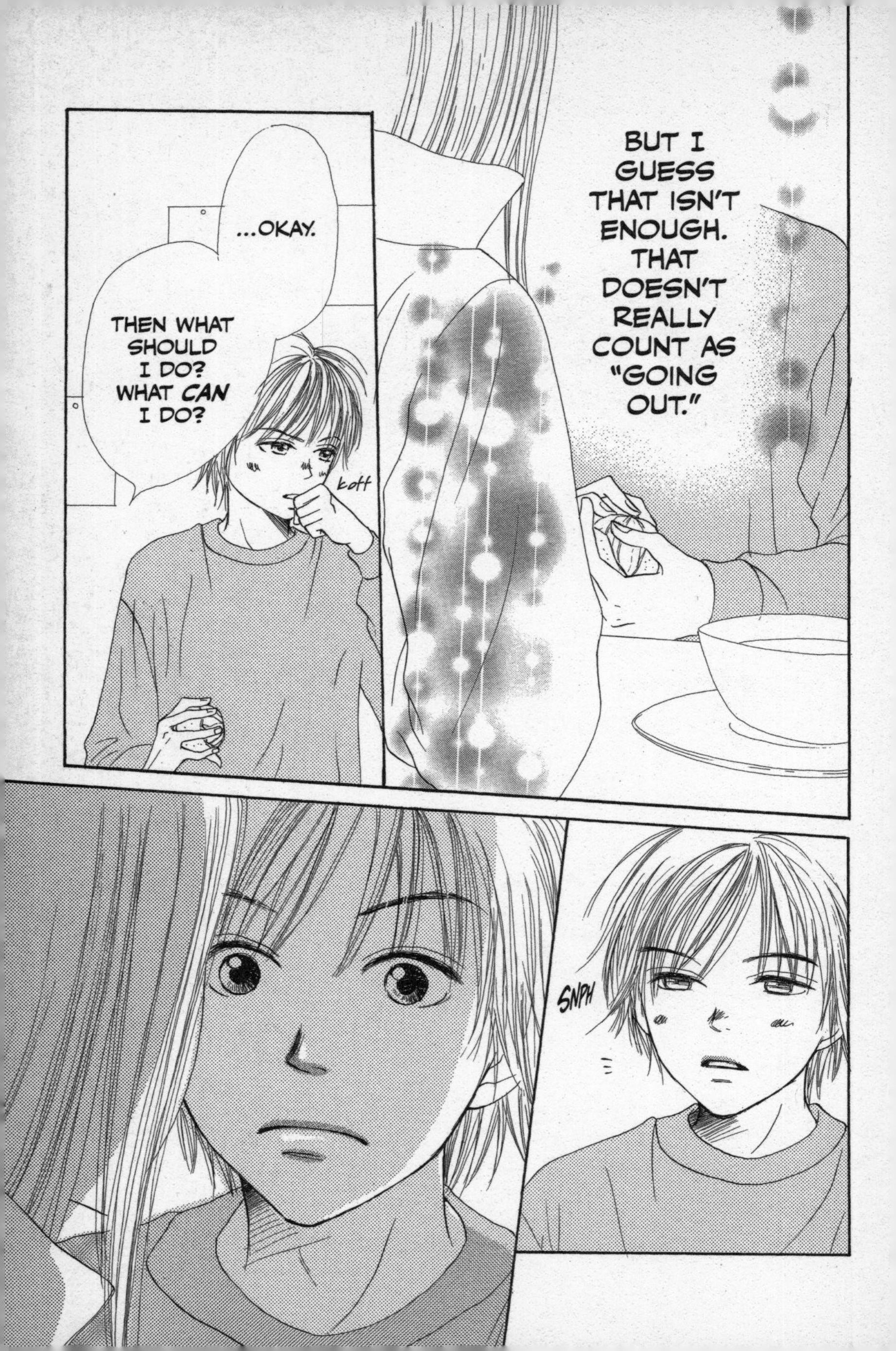
BUT I GUESS THAT ISN'T ENOUGH. THAT DOESN'T REALLY COUNT AS "GOING OUT."
...OKAY.
THEN WHAT SHOULD I DO? WHAT CAN I DO?
koff
SNPH

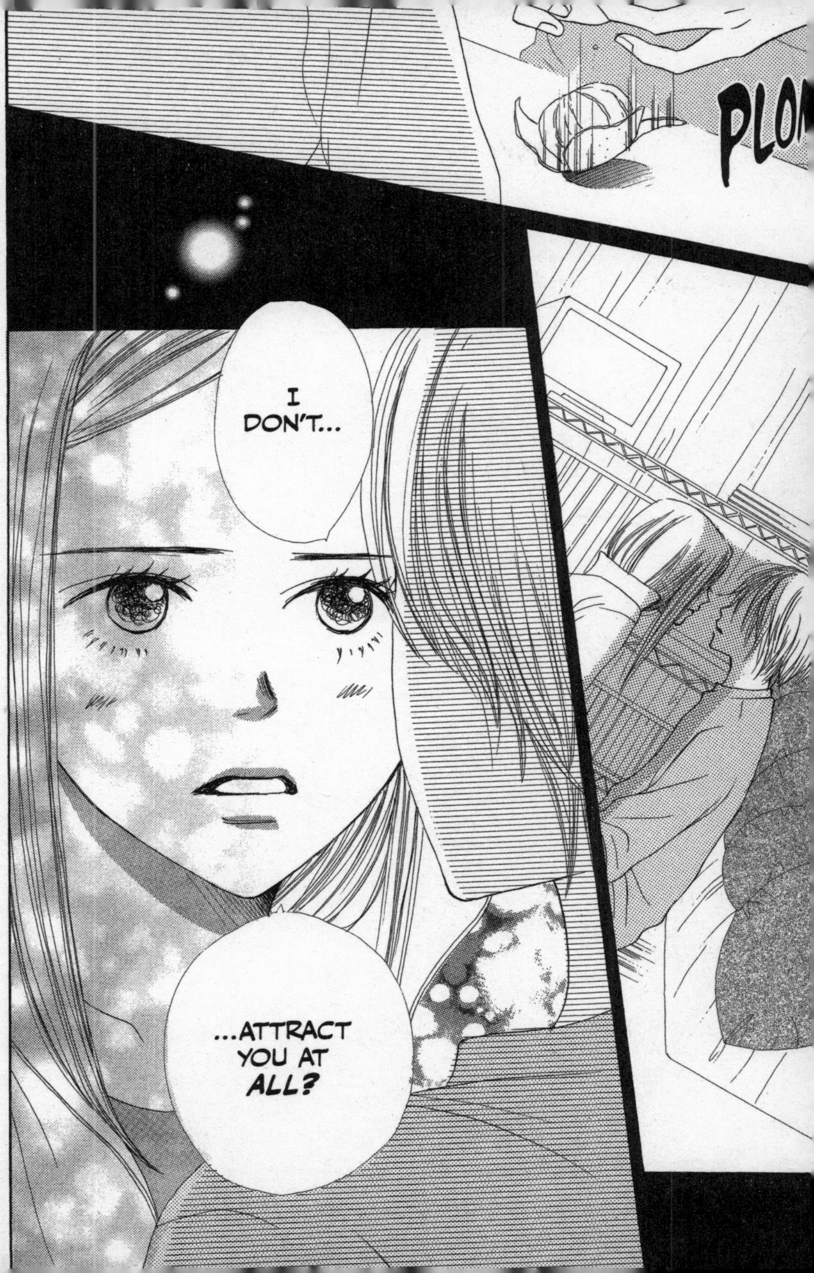
PLO
I DON'T...
...ATTRACT YOU AT ALL?

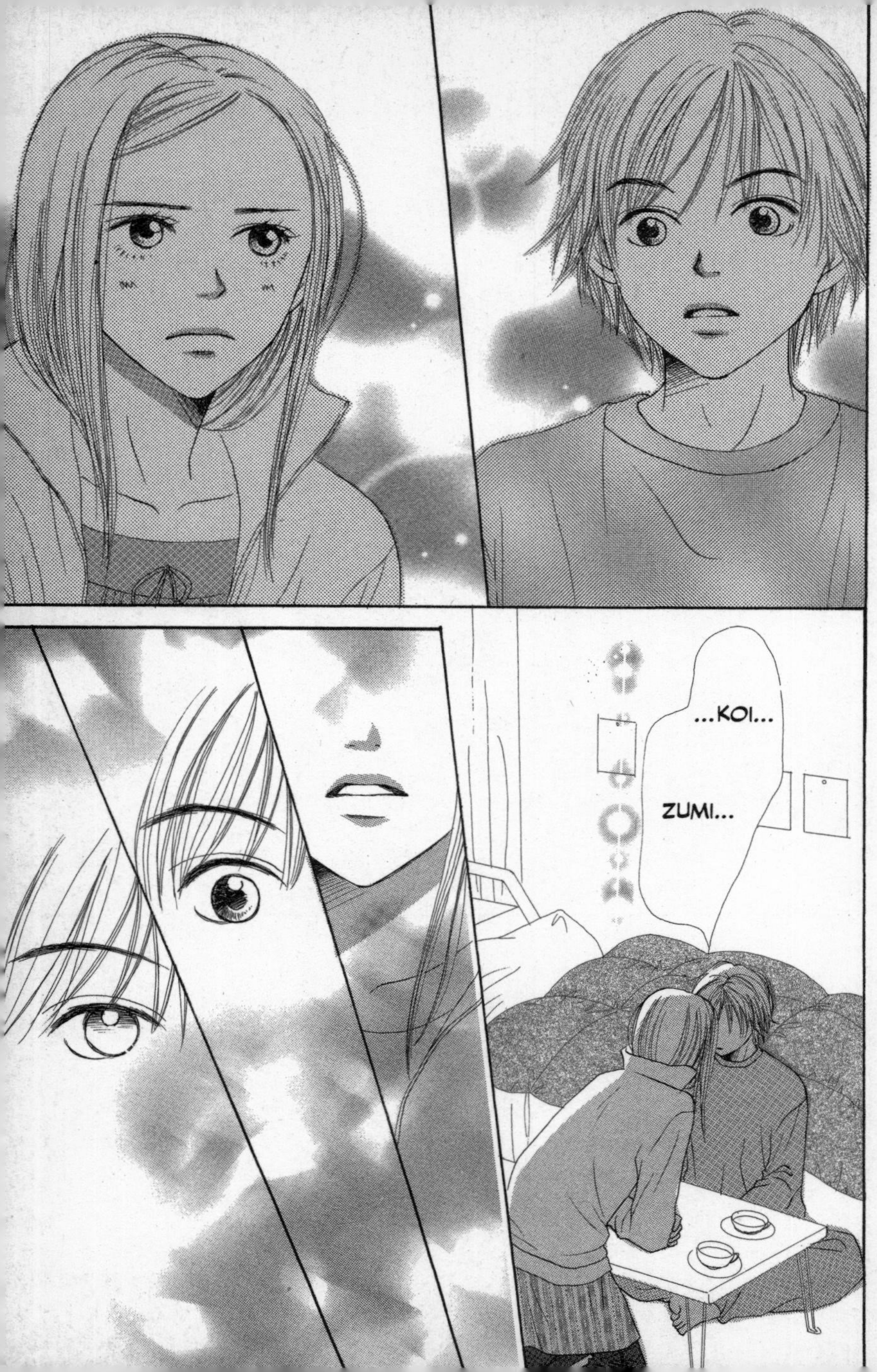
...KOI...
ZUMI...

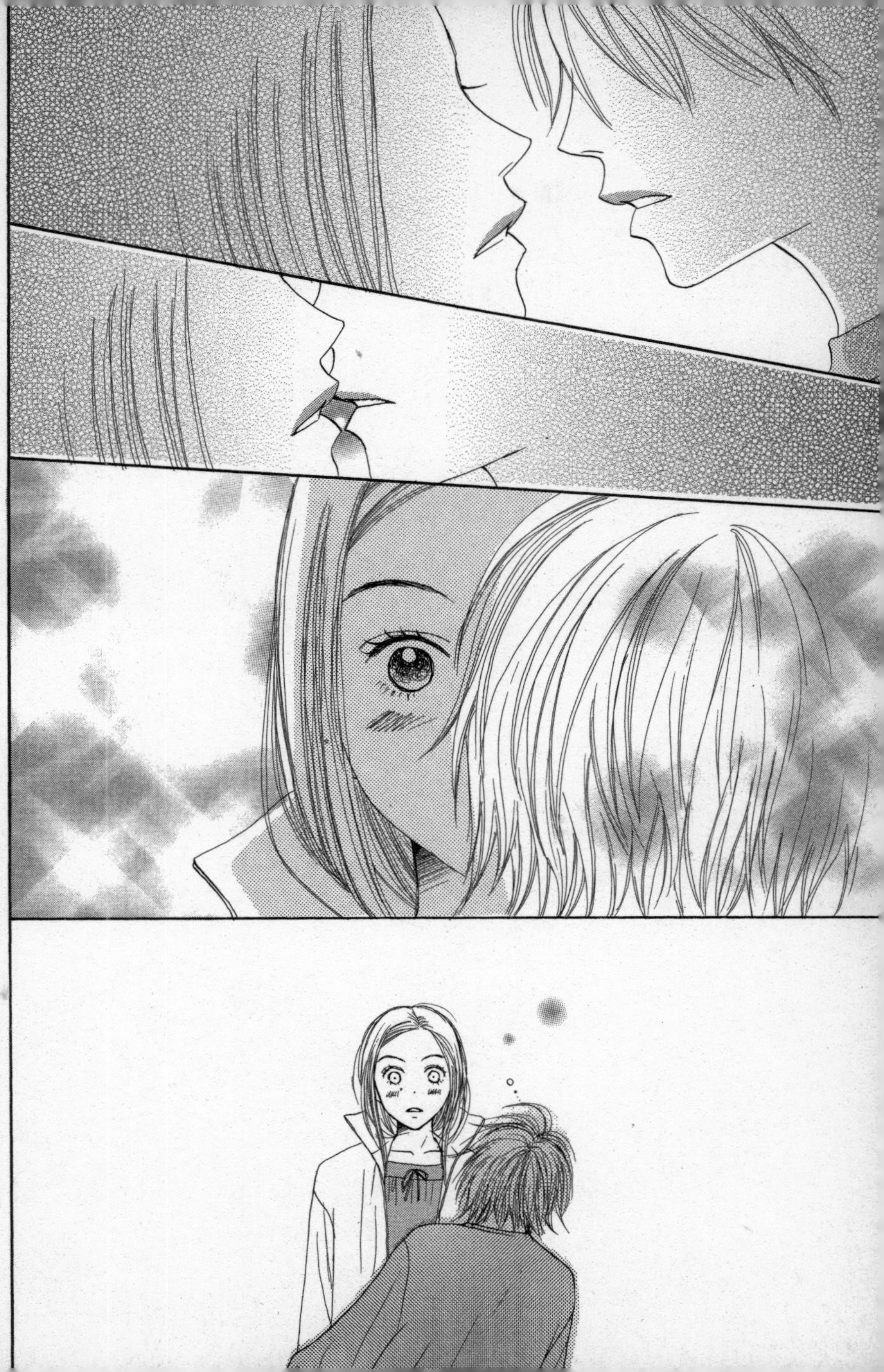

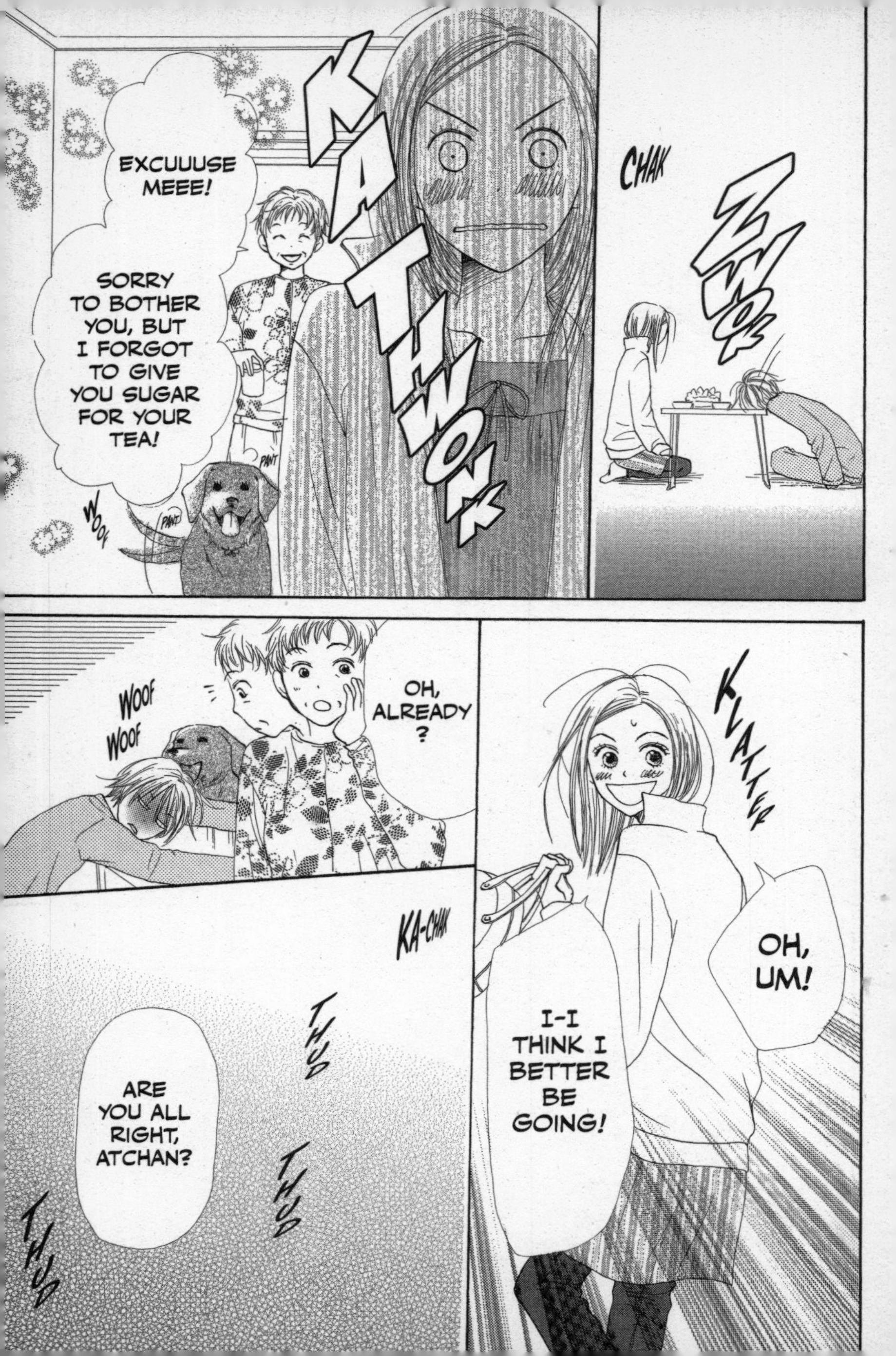
CHAK
KATHWONK
EXCUUUSE MEEE!
SORRY TO BOTHER YOU, BUT I FORGOT TO GIVE YOU SUGAR FOR YOUR TEA!
PANT
PANT
WOOF
KLATTER
OH, UM!
I-I THINK I BETTER BE GOING!
OH, ALREADY?
WOOF
WOOF
KA-CHAK
THUD
THUD
THUD
ARE YOU ALL RIGHT, ATCHAN?

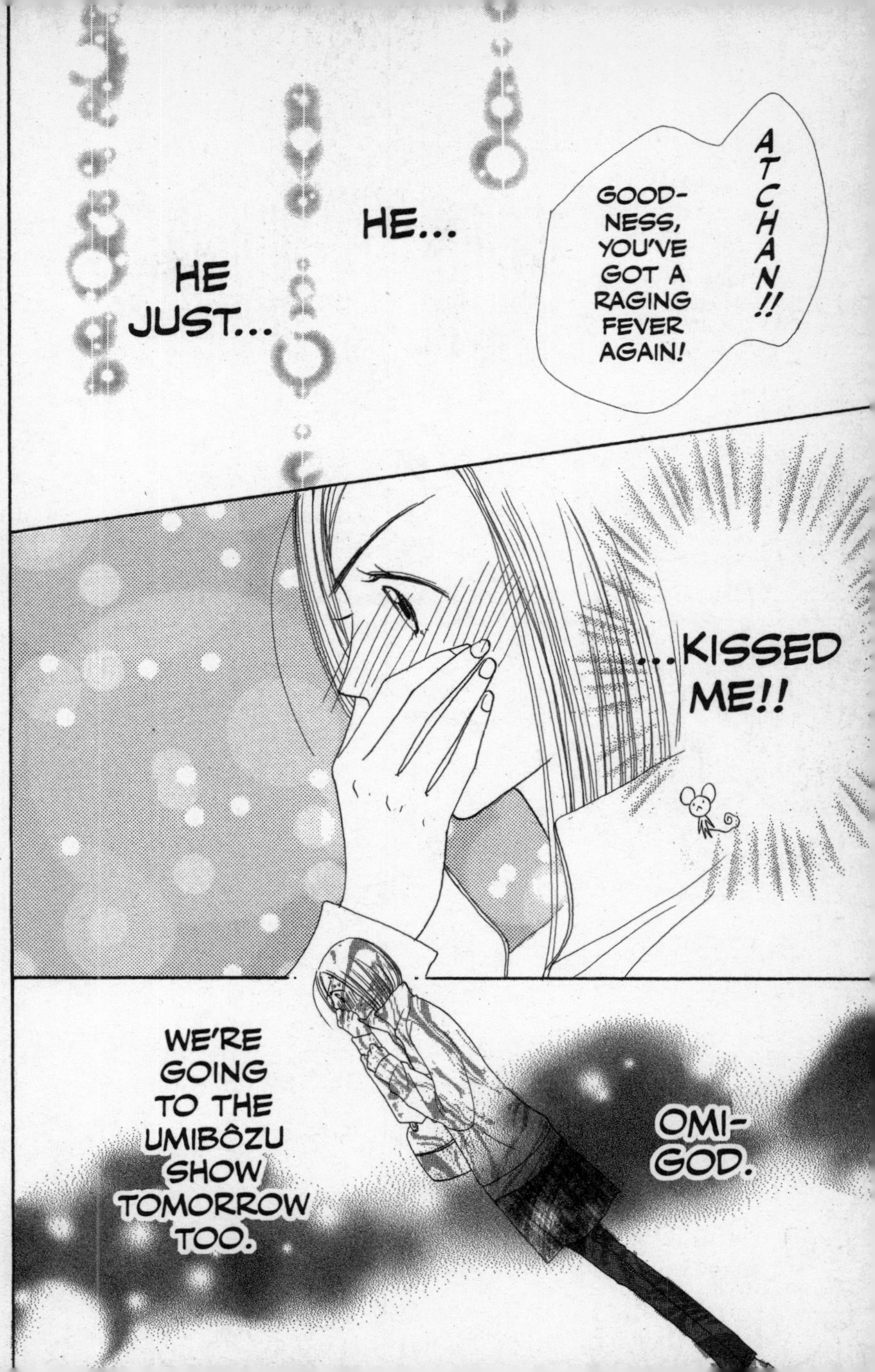
ATCHAN!!
GOODNESS, YOU'VE GOT A RAGING FEVER AGAIN!
HE...
HE JUST...
...KISSED ME!!
OMI-GOD.
WE'RE GOING TO THE UMIBÔZU SHOW TOMORROW TOO.

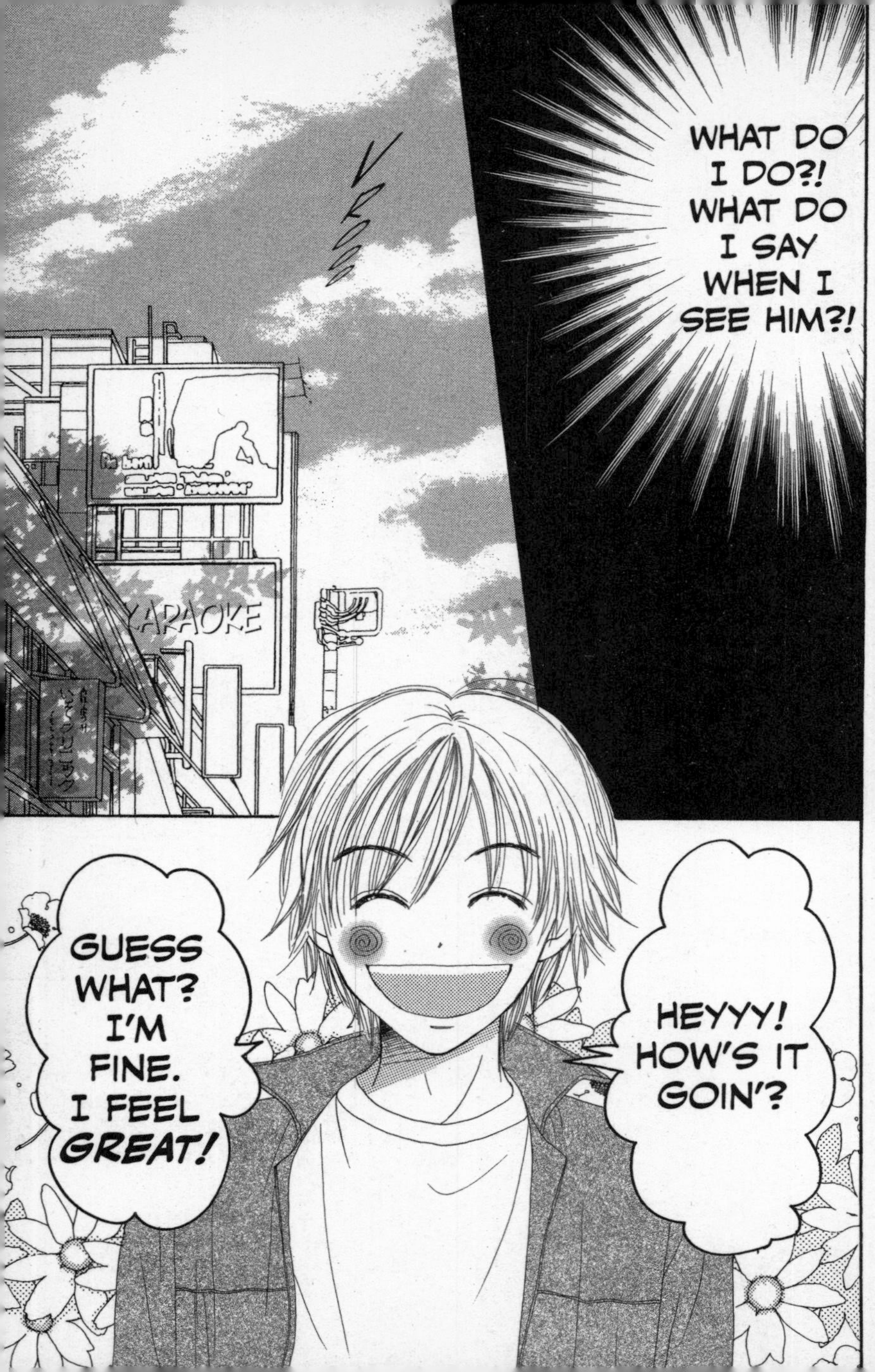
WHAT DO I DO?! WHAT DO I SAY WHEN I SEE HIM?!
VROOO
KARAOKE
HEYYY! HOW'S IT GOIN'?
GUESS WHAT? I'M FINE. I FEEL *GREAT!*

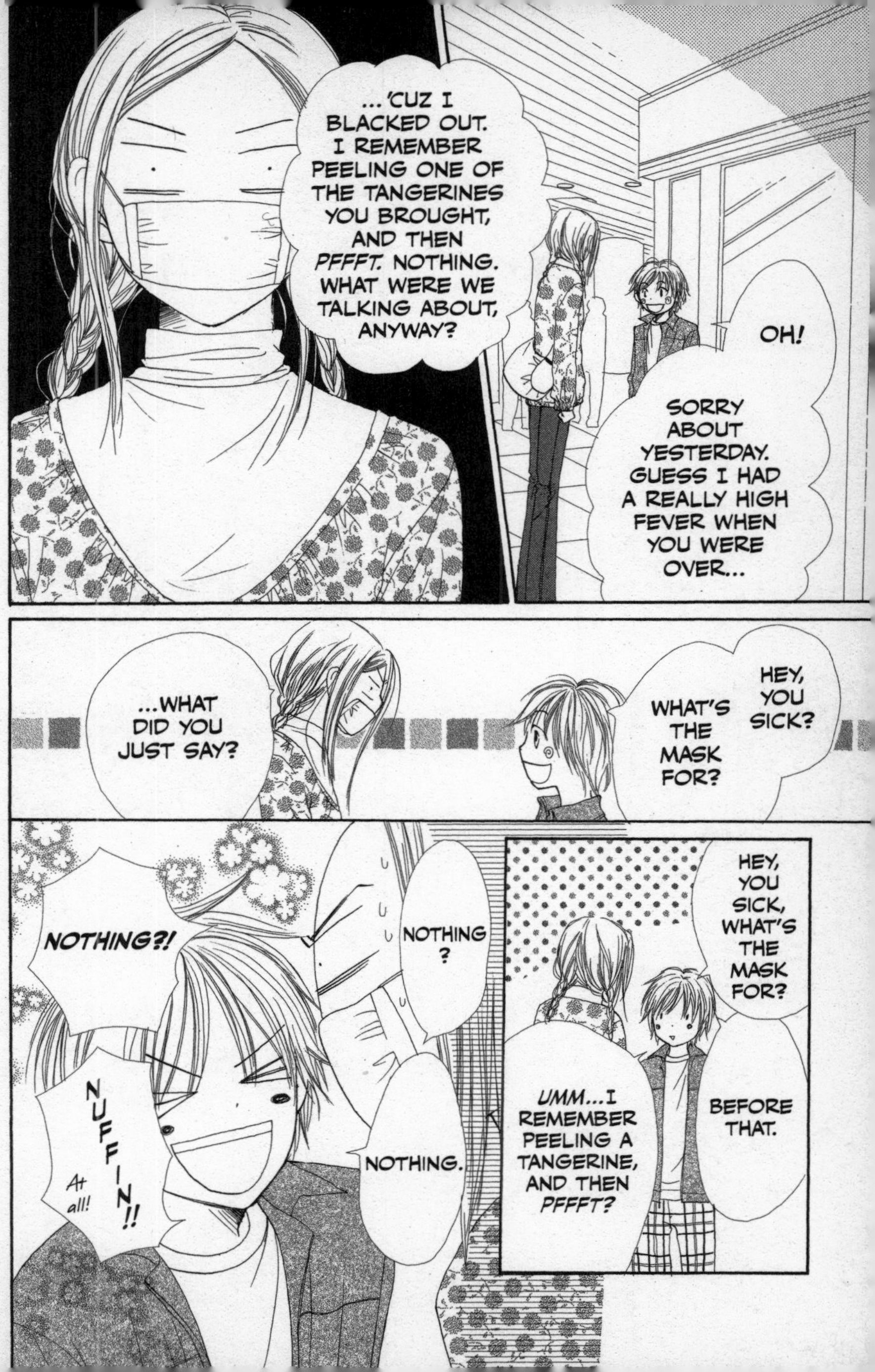
OH!
SORRY ABOUT YESTERDAY. GUESS I HAD A REALLY HIGH FEVER WHEN YOU WERE OVER...
...'CUZ I BLACKED OUT. I REMEMBER PEELING ONE OF THE TANGERINES YOU BROUGHT, AND THEN PFFFT. NOTHING. WHAT WERE WE TALKING ABOUT, ANYWAY?
HEY, YOU SICK?
WHAT'S THE MASK FOR?
...WHAT DID YOU JUST SAY?
HEY, YOU SICK, WHAT'S THE MASK FOR?
BEFORE THAT.
UMM...I REMEMBER PEELING A TANGERINE, AND THEN PFFFT?
NOTHING?
NOTHING?!
NOTHING.
NUFFIN!!
At all!

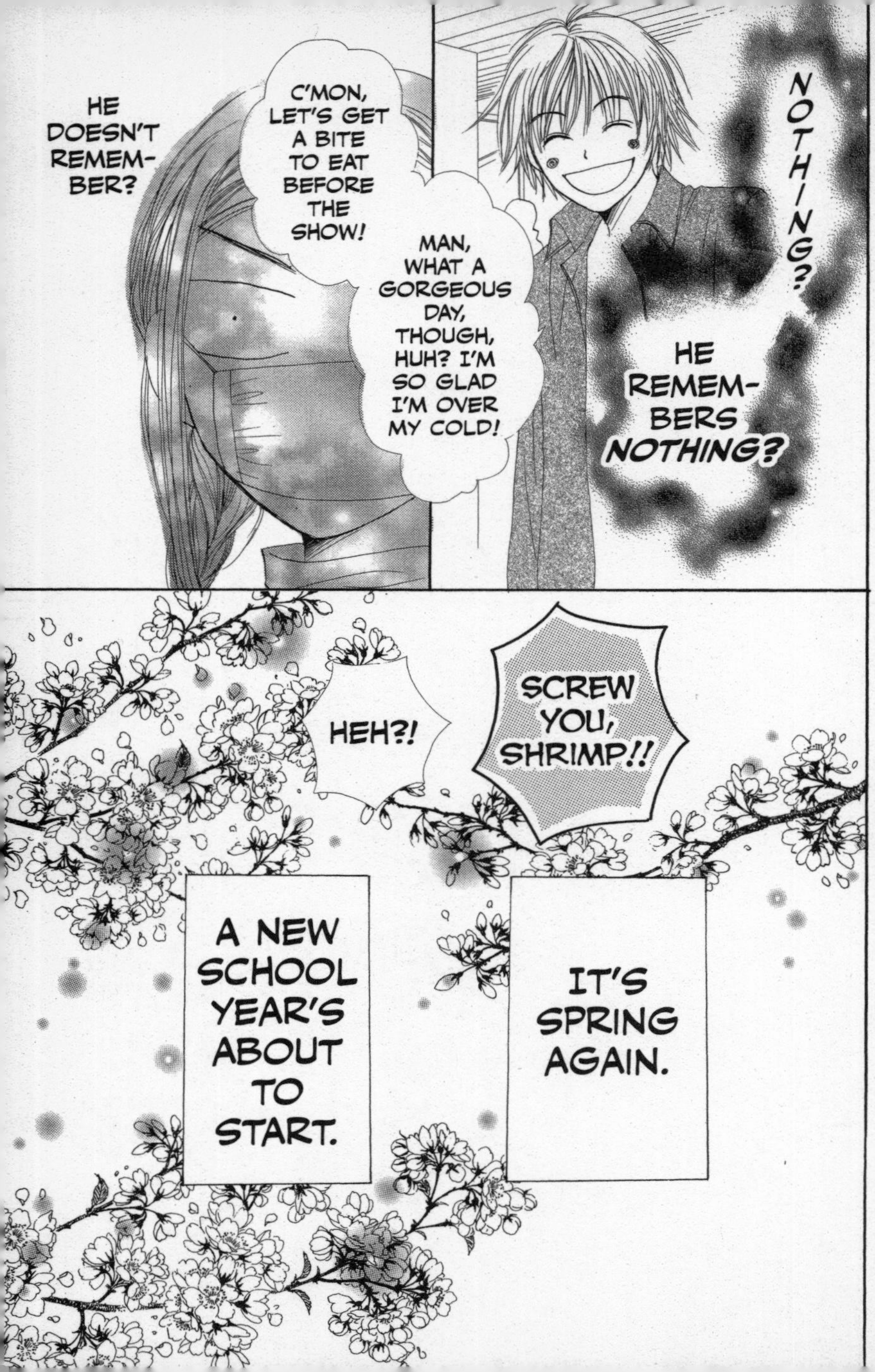
NOTHING?
HE REMEMBERS NOTHING?
MAN, WHAT A GORGEOUS DAY, THOUGH, HUH? I'M SO GLAD I'M OVER MY COLD!
C'MON, LET'S GET A BITE TO EAT BEFORE THE SHOW!
HE DOESN'T REMEMBER?
SCREW YOU, SHRIMP!!
HEH?!
IT'S SPRING AGAIN.
A NEW SCHOOL YEAR'S ABOUT TO START.

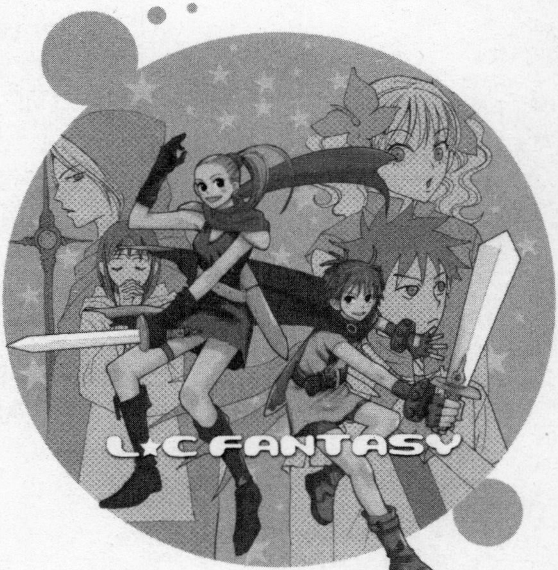
L★C FANTASY

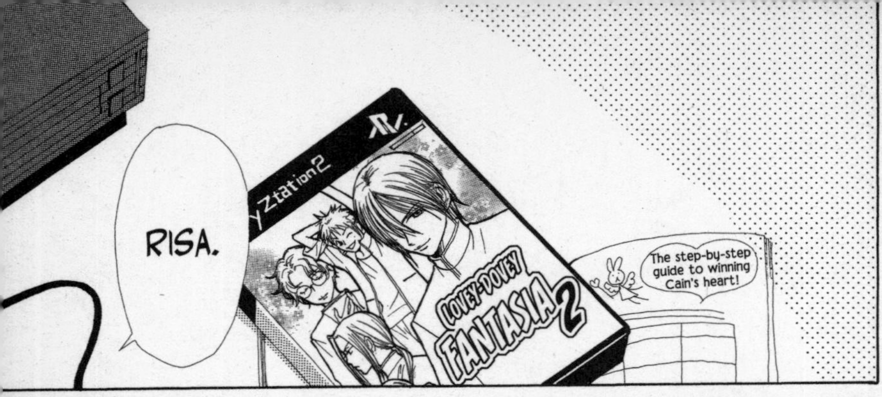
RISA.
yZtation2
LOVEY-DOVEY FANTASIA 2
The step-by-step guide to winning Cain's heart!

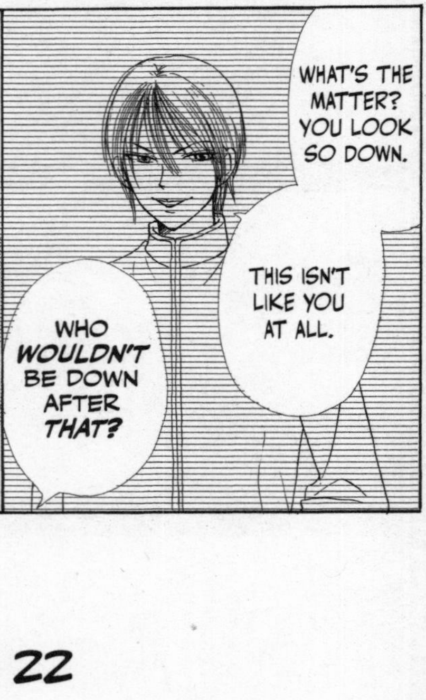
WHAT'S THE MATTER? YOU LOOK SO DOWN.
THIS ISN'T LIKE YOU AT ALL.
WHO *WOULDN'T* BE DOWN AFTER *THAT?*

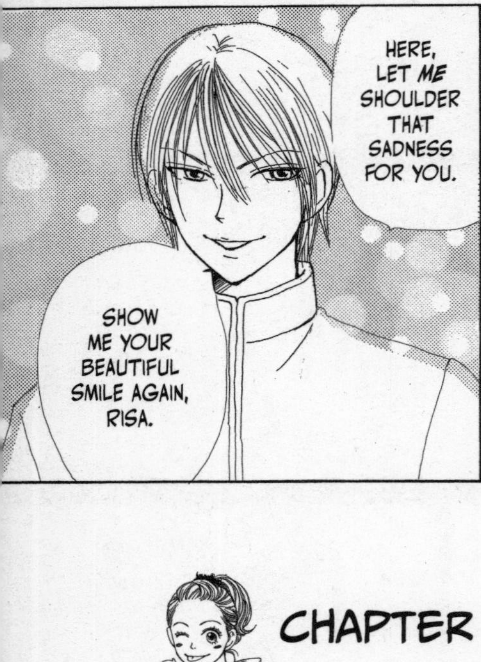
HERE, LET *ME* SHOULDER THAT SADNESS FOR YOU.
SHOW ME YOUR BEAUTIFUL SMILE AGAIN, RISA.

CHAPTER 22

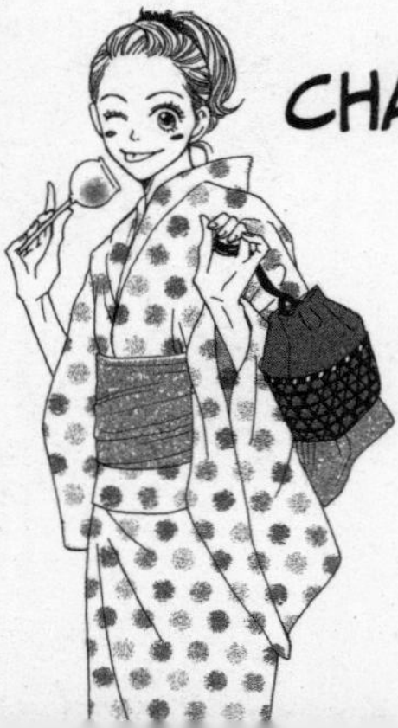

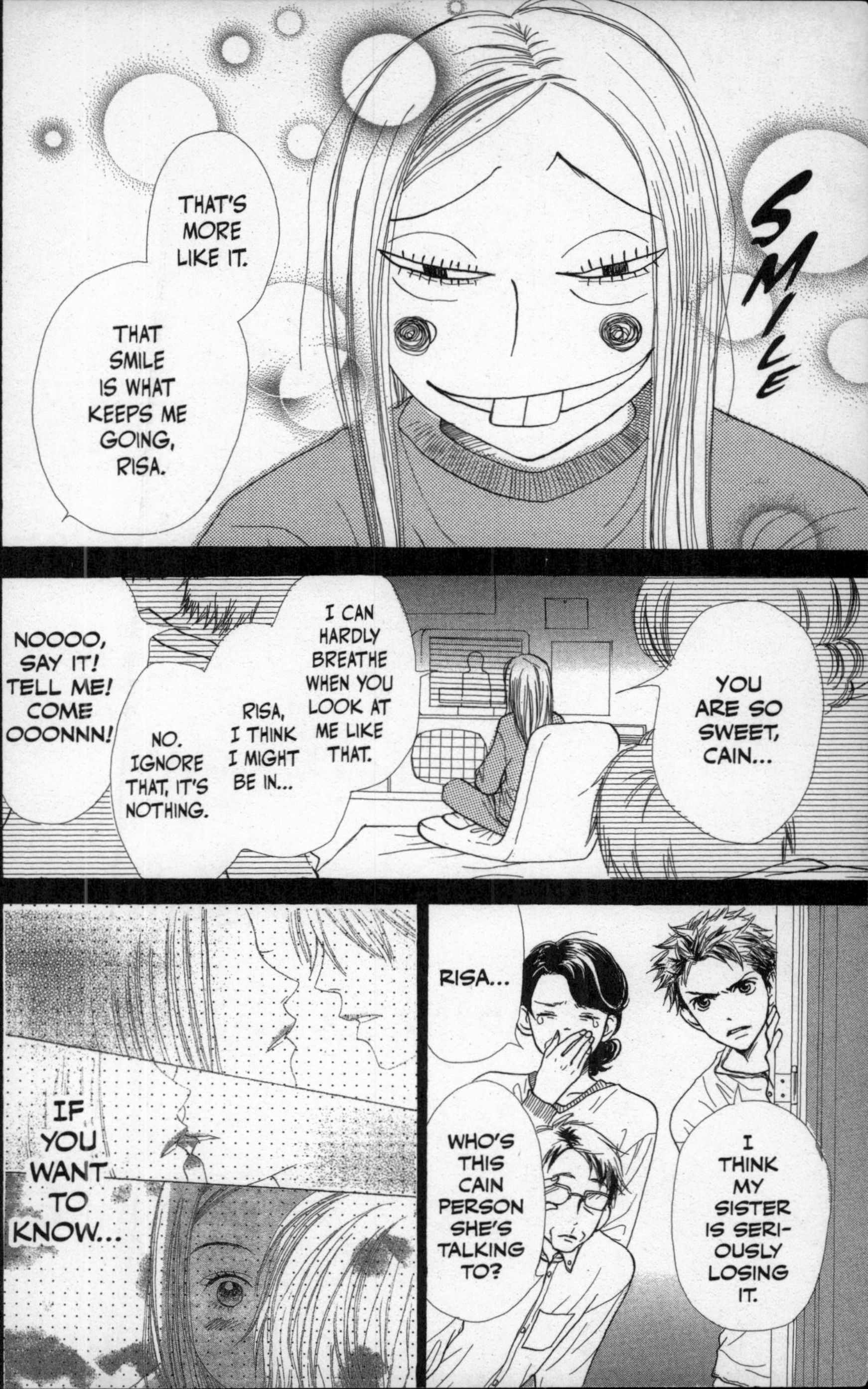
SMILE
THAT'S MORE LIKE IT.
THAT SMILE IS WHAT KEEPS ME GOING, RISA.
YOU ARE SO SWEET, CAIN...
I CAN HARDLY BREATHE WHEN YOU LOOK AT ME LIKE THAT.
RISA, I THINK I MIGHT BE IN...
NO. IGNORE THAT, IT'S NOTHING.
NOOOO, SAY IT! TELL ME! COME OOONNN!
RISA...
I THINK MY SISTER IS SERI-OUSLY LOSING IT.
WHO'S THIS CAIN PERSON SHE'S TALKING TO?
IF YOU WANT TO KNOW...

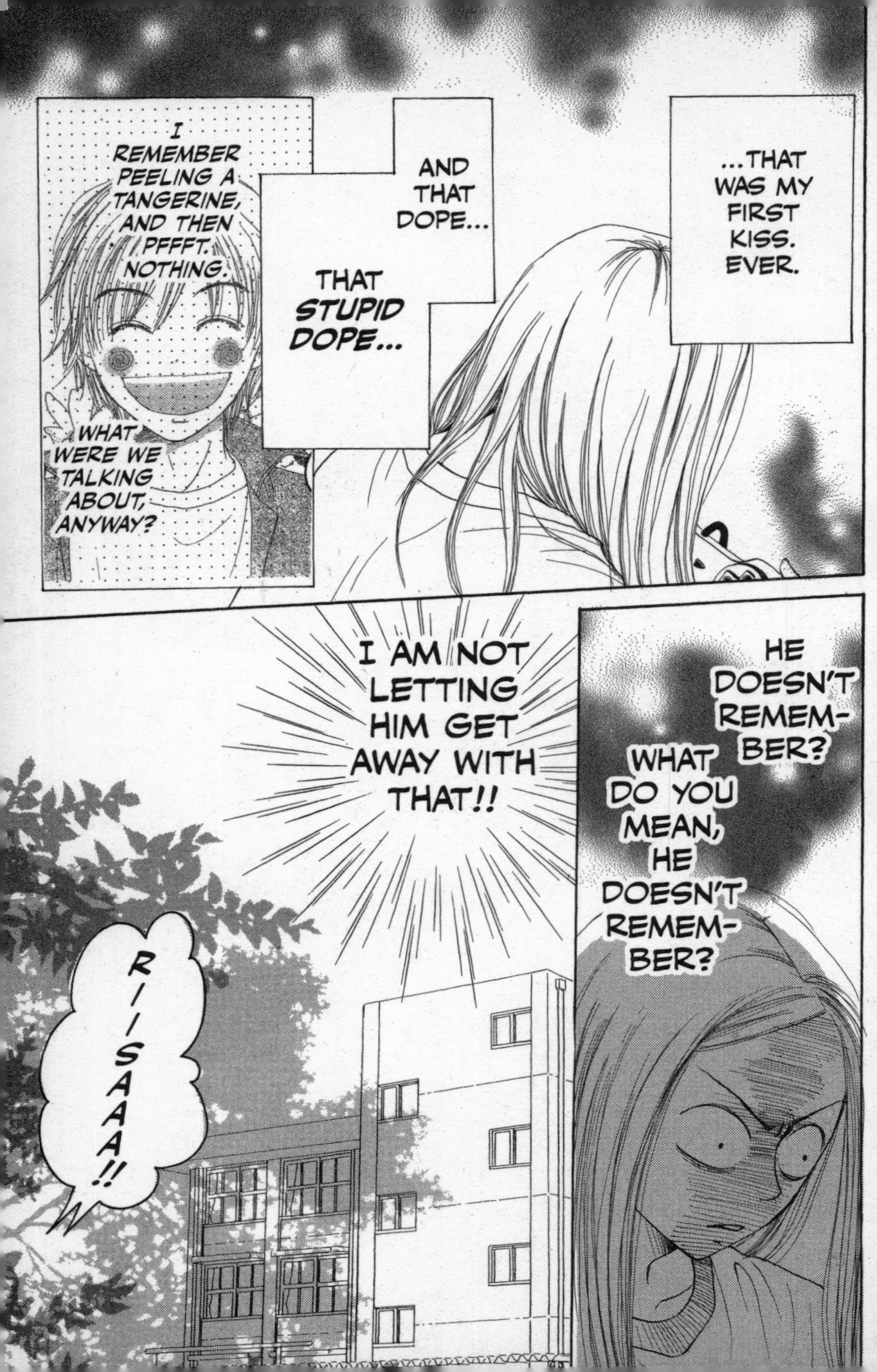
...THAT WAS MY FIRST KISS. EVER.
AND THAT DOPE...
THAT STUPID DOPE...
I REMEMBER PEELING A TANGERINE, AND THEN PFFFT. NOTHING.
WHAT WERE WE TALKING ABOUT, ANYWAY?
HE DOESN'T REMEM-BER?
WHAT DO YOU MEAN, HE DOESN'T REMEM-BER?
I AM NOT LETTING HIM GET AWAY WITH THAT!!
RIISAAAA!!

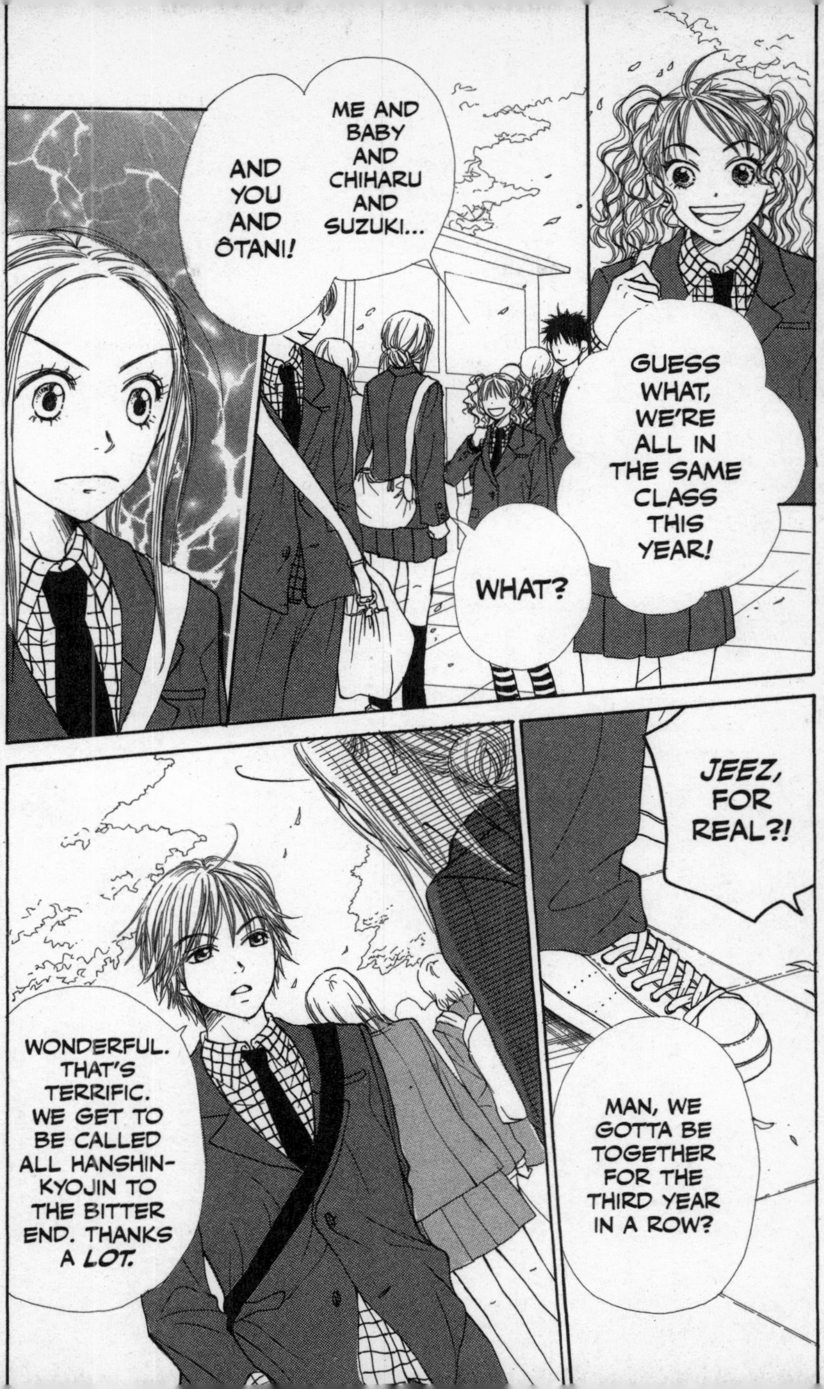
GUESS WHAT, WE'RE ALL IN THE SAME CLASS THIS YEAR!
WHAT?
ME AND BABY AND CHIHARU AND SUZUKI...
AND YOU AND ÔTANI!
JEEZ, FOR REAL?!
MAN, WE GOTTA BE TOGETHER FOR THE THIRD YEAR IN A ROW?
WONDERFUL. THAT'S TERRIFIC. WE GET TO BE CALLED ALL HANSHIN-KYOJIN TO THE BITTER END. THANKS A *LOT.*

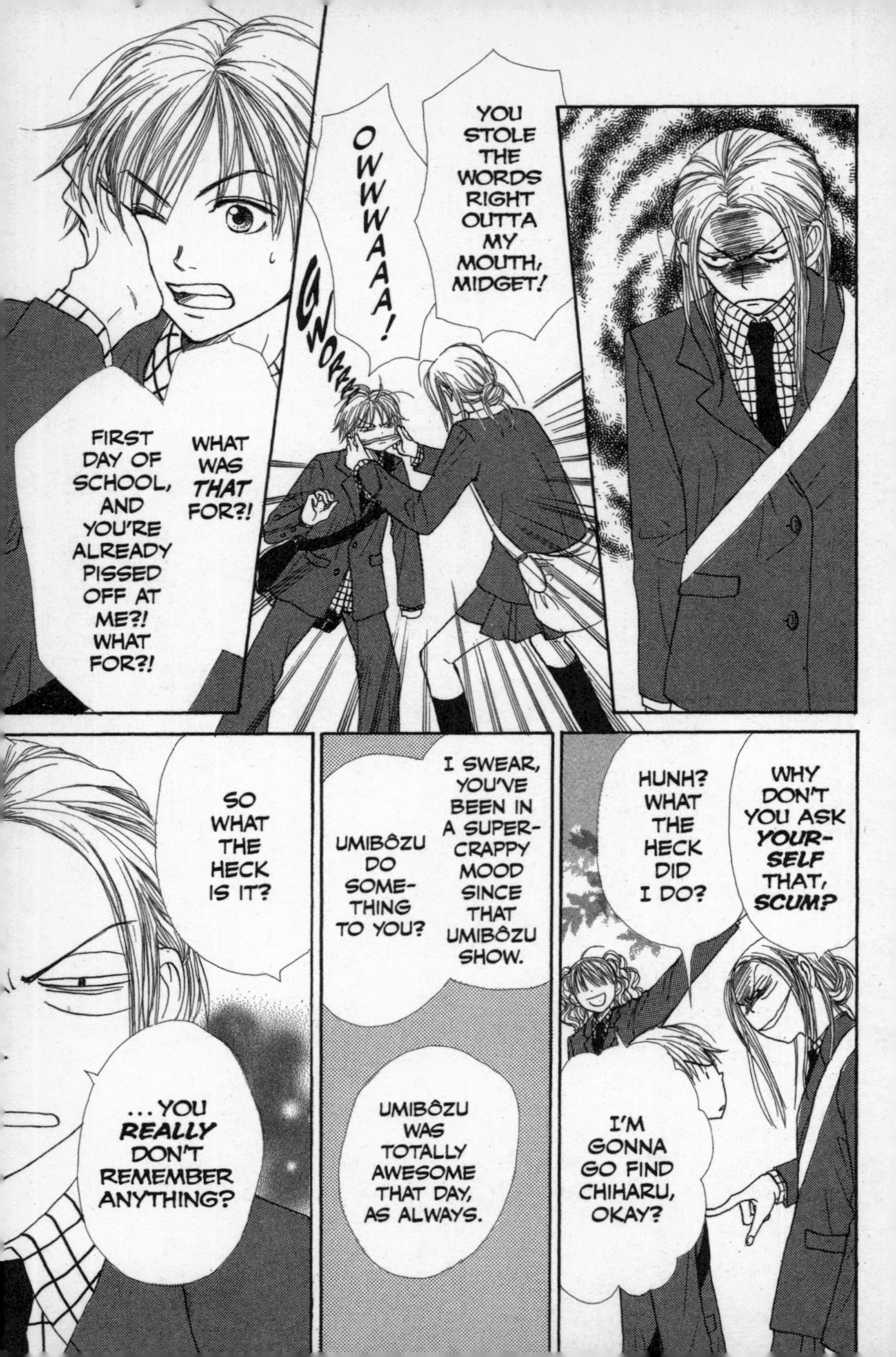
YOU STOLE THE WORDS RIGHT OUTTA MY MOUTH, MIDGET!
OWWWAAA!
WHAT WAS *THAT* FOR?!
FIRST DAY OF SCHOOL, AND YOU'RE ALREADY PISSED OFF AT ME?! WHAT FOR?!
WHY DON'T YOU ASK ***YOURSELF*** THAT, ***SCUM?***
HUNH? WHAT THE HECK DID I DO?
I'M GONNA GO FIND CHIHARU, OKAY?
I SWEAR, YOU'VE BEEN IN A SUPER-CRAPPY MOOD SINCE THAT UMIBÔZU SHOW.
UMIBÔZU DO SOMETHING TO YOU?
UMIBÔZU WAS TOTALLY AWESOME THAT DAY, AS ALWAYS.
SO WHAT THE HECK IS IT?
...YOU ***REALLY*** DON'T REMEMBER ANYTHING?

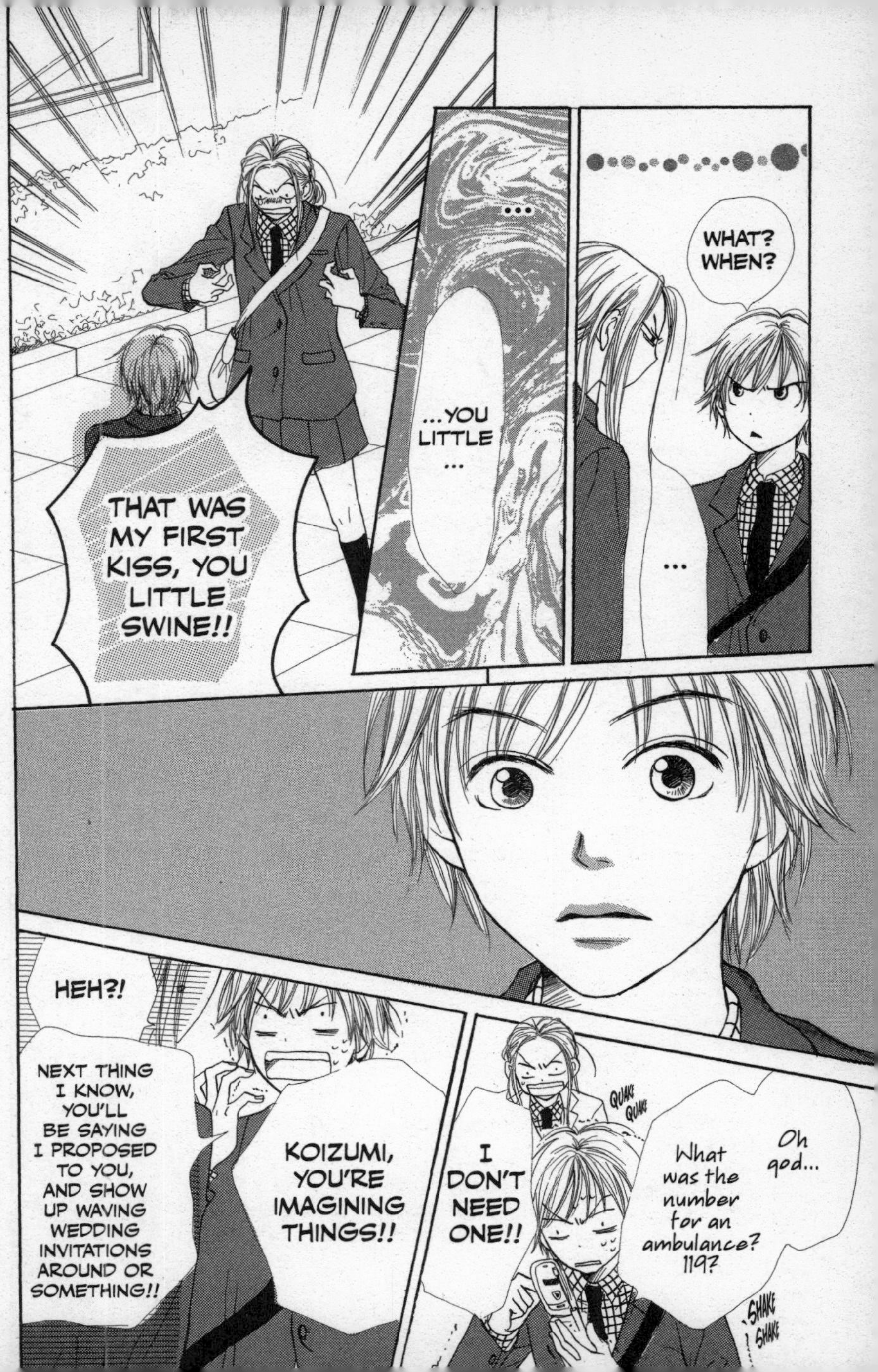

WHAT? WHEN?
...
...
...YOU LITTLE ...
THAT WAS MY FIRST KISS, YOU LITTLE SWINE!!
Oh god...
What was the number for an ambulance? 119?
QUAKE QUAKE
SHAKE SHAKE
I DON'T NEED ONE!!
KOIZUMI, YOU'RE IMAGINING THINGS!!
HEH?!
NEXT THING I KNOW, YOU'LL BE SAYING I PROPOSED TO YOU, AND SHOW UP WAVING WEDDING INVITATIONS AROUND OR SOMETHING!!

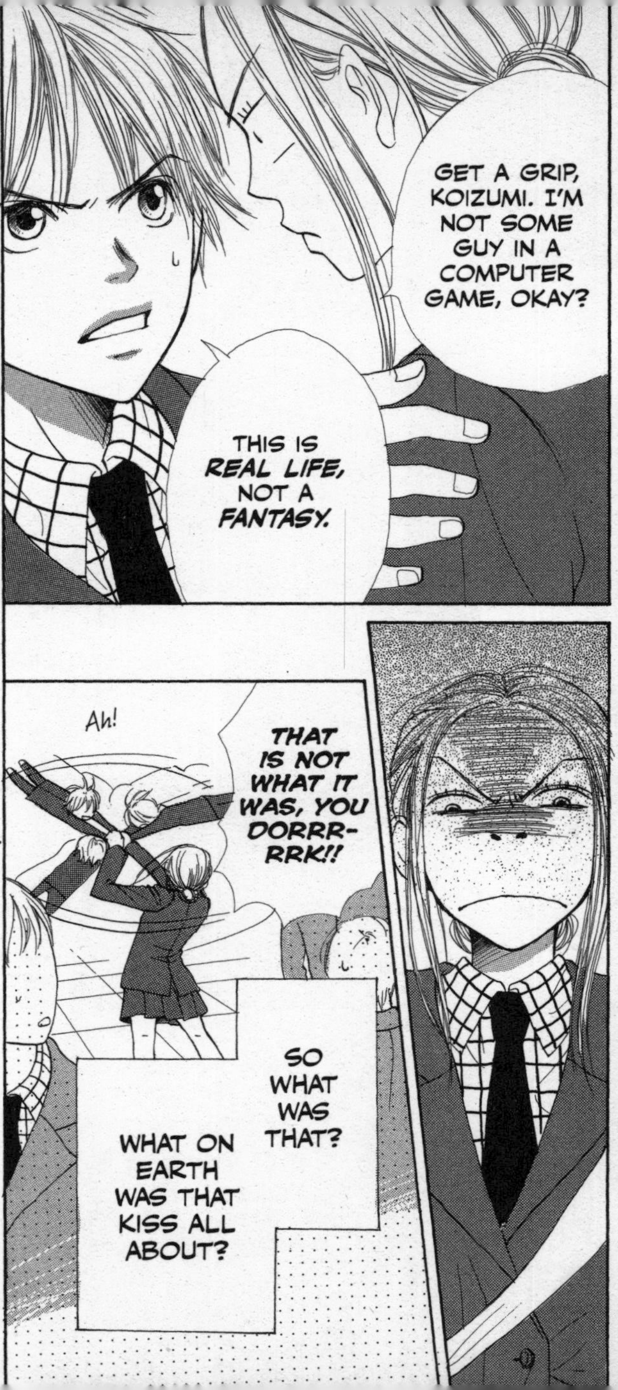
GET A GRIP, KOIZUMI. I'M NOT SOME GUY IN A COMPUTER GAME, OKAY?
THIS IS *REAL LIFE,* NOT A *FANTASY.*
Ah!
THAT IS NOT WHAT IT WAS, YOU DORRRR-RRK!!
SO WHAT WAS THAT?
WHAT ON EARTH WAS THAT KISS ALL ABOUT?

🐰 ②

So...guess what? They're going to put out a Love★Com drama CD. Ta-da! Heh heh heh heh.

There must be at least some of you asking, what does that mean? Well, it's a CD with a special Love★Com episode on it. With voice actors giving life to all the characters. Oooh! ✧✧

As I write this, it's still in the planning stages. I'd like to be involved as much as I can, to help make it a really fun CD.

Right now I'm coming up with some new story lines for it.

Hope you'll be interested...♡

I'm the type of person who, once she gets into something, gets into it all the way, i.e. a pretty big otaku, so I happen to own a lot of these drama CDs. But I listen to them because I love the manga, so, well, sorry to say this, but I was never very up on the voice actors in them. Was! Ulp!! Mommy, she switched to past tense in the middle of the sentence!! Now I kinda know who all the different voice actors are. heh heh heh

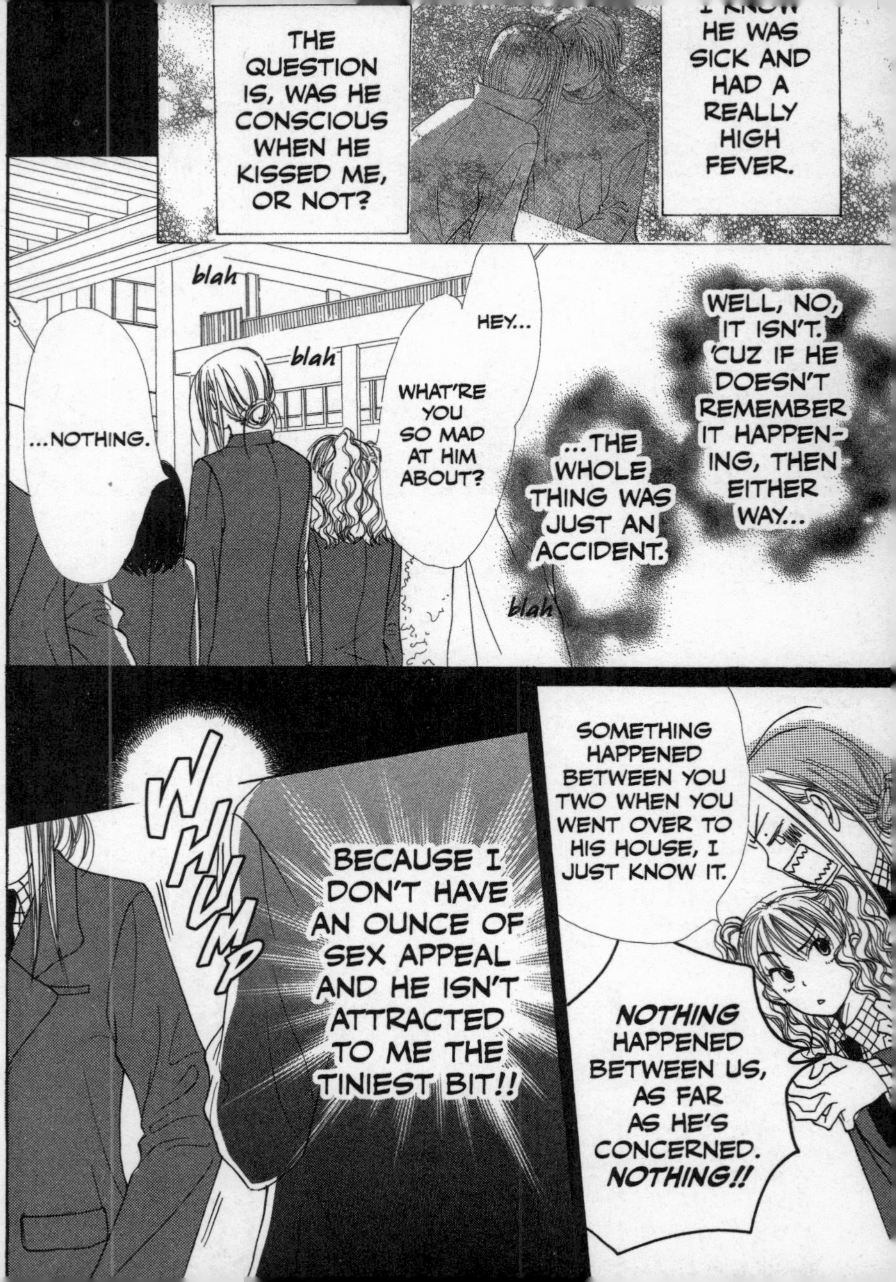
HE WAS SICK AND HAD A REALLY HIGH FEVER.
THE QUESTION IS, WAS HE CONSCIOUS WHEN HE KISSED ME, OR NOT?
WELL, NO, IT ISN'T. 'CUZ IF HE DOESN'T REMEMBER IT HAPPEN-ING, THEN EITHER WAY...
...THE WHOLE THING WAS JUST AN ACCIDENT.
blah
HEY...
WHAT'RE YOU SO MAD AT HIM ABOUT?
blah
blah
...NOTHING.
SOMETHING HAPPENED BETWEEN YOU TWO WHEN YOU WENT OVER TO HIS HOUSE, I JUST KNOW IT.
NOTHING HAPPENED BETWEEN US, AS FAR AS HE'S CONCERNED. *NOTHING!!*
WHUMP
BECAUSE I DON'T HAVE AN OUNCE OF SEX APPEAL AND HE ISN'T ATTRACTED TO ME THE TINIEST BIT!!

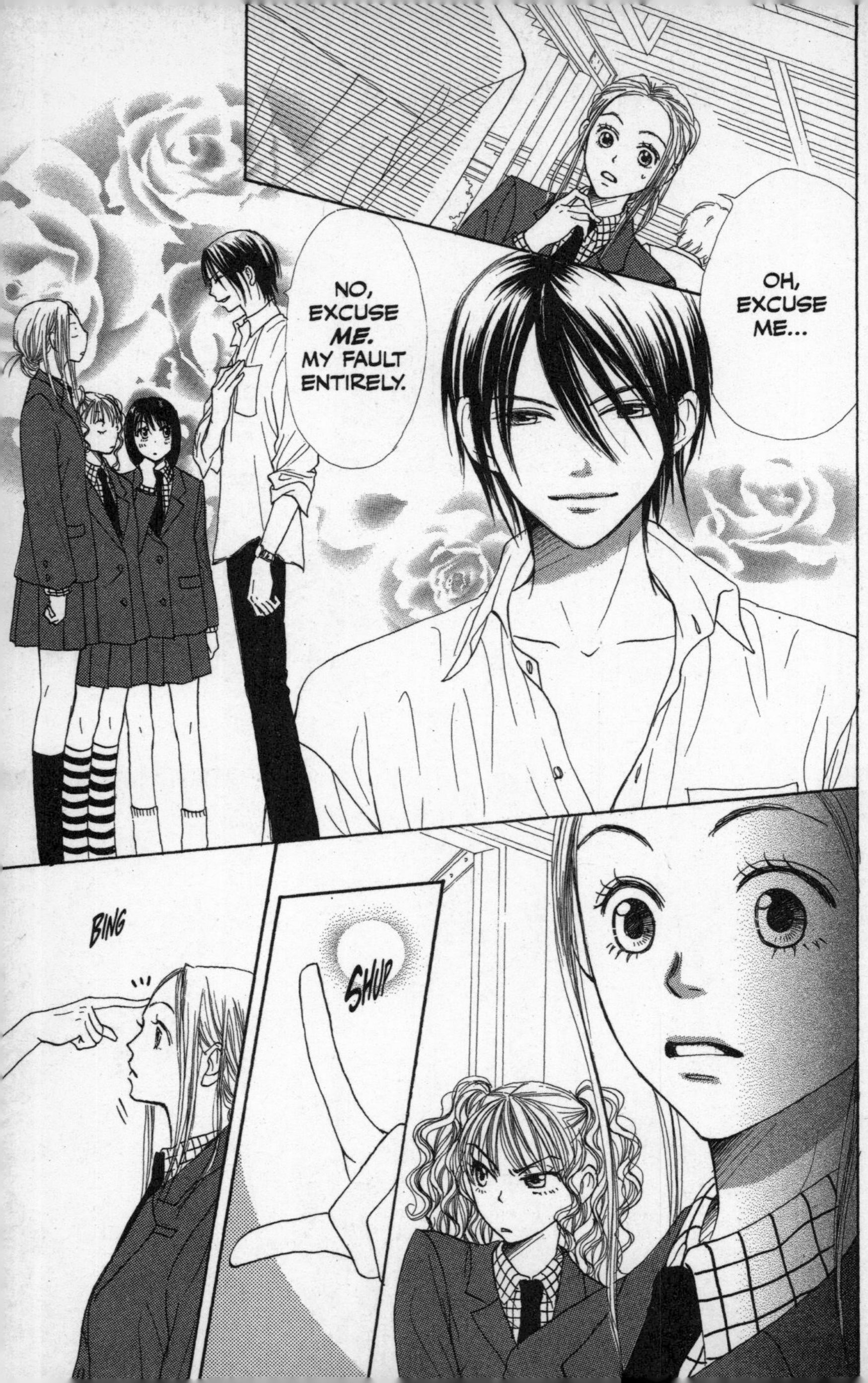
OH, EXCUSE ME...
NO, EXCUSE *ME.* MY FAULT ENTIRELY.
SHUP
BING

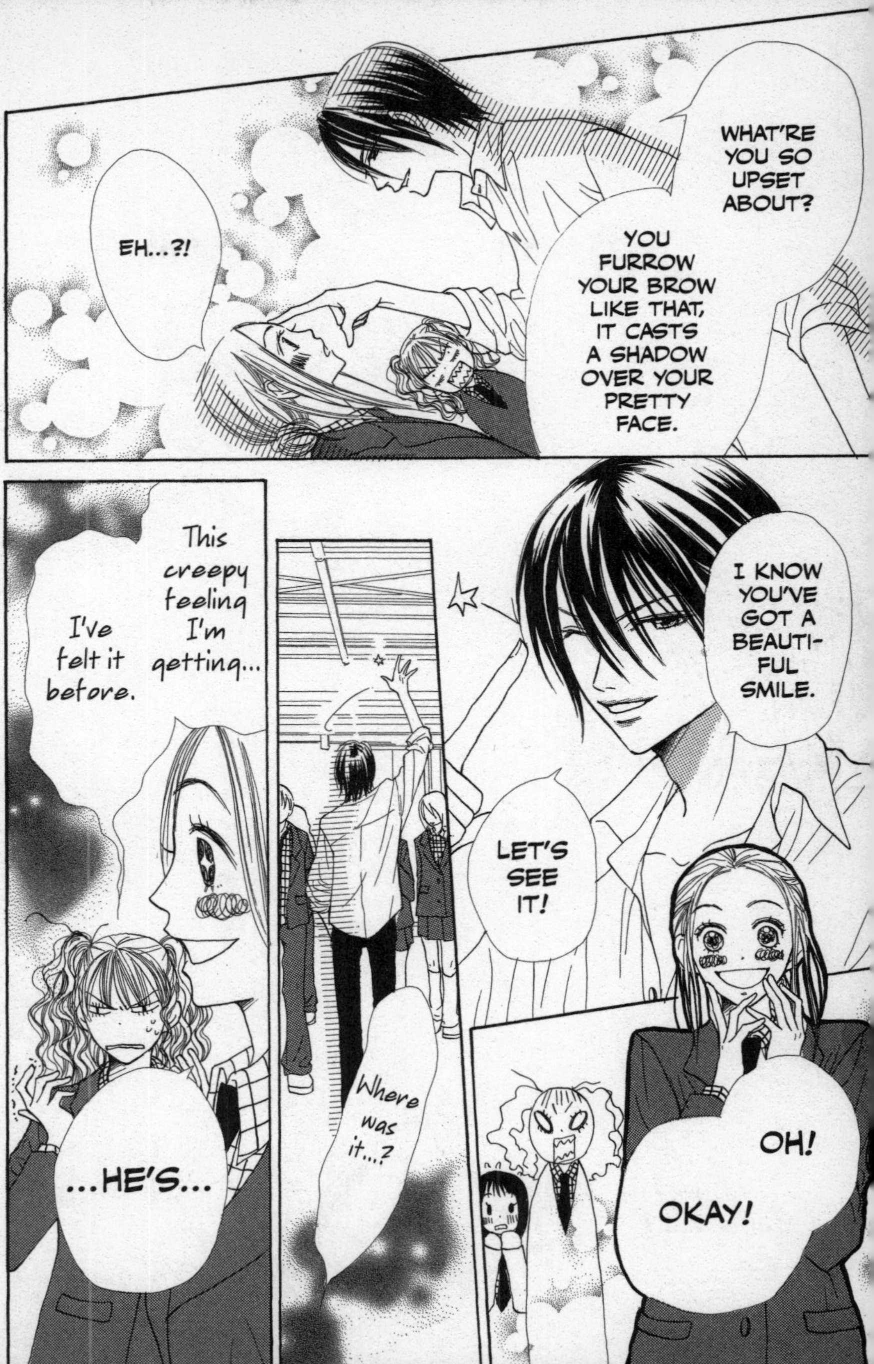
WHAT'RE YOU SO UPSET ABOUT?
YOU FURROW YOUR BROW LIKE THAT, IT CASTS A SHADOW OVER YOUR PRETTY FACE.
EH...?!
I KNOW YOU'VE GOT A BEAUTI-FUL SMILE.
LET'S SEE IT!
OH!
OKAY!
Where was it...?
This creepy feeling I'm getting...
I've felt it before.
...HE'S...

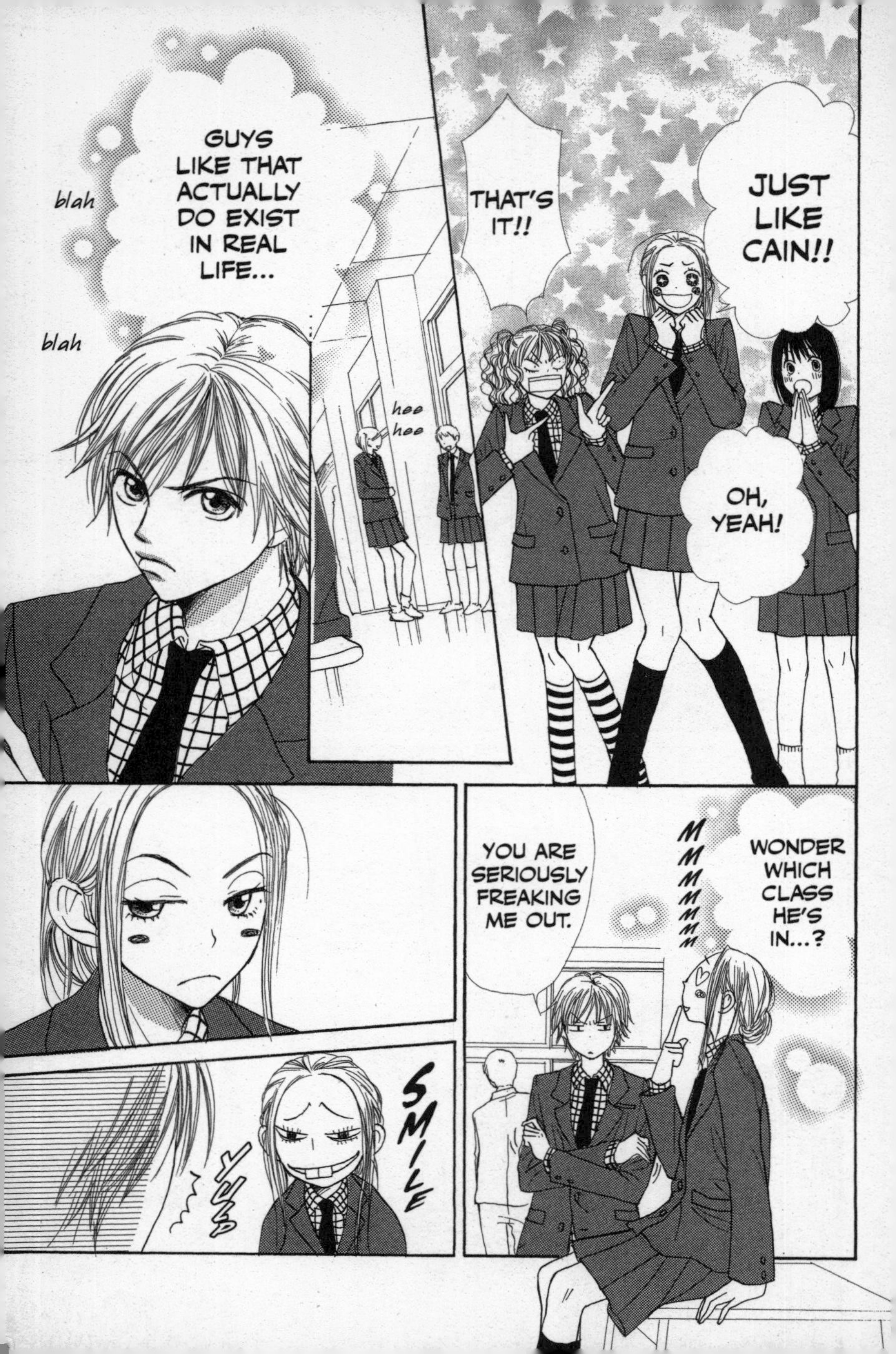
JUST LIKE CAIN!!
THAT'S IT!!
OH, YEAH!
hee hee
GUYS LIKE THAT ACTUALLY DO EXIST IN REAL LIFE...
blah
blah
WONDER WHICH CLASS HE'S IN...?
MMMMMMMM
YOU ARE SERIOUSLY FREAKING ME OUT.
SMILE
YUMP

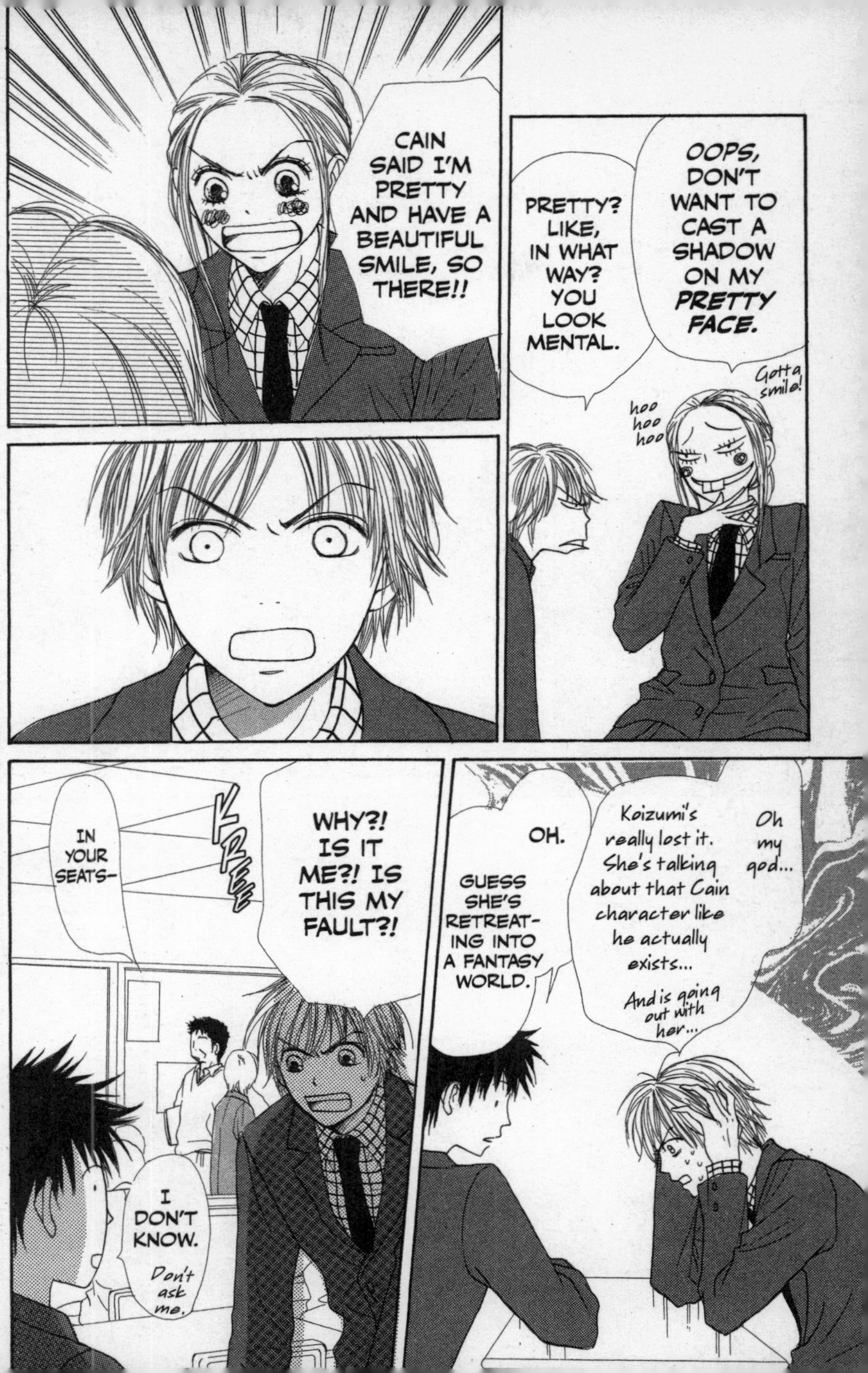

OOPS, DON'T WANT TO CAST A SHADOW ON MY *PRETTY FACE.*
PRETTY? LIKE, IN WHAT WAY? YOU LOOK MENTAL.
Gotta smile!
hoo hoo hoo
CAIN SAID I'M PRETTY AND HAVE A BEAUTIFUL SMILE, SO THERE!!
Oh my god...
Koizumi's really lost it. She's talking about that Cain character like he actually exists...
And is going out with her...
OH.
GUESS SHE'S RETREAT-ING INTO A FANTASY WORLD.
WHY?! IS IT ME?! IS THIS MY FAULT?!
KREE
IN YOUR SEATS-
I DON'T KNOW.
Don't ask me.

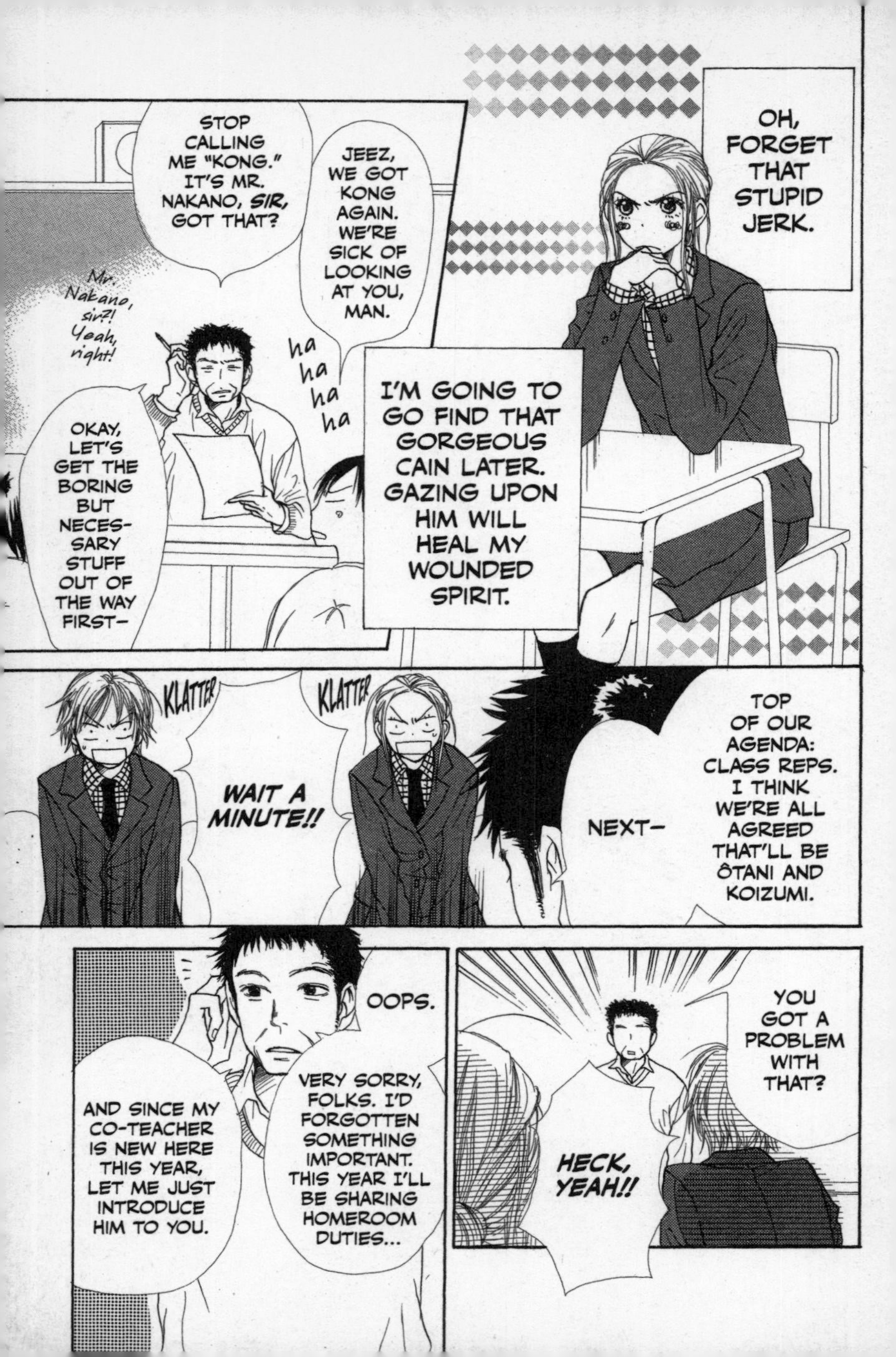
OH, FORGET THAT STUPID JERK.
I'M GOING TO GO FIND THAT GORGEOUS CAIN LATER. GAZING UPON HIM WILL HEAL MY WOUNDED SPIRIT.
JEEZ, WE GOT KONG AGAIN. WE'RE SICK OF LOOKING AT YOU, MAN.
ha ha ha ha
STOP CALLING ME "KONG." IT'S MR. NAKANO, *SIR,* GOT THAT?
Mr. Nakano, sir?! Yeah, right!
OKAY, LET'S GET THE BORING BUT NECES-SARY STUFF OUT OF THE WAY FIRST–
TOP OF OUR AGENDA: CLASS REPS. I THINK WE'RE ALL AGREED THAT'LL BE ŌTANI AND KOIZUMI.
NEXT–
KLATTER
WAIT A MINUTE!!
KLATTER
YOU GOT A PROBLEM WITH THAT?
HECK, YEAH!!
OOPS.
VERY SORRY, FOLKS. I'D FORGOTTEN SOMETHING IMPORTANT. THIS YEAR I'LL BE SHARING HOMEROOM DUTIES...
AND SINCE MY CO-TEACHER IS NEW HERE THIS YEAR, LET ME JUST INTRODUCE HIM TO YOU.

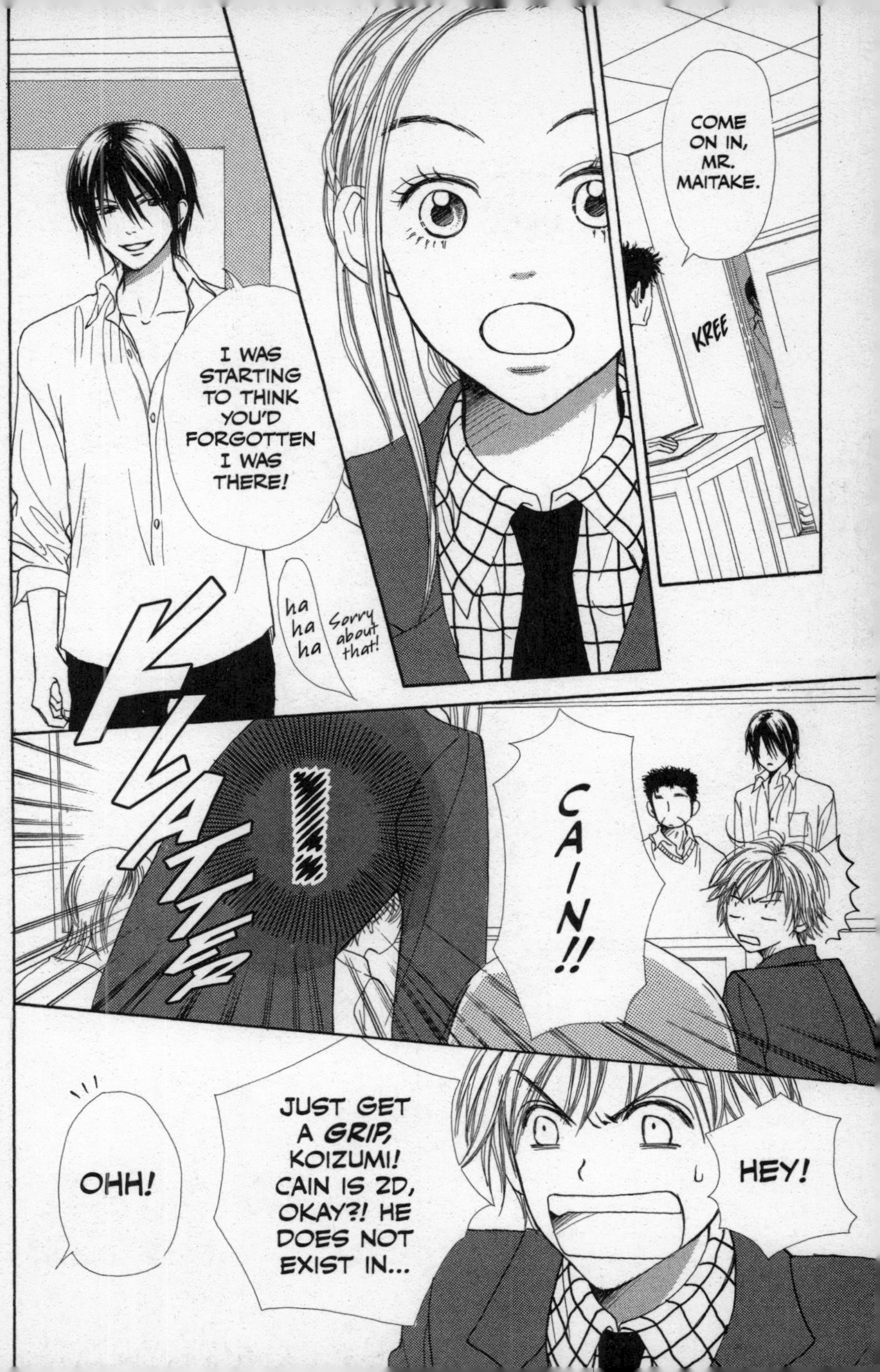
COME ON IN, MR. MAITAKE.
KREE
I WAS STARTING TO THINK YOU'D FORGOTTEN I WAS THERE!
Sorry about that!
ha ha ha
CAIN!!
HEY!
JUST GET A *GRIP,* KOIZUMI! CAIN IS 2D, OKAY?! HE DOES NOT EXIST IN...
OHH!

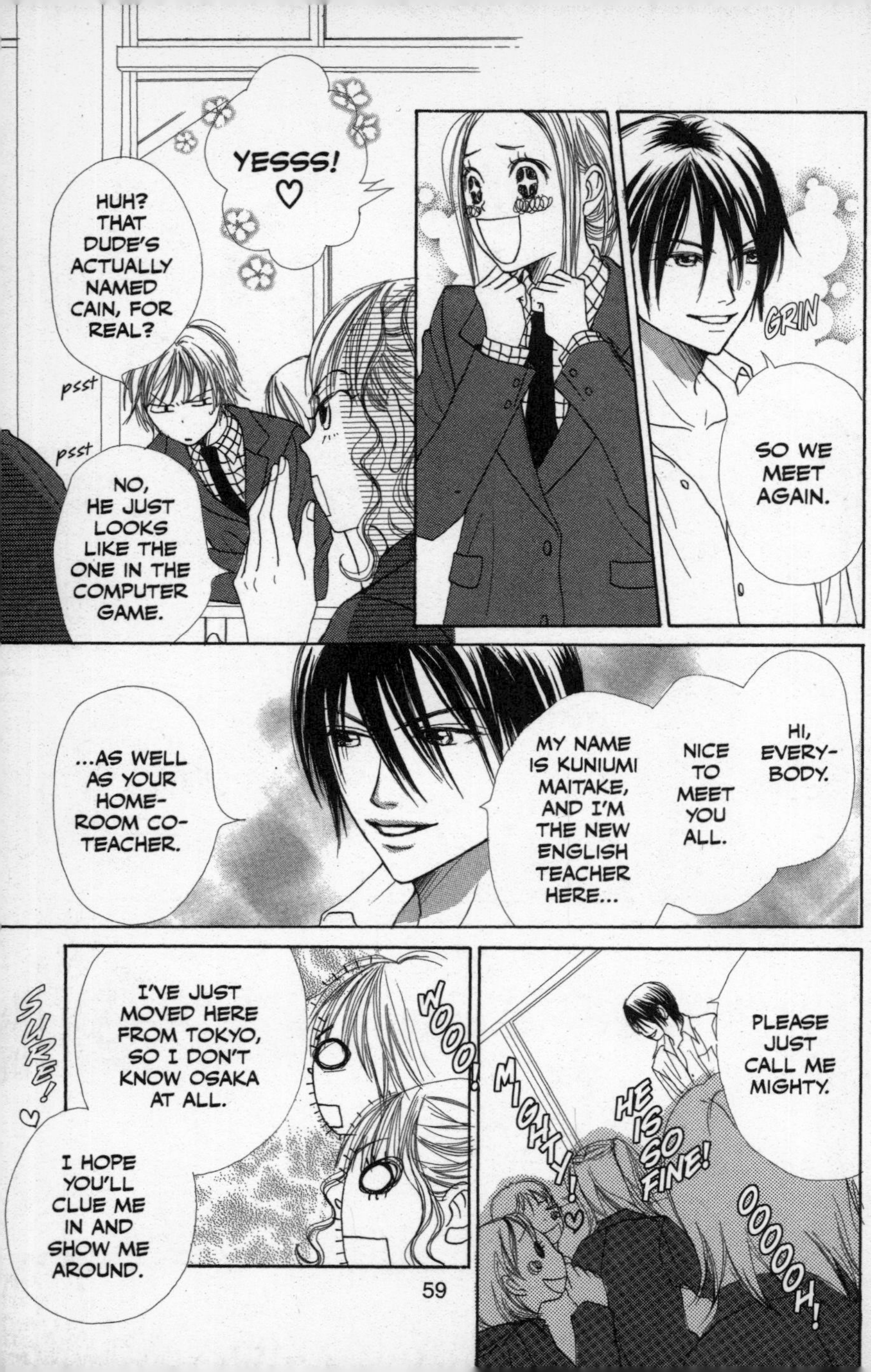
GRIN
SO WE MEET AGAIN.
YESSS! ♥
HUH? THAT DUDE'S ACTUALLY NAMED CAIN, FOR REAL?
psst
psst
NO, HE JUST LOOKS LIKE THE ONE IN THE COMPUTER GAME.
HI, EVERYBODY.
NICE TO MEET YOU ALL.
MY NAME IS KUNIUMI MAITAKE, AND I'M THE NEW ENGLISH TEACHER HERE...
...AS WELL AS YOUR HOME-ROOM CO-TEACHER.
PLEASE JUST CALL ME MIGHTY.
OOOOOH!
HE IS SO FINE!
MIGHTY! ♥
WOOO!
I'VE JUST MOVED HERE FROM TOKYO, SO I DON'T KNOW OSAKA AT ALL.
SURE! ♥
I HOPE YOU'LL CLUE ME IN AND SHOW ME AROUND.

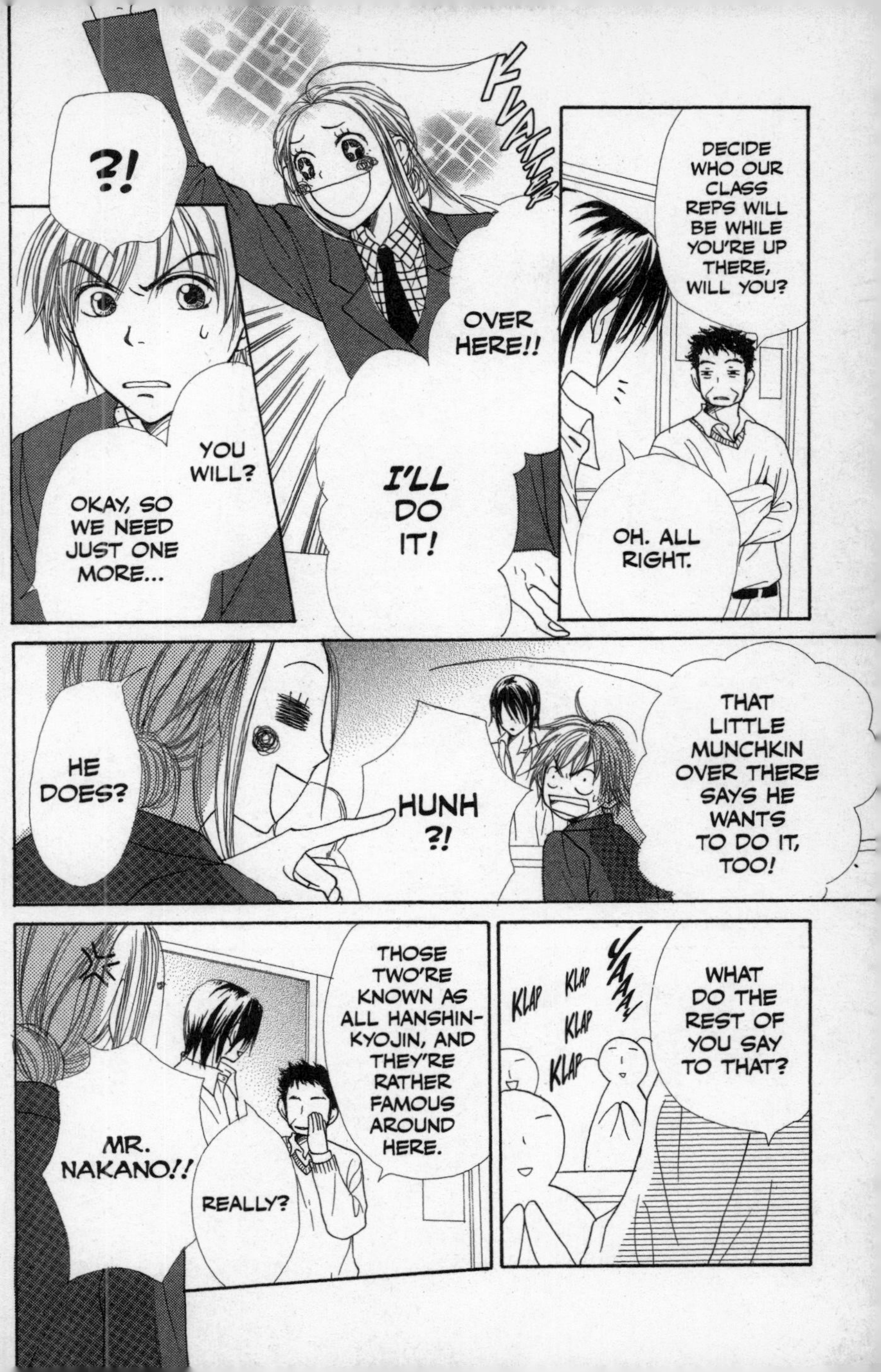
DECIDE WHO OUR CLASS REPS WILL BE WHILE YOU'RE UP THERE, WILL YOU?
OH. ALL RIGHT.
OVER HERE!!
I'LL DO IT!
?!
YOU WILL?
OKAY, SO WE NEED JUST ONE MORE...
THAT LITTLE MUNCHKIN OVER THERE SAYS HE WANTS TO DO IT, TOO!
HUNH ?!
HE DOES?
WHAT DO THE REST OF YOU SAY TO THAT?
KLAP
KLAP
KLAP
KLAP
THOSE TWO'RE KNOWN AS ALL HANSHIN-KYOJIN, AND THEY'RE RATHER FAMOUS AROUND HERE.
REALLY?
MR. NAKANO!!

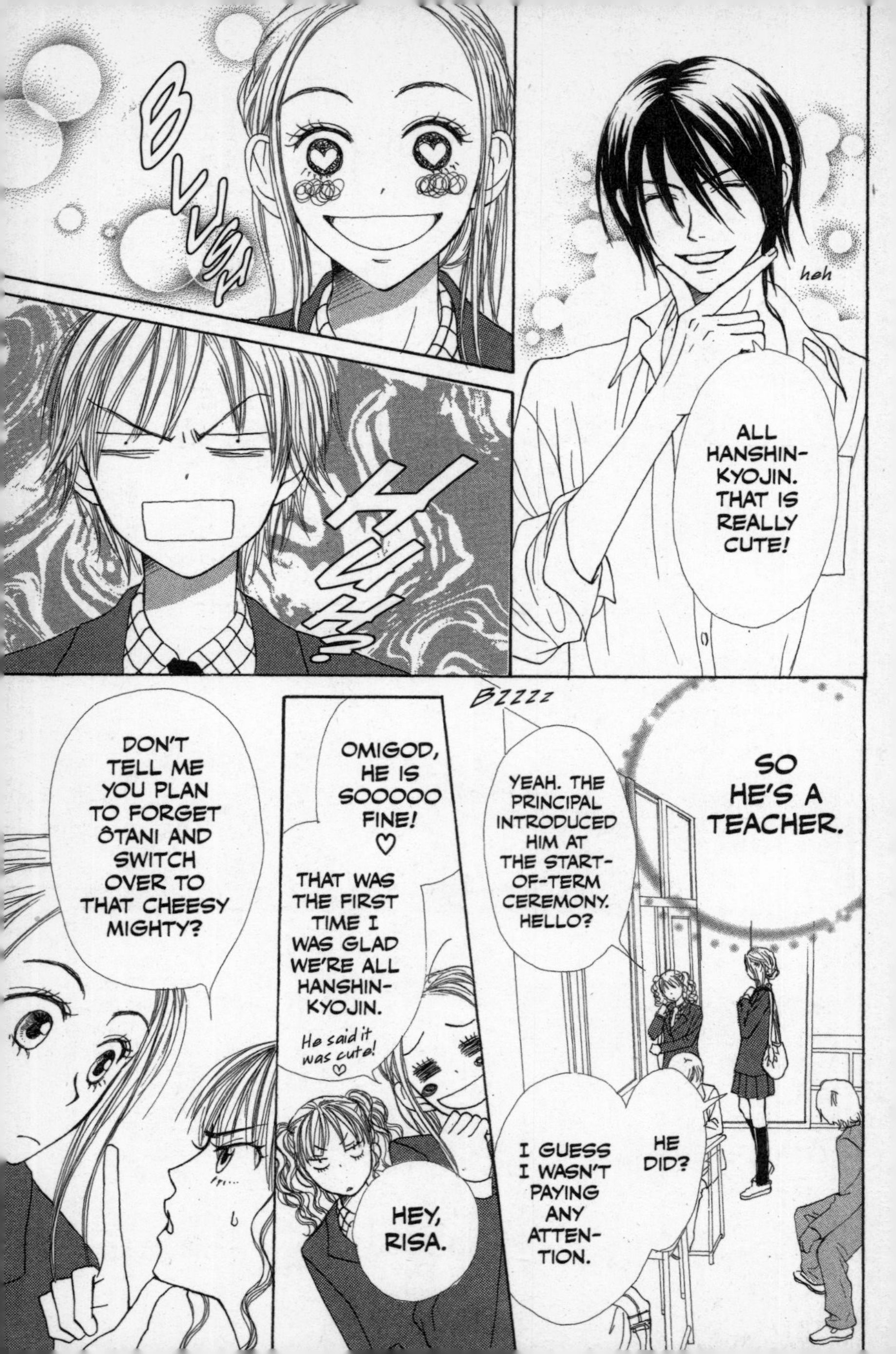
heh
ALL HANSHIN-KYOJIN. THAT IS REALLY CUTE!
BLUSH
SO HE'S A TEACHER.
BZZZZ
YEAH. THE PRINCIPAL INTRODUCED HIM AT THE START-OF-TERM CEREMONY. HELLO?
HE DID?
I GUESS I WASN'T PAYING ANY ATTEN-TION.
OMIGOD, HE IS SOOOOO FINE! ♡
THAT WAS THE FIRST TIME I WAS GLAD WE'RE ALL HANSHIN-KYOJIN.
He said it was cute! ♡
HEY, RISA.
DON'T TELL ME YOU PLAN TO FORGET ÔTANI AND SWITCH OVER TO THAT CHEESY MIGHTY?

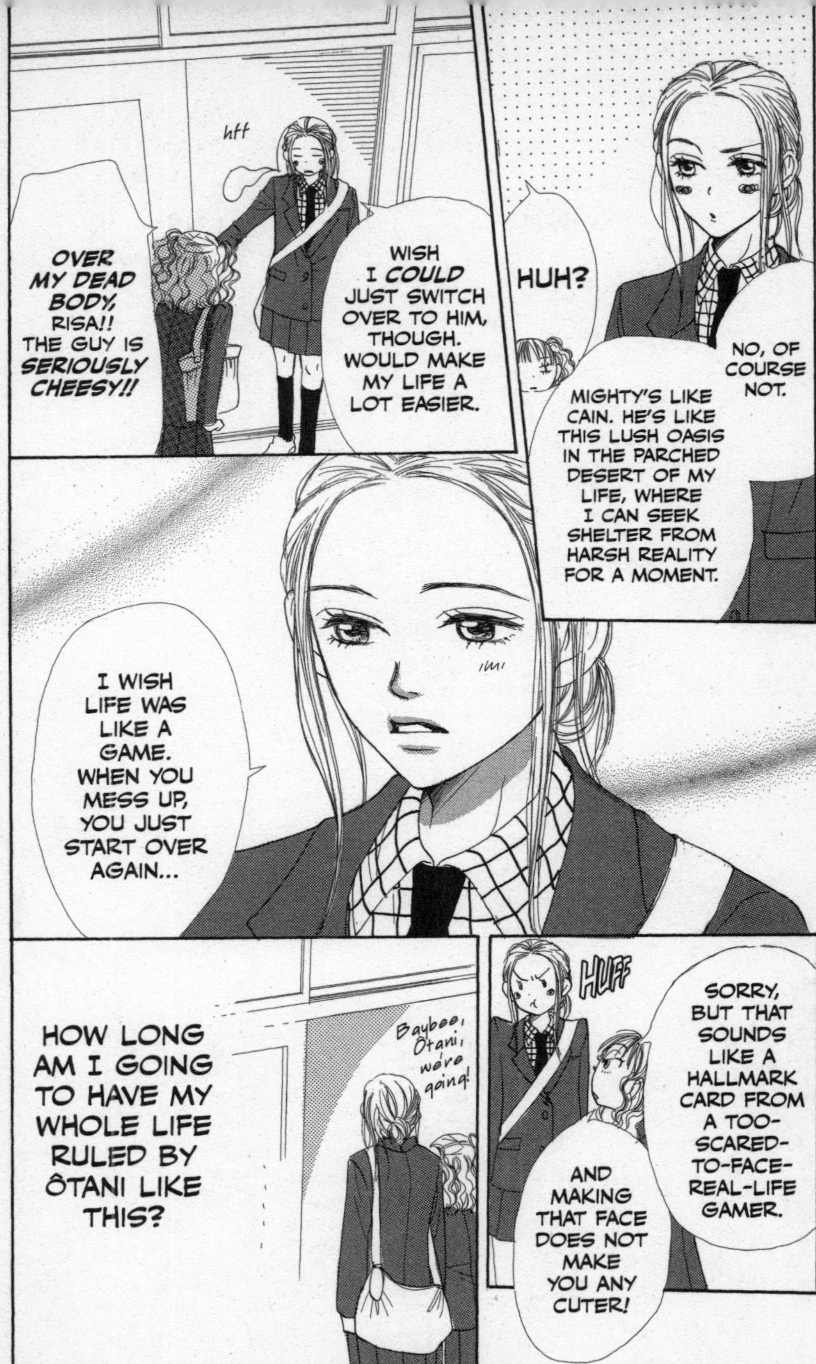
HUH?
NO, OF COURSE NOT.
MIGHTY'S LIKE CAIN. HE'S LIKE THIS LUSH OASIS IN THE PARCHED DESERT OF MY LIFE, WHERE I CAN SEEK SHELTER FROM HARSH REALITY FOR A MOMENT.
hff
WISH I *COULD* JUST SWITCH OVER TO HIM, THOUGH. WOULD MAKE MY LIFE A LOT EASIER.
OVER MY DEAD BODY, RISA!! THE GUY IS *SERIOUSLY CHEESY!!*
I WISH LIFE WAS LIKE A GAME. WHEN YOU MESS UP, YOU JUST START OVER AGAIN...
HUFF
SORRY, BUT THAT SOUNDS LIKE A HALLMARK CARD FROM A TOO-SCARED-TO-FACE-REAL-LIFE GAMER.
AND MAKING THAT FACE DOES NOT MAKE YOU ANY CUTER!
Baybee, Ōtani, we're going!
HOW LONG AM I GOING TO HAVE MY WHOLE LIFE RULED BY ŌTANI LIKE THIS?

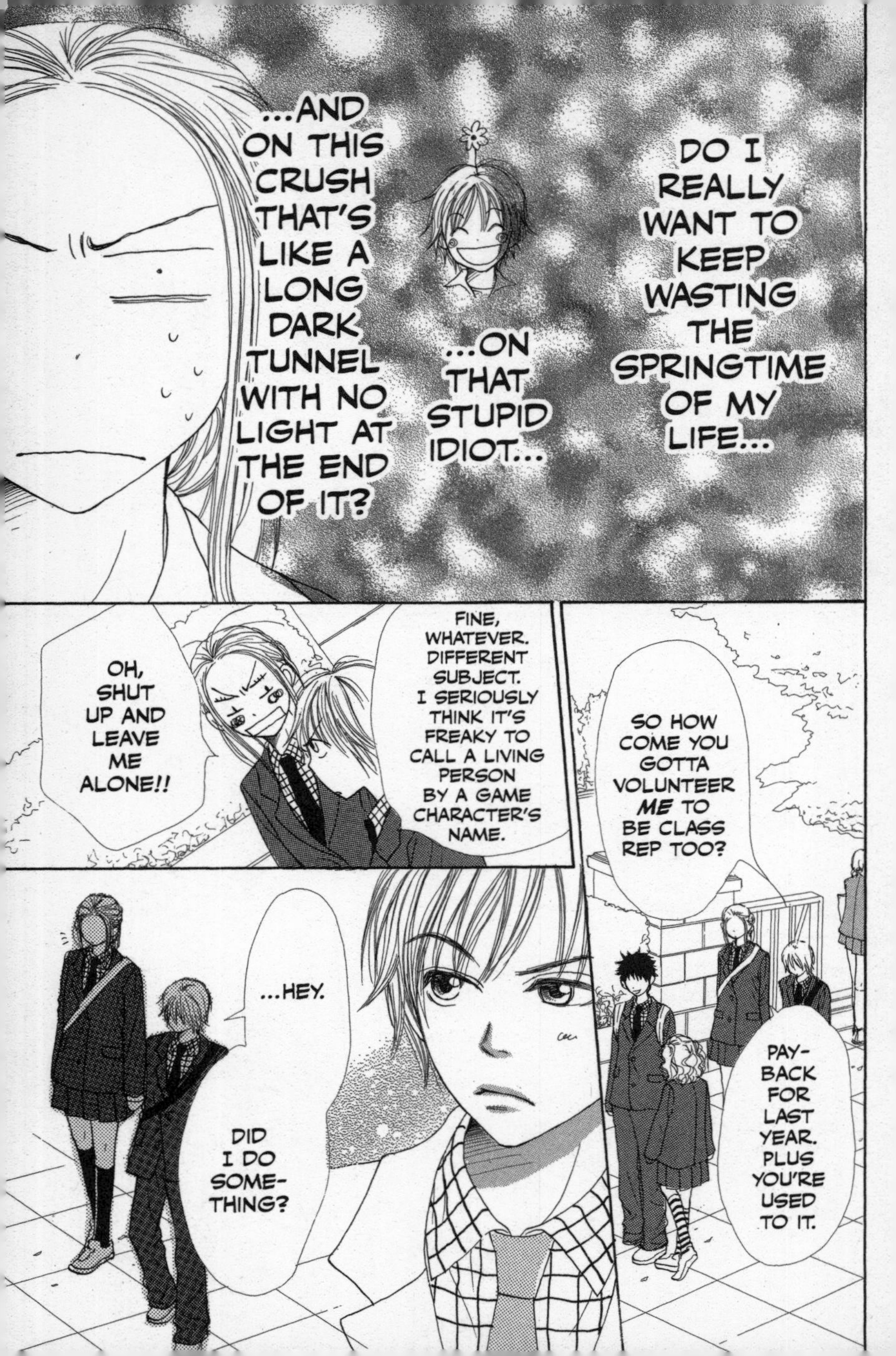
DO I REALLY WANT TO KEEP WASTING THE SPRINGTIME OF MY LIFE...
...ON THAT STUPID IDIOT...
...AND ON THIS CRUSH THAT'S LIKE A LONG DARK TUNNEL WITH NO LIGHT AT THE END OF IT?
SO HOW COME YOU GOTTA VOLUNTEER *ME* TO BE CLASS REP TOO?
FINE, WHATEVER. DIFFERENT SUBJECT. I SERIOUSLY THINK IT'S FREAKY TO CALL A LIVING PERSON BY A GAME CHARACTER'S NAME.
OH, SHUT UP AND LEAVE ME ALONE!!
PAY-BACK FOR LAST YEAR. PLUS YOU'RE USED TO IT.
...HEY.
DID I DO SOME-THING?

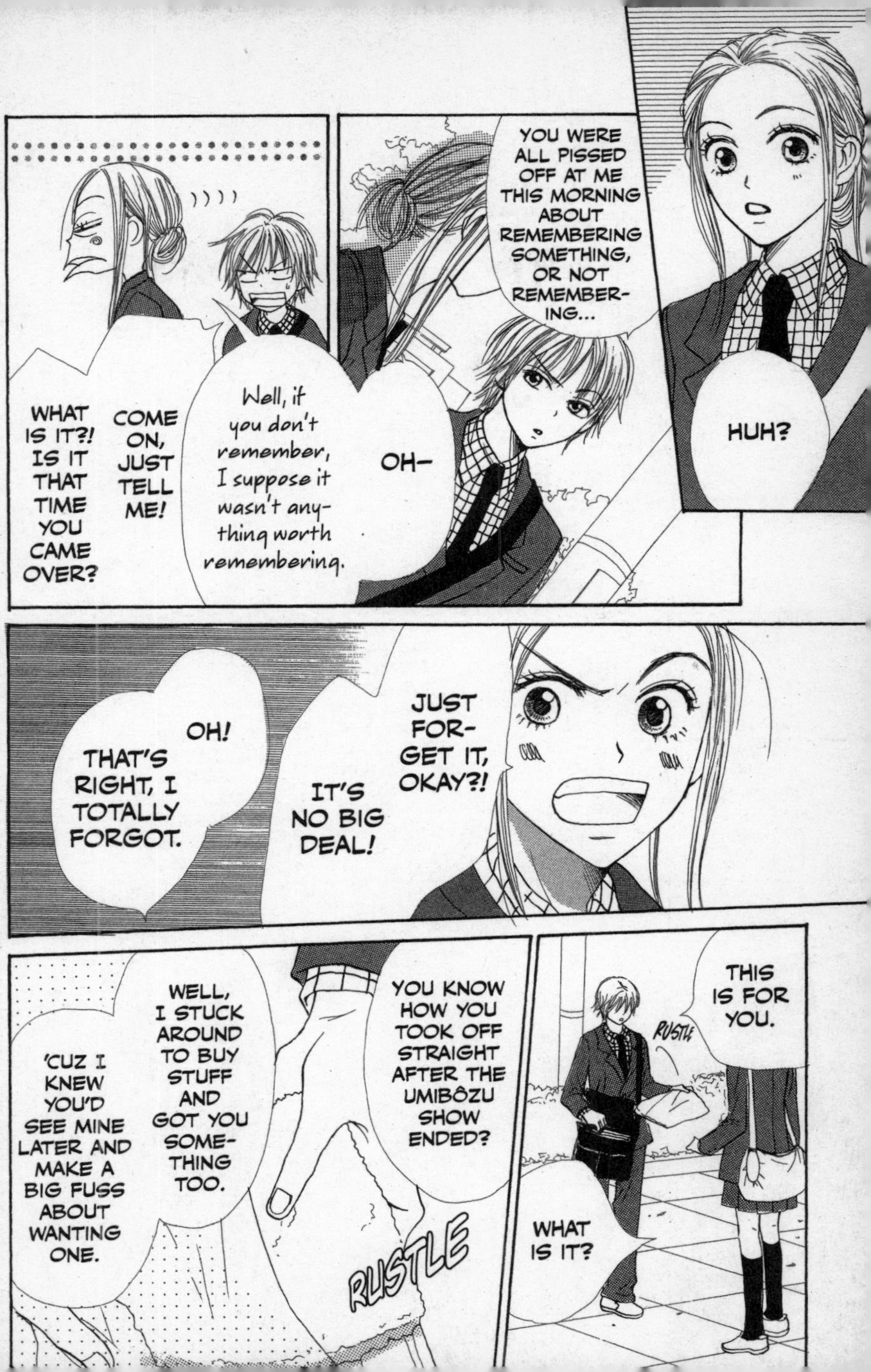
HUH?
YOU WERE ALL PISSED OFF AT ME THIS MORNING ABOUT REMEMBERING SOMETHING, OR NOT REMEMBERING...
OH—
Well, if you don't remember, I suppose it wasn't anything worth remembering.
COME ON, JUST TELL ME!
WHAT IS IT?! IS IT THAT TIME YOU CAME OVER?
JUST FORGET IT, OKAY?!
IT'S NO BIG DEAL!
OH! THAT'S RIGHT, I TOTALLY FORGOT.
THIS IS FOR YOU.
RUSTLE
WHAT IS IT?
YOU KNOW HOW YOU TOOK OFF STRAIGHT AFTER THE UMIBÔZU SHOW ENDED?
WELL, I STUCK AROUND TO BUY STUFF AND GOT YOU SOMETHING TOO.
'CUZ I KNEW YOU'D SEE MINE LATER AND MAKE A BIG FUSS ABOUT WANTING ONE.
RUSTLE

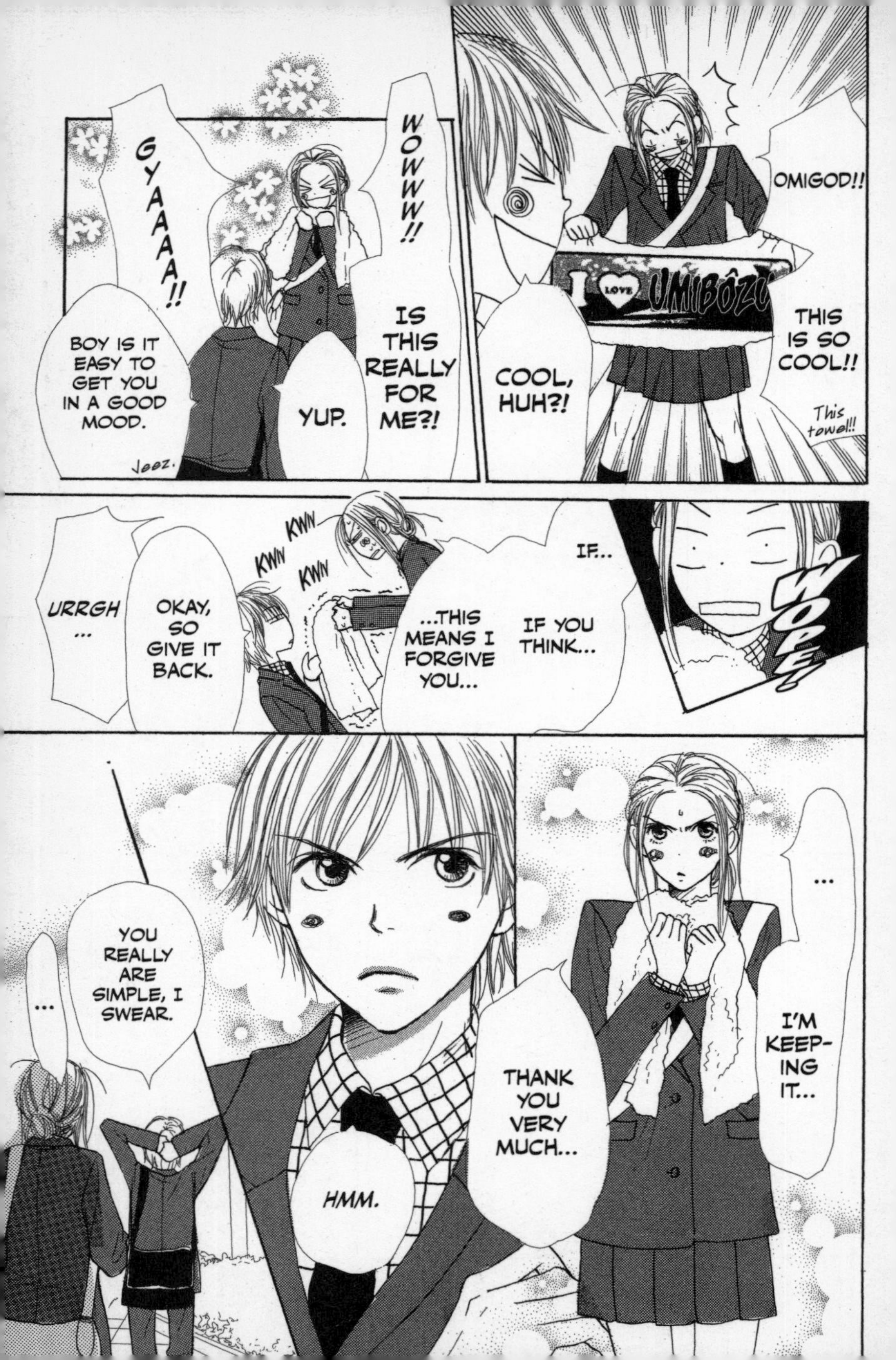
OMIGOD!!
THIS IS SO COOL!!
This towel!!
COOL, HUH?!
WOWWWW!!
IS THIS REALLY FOR ME?!
YUP.
GYAAAA!!
BOY IS IT EASY TO GET YOU IN A GOOD MOOD.
Jeez.
NOPE!
IF...
IF YOU THINK...
...THIS MEANS I FORGIVE YOU...
KWN
KWN
KWN
OKAY, SO GIVE IT BACK.
URRGH...
...
I'M KEEPING IT...
THANK YOU VERY MUCH...
HMM.
YOU REALLY ARE SIMPLE, I SWEAR.
...

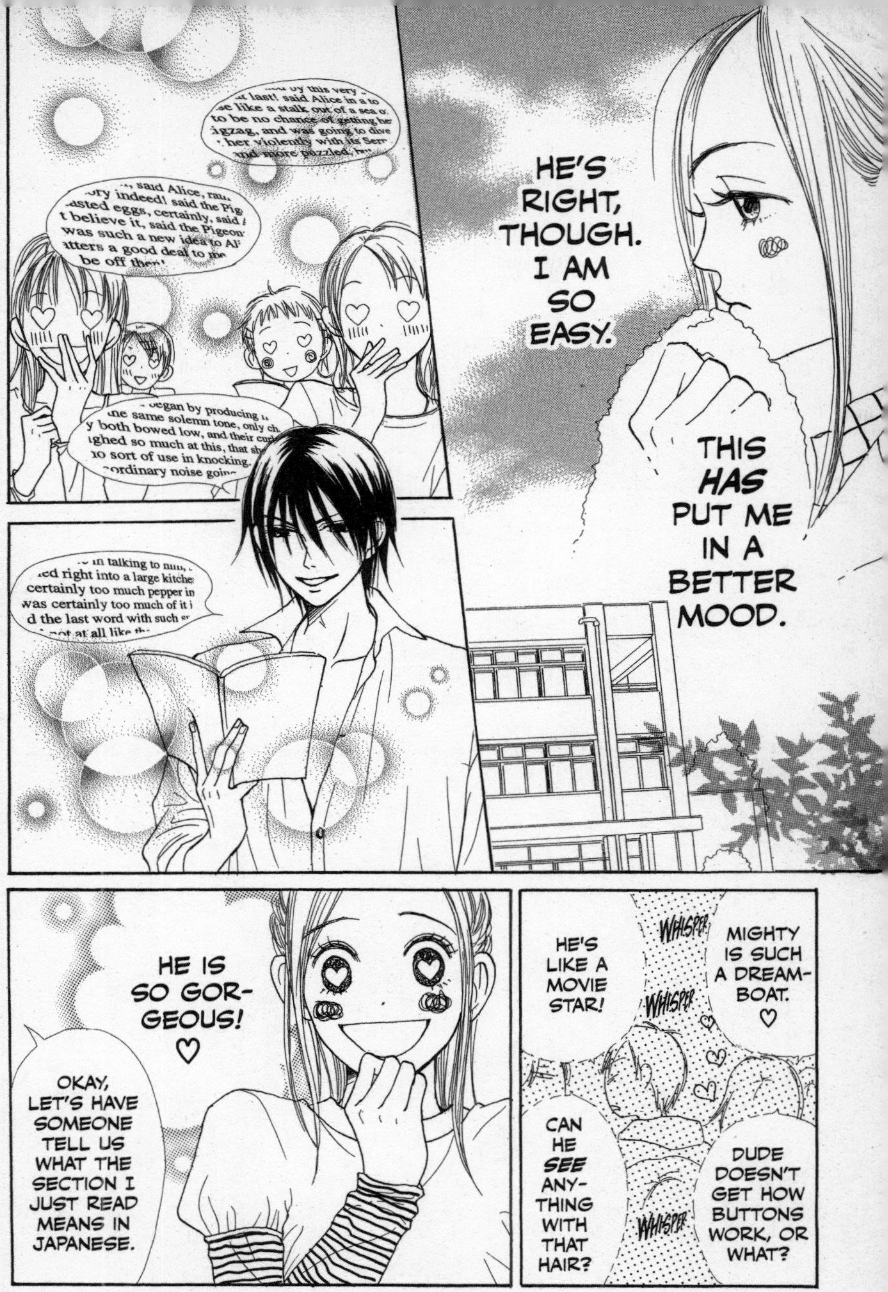
HE'S RIGHT, THOUGH. I AM SO EASY.
THIS *HAS* PUT ME IN A BETTER MOOD.
said Alice in a
se like a stalk out of a sea
to be no chance of getting
igzag, and was going to dive
her violently with its
and more puzzled,
said Alice,
ory indeed! said the Pig
asted eggs, certainly, said
t believe it, said the Pigeon
was such a new idea to Ali
atters a good deal to me
be off then!
egan by producing
he same solemn tone, only ch
y both bowed low, and their curl
ghed so much at this, that sh
o sort of use in knocking.
ordinary noise going
in talking to him,
ed right into a large kitche
certainly too much pepper in
was certainly too much of it i
d the last word with such
not at all like th
MIGHTY IS SUCH A DREAM-BOAT. ♡
WHISPER
HE'S LIKE A MOVIE STAR!
WHISPER
DUDE DOESN'T GET HOW BUTTONS WORK, OR WHAT?
WHISPER
CAN HE *SEE* ANYTHING WITH THAT HAIR?
HE IS SO GOR-GEOUS! ♡
OKAY, LET'S HAVE SOMEONE TELL US WHAT THE SECTION I JUST READ MEANS IN JAPANESE.

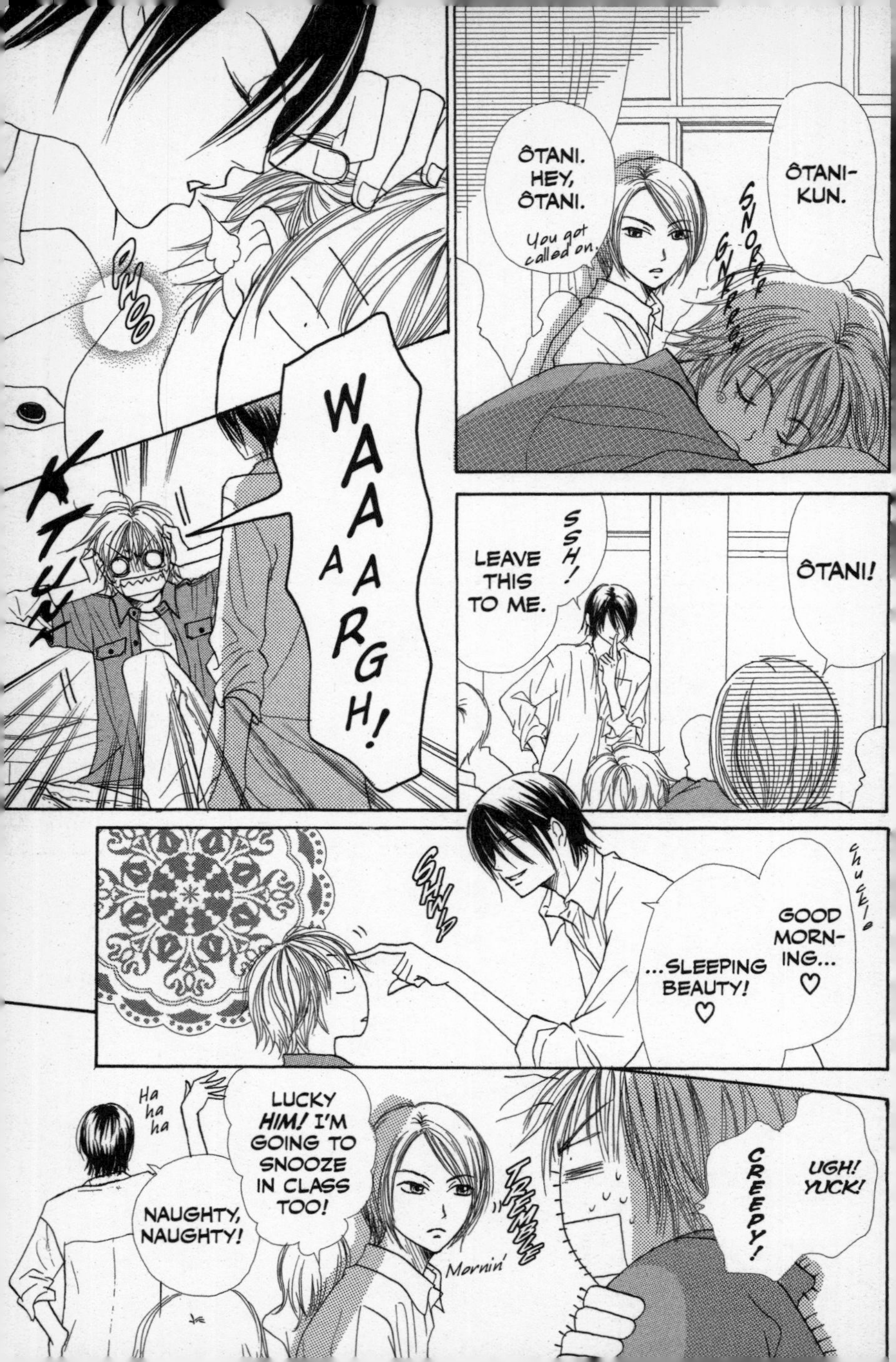
ÔTANI-KUN.
ÔTANI. HEY, ÔTANI.
You got called on.
ÔTANI!
SSH!
LEAVE THIS TO ME.
PHOO
WAAAARGH!
KTUNK
chuckle
GOOD MORN-ING... ♥
...SLEEPING BEAUTY! ♥
UGH! YUCK!
CREEPY!
Mornin'
LUCKY HIM! I'M GOING TO SNOOZE IN CLASS TOO!
Ha ha ha
NAUGHTY, NAUGHTY!

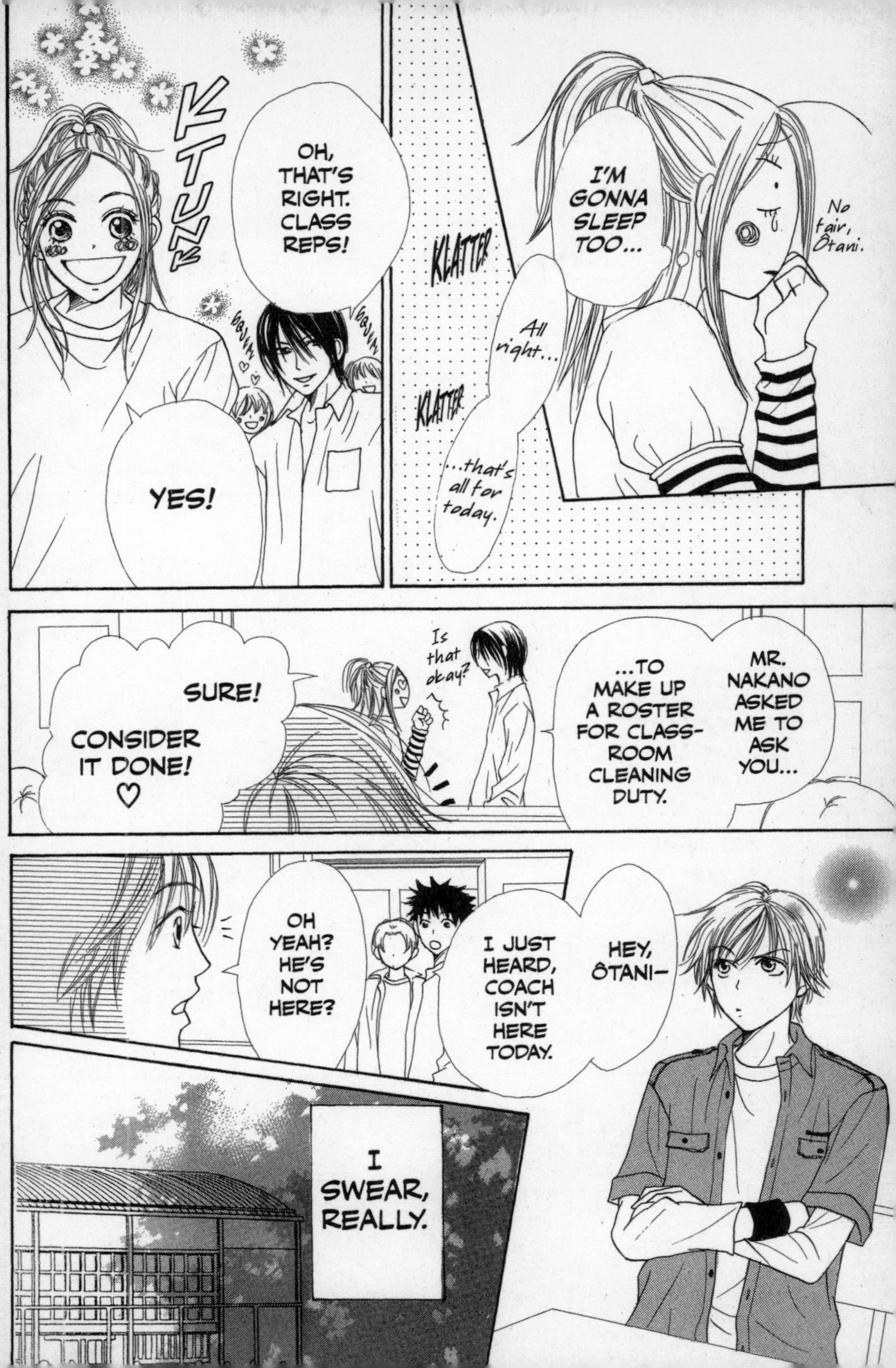
No fair, Ōtani.
I'M GONNA SLEEP TOO...
KLATTER
All right...
KLATTER
...that's all for today.
KTUNK
OH, THAT'S RIGHT. CLASS REPS!
YES!
MR. NAKANO ASKED ME TO ASK YOU...
...TO MAKE UP A ROSTER FOR CLASS-ROOM CLEANING DUTY.
Is that okay?
SURE!
CONSIDER IT DONE! ♡
HEY, ŌTANI—
I JUST HEARD, COACH ISN'T HERE TODAY.
OH YEAH? HE'S NOT HERE?
I SWEAR, REALLY.

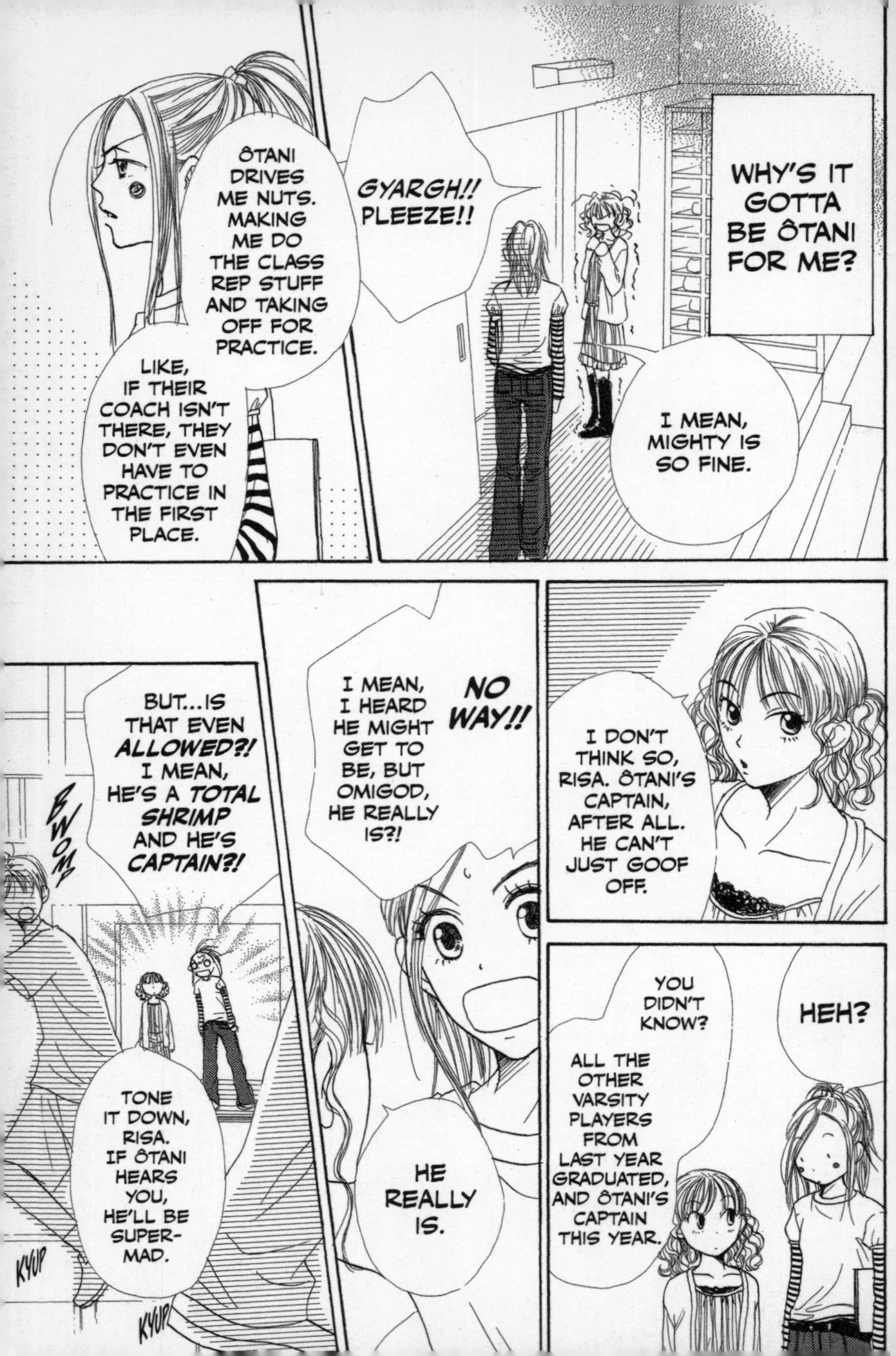
WHY'S IT GOTTA BE ÔTANI FOR ME?
I MEAN, MIGHTY IS SO FINE.
GYARGH!! PLEEZE!!
ÔTANI DRIVES ME NUTS. MAKING ME DO THE CLASS REP STUFF AND TAKING OFF FOR PRACTICE.
LIKE, IF THEIR COACH ISN'T THERE, THEY DON'T EVEN HAVE TO PRACTICE IN THE FIRST PLACE.
I DON'T THINK SO, RISA. ÔTANI'S CAPTAIN, AFTER ALL. HE CAN'T JUST GOOF OFF.
HEH?
YOU DIDN'T KNOW?
ALL THE OTHER VARSITY PLAYERS FROM LAST YEAR GRADUATED, AND ÔTANI'S CAPTAIN THIS YEAR.
NO WAY!!
I MEAN, I HEARD HE MIGHT GET TO BE, BUT OMIGOD, HE REALLY IS?!
HE REALLY IS.
BUT...IS THAT EVEN ALLOWED?! I MEAN, HE'S A TOTAL SHRIMP AND HE'S CAPTAIN?!
BWOMP
TONE IT DOWN, RISA. IF ÔTANI HEARS YOU, HE'LL BE SUPER-MAD.
KYUP
KYUP

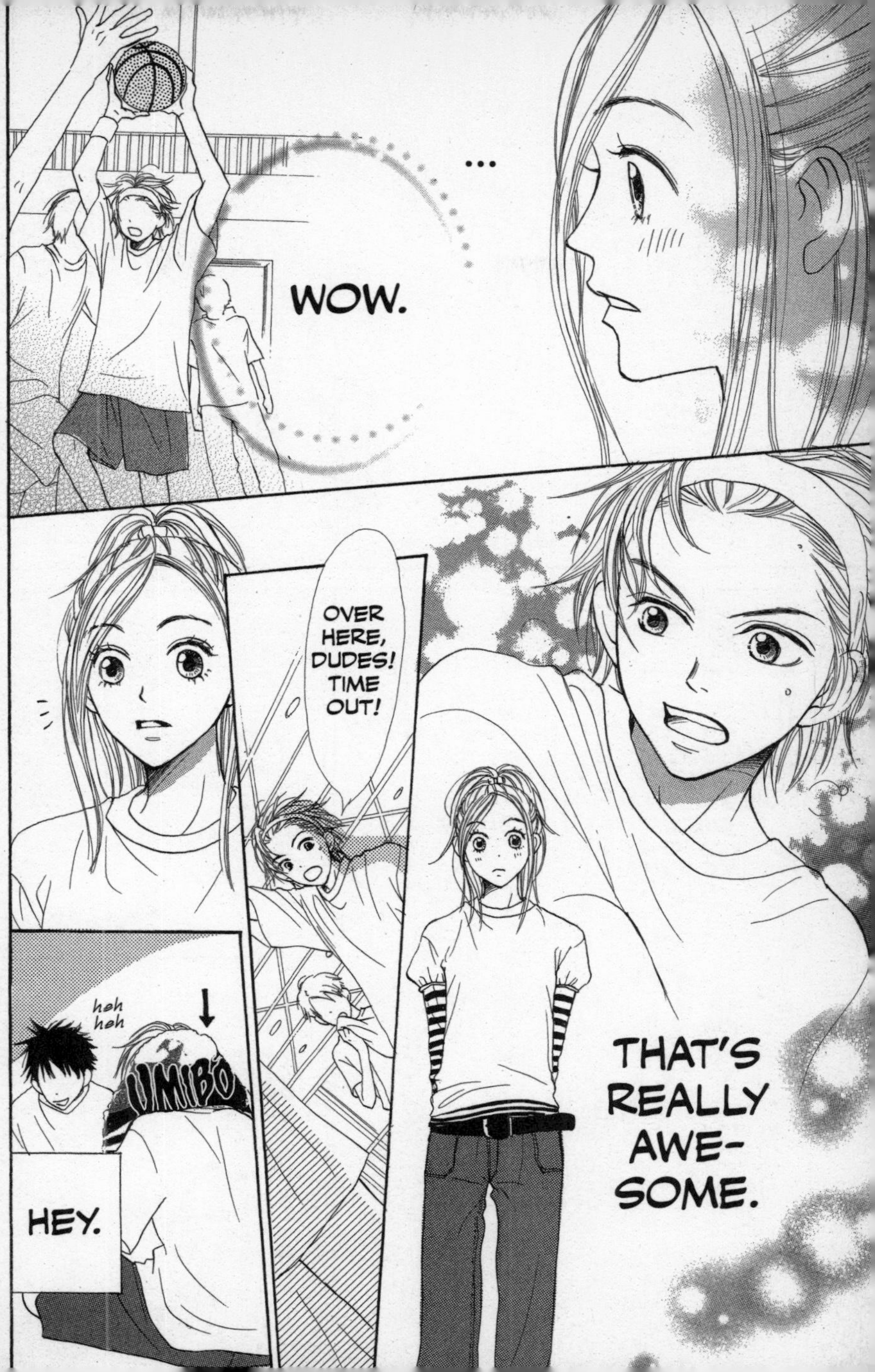
...
WOW.
THAT'S REALLY AWE-SOME.
OVER HERE, DUDES! TIME OUT!
heh heh
UMIBO
HEY.

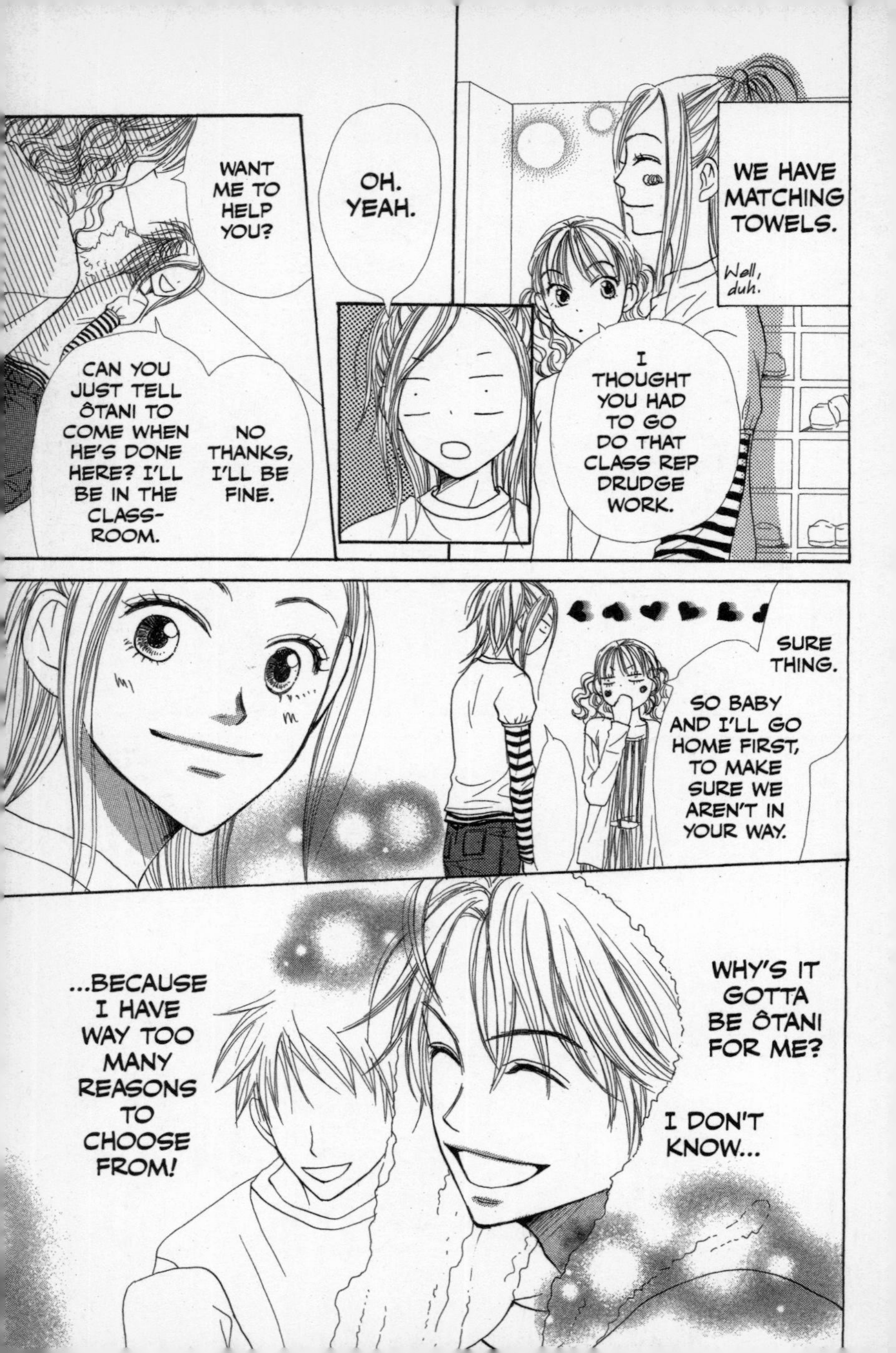
WE HAVE MATCHING TOWELS.
Well, duh.
I THOUGHT YOU HAD TO GO DO THAT CLASS REP DRUDGE WORK.
OH. YEAH.
WANT ME TO HELP YOU?
NO THANKS, I'LL BE FINE.
CAN YOU JUST TELL ÔTANI TO COME WHEN HE'S DONE HERE? I'LL BE IN THE CLASS-ROOM.
SURE THING.
SO BABY AND I'LL GO HOME FIRST, TO MAKE SURE WE AREN'T IN YOUR WAY.
WHY'S IT GOTTA BE ÔTANI FOR ME?
I DON'T KNOW...
...BECAUSE I HAVE WAY TOO MANY REASONS TO CHOOSE FROM!

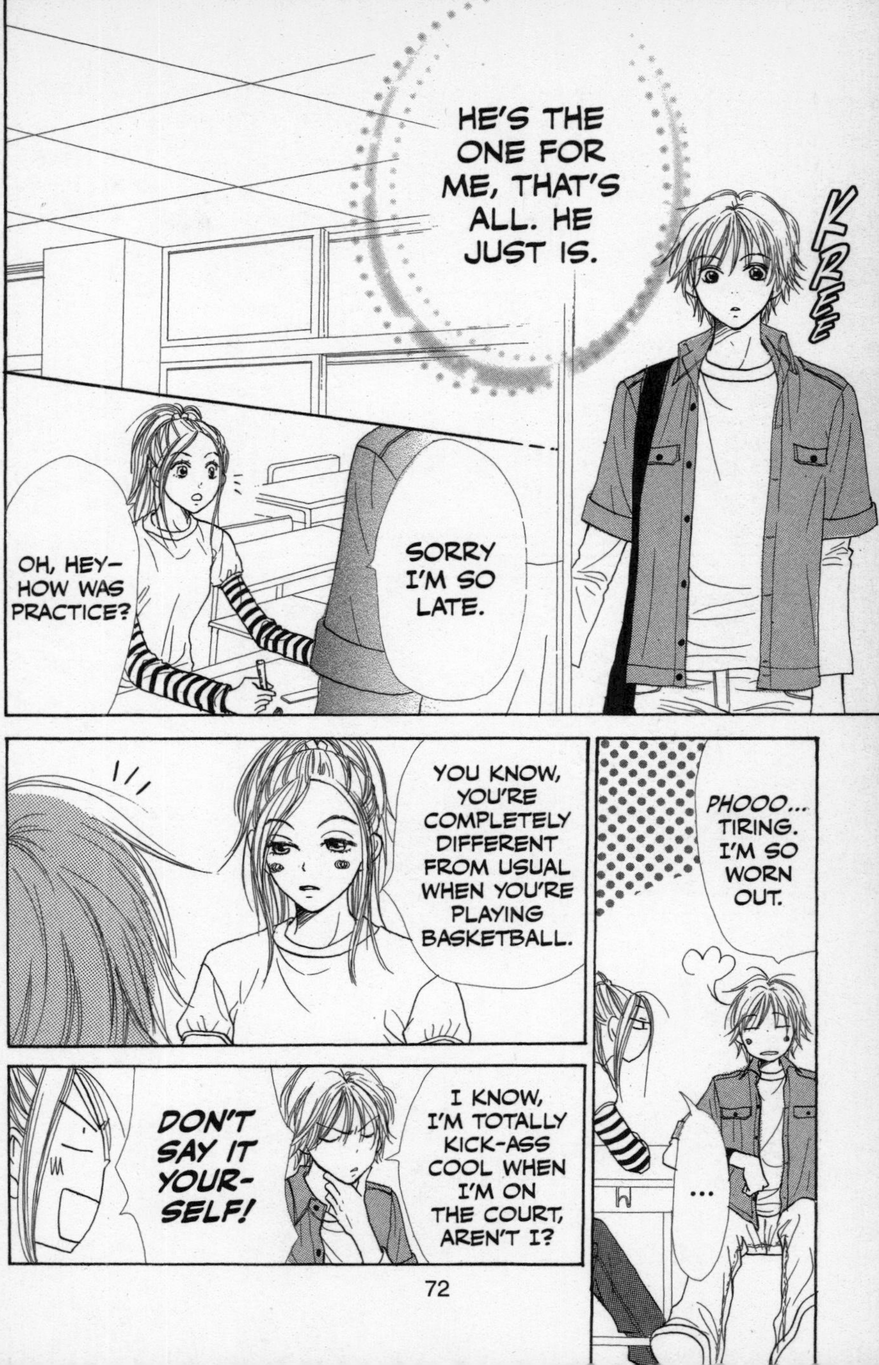
HE'S THE ONE FOR ME, THAT'S ALL. HE JUST IS.
KREE
SORRY I'M SO LATE.
OH, HEY— HOW WAS PRACTICE?
PHOOO... TIRING. I'M SO WORN OUT.
...
YOU KNOW, YOU'RE COMPLETELY DIFFERENT FROM USUAL WHEN YOU'RE PLAYING BASKETBALL.
I KNOW, I'M TOTALLY KICK-ASS COOL WHEN I'M ON THE COURT, AREN'T I?
DON'T SAY IT YOURSELF!

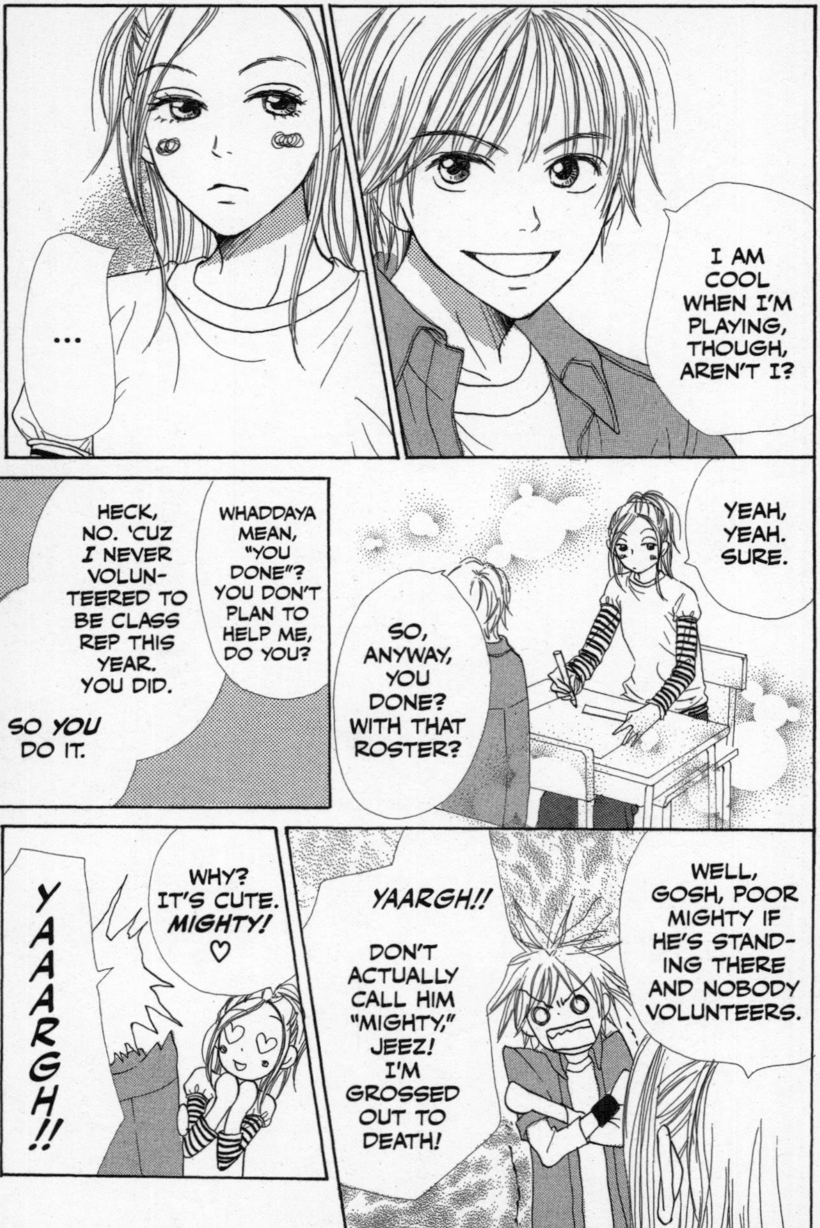
I AM COOL WHEN I'M PLAYING, THOUGH, AREN'T I?
...
YEAH, YEAH. SURE.
SO, ANYWAY, YOU DONE? WITH THAT ROSTER?
WHADDAYA MEAN, "YOU DONE"? YOU DON'T PLAN TO HELP ME, DO YOU?
HECK, NO. 'CUZ *I* NEVER VOLUN-TEERED TO BE CLASS REP THIS YEAR. YOU DID.
SO *YOU* DO IT.
WELL, GOSH, POOR MIGHTY IF HE'S STAND-ING THERE AND NOBODY VOLUNTEERS.
YAARGH!!
DON'T ACTUALLY CALL HIM "MIGHTY," JEEZ! I'M GROSSED OUT TO DEATH!
WHY? IT'S CUTE. *MIGHTY!* ♡
YAAAARGH!!

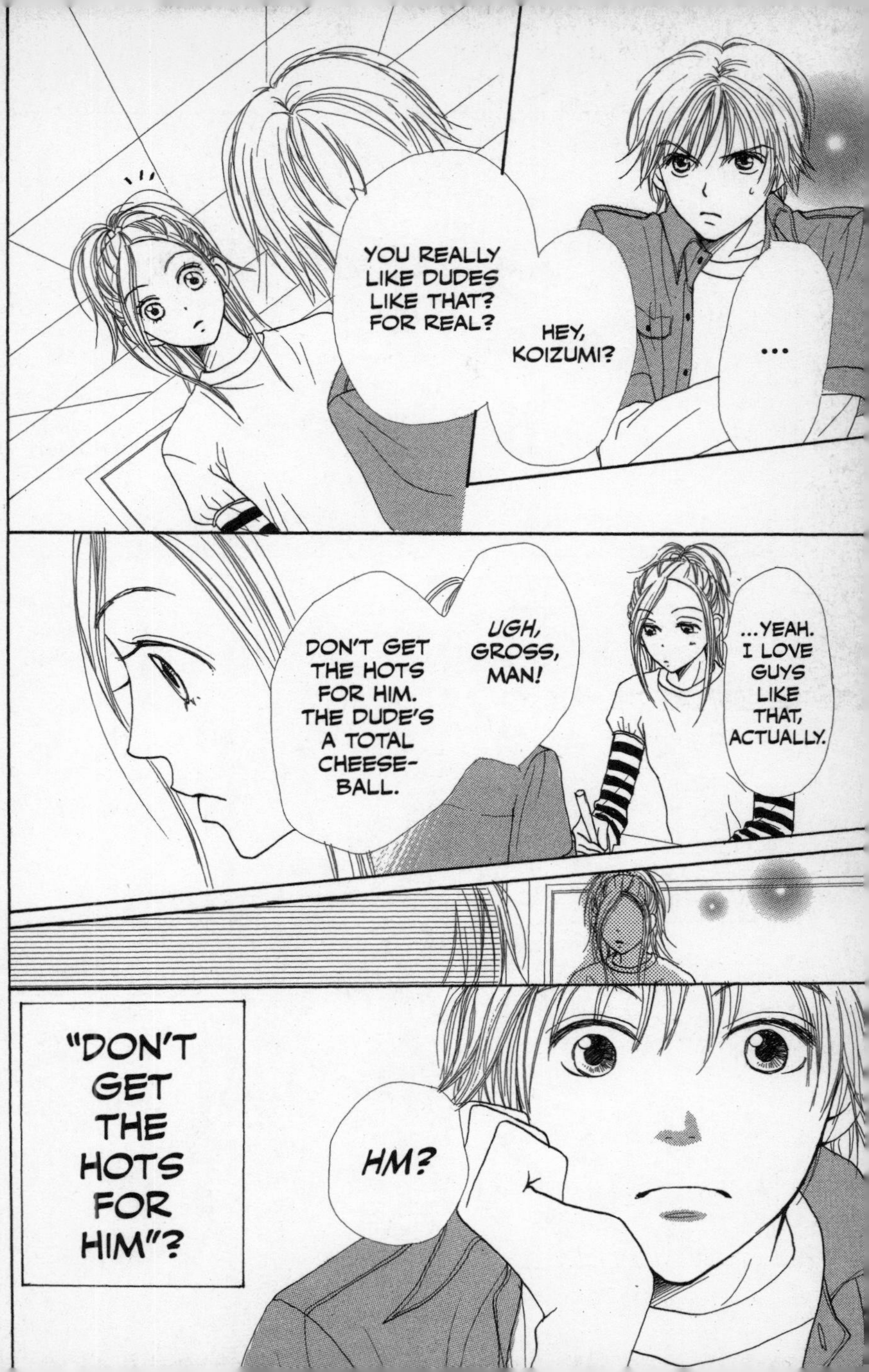
...
HEY, KOIZUMI?
YOU REALLY LIKE DUDES LIKE THAT? FOR REAL?
...YEAH. I LOVE GUYS LIKE THAT, ACTUALLY.
UGH, GROSS, MAN!
DON'T GET THE HOTS FOR HIM. THE DUDE'S A TOTAL CHEESE-BALL.
HM?
"DON'T GET THE HOTS FOR HIM"?

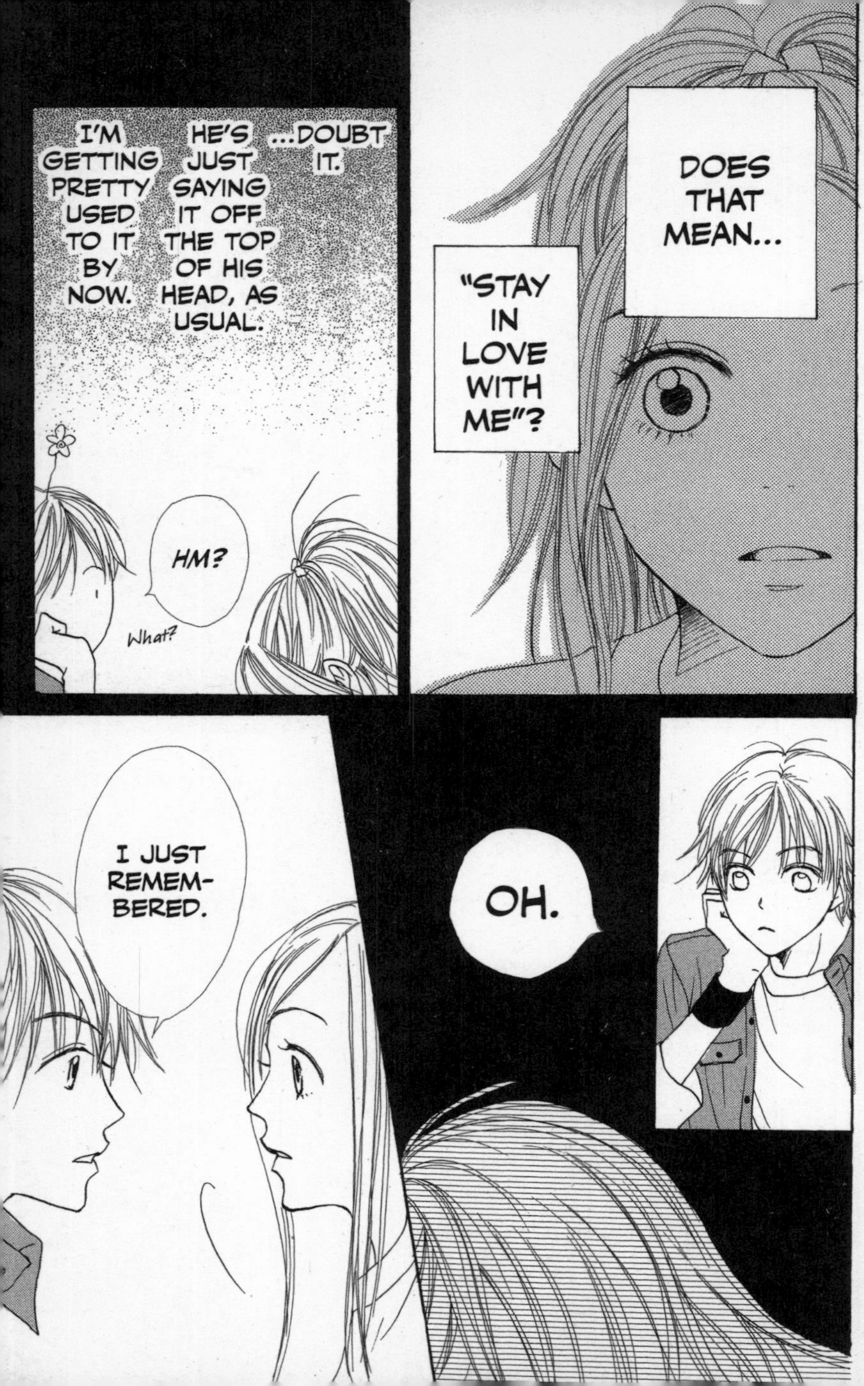

DOES THAT MEAN...
"STAY IN LOVE WITH ME"?
...DOUBT IT.
HE'S JUST SAYING IT OFF THE TOP OF HIS HEAD, AS USUAL.
I'M GETTING PRETTY USED TO IT BY NOW.
HM?
What?
OH.
I JUST REMEMBERED.

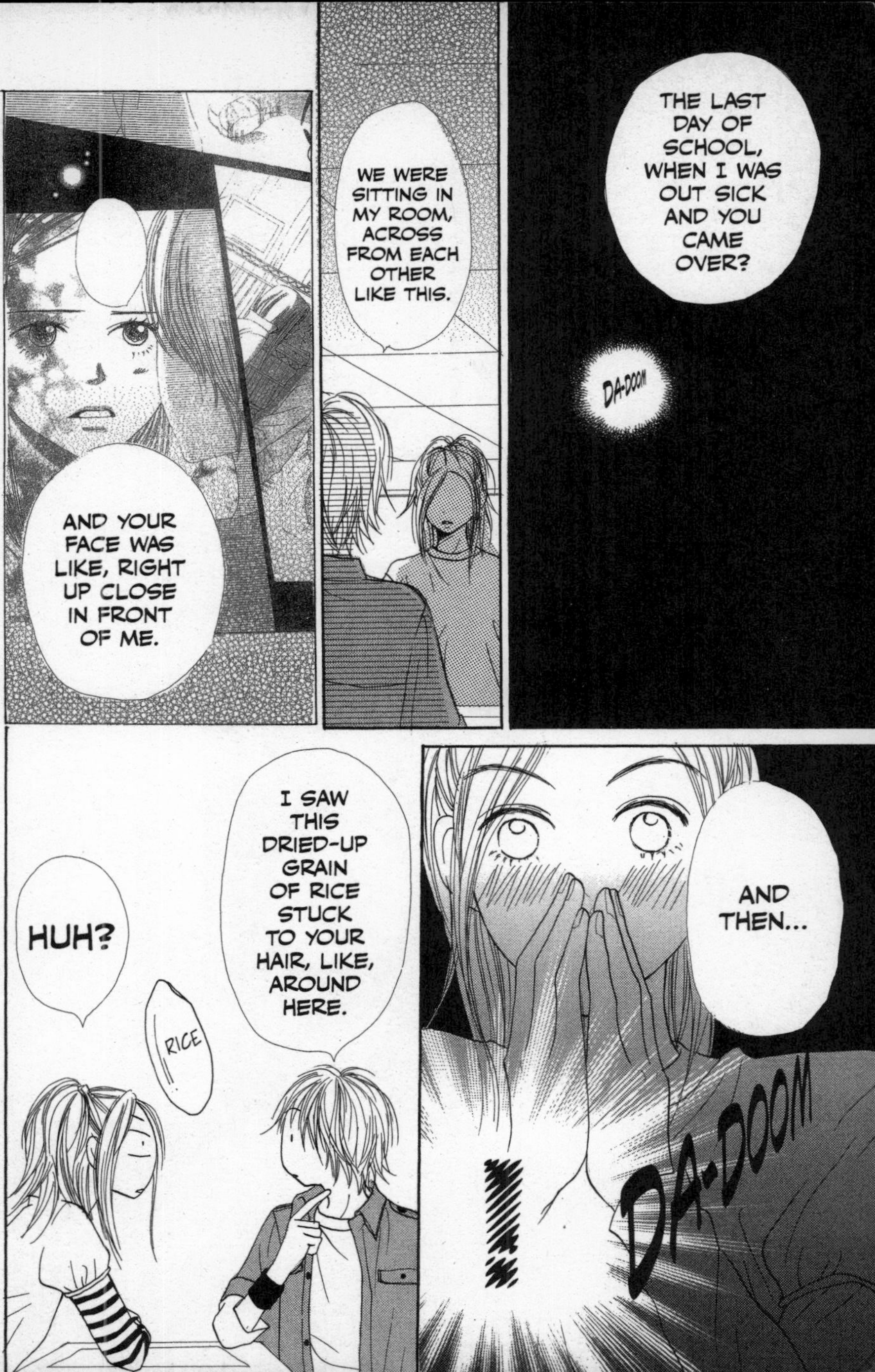
THE LAST DAY OF SCHOOL, WHEN I WAS OUT SICK AND YOU CAME OVER?
DA-DOOM
WE WERE SITTING IN MY ROOM, ACROSS FROM EACH OTHER LIKE THIS.
AND YOUR FACE WAS LIKE, RIGHT UP CLOSE IN FRONT OF ME.
AND THEN...
!!
DA-DOOM
I SAW THIS DRIED-UP GRAIN OF RICE STUCK TO YOUR HAIR, LIKE, AROUND HERE.
RICE
HUH?

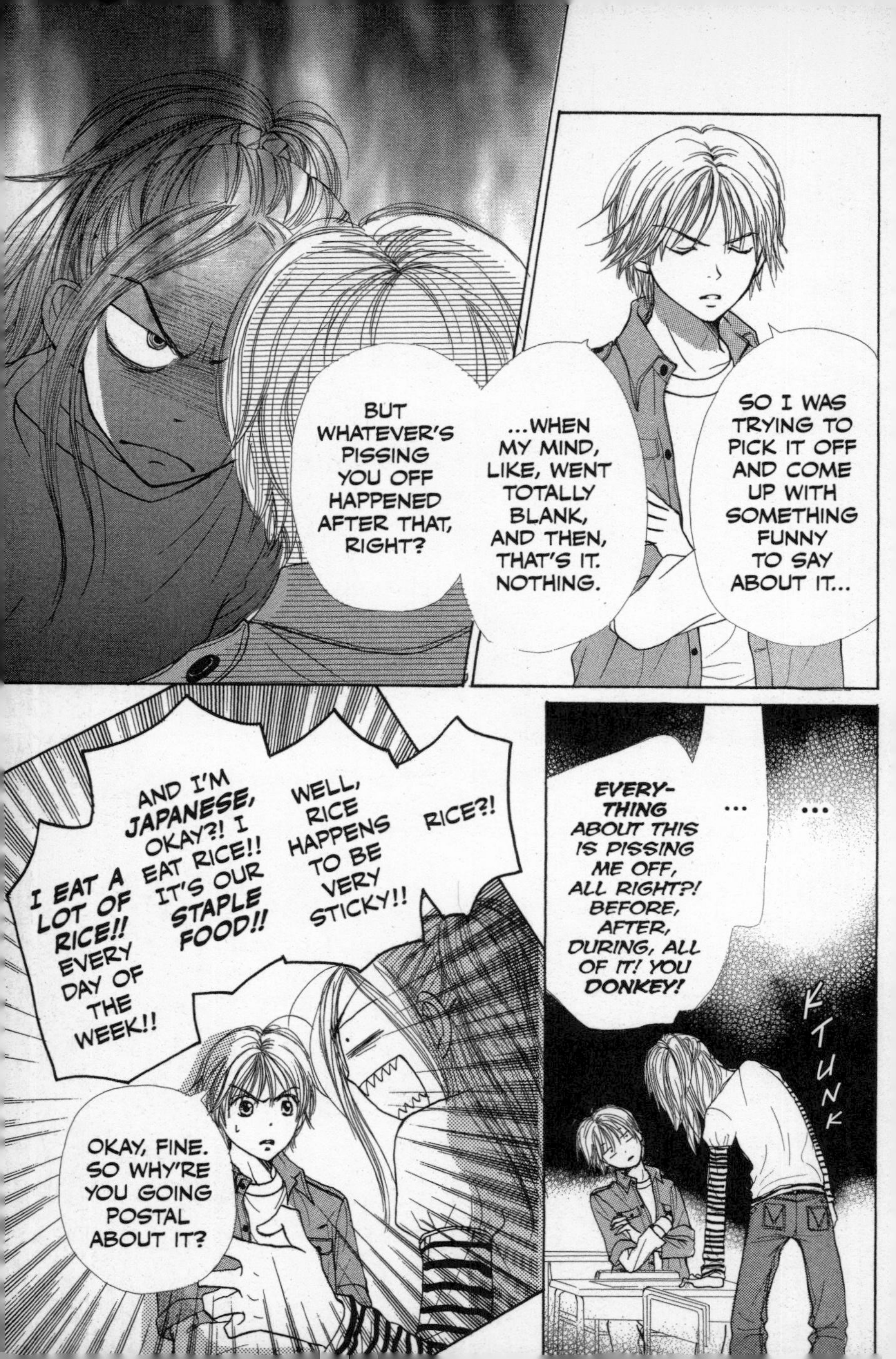
SO I WAS TRYING TO PICK IT OFF AND COME UP WITH SOMETHING FUNNY TO SAY ABOUT IT...
...WHEN MY MIND, LIKE, WENT TOTALLY BLANK, AND THEN, THAT'S IT. NOTHING.
BUT WHATEVER'S PISSING YOU OFF HAPPENED AFTER THAT, RIGHT?
...
...
EVERY-THING ABOUT THIS IS PISSING ME OFF, ALL RIGHT?! BEFORE, AFTER, DURING, ALL OF IT! YOU DONKEY!
KTUNK
RICE?!
WELL, RICE HAPPENS TO BE VERY STICKY!!
AND I'M JAPANESE, OKAY?! I EAT RICE!! IT'S OUR STAPLE FOOD!!
I EAT A LOT OF RICE!! EVERY DAY OF THE WEEK!!
OKAY, FINE. SO WHY'RE YOU GOING POSTAL ABOUT IT?

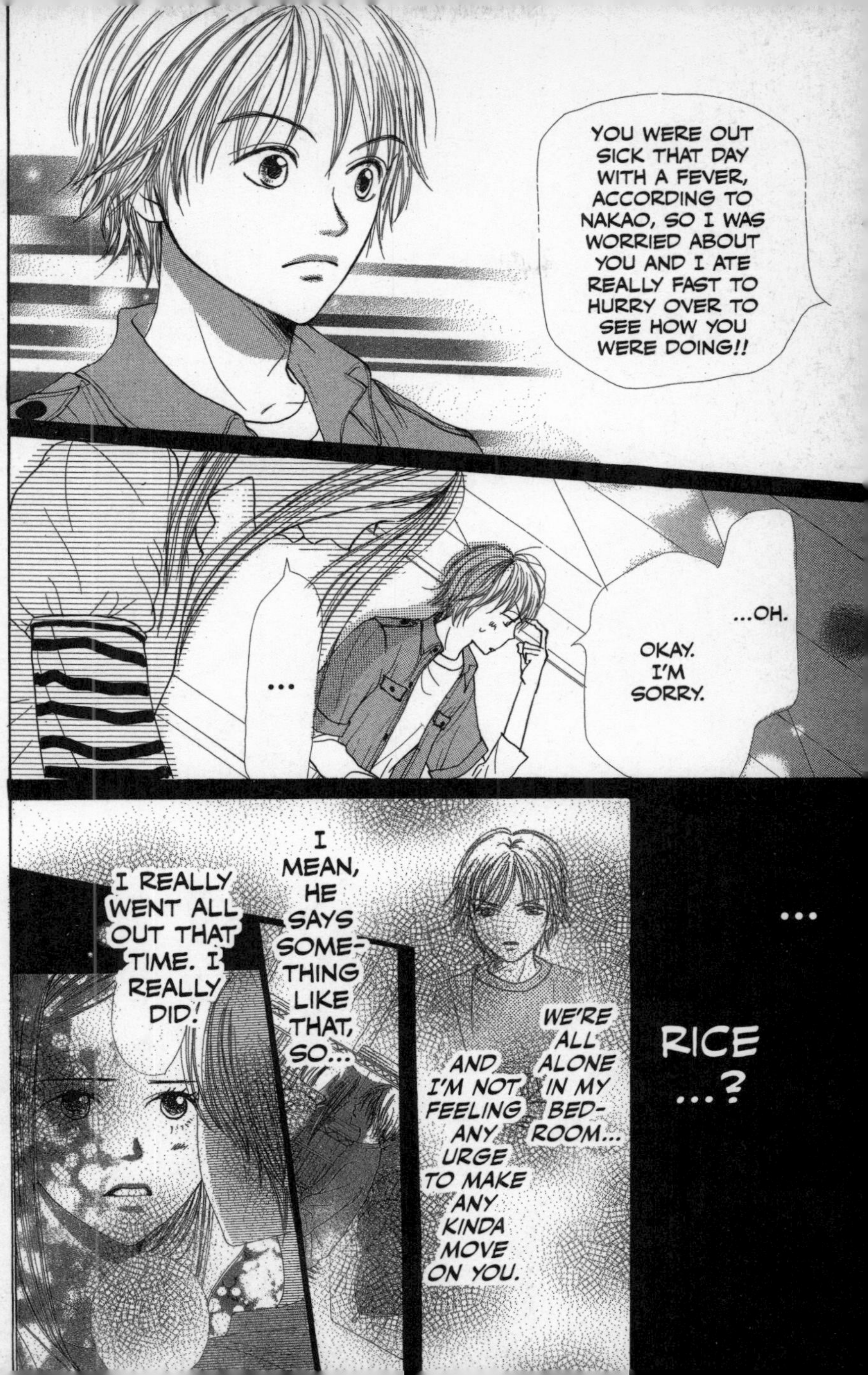
YOU WERE OUT SICK THAT DAY WITH A FEVER, ACCORDING TO NAKAO, SO I WAS WORRIED ABOUT YOU AND I ATE REALLY FAST TO HURRY OVER TO SEE HOW YOU WERE DOING!!
...OH.
OKAY. I'M SORRY.
...
...
RICE ...?
WE'RE ALL ALONE IN MY BEDROOM...
AND I'M NOT FEELING ANY URGE TO MAKE ANY KINDA MOVE ON YOU.
I MEAN, HE SAYS SOMETHING LIKE THAT, SO...
I REALLY WENT ALL OUT THAT TIME. I REALLY DID!

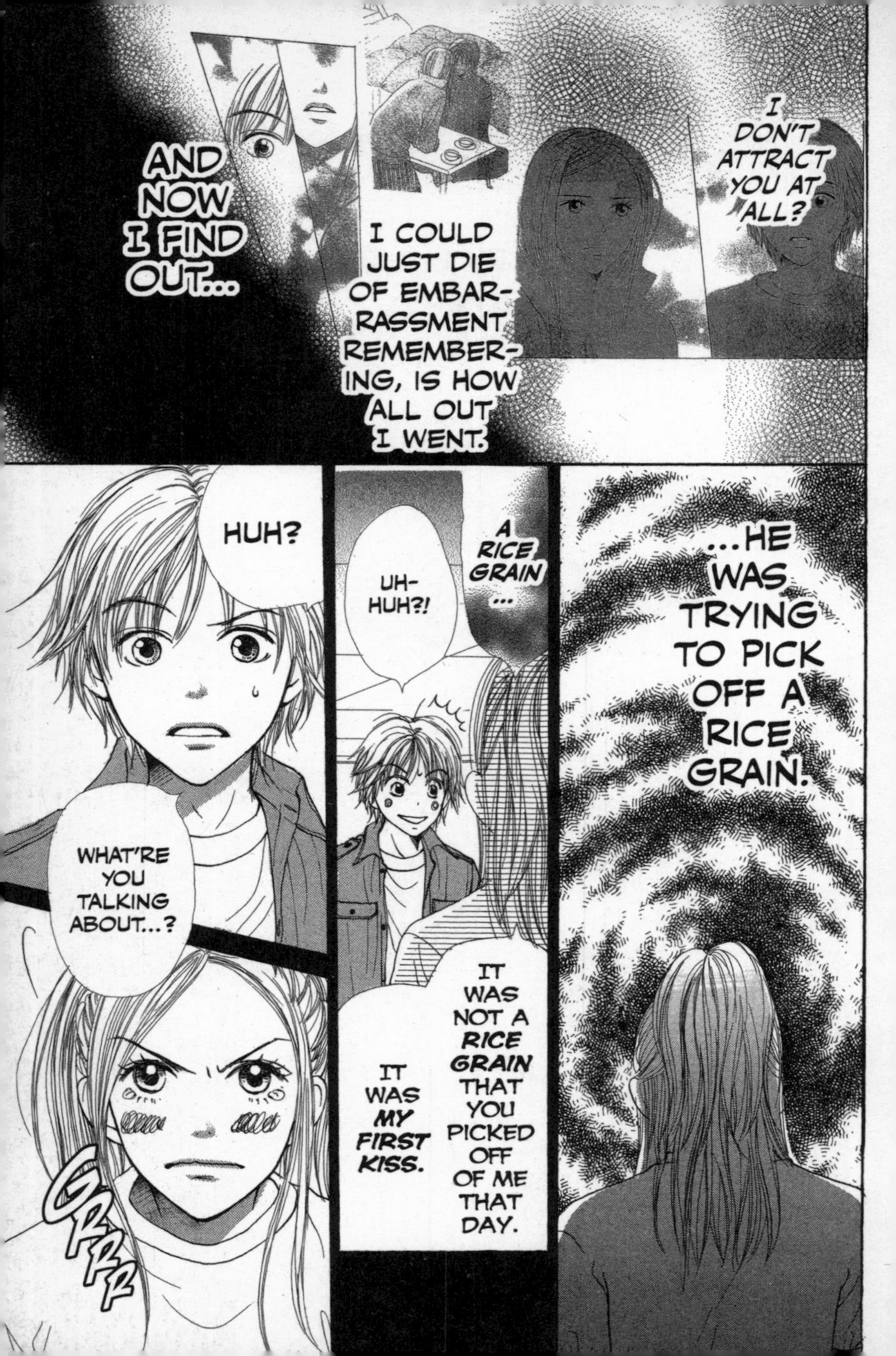
I DON'T ATTRACT YOU AT ALL?
I COULD JUST DIE OF EMBARRASSMENT REMEMBERING, IS HOW ALL OUT I WENT.
AND NOW I FIND OUT...
...HE WAS TRYING TO PICK OFF A RICE GRAIN.
A RICE GRAIN...
UH-HUH?!
IT WAS NOT A RICE GRAIN THAT YOU PICKED OFF OF ME THAT DAY.
IT WAS MY FIRST KISS.
HUH?
WHAT'RE YOU TALKING ABOUT...?
GRRR

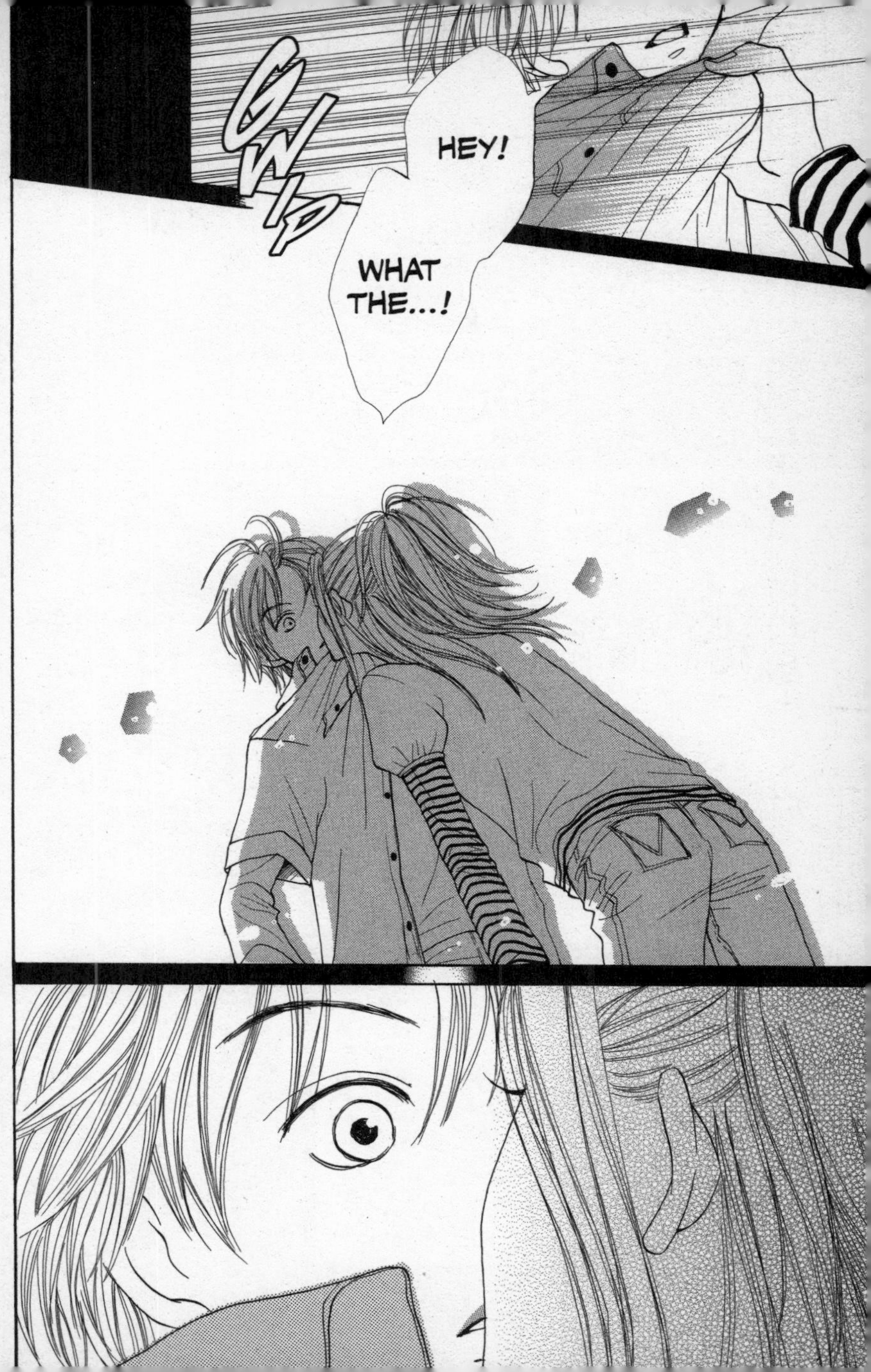
GWIP
HEY!
WHAT THE...!

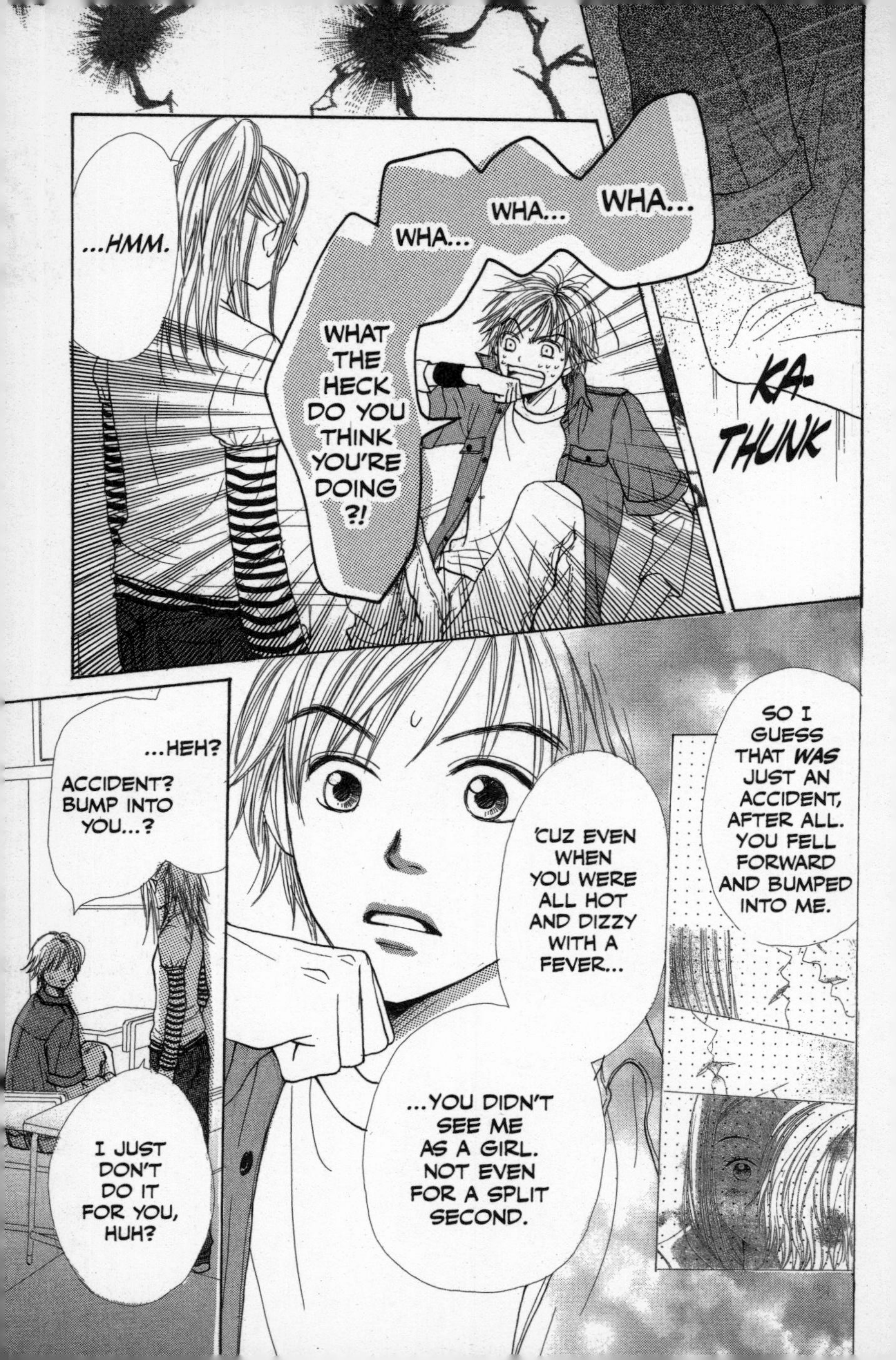
KA-THUNK
WHA...
WHA...
WHA...
WHAT THE HECK DO YOU THINK YOU'RE DOING ?!
...HMM.
SO I GUESS THAT *WAS* JUST AN ACCIDENT, AFTER ALL. YOU FELL FORWARD AND BUMPED INTO ME.
'CUZ EVEN WHEN YOU WERE ALL HOT AND DIZZY WITH A FEVER...
...YOU DIDN'T SEE ME AS A GIRL. NOT EVEN FOR A SPLIT SECOND.
...HEH?
ACCIDENT? BUMP INTO YOU...?
I JUST DON'T DO IT FOR YOU, HUH?

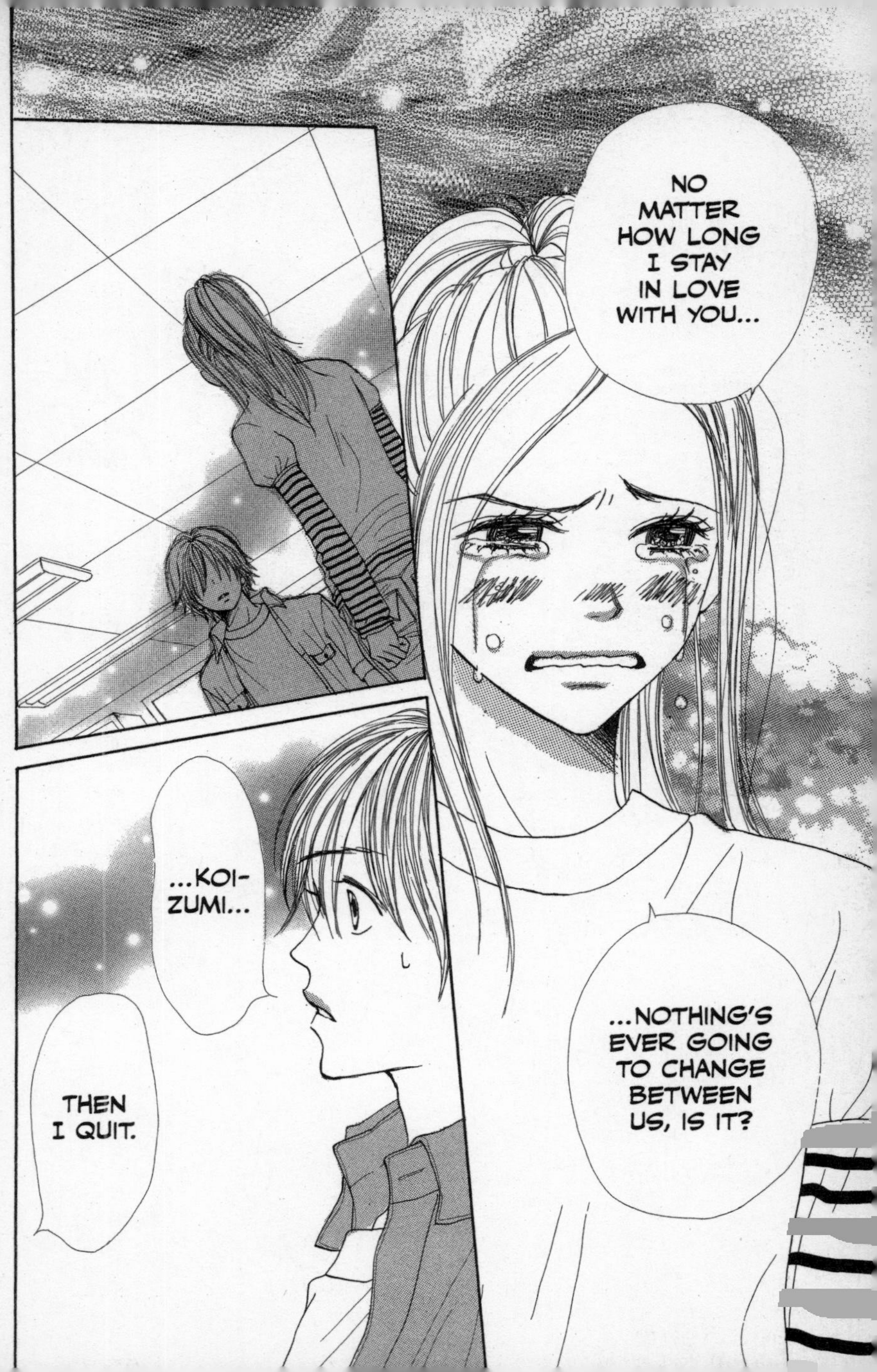
NO MATTER HOW LONG I STAY IN LOVE WITH YOU...
...NOTHING'S EVER GOING TO CHANGE BETWEEN US, IS IT?
...KOI-ZUMI...
THEN I QUIT.

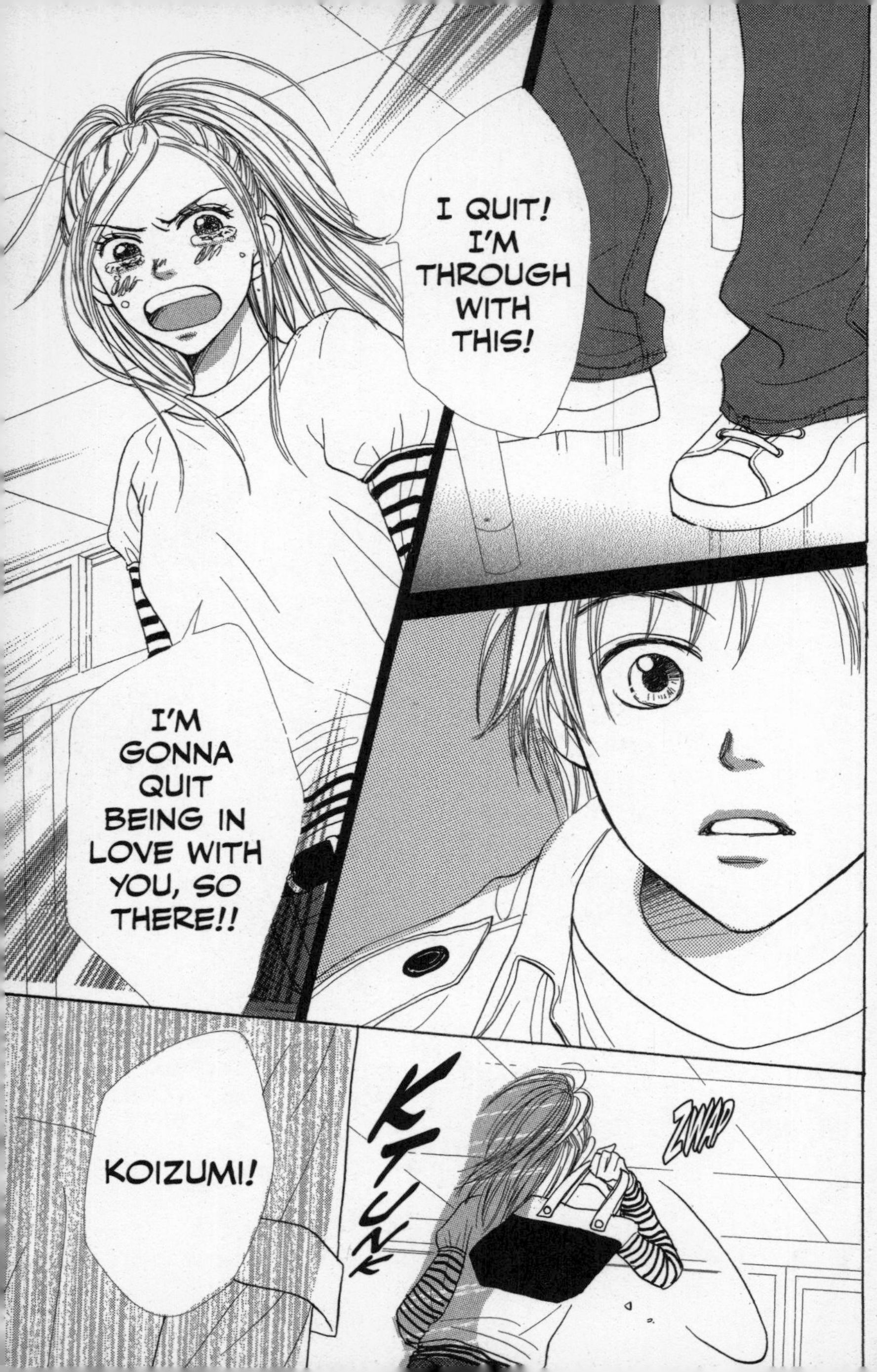
I QUIT! I'M THROUGH WITH THIS!
I'M GONNA QUIT BEING IN LOVE WITH YOU, SO THERE!!
KTUNK
ZWAP
KOIZUMI!

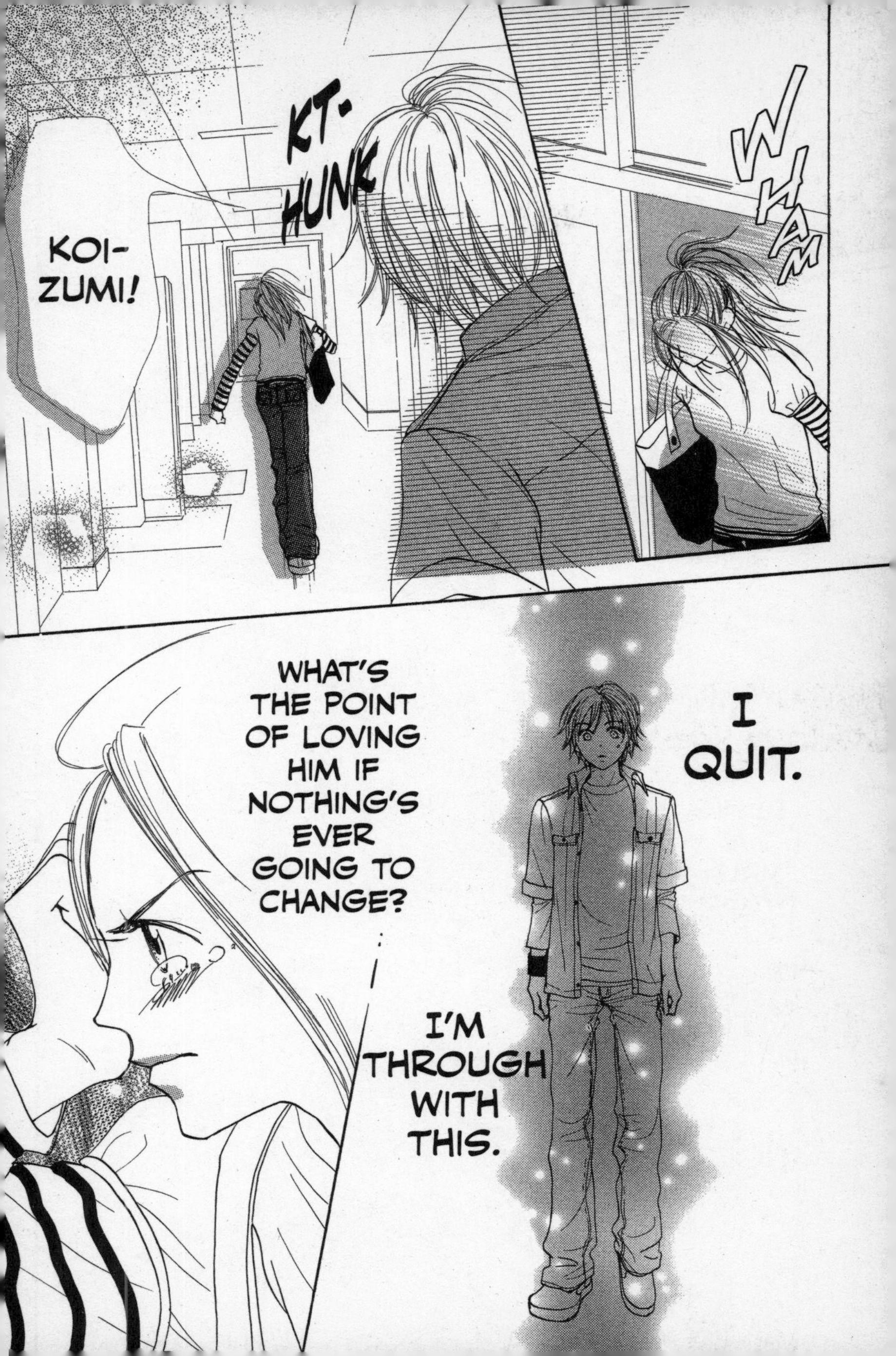
WHAM
KT-HUNK
KOI-ZUMI!
I QUIT.
WHAT'S THE POINT OF LOVING HIM IF NOTHING'S EVER GOING TO CHANGE?
I'M THROUGH WITH THIS.

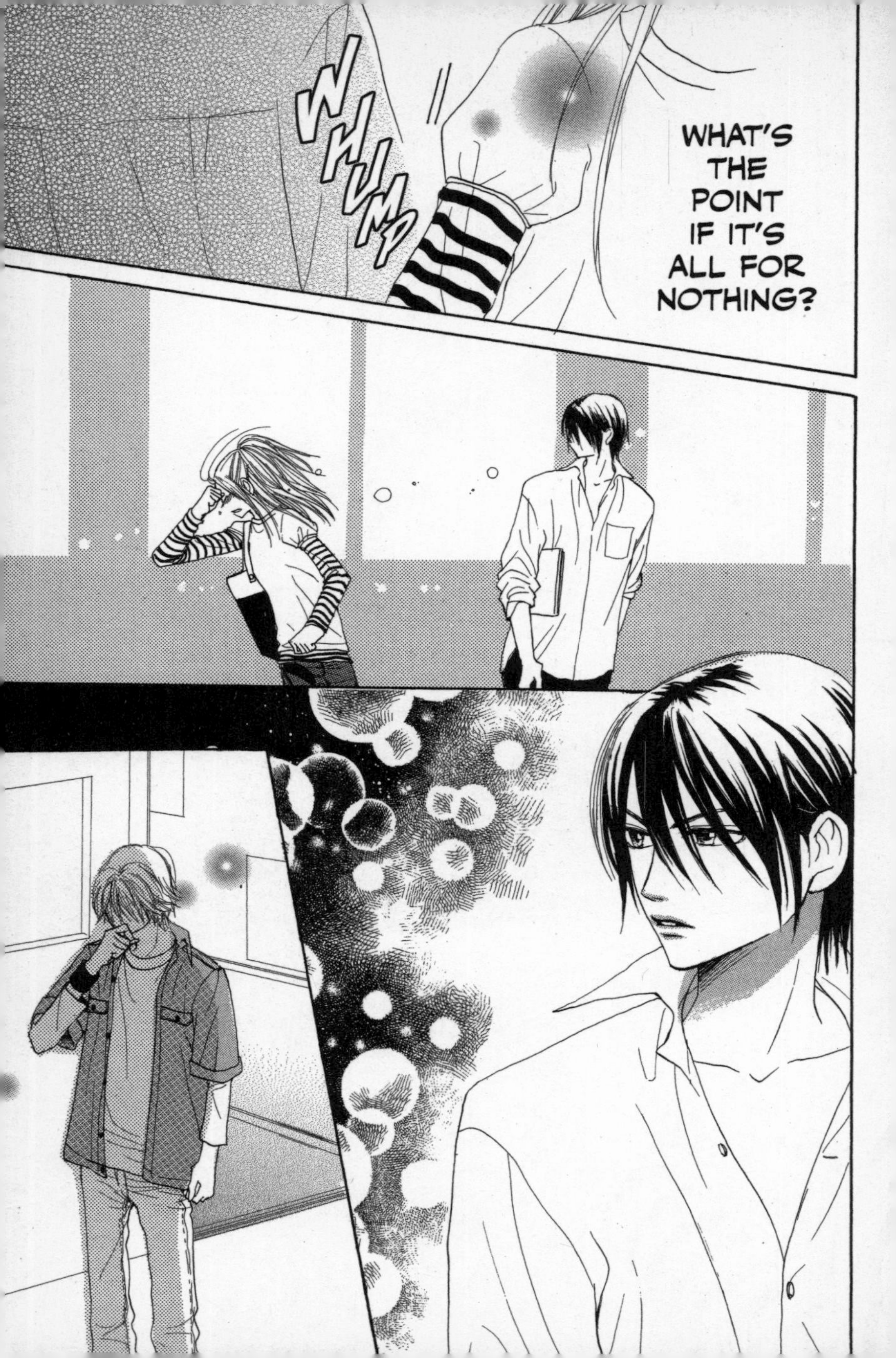
WHAT'S THE POINT IF IT'S ALL FOR NOTHING?
WHUMP

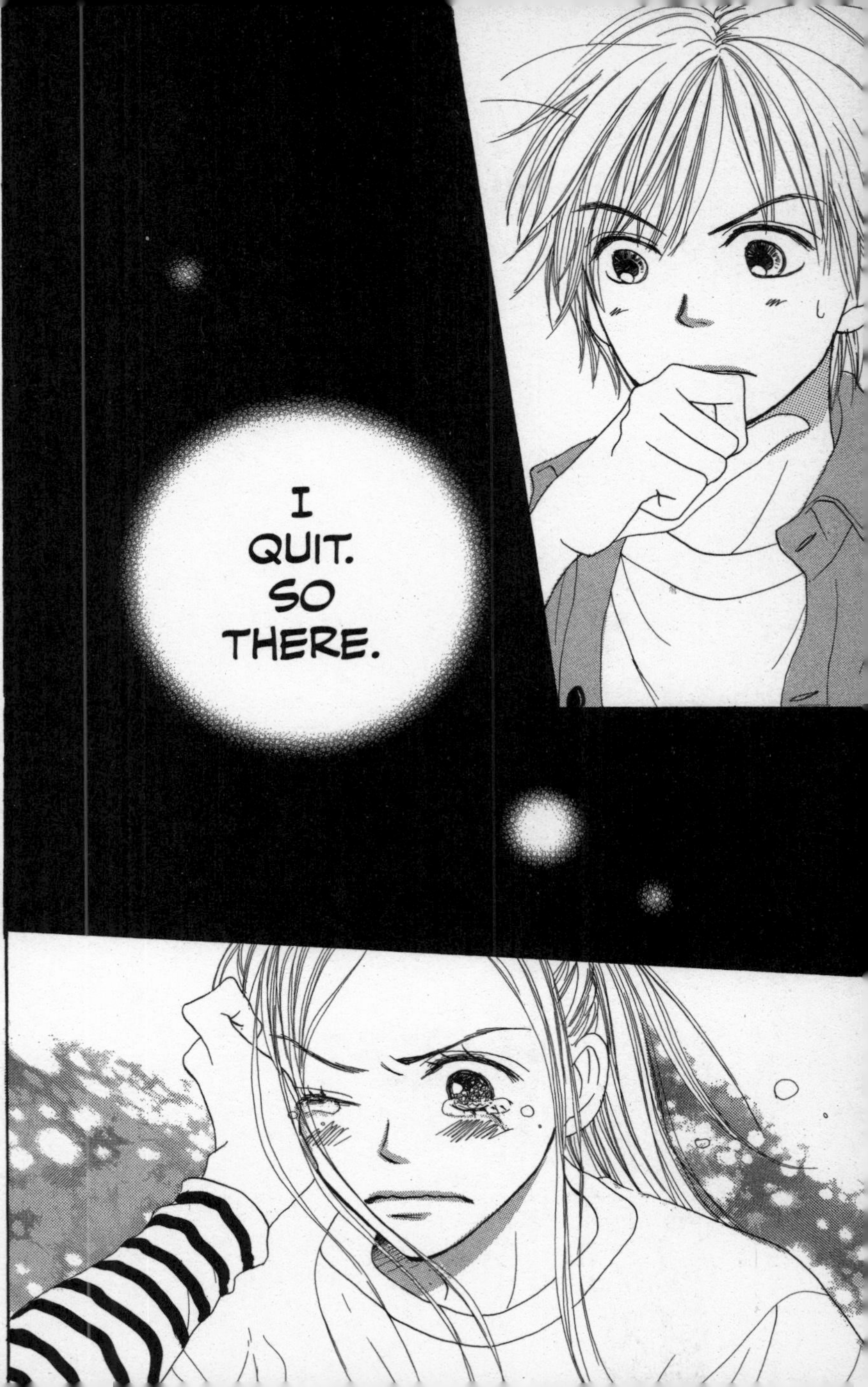
I QUIT. SO THERE.

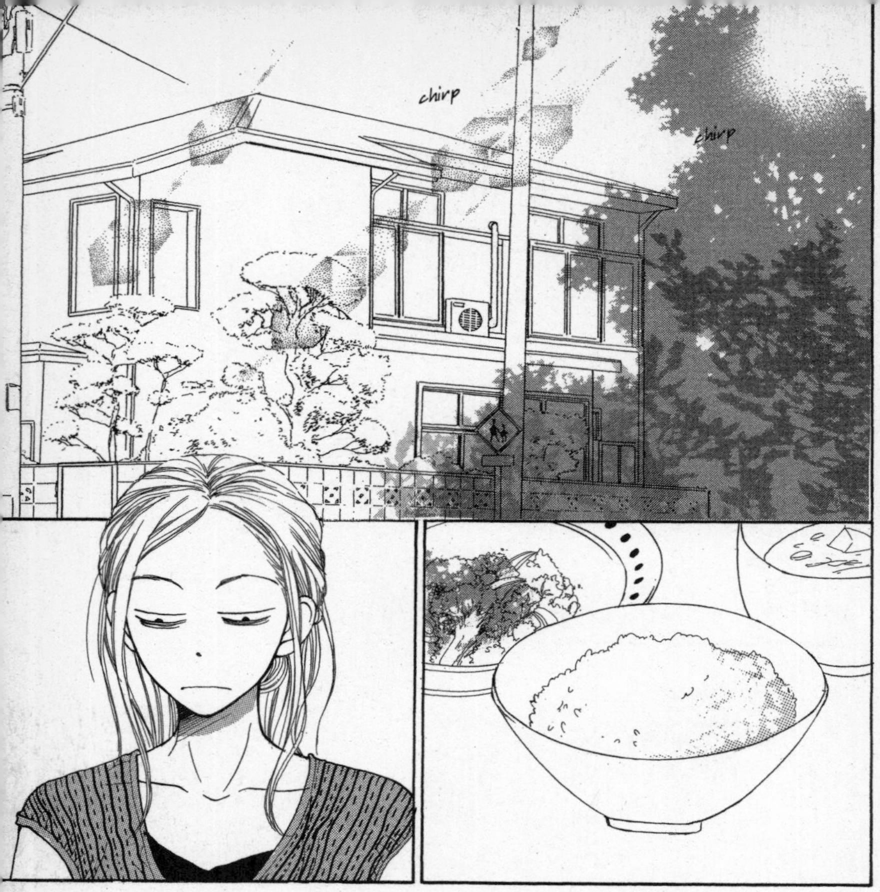
chirp
chirp

CHAPTER 23

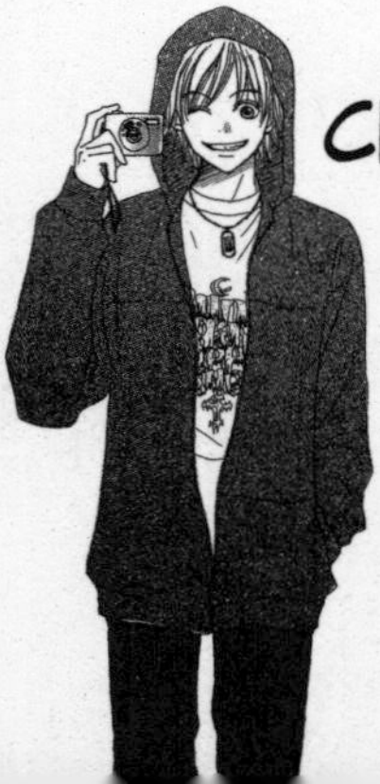

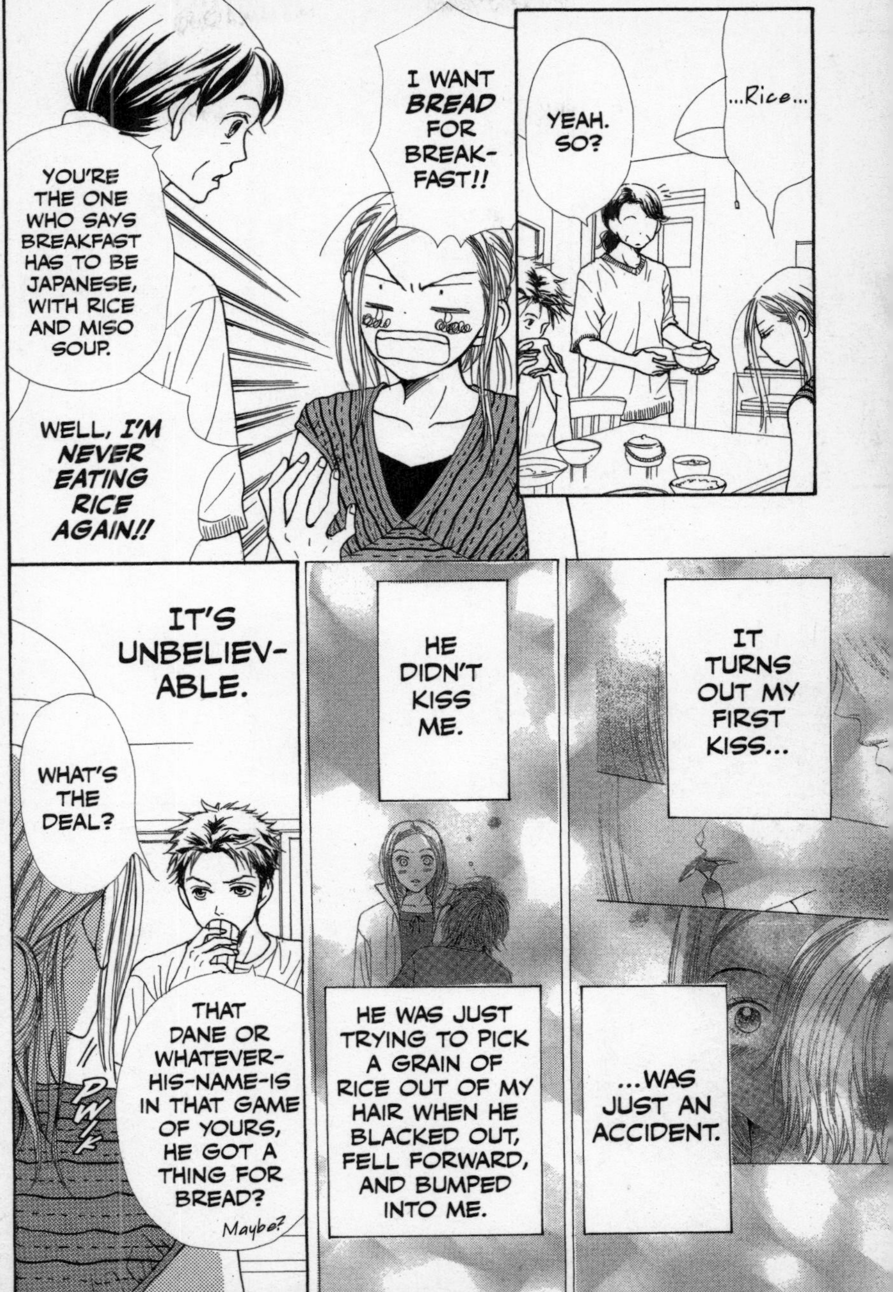
...Rice...
YEAH. SO?
I WANT BREAD FOR BREAK-FAST!!
YOU'RE THE ONE WHO SAYS BREAKFAST HAS TO BE JAPANESE, WITH RICE AND MISO SOUP.
WELL, I'M NEVER EATING RICE AGAIN!!
IT TURNS OUT MY FIRST KISS...
...WAS JUST AN ACCIDENT.
HE DIDN'T KISS ME.
HE WAS JUST TRYING TO PICK A GRAIN OF RICE OUT OF MY HAIR WHEN HE BLACKED OUT, FELL FORWARD, AND BUMPED INTO ME.
IT'S UNBELIEV-ABLE.
WHAT'S THE DEAL?
THAT DANE OR WHATEVER-HIS-NAME-IS IN THAT GAME OF YOURS, HE GOT A THING FOR BREAD?
PWIK
Maybe?

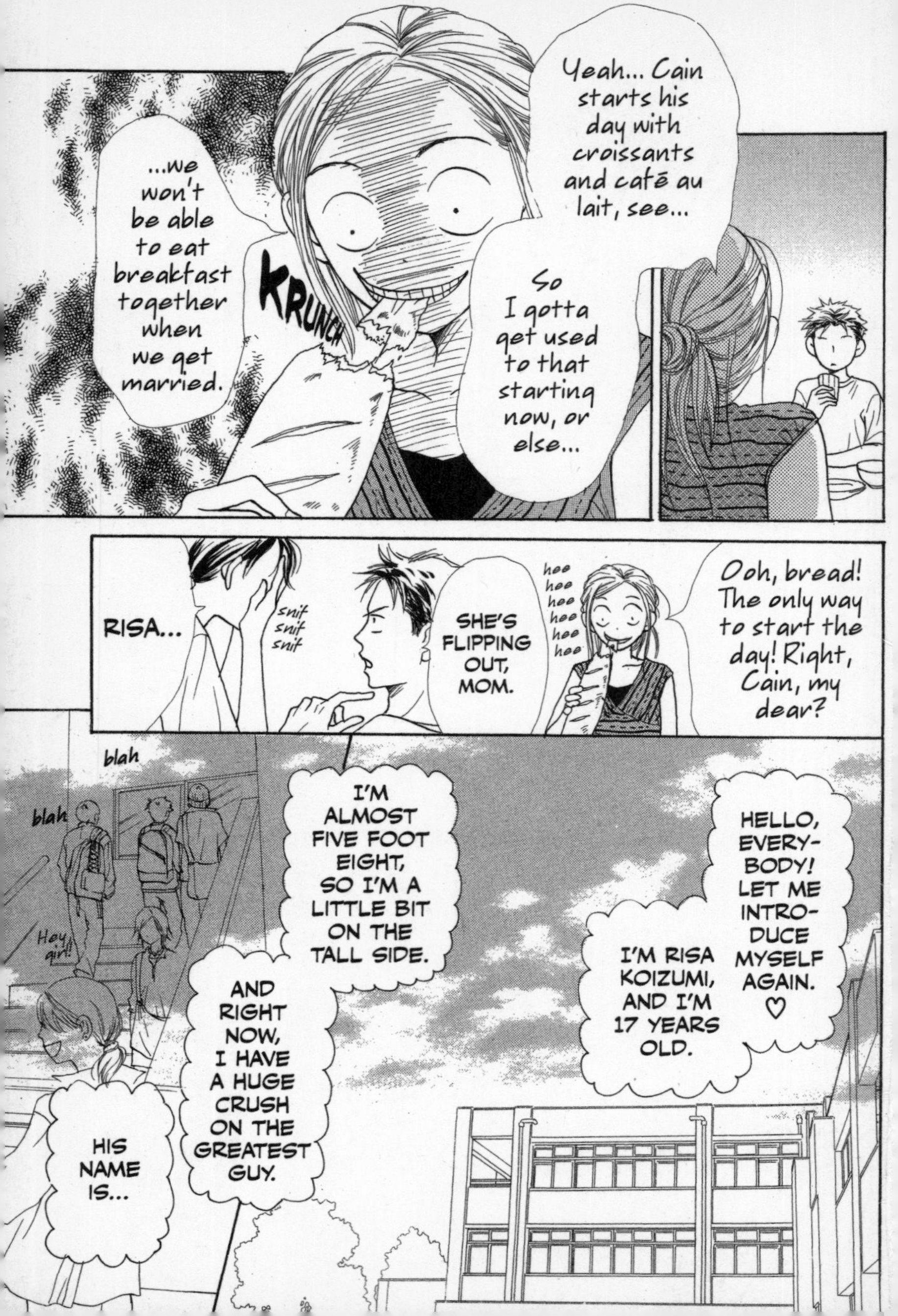
Yeah... Cain starts his day with croissants and café au lait, see...
...we won't be able to eat breakfast together when we get married.
KRUNCH
So I gotta get used to that starting now, or else...
Ooh, bread! The only way to start the day! Right, Cain, my dear?
hee hee hee hee hee hee
SHE'S FLIPPING OUT, MOM.
snif snif snif
RISA...
HELLO, EVERYBODY! LET ME INTRODUCE MYSELF AGAIN. ♡
I'M RISA KOIZUMI, AND I'M 17 YEARS OLD.
I'M ALMOST FIVE FOOT EIGHT, SO I'M A LITTLE BIT ON THE TALL SIDE.
AND RIGHT NOW, I HAVE A HUGE CRUSH ON THE GREATEST GUY.
blah
blah
Hey girl!
HIS NAME IS...

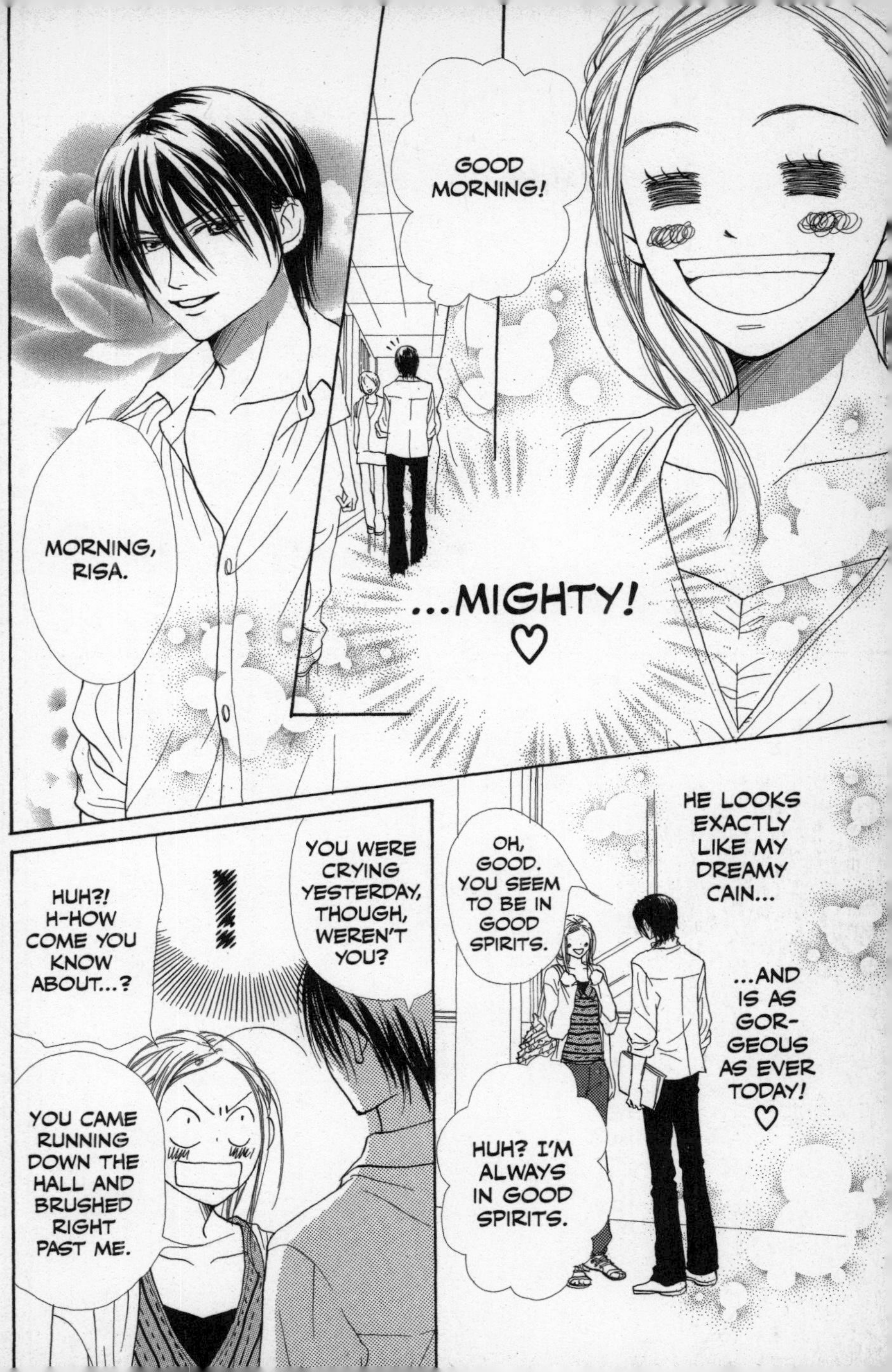
GOOD MORNING!
...MIGHTY! ♡
MORNING, RISA.
HE LOOKS EXACTLY LIKE MY DREAMY CAIN...
...AND IS AS GOR-GEOUS AS EVER TODAY! ♡
OH, GOOD. YOU SEEM TO BE IN GOOD SPIRITS.
HUH? I'M ALWAYS IN GOOD SPIRITS.
YOU WERE CRYING YESTERDAY, THOUGH, WEREN'T YOU?
HUH?! H-HOW COME YOU KNOW ABOUT...?
YOU CAME RUNNING DOWN THE HALL AND BRUSHED RIGHT PAST ME.

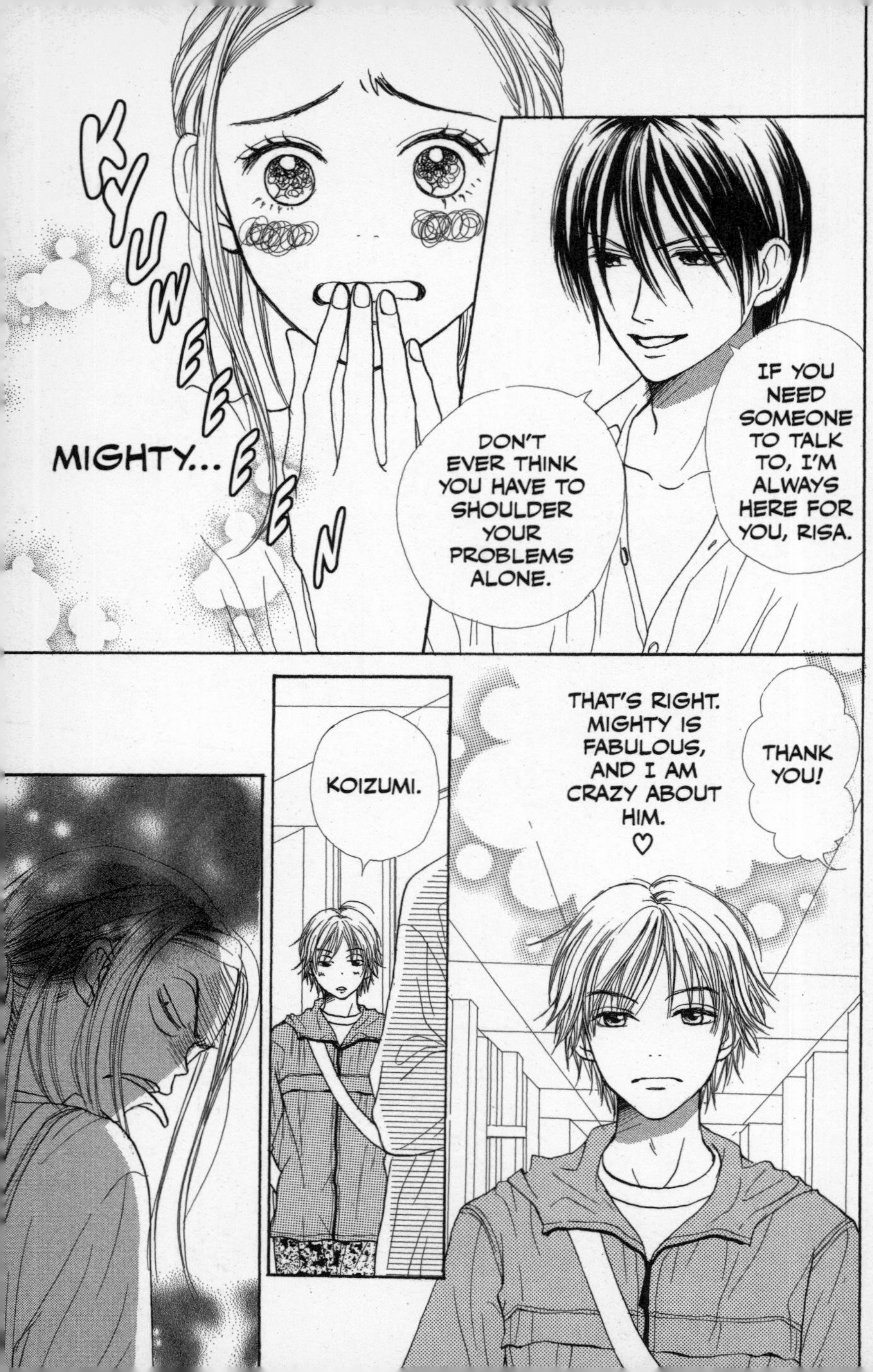
IF YOU NEED SOMEONE TO TALK TO, I'M ALWAYS HERE FOR YOU, RISA.
DON'T EVER THINK YOU HAVE TO SHOULDER YOUR PROBLEMS ALONE.
KYUWEEEEN
MIGHTY...
THANK YOU!
THAT'S RIGHT. MIGHTY IS FABULOUS, AND I AM CRAZY ABOUT HIM. ♡
KOIZUMI.

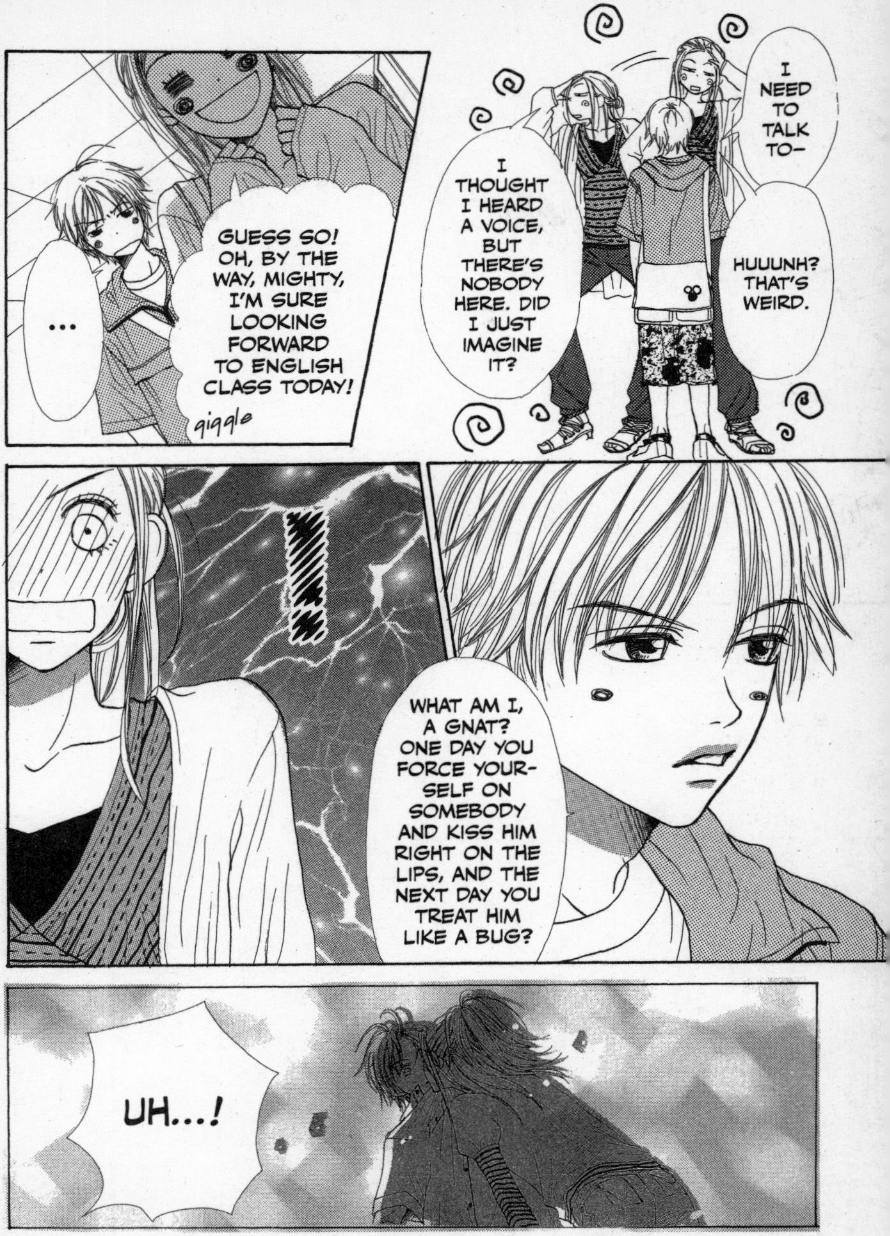
I NEED TO TALK TO—
HUUUNH? THAT'S WEIRD.
I THOUGHT I HEARD A VOICE, BUT THERE'S NOBODY HERE. DID I JUST IMAGINE IT?
GUESS SO! OH, BY THE WAY, MIGHTY, I'M SURE LOOKING FORWARD TO ENGLISH CLASS TODAY!
giggle
...
WHAT AM I, A GNAT? ONE DAY YOU FORCE YOUR-SELF ON SOMEBODY AND KISS HIM RIGHT ON THE LIPS, AND THE NEXT DAY YOU TREAT HIM LIKE A BUG?
!
UH...!

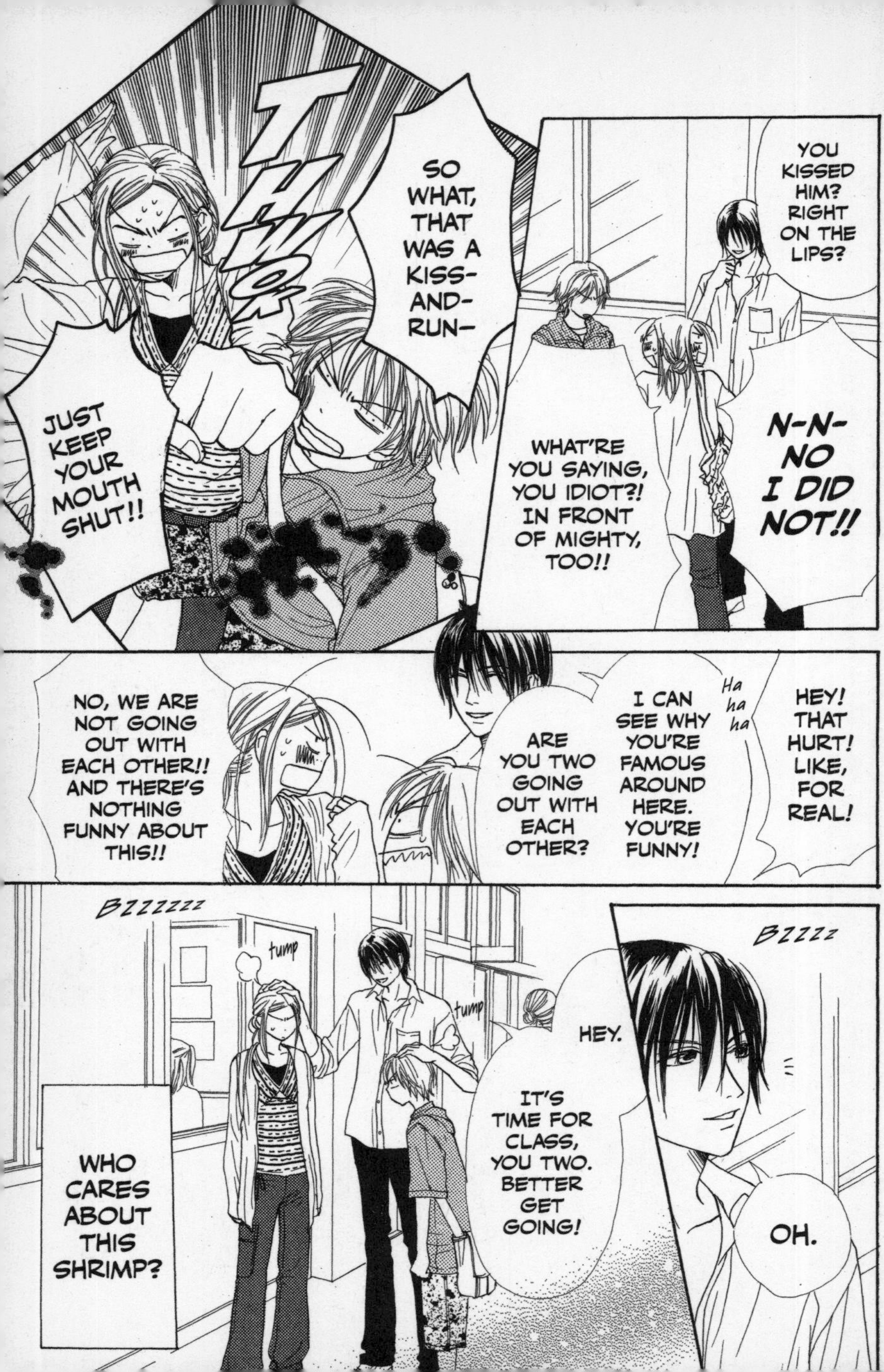
YOU KISSED HIM? RIGHT ON THE LIPS?
N-N-NO I DID NOT!!
WHAT'RE YOU SAYING, YOU IDIOT?! IN FRONT OF MIGHTY, TOO!!
SO WHAT, THAT WAS A KISS-AND-RUN—
THWOK
JUST KEEP YOUR MOUTH SHUT!!
HEY! THAT HURT! LIKE, FOR REAL!
Ha ha ha
I CAN SEE WHY YOU'RE FAMOUS AROUND HERE. YOU'RE FUNNY!
ARE YOU TWO GOING OUT WITH EACH OTHER?
NO, WE ARE NOT GOING OUT WITH EACH OTHER!! AND THERE'S NOTHING FUNNY ABOUT THIS!!
Bzzzz
OH.
Bzzzzzzz
tump
tump
HEY.
IT'S TIME FOR CLASS, YOU TWO. BETTER GET GOING!
WHO CARES ABOUT THIS SHRIMP?

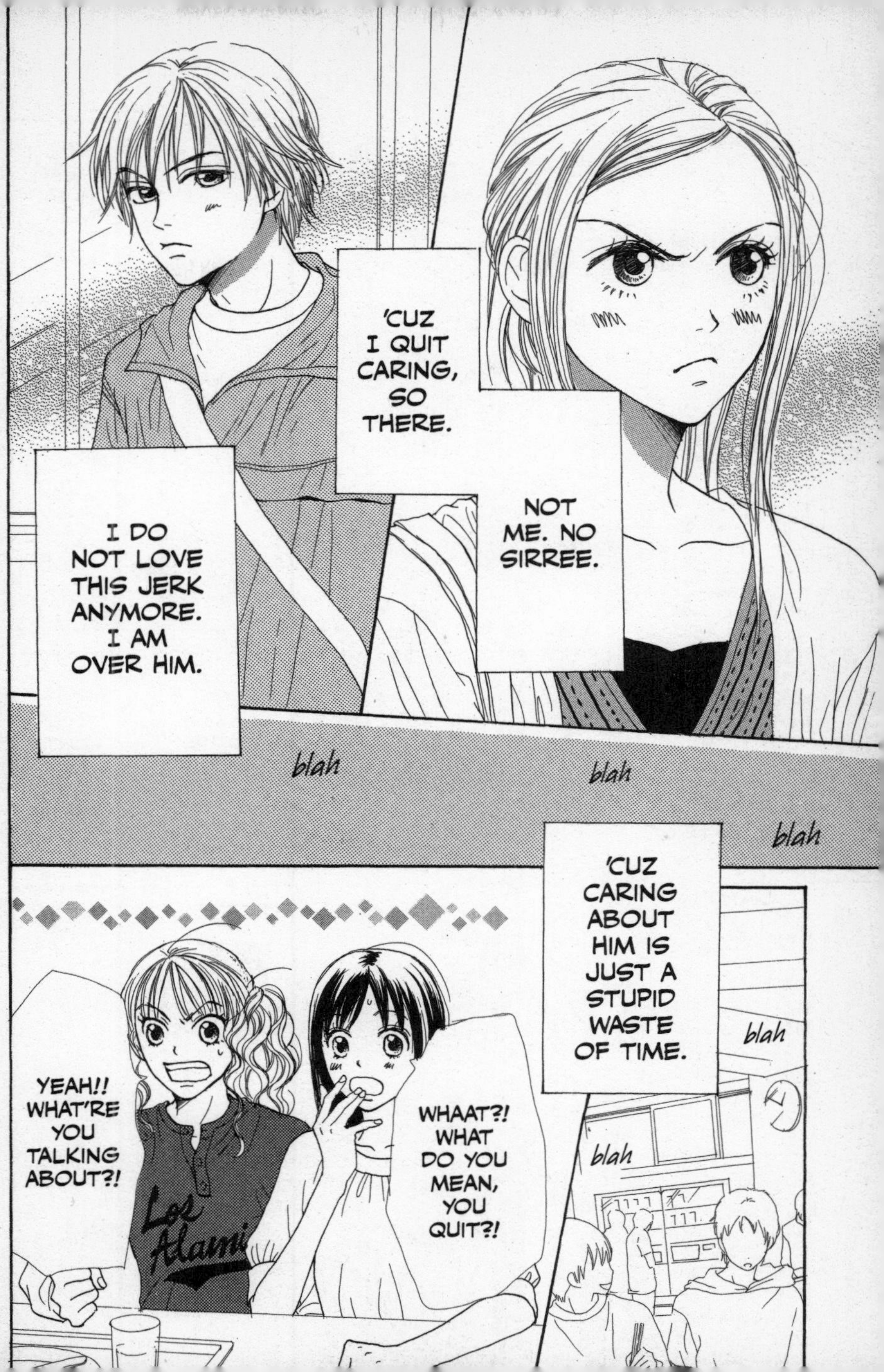

'CUZ I QUIT CARING, SO THERE.
NOT ME. NO SIRREE.
I DO NOT LOVE THIS JERK ANYMORE. I AM OVER HIM.
blah
blah
blah
'CUZ CARING ABOUT HIM IS JUST A STUPID WASTE OF TIME.
blah
blah
WHAAT?! WHAT DO YOU MEAN, YOU QUIT?!
YEAH!! WHAT'RE YOU TALKING ABOUT?!
Los Alami

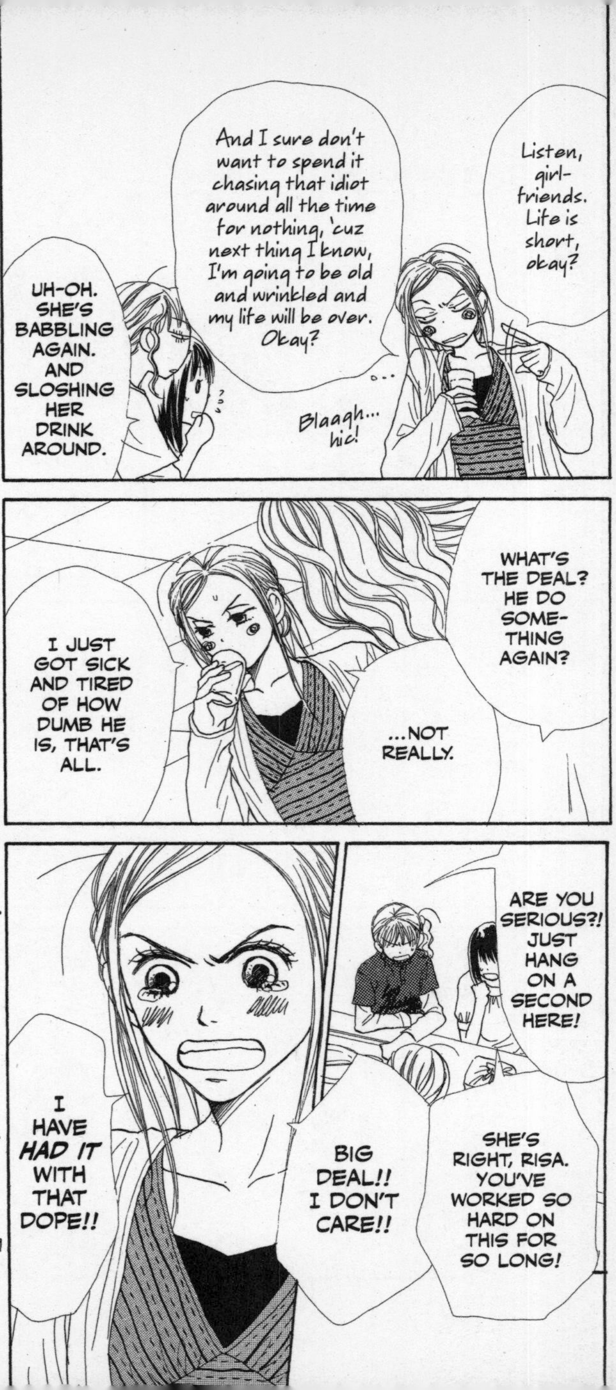
Listen, girl-friends. Life is short, okay?
And I sure don't want to spend it chasing that idiot around all the time for nothing, 'cuz next thing I know, I'm going to be old and wrinkled and my life will be over. Okay?
...
Blaagh... hic!
UH-OH. SHE'S BABBLING AGAIN. AND SLOSHING HER DRINK AROUND.
WHAT'S THE DEAL? HE DO SOME-THING AGAIN?
...NOT REALLY.
I JUST GOT SICK AND TIRED OF HOW DUMB HE IS, THAT'S ALL.
ARE YOU SERIOUS?! JUST HANG ON A SECOND HERE!
SHE'S RIGHT, RISA. YOU'VE WORKED SO HARD ON THIS FOR SO LONG!
BIG DEAL!! I DON'T CARE!!
I HAVE *HAD IT* WITH THAT DOPE!!

3

That UmibÔzu towel that Ôtani bought for himself and Risa at the show in this volume has been produced for real. It is very fluffy. Besides the towel, there's also a makeup bag, a coin purse, badges, key holders, a bag...

Bessatsu Margaret, the magazine, has been making Love☆Com products to give away. To 1,000 lucky readers (almost) every month! Which means, I would think, that if you write in for one, you will almost surely get it...

It is so much fun coming up with designs for Love☆Com goods.

↑
I love making stuff like this. In fact, this is what I originally wanted to do for a living, but unfortunately... well, what you see here is the best I can come up with.

But now I'm really glad I got to be a manga artist instead!

So anyway, I thought I'd plug Bessatsu Margaret to you all in this rather roundabout fashion. Isn't that sneaky?!

But please do check out Bessatsu Margaret, too. ♡

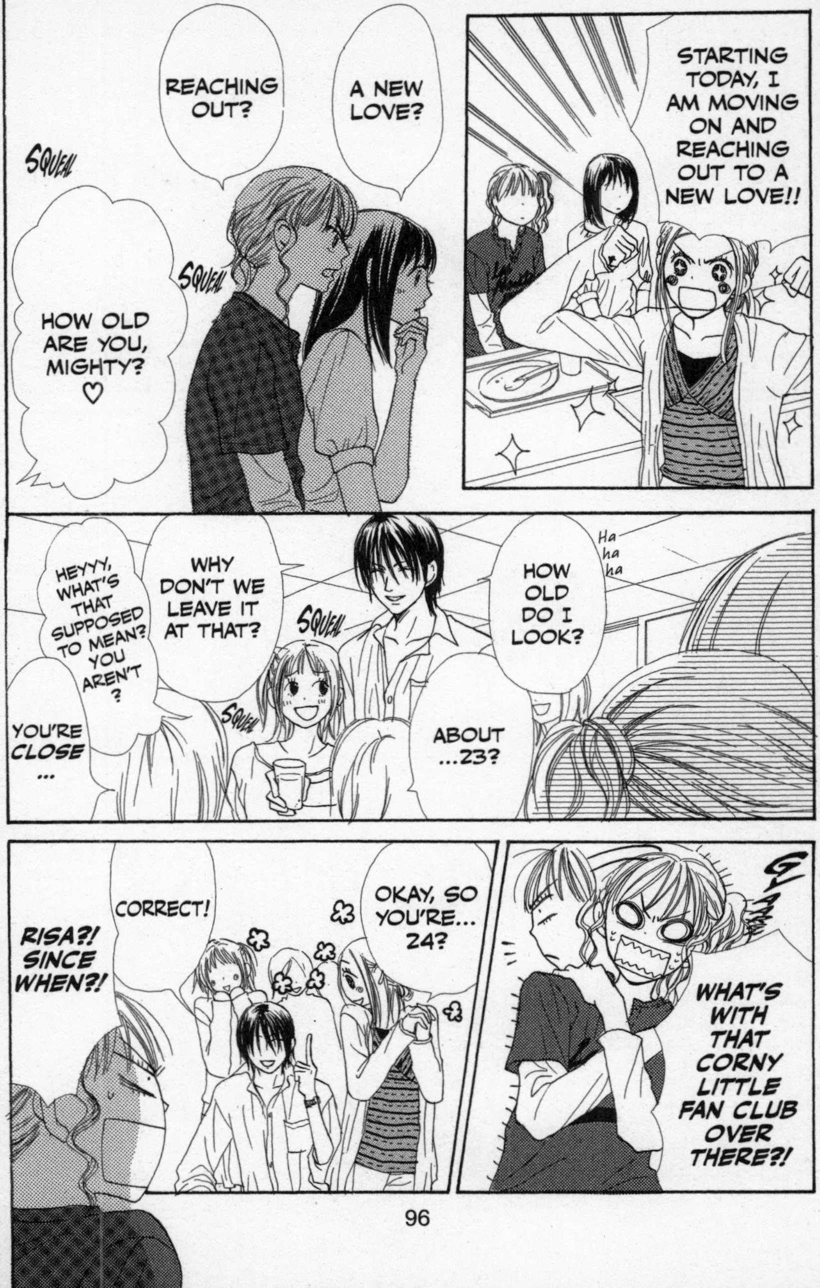
STARTING TODAY, I AM MOVING ON AND REACHING OUT TO A NEW LOVE!!
A NEW LOVE?
REACHING OUT?
SQUEAL
SQUEAL
HOW OLD ARE YOU, MIGHTY? ♡
Ha ha ha
HOW OLD DO I LOOK?
ABOUT ...23?
SQUEAL
WHY DON'T WE LEAVE IT AT THAT?
SQUEAL
HEYYY, WHAT'S THAT SUPPOSED TO MEAN? YOU AREN'T ?
YOU'RE CLOSE ...
WHAT'S WITH THAT CORNY LITTLE FAN CLUB OVER THERE?!
OKAY, SO YOU'RE... 24?
CORRECT!
RISA?! SINCE WHEN?!

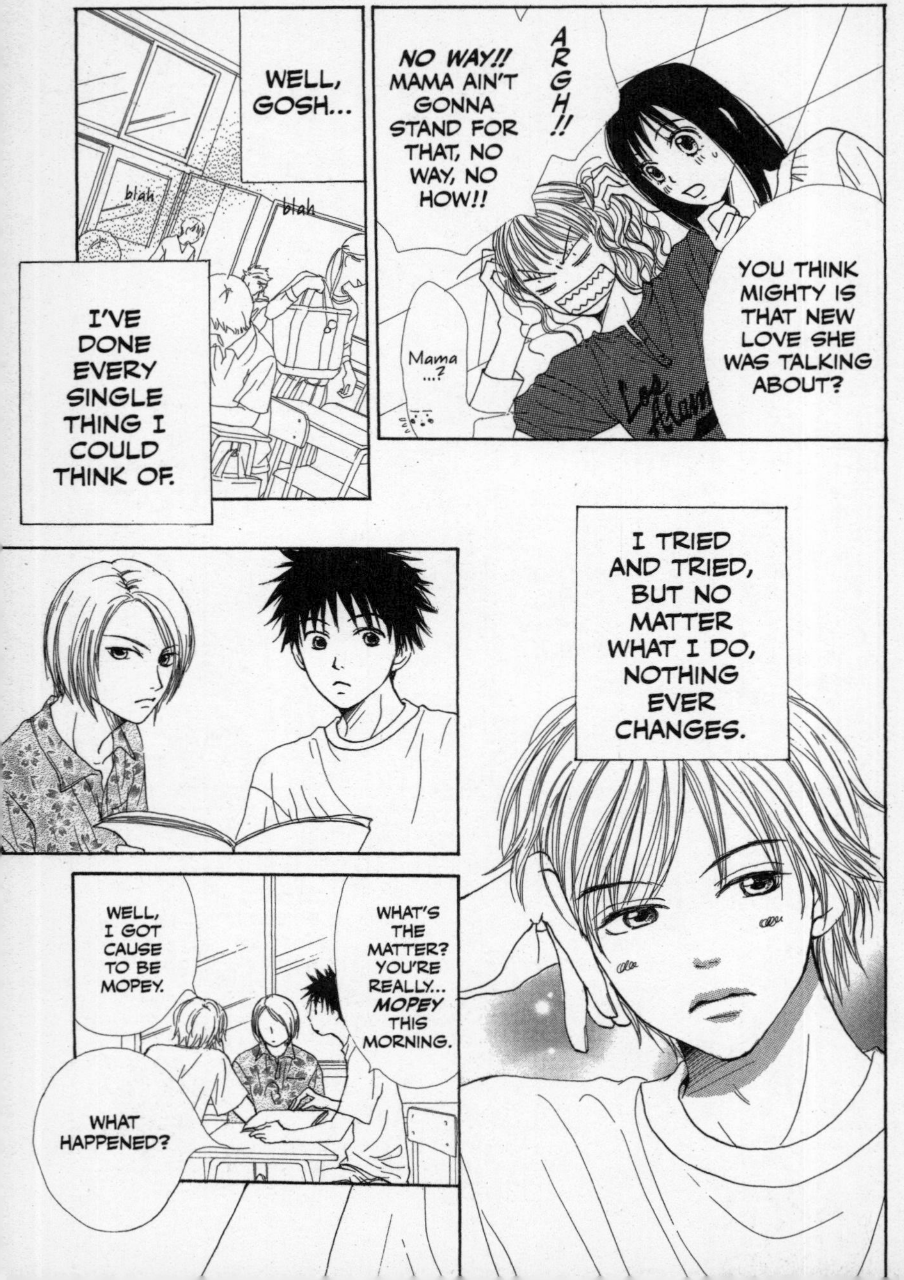
ARGH!!
NO WAY!! MAMA AIN'T GONNA STAND FOR THAT, NO WAY, NO HOW!!
YOU THINK MIGHTY IS THAT NEW LOVE SHE WAS TALKING ABOUT?
Mama ...?
WELL, GOSH...
blah
blah
I'VE DONE EVERY SINGLE THING I COULD THINK OF.
I TRIED AND TRIED, BUT NO MATTER WHAT I DO, NOTHING EVER CHANGES.
WHAT'S THE MATTER? YOU'RE REALLY... MOPEY THIS MORNING.
WELL, I GOT CAUSE TO BE MOPEY.
WHAT HAPPENED?

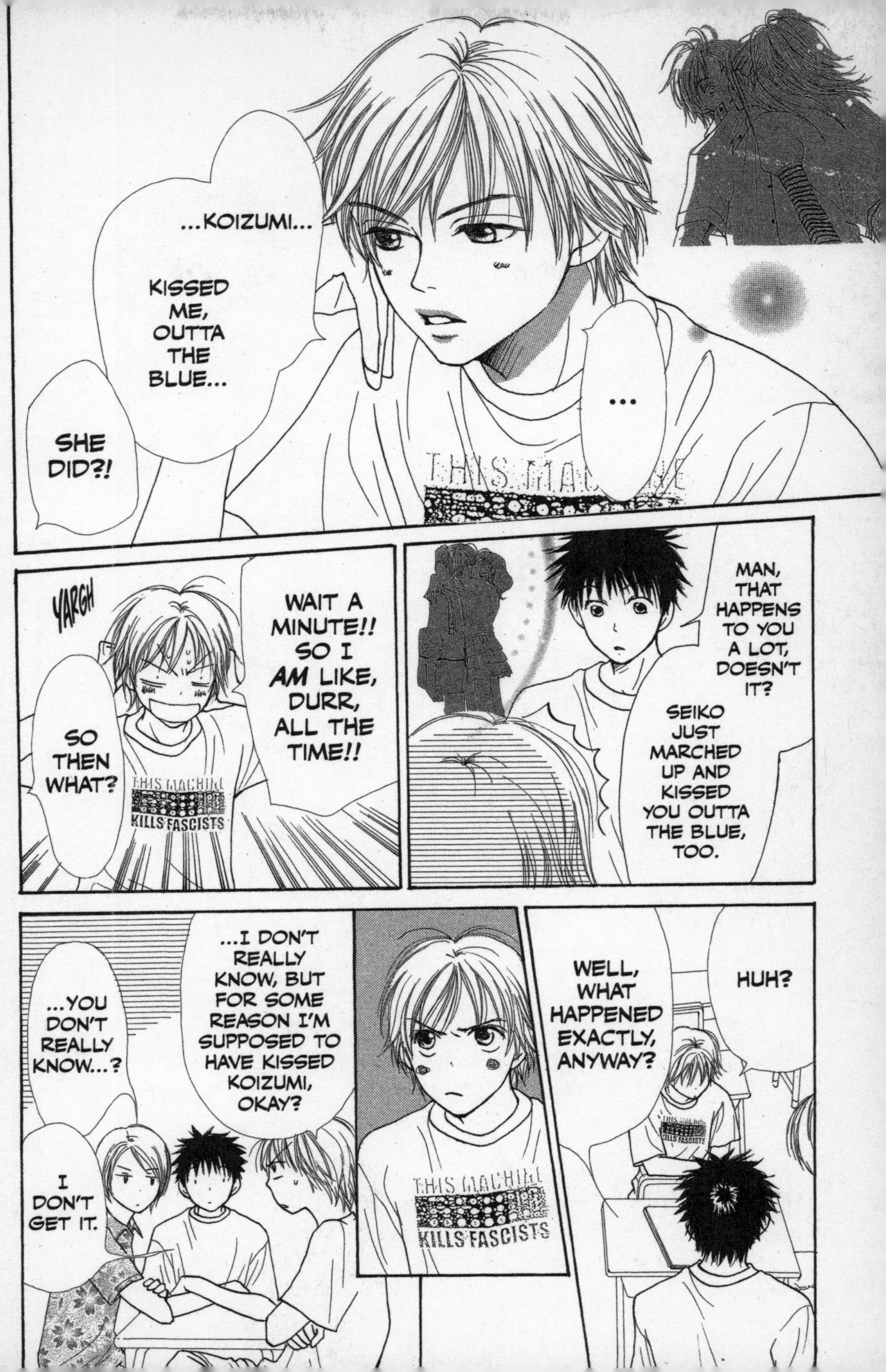
...
...KOIZUMI... KISSED ME, OUTTA THE BLUE...
SHE DID?!
MAN, THAT HAPPENS TO YOU A LOT, DOESN'T IT?
SEIKO JUST MARCHED UP AND KISSED YOU OUTTA THE BLUE, TOO.
WAIT A MINUTE!! SO I *AM* LIKE, DURR, ALL THE TIME!!
YARGH
SO THEN WHAT?
HUH?
WELL, WHAT HAPPENED EXACTLY, ANYWAY?
...I DON'T REALLY KNOW, BUT FOR SOME REASON I'M SUPPOSED TO HAVE KISSED KOIZUMI, OKAY?
...YOU DON'T REALLY KNOW...?
I DON'T GET IT.

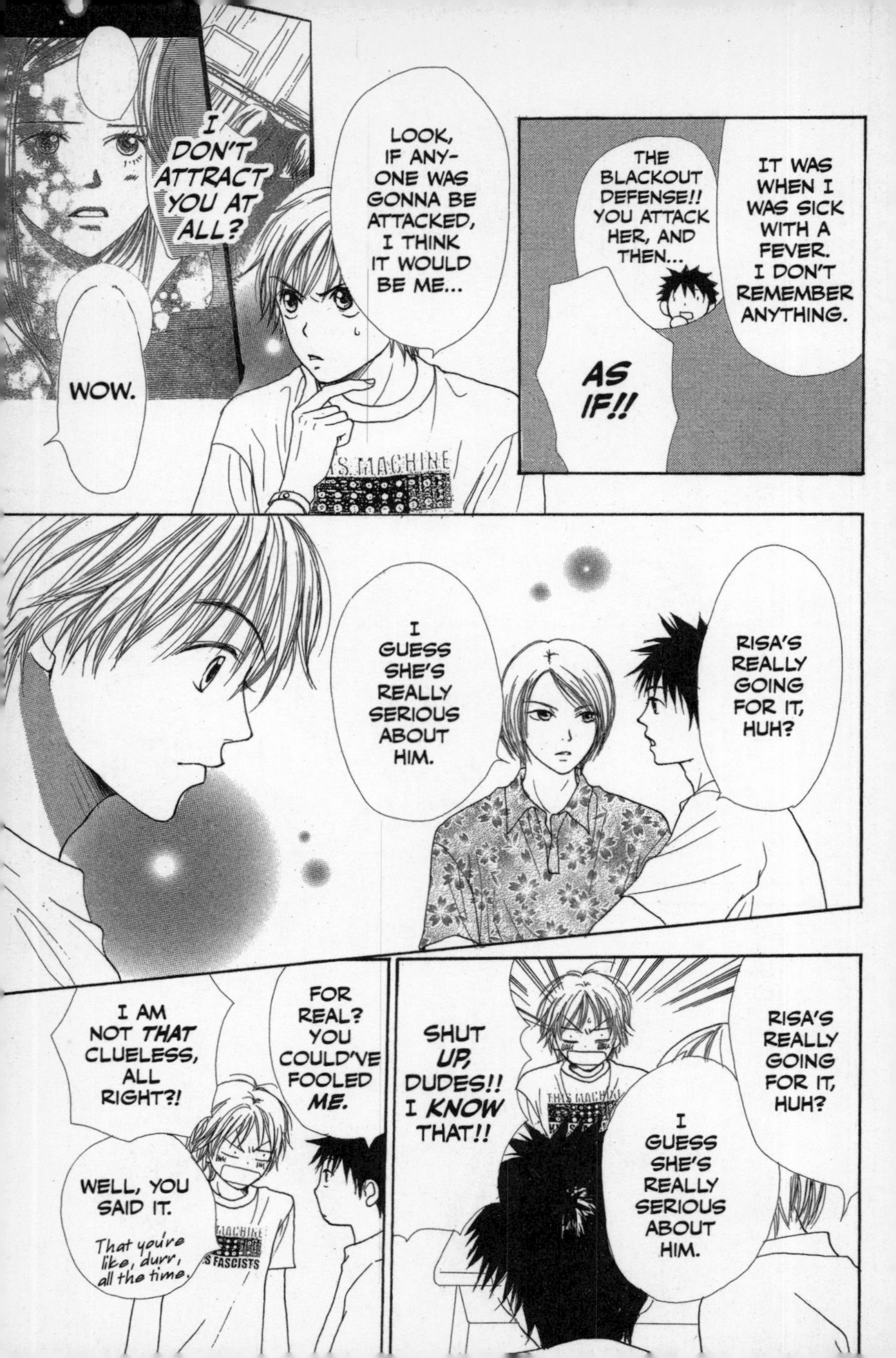
IT WAS WHEN I WAS SICK WITH A FEVER. I DON'T REMEMBER ANYTHING.
THE BLACKOUT DEFENSE!! YOU ATTACK HER, AND THEN...
AS IF!!
LOOK, IF ANYONE WAS GONNA BE ATTACKED, I THINK IT WOULD BE ME...
I DON'T ATTRACT YOU AT ALL?
WOW.
RISA'S REALLY GOING FOR IT, HUH?
I GUESS SHE'S REALLY SERIOUS ABOUT HIM.
RISA'S REALLY GOING FOR IT, HUH?
I GUESS SHE'S REALLY SERIOUS ABOUT HIM.
SHUT *UP*, DUDES!! I *KNOW* THAT!!
FOR REAL? YOU COULD'VE FOOLED *ME*.
I AM NOT *THAT* CLUELESS, ALL RIGHT?!
WELL, YOU SAID IT.
That you're like, durr, all the time.

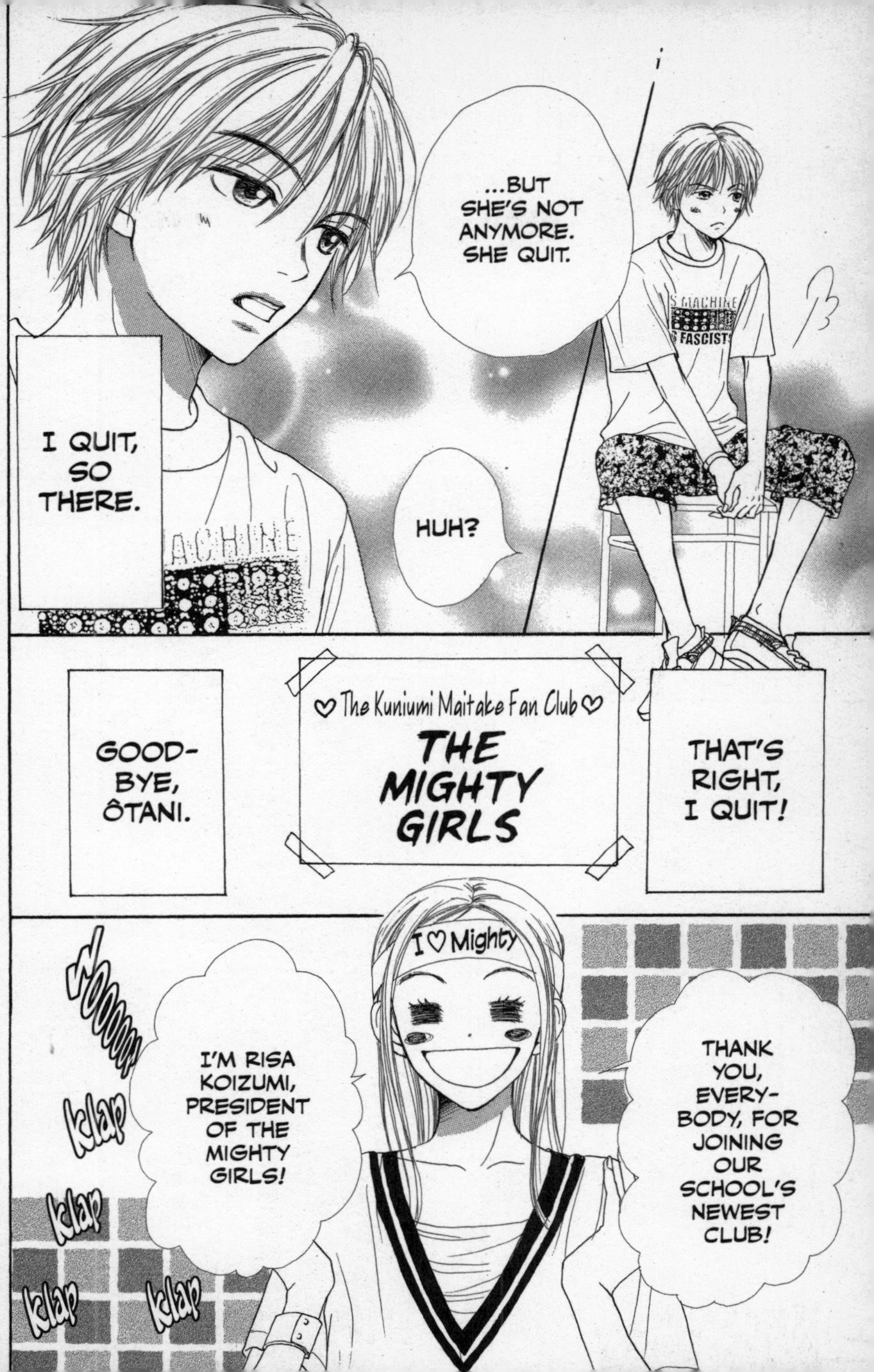

...BUT SHE'S NOT ANYMORE. SHE QUIT.
HUH?
I QUIT, SO THERE.
THAT'S RIGHT, I QUIT!
♡ The Kuniumi Maitake Fan Club ♡
THE MIGHTY GIRLS
GOOD-BYE, ÔTANI.
THANK YOU, EVERYBODY, FOR JOINING OUR SCHOOL'S NEWEST CLUB!
I ♡ Mighty
I'M RISA KOIZUMI, PRESIDENT OF THE MIGHTY GIRLS!
klap
klap
klap
klap

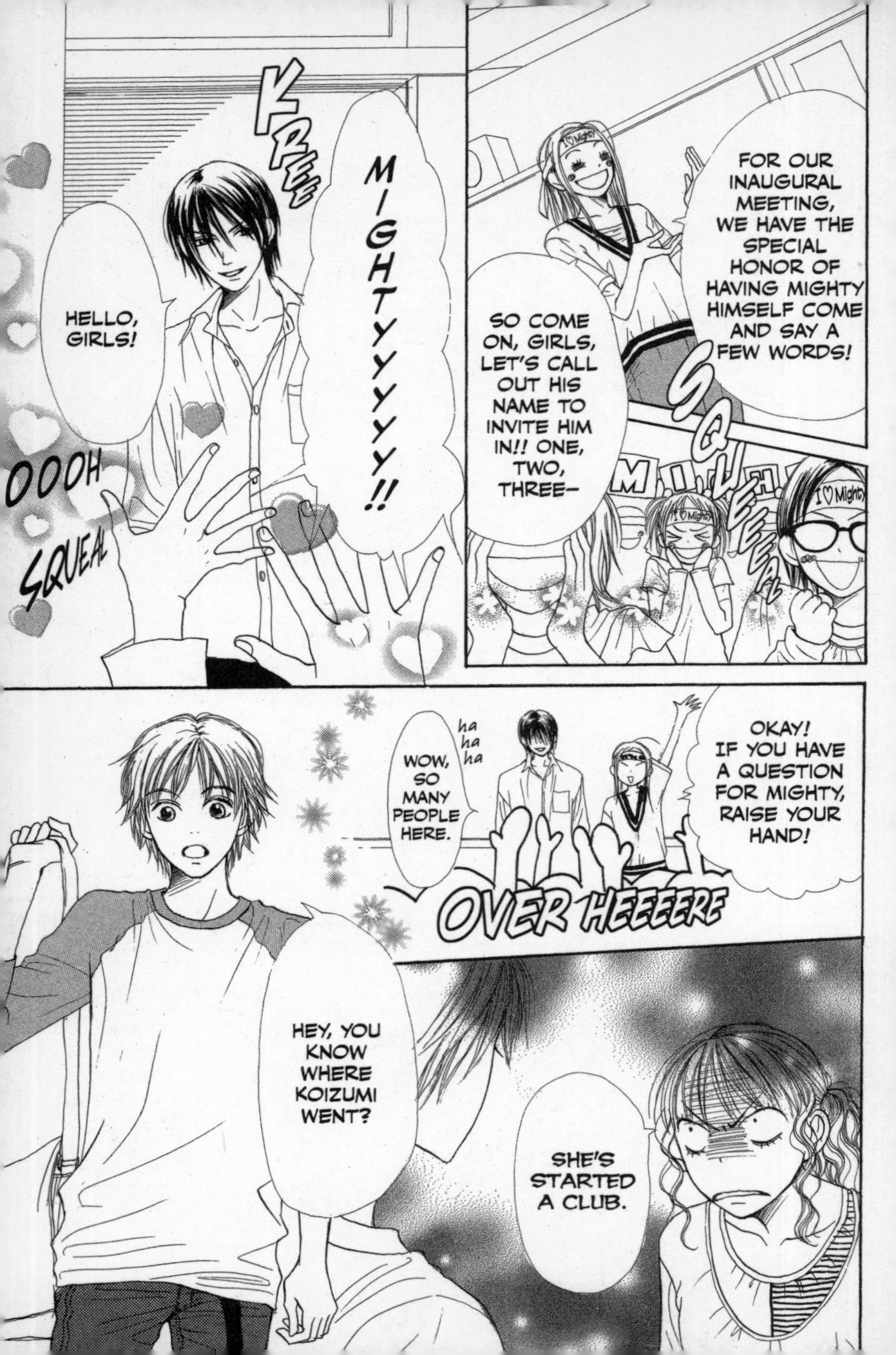
FOR OUR INAUGURAL MEETING, WE HAVE THE SPECIAL HONOR OF HAVING MIGHTY HIMSELF COME AND SAY A FEW WORDS!
SO COME ON, GIRLS, LET'S CALL OUT HIS NAME TO INVITE HIM IN!! ONE, TWO, THREE–
SQUEEEEAL
I ♡ Mighty
KREE
MIGHTYYYYYY!!
HELLO, GIRLS!
OOOH
SQUEAL
OKAY! IF YOU HAVE A QUESTION FOR MIGHTY, RAISE YOUR HAND!
ha ha ha
WOW, SO MANY PEOPLE HERE.
OVER HEEEERE
HEY, YOU KNOW WHERE KOIZUMI WENT?
SHE'S STARTED A CLUB.

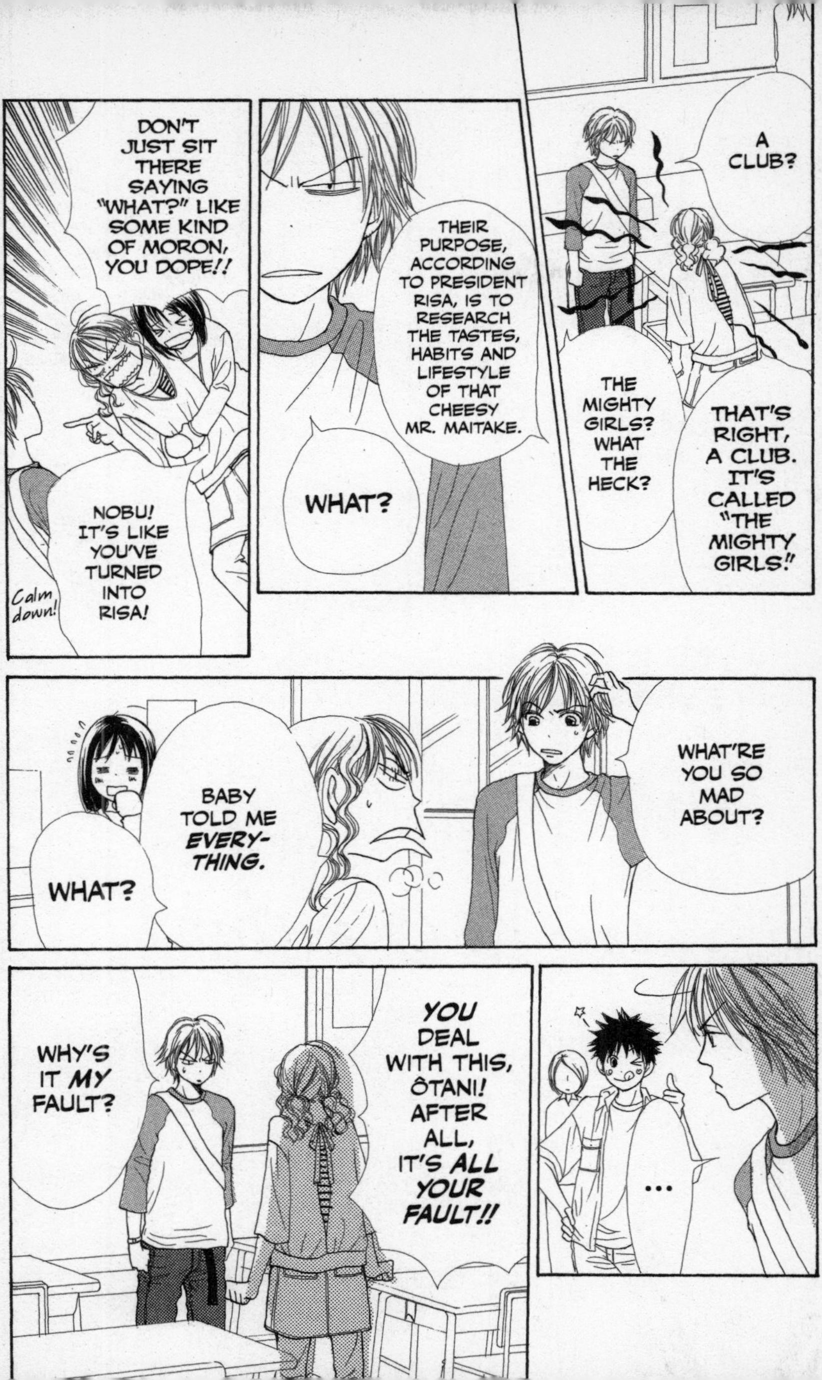
A CLUB?
THAT'S RIGHT, A CLUB. IT'S CALLED "THE MIGHTY GIRLS!"
THE MIGHTY GIRLS? WHAT THE HECK?
THEIR PURPOSE, ACCORDING TO PRESIDENT RISA, IS TO RESEARCH THE TASTES, HABITS AND LIFESTYLE OF THAT CHEESY MR. MAITAKE.
WHAT?
DON'T JUST SIT THERE SAYING "WHAT?" LIKE SOME KIND OF MORON, YOU DOPE!!
NOBU! IT'S LIKE YOU'VE TURNED INTO RISA!
Calm down!
WHAT'RE YOU SO MAD ABOUT?
BABY TOLD ME EVERYTHING.
WHAT?
...
YOU DEAL WITH THIS, ÔTANI! AFTER ALL, IT'S ALL YOUR FAULT!!
WHY'S IT MY FAULT?

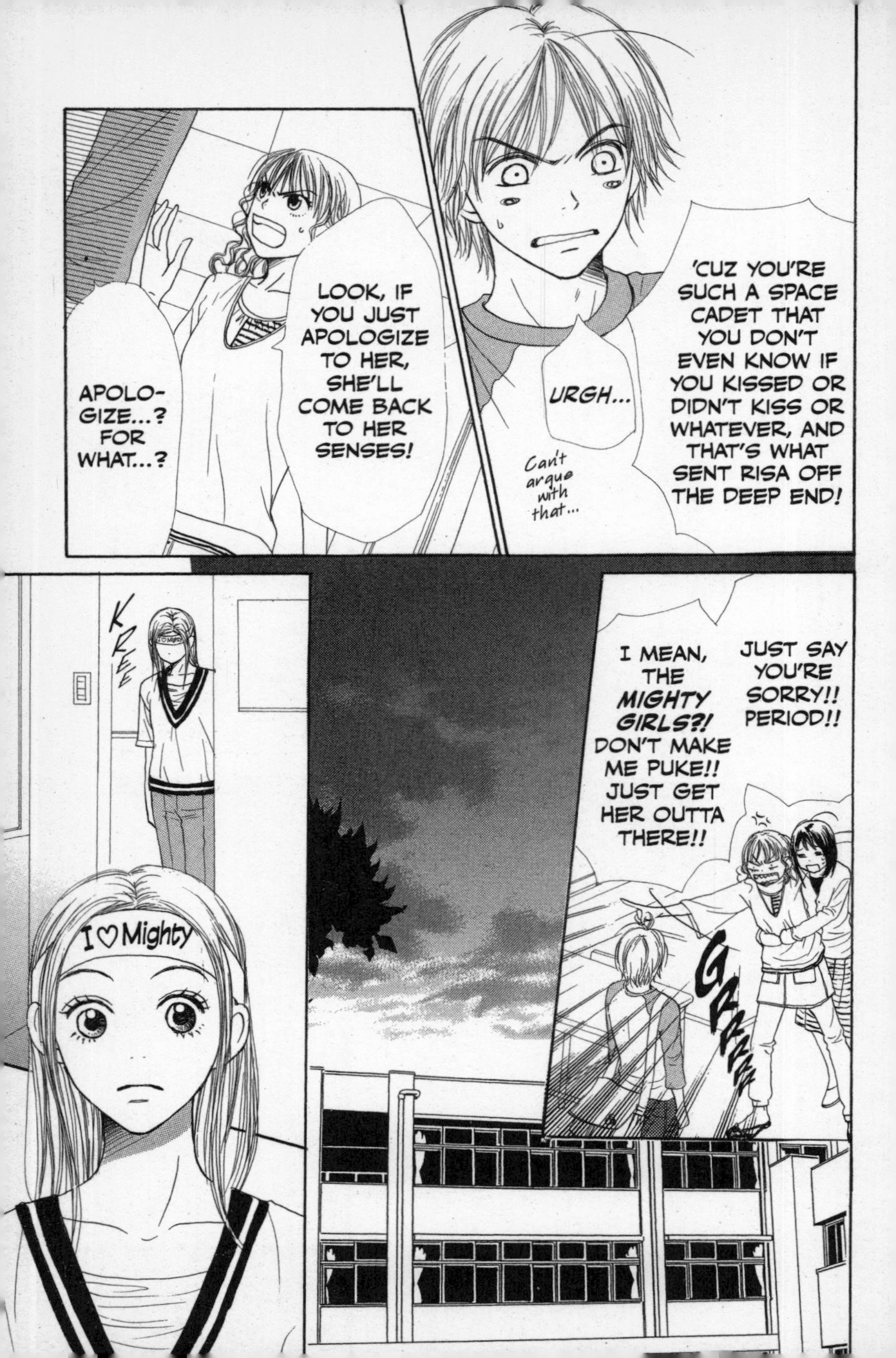
'CUZ YOU'RE SUCH A SPACE CADET THAT YOU DON'T EVEN KNOW IF YOU KISSED OR DIDN'T KISS OR WHATEVER, AND THAT'S WHAT SENT RISA OFF THE DEEP END!
URGH...
Can't argue with that...
LOOK, IF YOU JUST APOLOGIZE TO HER, SHE'LL COME BACK TO HER SENSES!
APOLO-GIZE...? FOR WHAT...?
JUST SAY YOU'RE SORRY!! PERIOD!!
I MEAN, THE *MIGHTY GIRLS?!* DON'T MAKE ME PUKE!! JUST GET HER OUTTA THERE!!
GRRRR
KREE
I ♡ Mighty

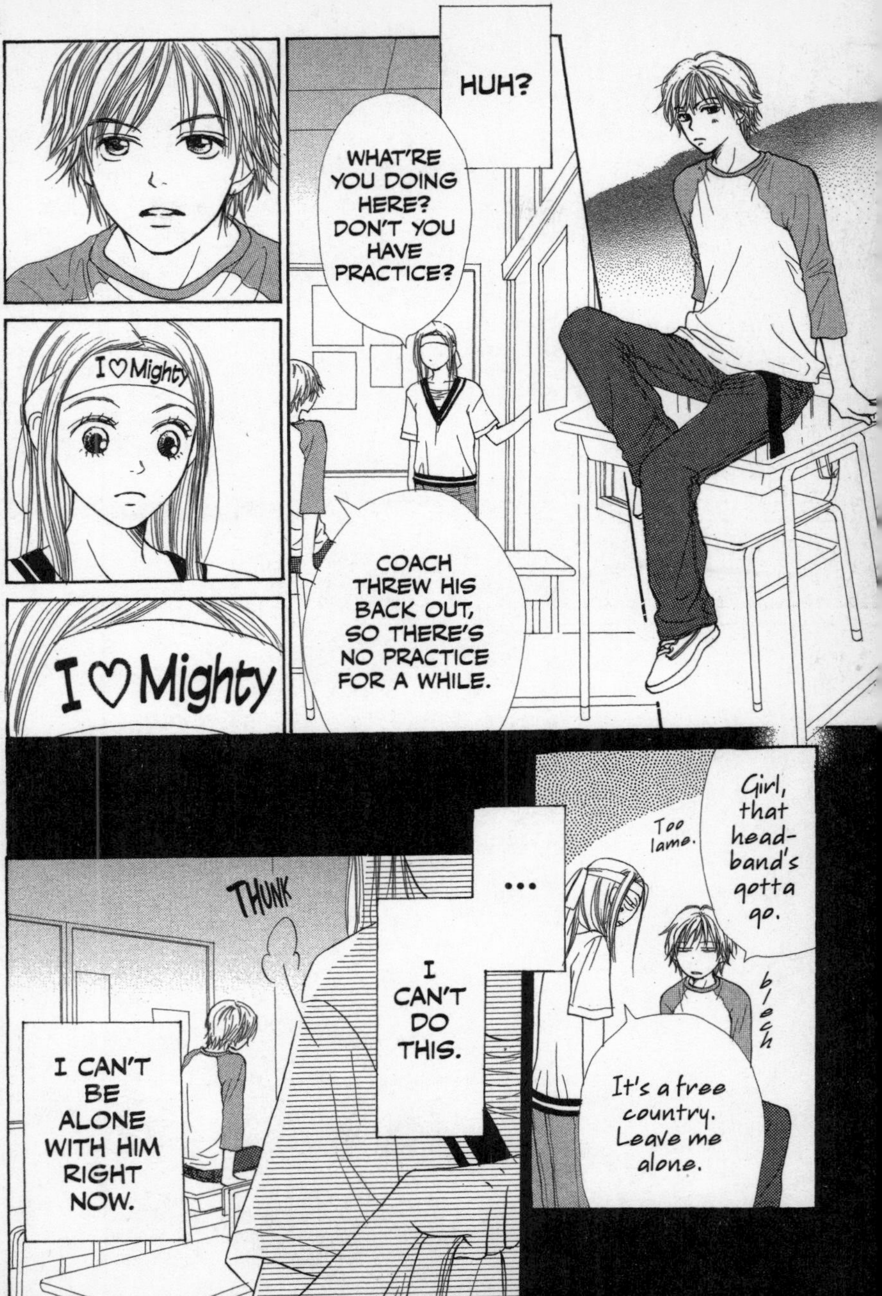
HUH?
WHAT'RE YOU DOING HERE? DON'T YOU HAVE PRACTICE?
COACH THREW HIS BACK OUT, SO THERE'S NO PRACTICE FOR A WHILE.
I ♡ Mighty
I ♡ Mighty
Girl, that head-band's gotta go.
Too lame.
blech
It's a free country. Leave me alone.
...
I CAN'T DO THIS.
THUNK
I CAN'T BE ALONE WITH HIM RIGHT NOW.

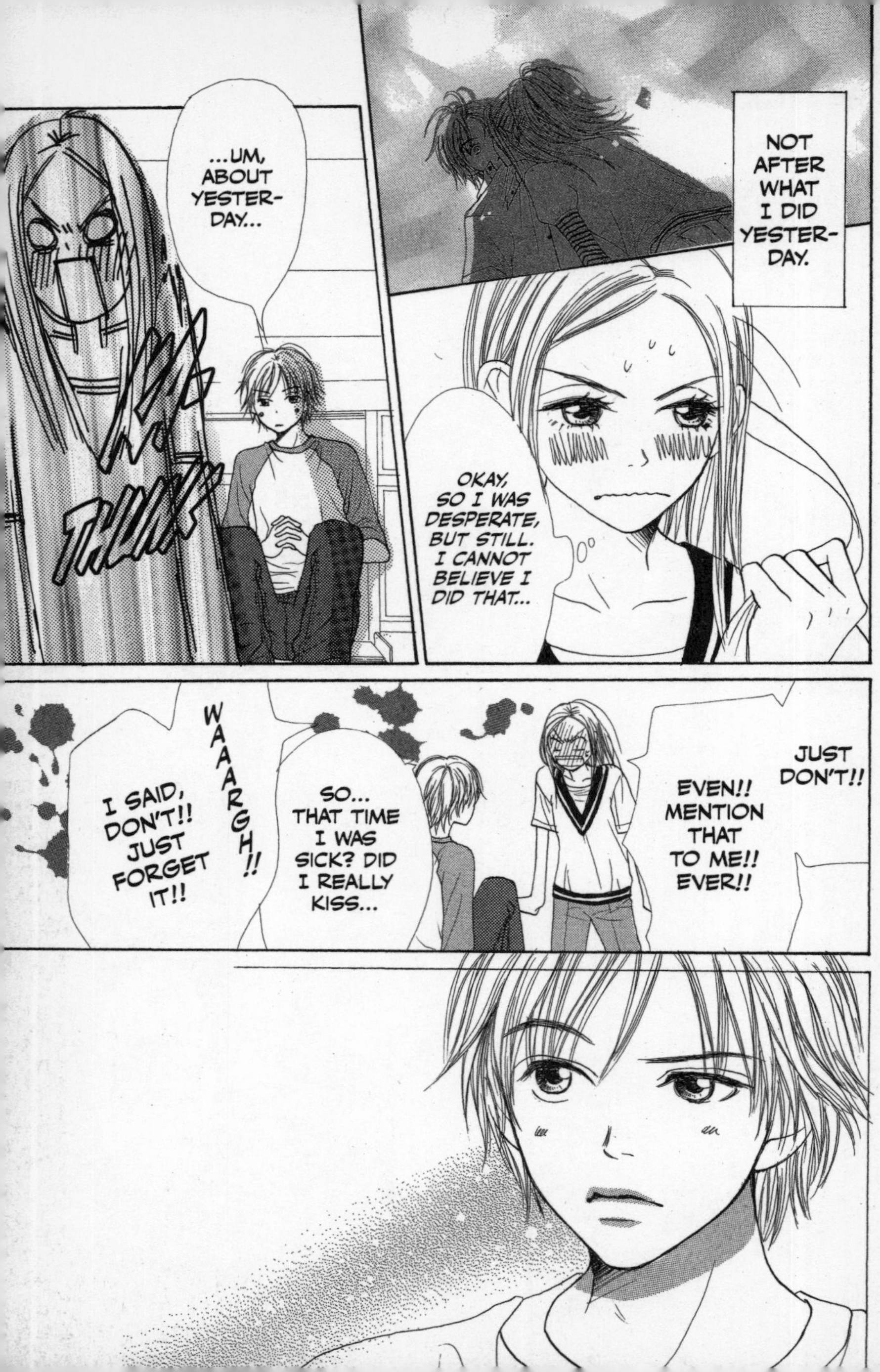
NOT AFTER WHAT I DID YESTER-DAY.
OKAY, SO I WAS DESPERATE, BUT STILL. I CANNOT BELIEVE I DID THAT...
...UM, ABOUT YESTER-DAY...
THUNK
JUST DON'T!!
EVEN!! MENTION THAT TO ME!! EVER!!
SO... THAT TIME I WAS SICK? DID I REALLY KISS...
WAAAARGH!!
I SAID, DON'T!! JUST FORGET IT!!

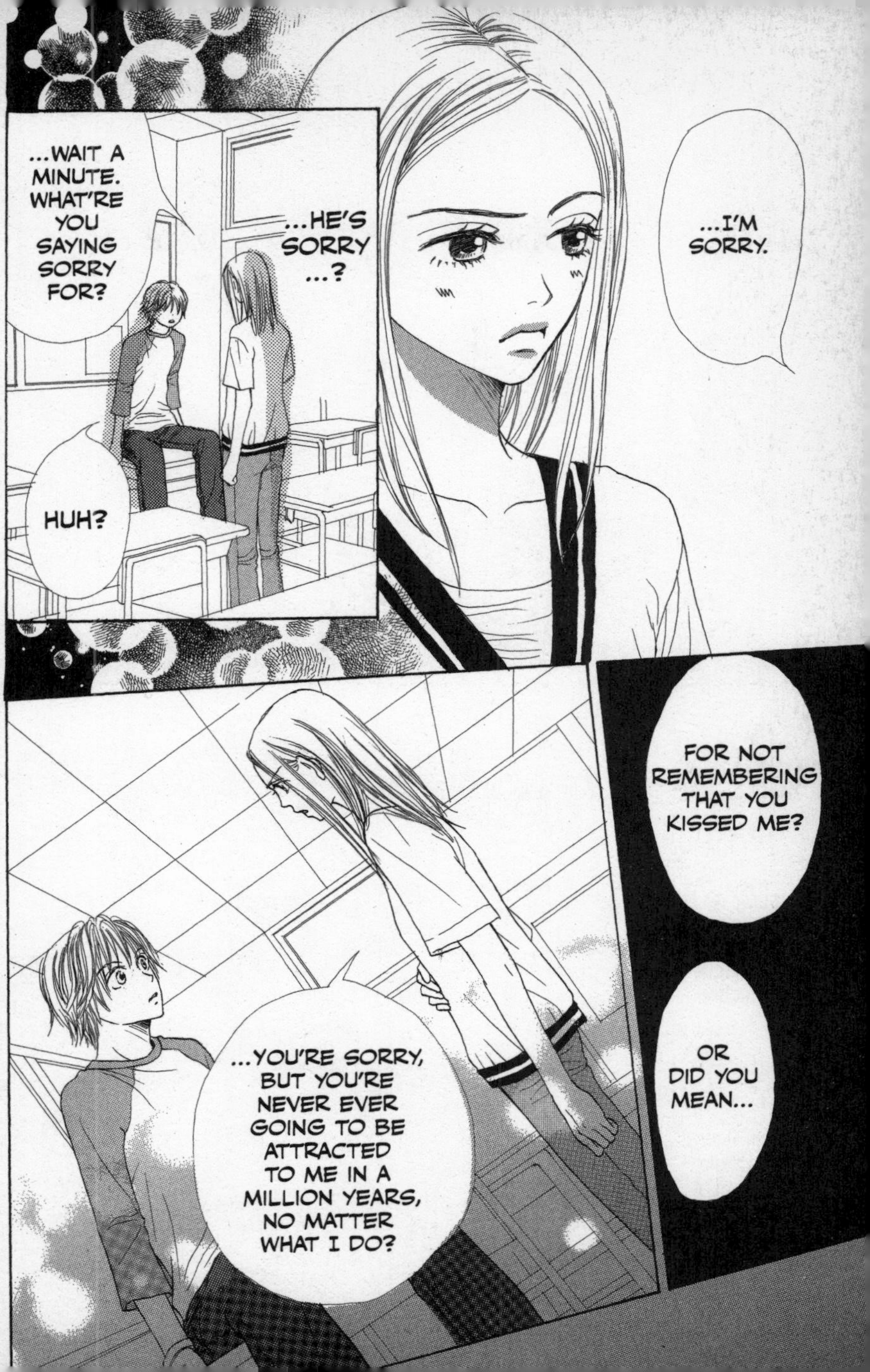
...I'M SORRY.
...HE'S SORRY ...?
...WAIT A MINUTE. WHAT'RE YOU SAYING SORRY FOR?
HUH?
FOR NOT REMEMBERING THAT YOU KISSED ME?
OR DID YOU MEAN...
...YOU'RE SORRY, BUT YOU'RE NEVER EVER GOING TO BE ATTRACTED TO ME IN A MILLION YEARS, NO MATTER WHAT I DO?

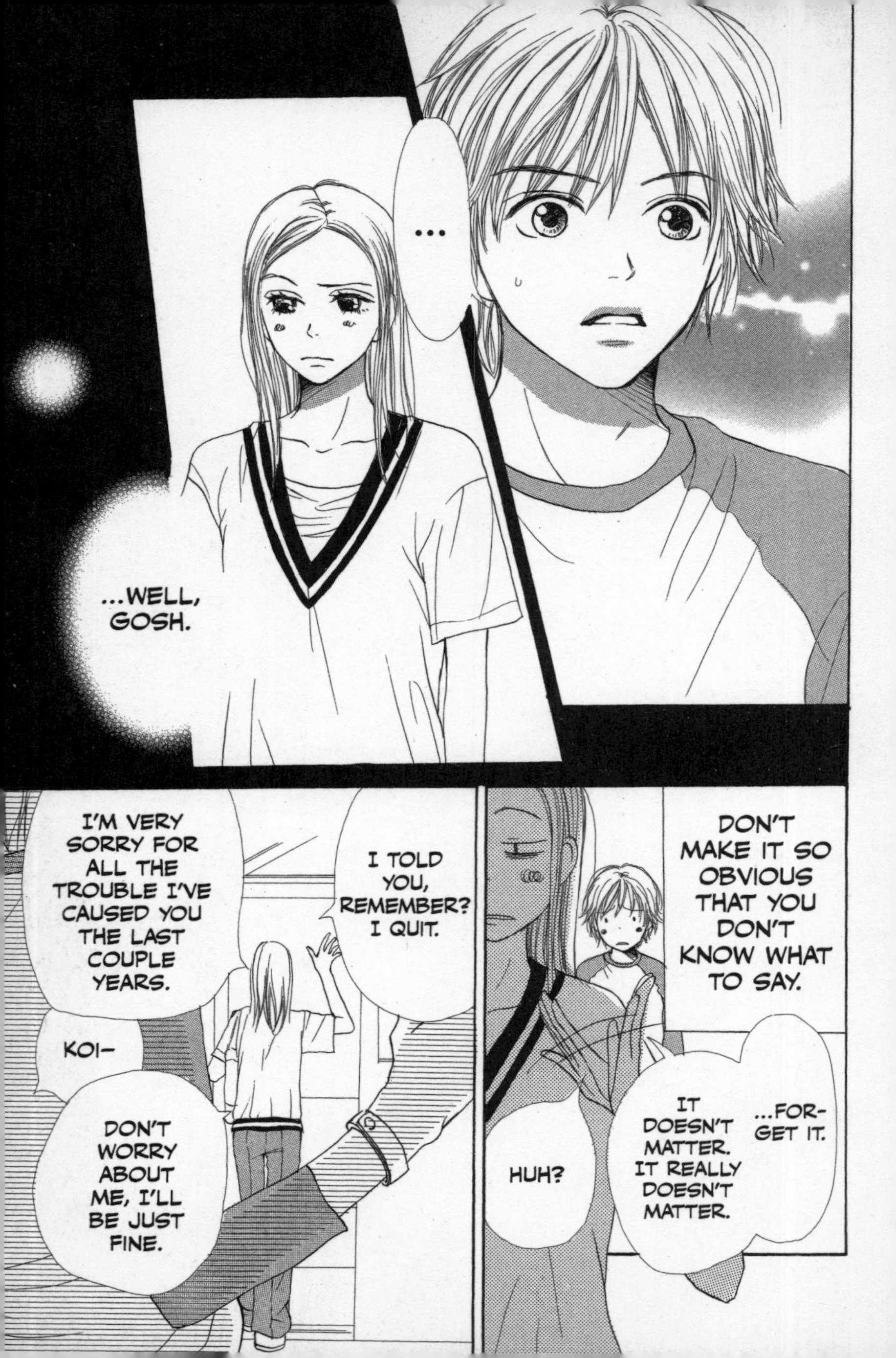
...
...WELL, GOSH.
DON'T MAKE IT SO OBVIOUS THAT YOU DON'T KNOW WHAT TO SAY.
...FOR-GET IT.
IT DOESN'T MATTER. IT REALLY DOESN'T MATTER.
HUH?
I TOLD YOU, REMEMBER? I QUIT.
I'M VERY SORRY FOR ALL THE TROUBLE I'VE CAUSED YOU THE LAST COUPLE YEARS.
KOI-
DON'T WORRY ABOUT ME, I'LL BE JUST FINE.

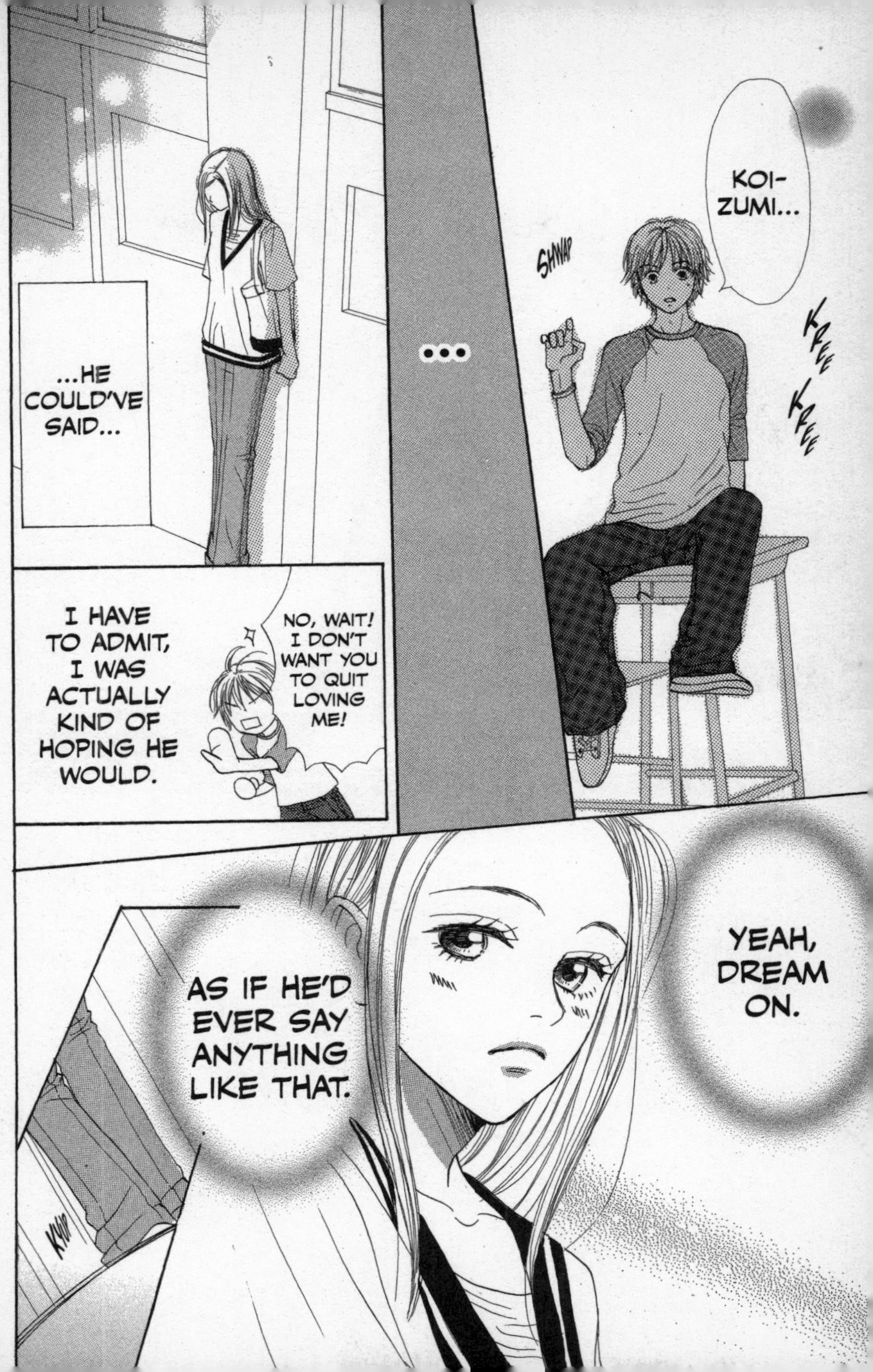
KOI-ZUMI...
SHWAP
KREE KREE
...
...HE COULD'VE SAID...
NO, WAIT! I DON'T WANT YOU TO QUIT LOVING ME!
I HAVE TO ADMIT, I WAS ACTUALLY KIND OF HOPING HE WOULD.
YEAH, DREAM ON.
AS IF HE'D EVER SAY ANYTHING LIKE THAT.
KYUP

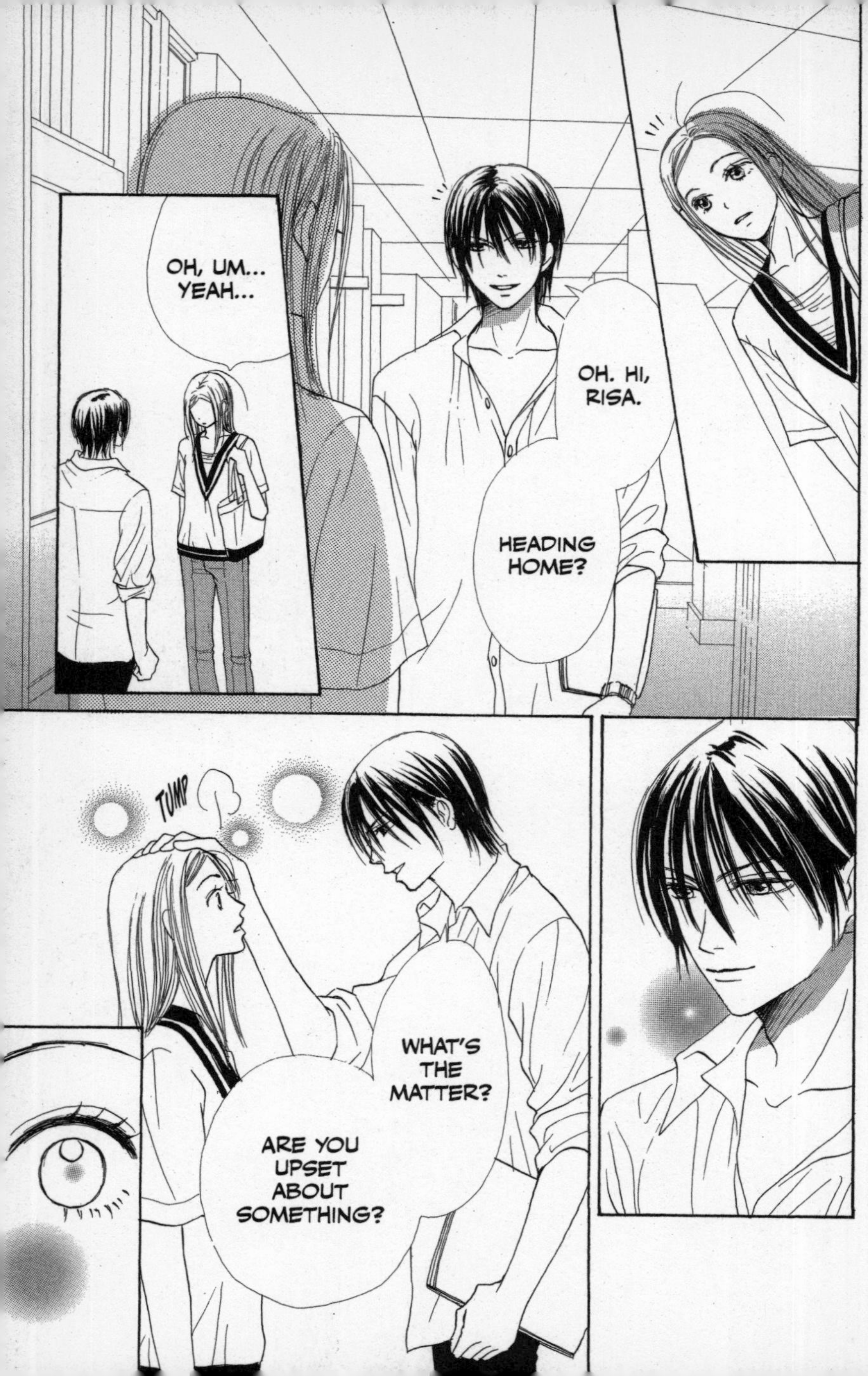
OH. HI, RISA.
HEADING HOME?
OH, UM... YEAH...
TUMP
WHAT'S THE MATTER?
ARE YOU UPSET ABOUT SOMETHING?

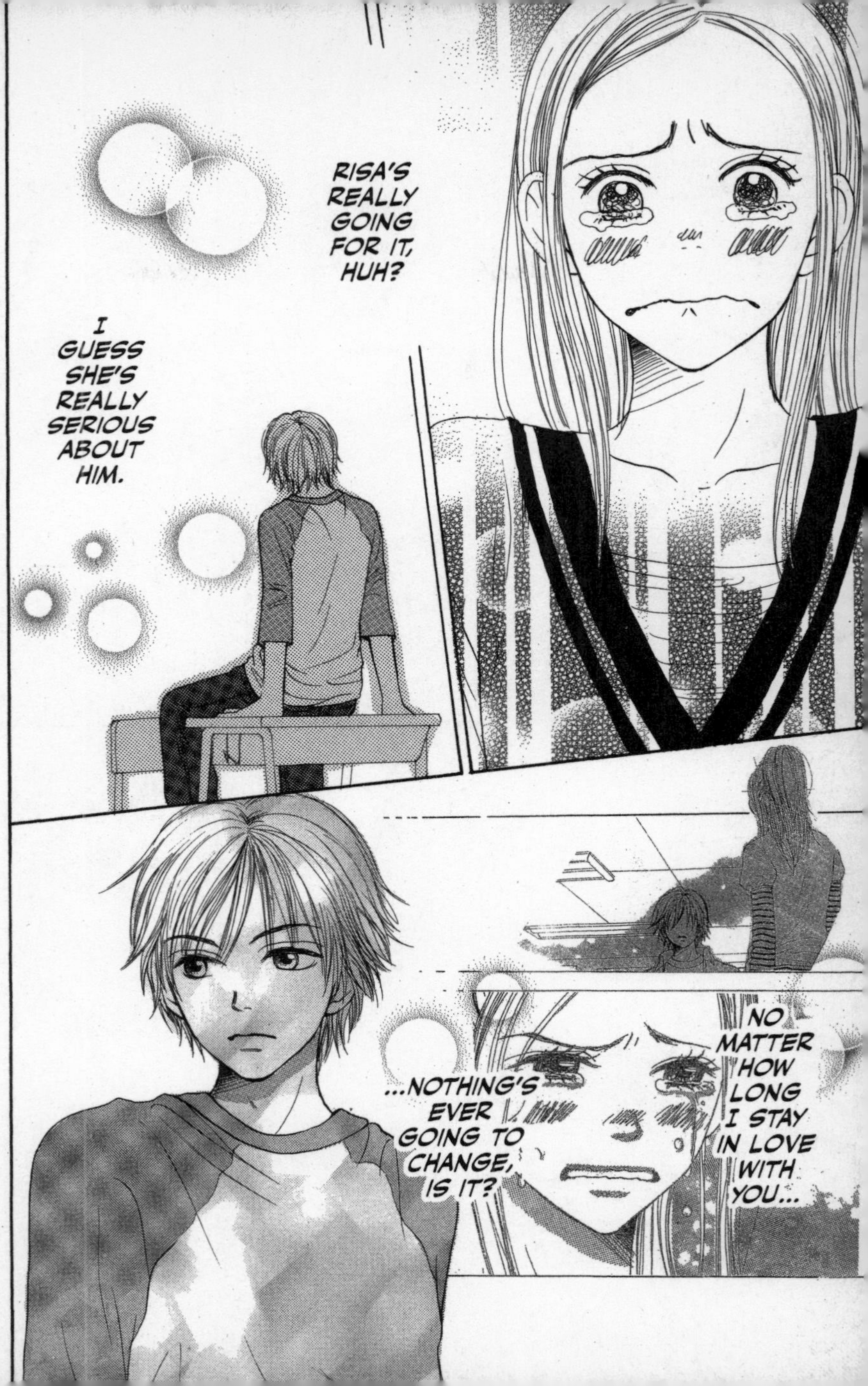
RISA'S REALLY GOING FOR IT, HUH?
I GUESS SHE'S REALLY SERIOUS ABOUT HIM.
NO MATTER HOW LONG I STAY IN LOVE WITH YOU...
...NOTHING'S EVER GOING TO CHANGE, IS IT?

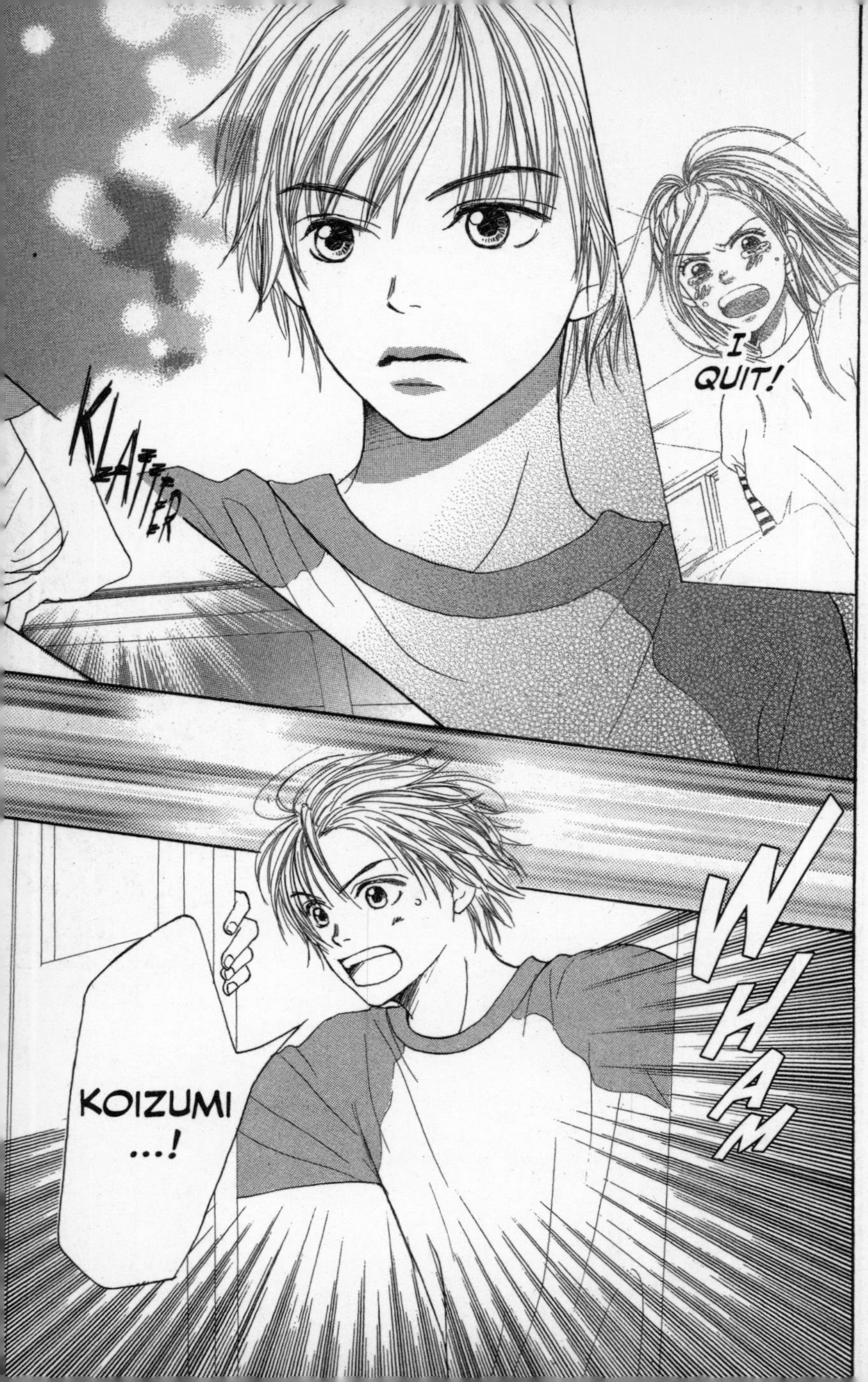
I QUIT!
KLATTER
WHAM
KOIZUMI ...!

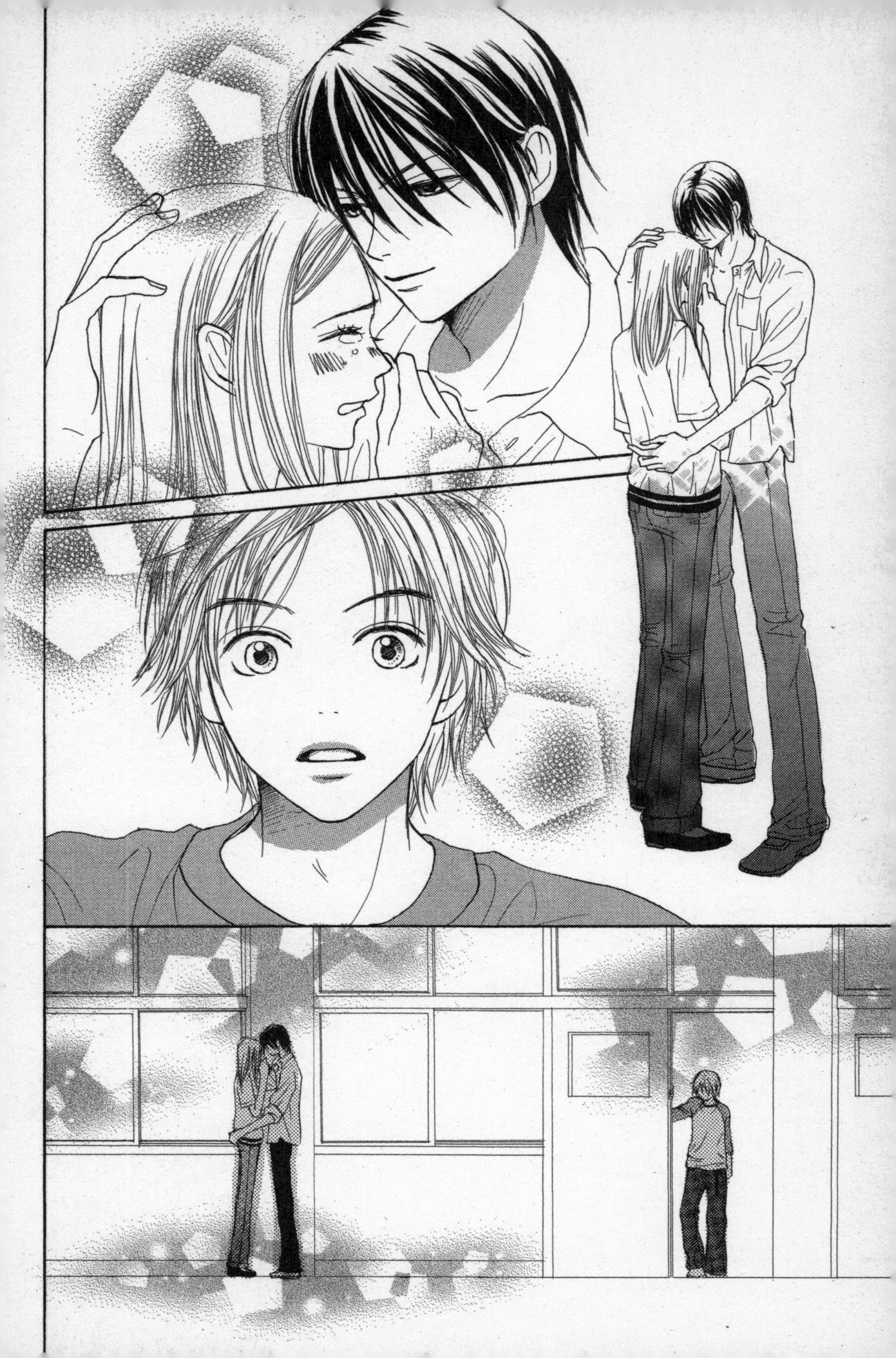

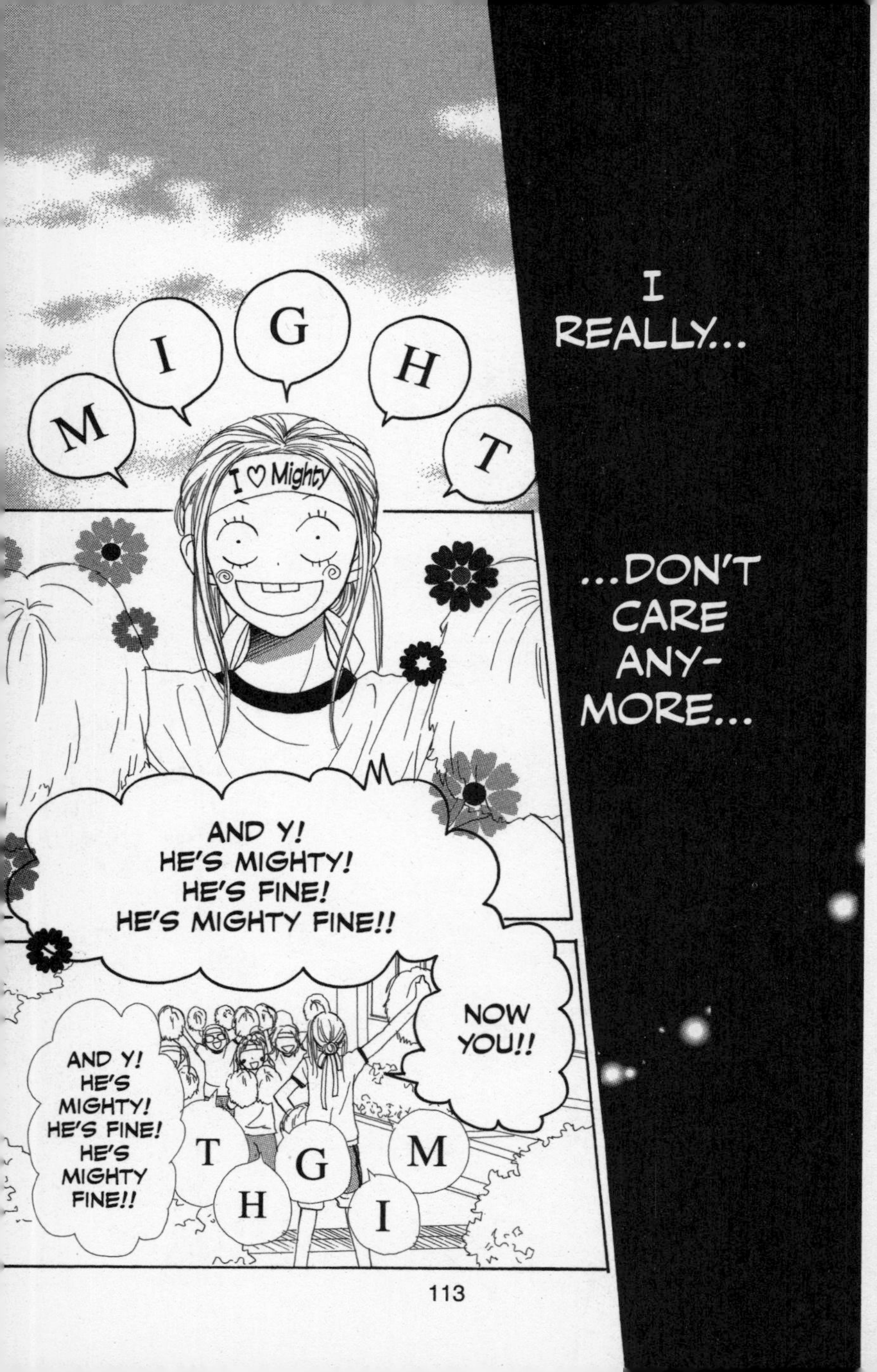
I REALLY...
...DON'T CARE ANYMORE...
M
I
G
H
T
I ♡ Mighty
AND Y! HE'S MIGHTY! HE'S FINE! HE'S MIGHTY FINE!!
NOW YOU!!
M
I
G
H
T
AND Y! HE'S MIGHTY! HE'S FINE! HE'S MIGHTY FINE!!

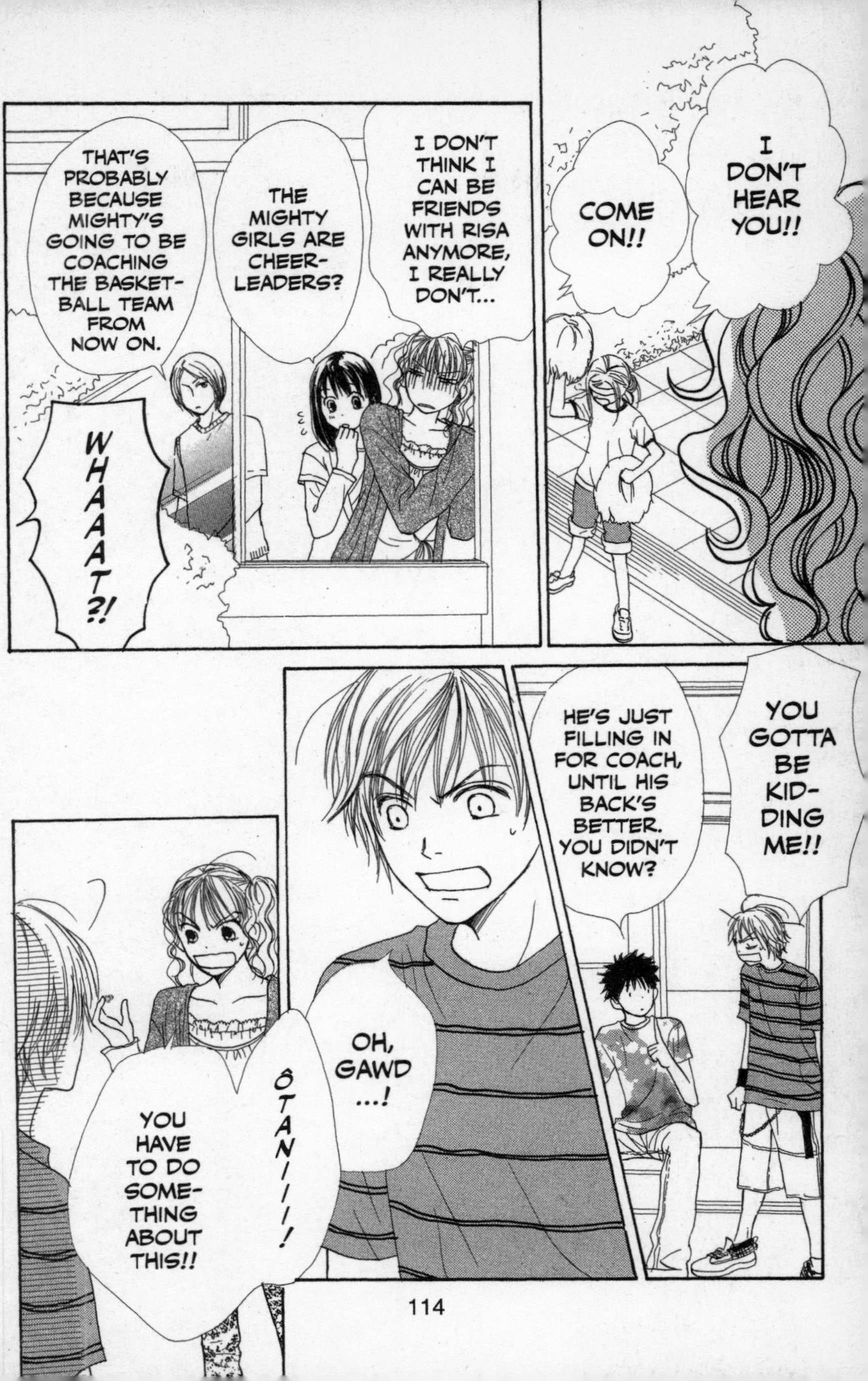
I DON'T HEAR YOU!!
COME ON!!
I DON'T THINK I CAN BE FRIENDS WITH RISA ANYMORE, I REALLY DON'T...
THE MIGHTY GIRLS ARE CHEER-LEADERS?
THAT'S PROBABLY BECAUSE MIGHTY'S GOING TO BE COACHING THE BASKET-BALL TEAM FROM NOW ON.
WHAAAAT?!
YOU GOTTA BE KID-DING ME!!
HE'S JUST FILLING IN FOR COACH, UNTIL HIS BACK'S BETTER. YOU DIDN'T KNOW?
OH, GAWD ...!
ÔTANI!!!!!
YOU HAVE TO DO SOME-THING ABOUT THIS!!

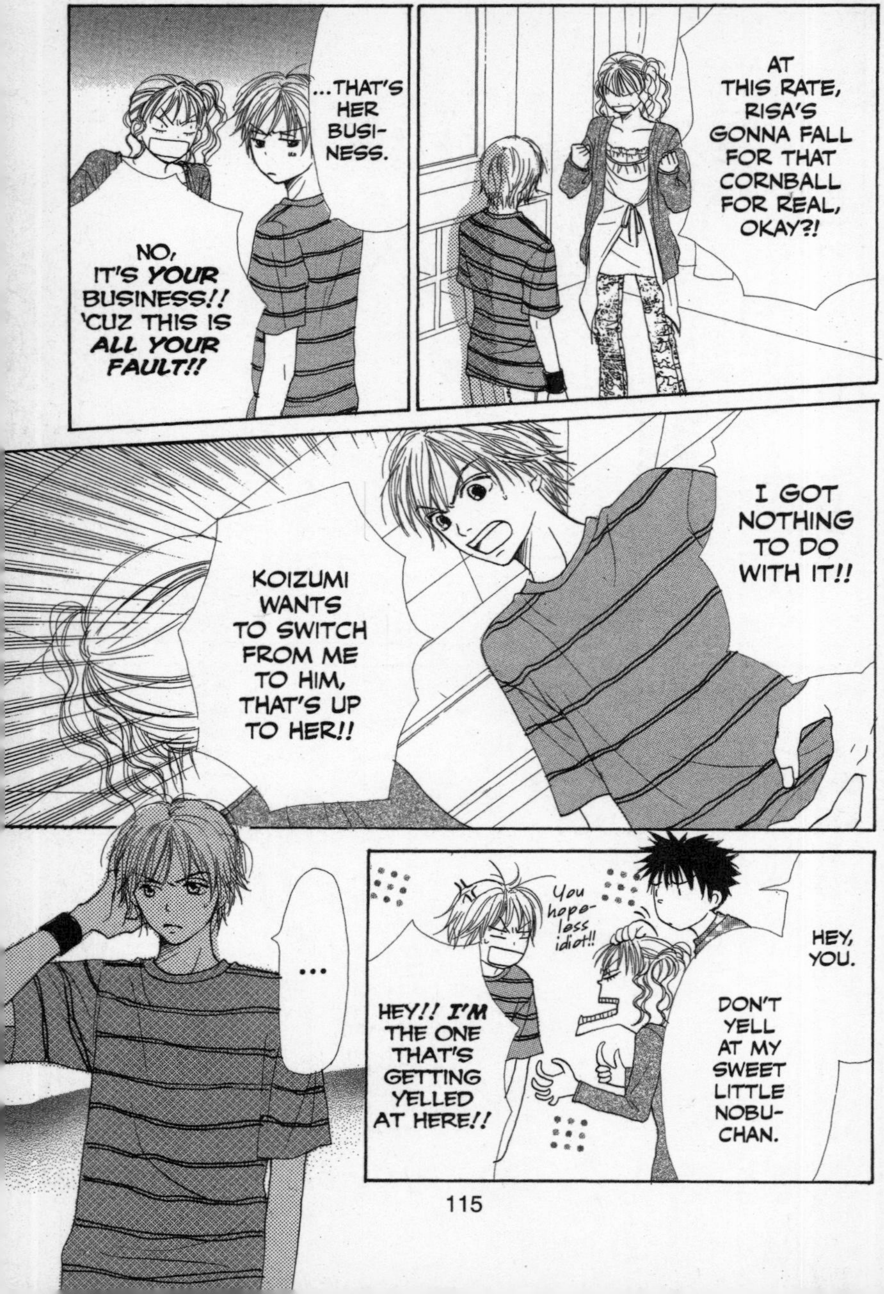
AT THIS RATE, RISA'S GONNA FALL FOR THAT CORNBALL FOR REAL, OKAY?!
...THAT'S HER BUSI-NESS.
NO, IT'S YOUR BUSINESS!! 'CUZ THIS IS ALL YOUR FAULT!!
I GOT NOTHING TO DO WITH IT!!
KOIZUMI WANTS TO SWITCH FROM ME TO HIM, THAT'S UP TO HER!!
HEY, YOU.
DON'T YELL AT MY SWEET LITTLE NOBU-CHAN.
You hope-less idiot!!
HEY!! I'M THE ONE THAT'S GETTING YELLED AT HERE!!
...

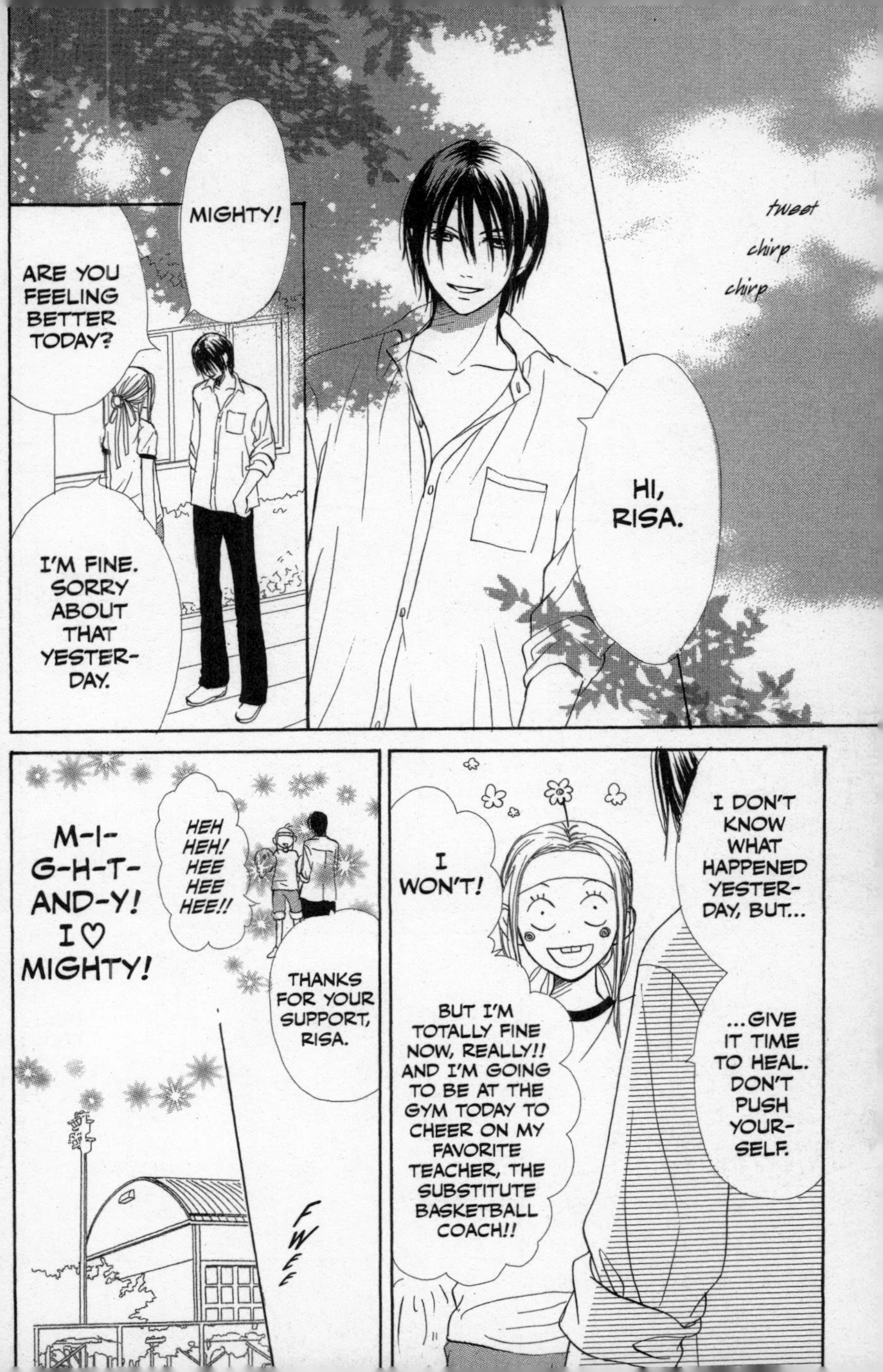
tweet
chirp
chirp
HI, RISA.
MIGHTY!
ARE YOU FEELING BETTER TODAY?
I'M FINE. SORRY ABOUT THAT YESTERDAY.
I DON'T KNOW WHAT HAPPENED YESTERDAY, BUT...
...GIVE IT TIME TO HEAL. DON'T PUSH YOURSELF.
I WON'T!
BUT I'M TOTALLY FINE NOW, REALLY!! AND I'M GOING TO BE AT THE GYM TODAY TO CHEER ON MY FAVORITE TEACHER, THE SUBSTITUTE BASKETBALL COACH!!
HEH HEH! HEE HEE HEE!!
M-I-G-H-T-AND-Y! I ♡ MIGHTY!
THANKS FOR YOUR SUPPORT, RISA.
FWEE

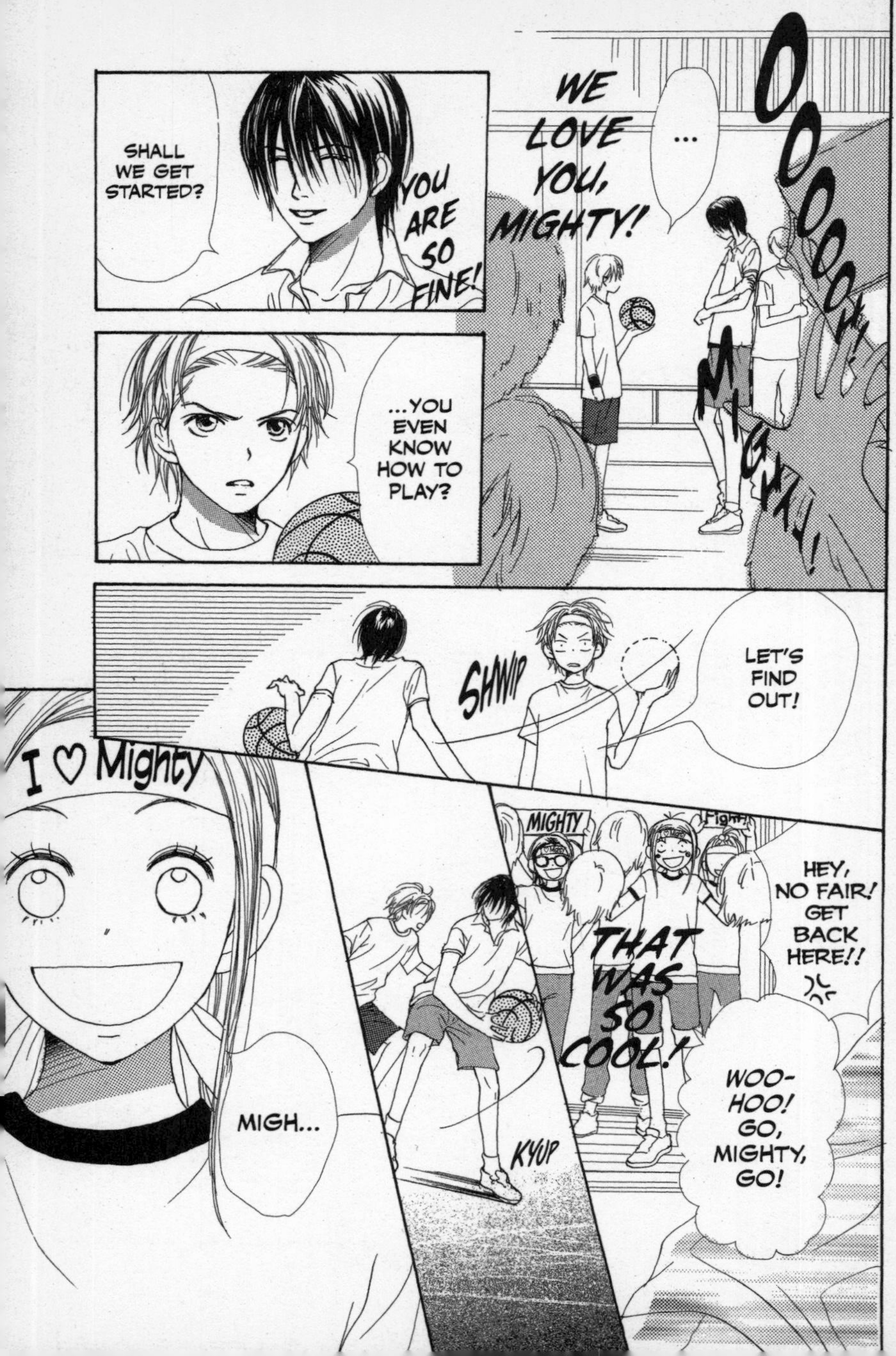
OOOOOH!
MIGHTY!
...
WE LOVE YOU, MIGHTY!
SHALL WE GET STARTED?
YOU ARE SO FINE!
...YOU EVEN KNOW HOW TO PLAY?
LET'S FIND OUT!
SHWIP
HEY, NO FAIR! GET BACK HERE!!
MIGHTY
Fight
THAT WAS SO COOL!
WOO-HOO! GO, MIGHTY, GO!
KYUP
I ♡ Mighty
MIGH...

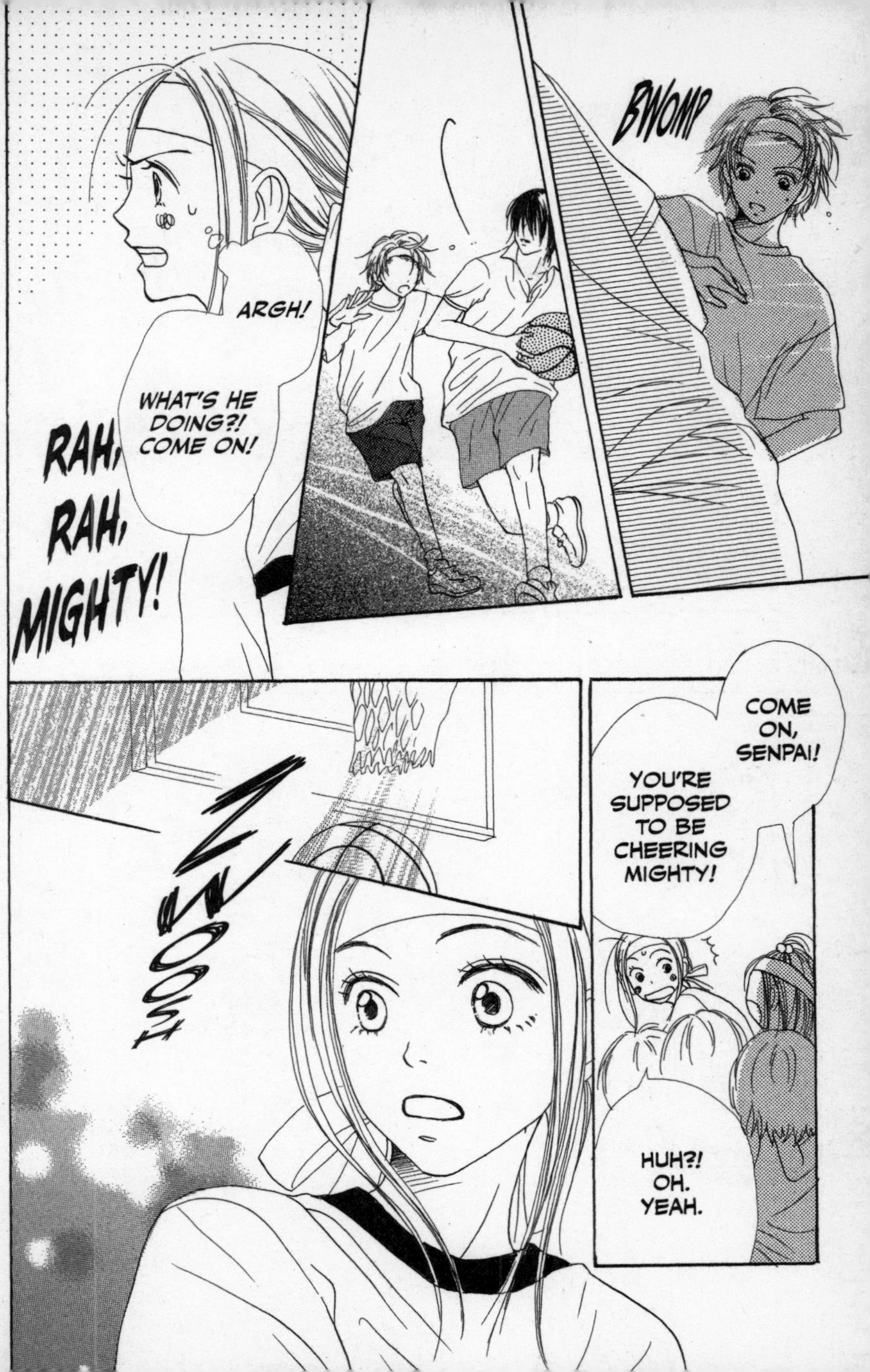
BWOMP
ARGH!
WHAT'S HE DOING?! COME ON!
RAH, RAH, MIGHTY!
COME ON, SENPAI!
YOU'RE SUPPOSED TO BE CHEERING MIGHTY!
HUH?! OH. YEAH.
WOOSH

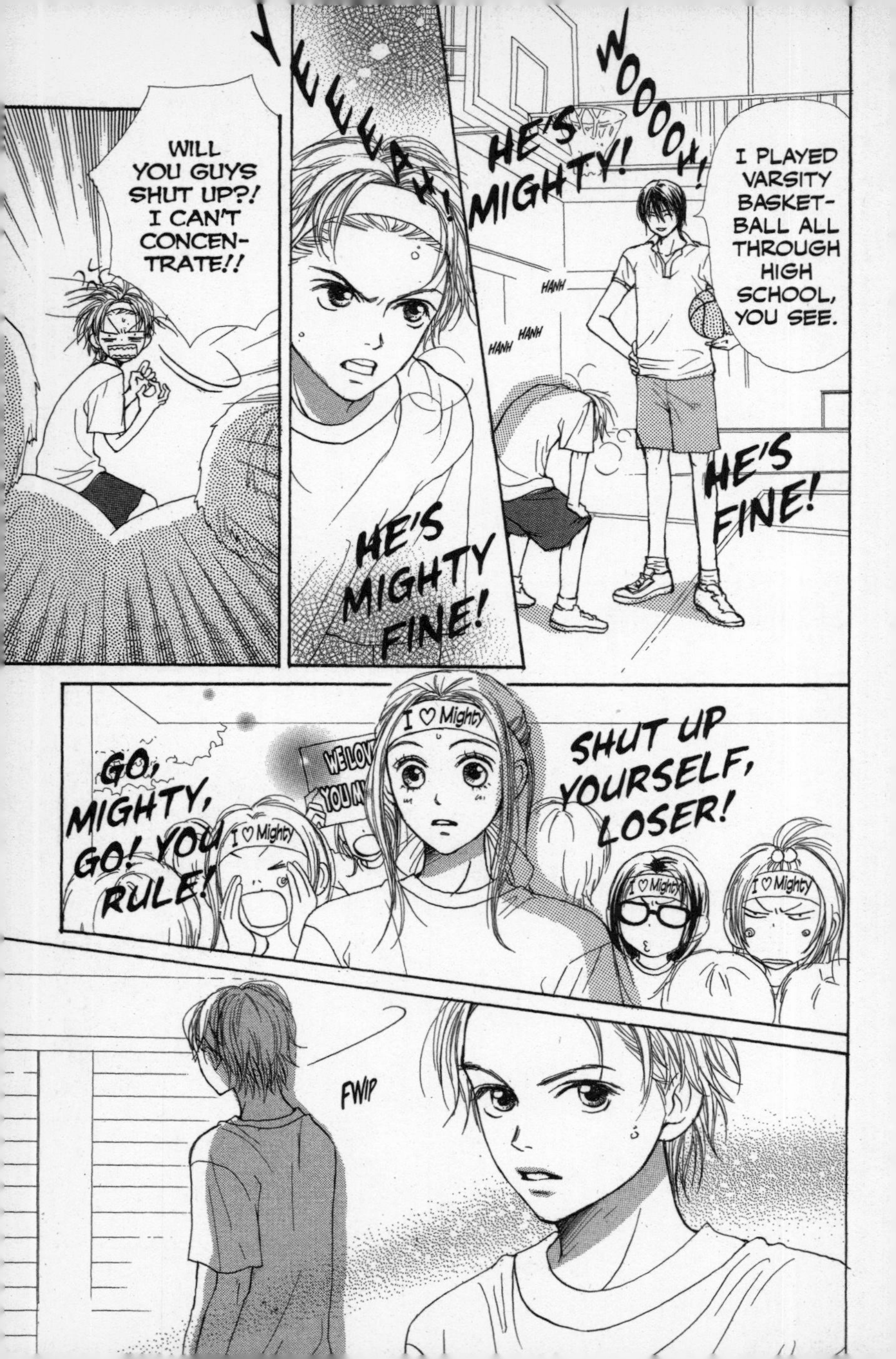
I PLAYED VARSITY BASKETBALL ALL THROUGH HIGH SCHOOL, YOU SEE.
WOOOOOH!
HE'S MIGHTY!
HANH
HANH
HANH
HE'S FINE!
YEEEEAH!
HE'S MIGHTY FINE!
WILL YOU GUYS SHUT UP?! I CAN'T CONCENTRATE!!
I ♡ Mighty
I ♡ Mighty
SHUT UP YOURSELF, LOSER!
I ♡ Mighty
I ♡ Mighty
GO, MIGHTY, GO! YOU RULE!
FWIP

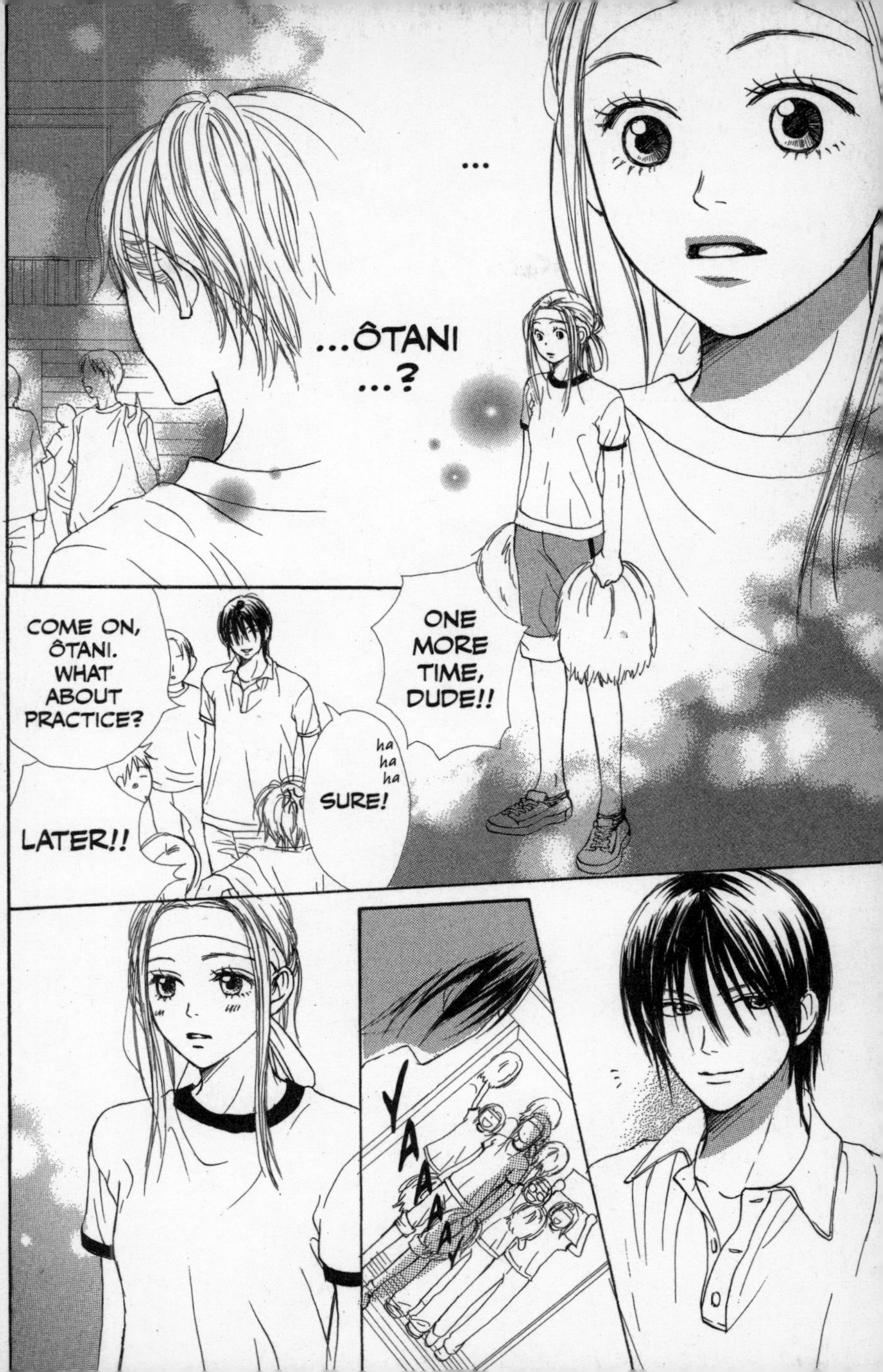
...
...ÔTANI
...?
ONE MORE TIME, DUDE!!
COME ON, ÔTANI. WHAT ABOUT PRACTICE?
ha ha ha
SURE!
LATER!!
YAAAA

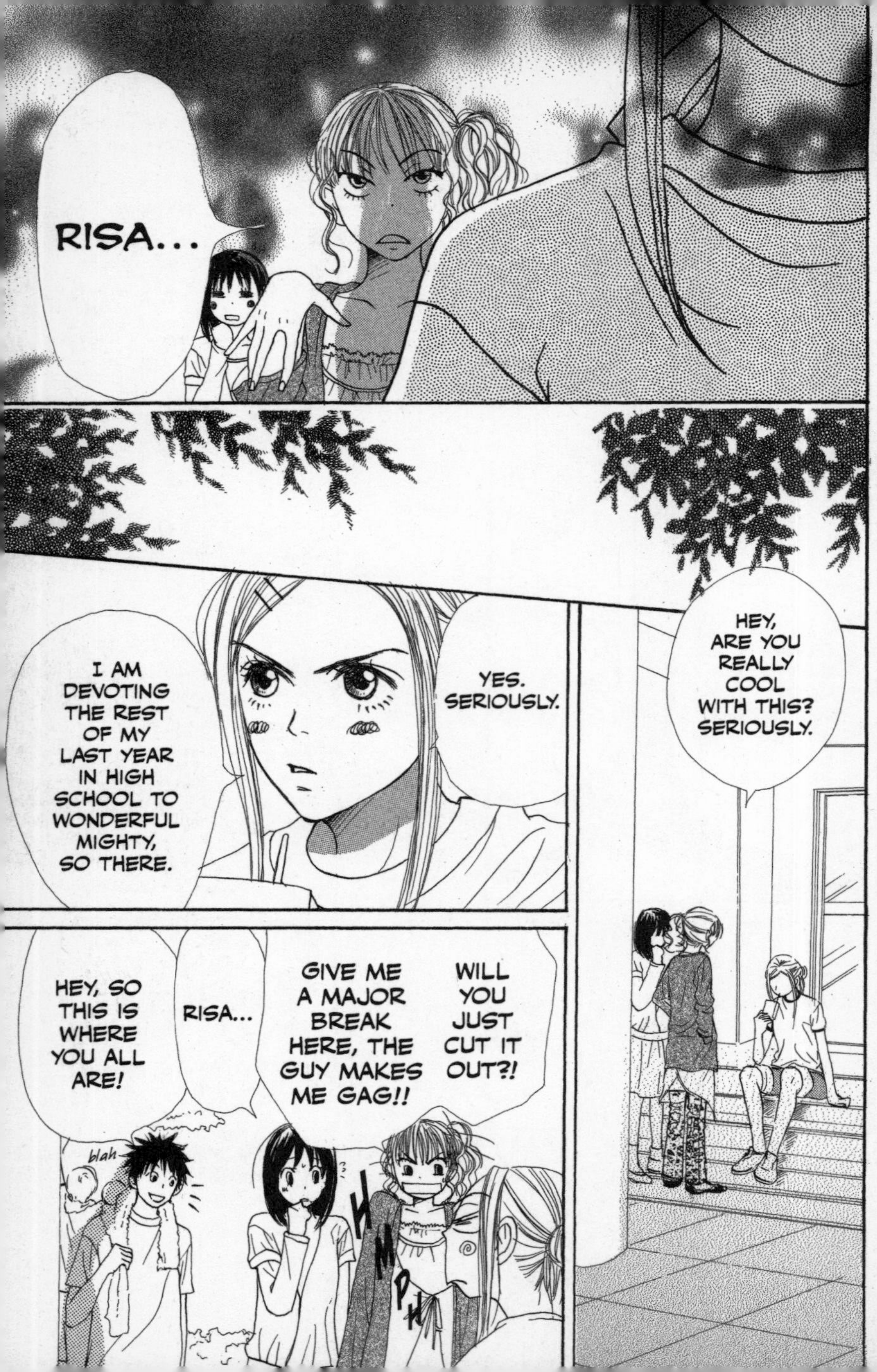
RISA...
HEY, ARE YOU REALLY COOL WITH THIS? SERIOUSLY.
YES. SERIOUSLY.
I AM DEVOTING THE REST OF MY LAST YEAR IN HIGH SCHOOL TO WONDERFUL MIGHTY, SO THERE.
WILL YOU JUST CUT IT OUT?!
GIVE ME A MAJOR BREAK HERE, THE GUY MAKES ME GAG!!
RISA...
HEY, SO THIS IS WHERE YOU ALL ARE!
HMPH
blah

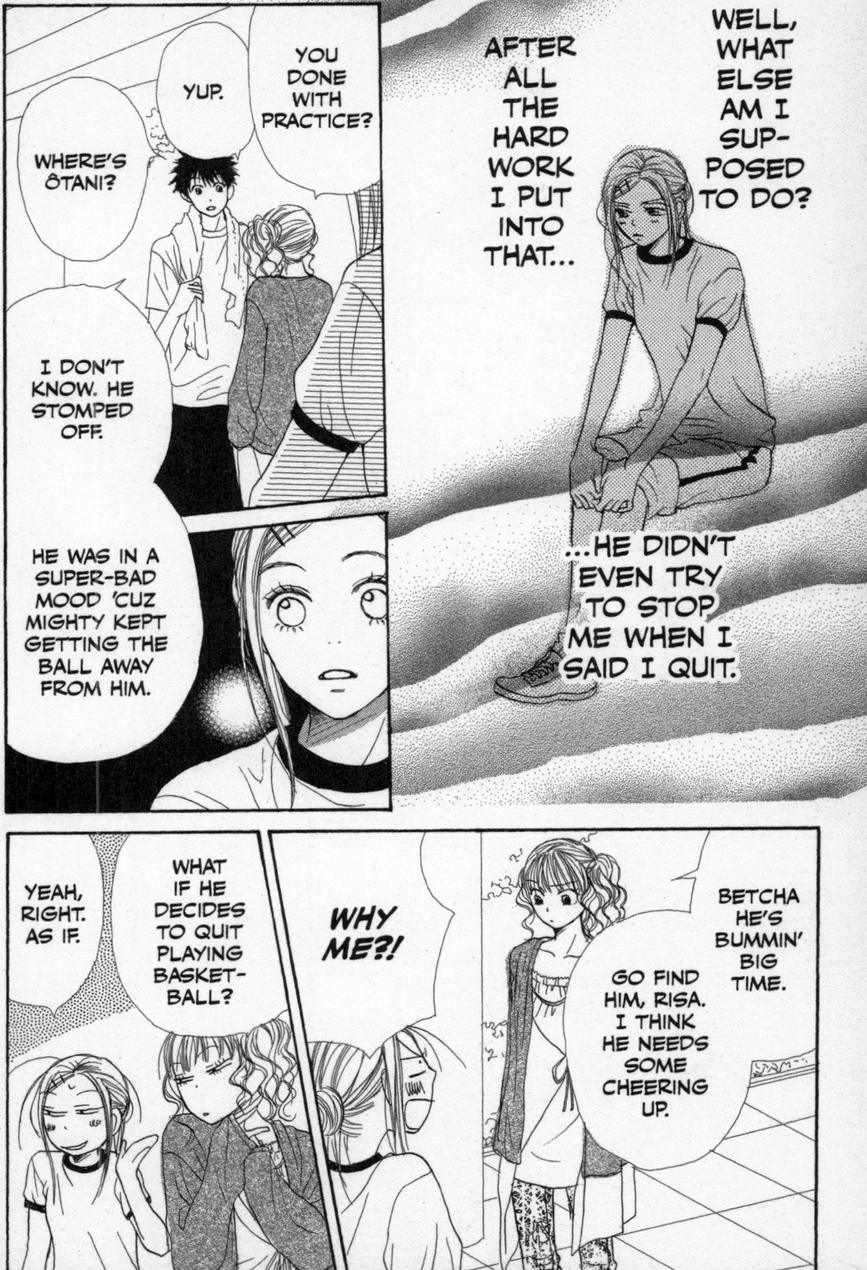
WELL, WHAT ELSE AM I SUP-POSED TO DO?
AFTER ALL THE HARD WORK I PUT INTO THAT...
...HE DIDN'T EVEN TRY TO STOP ME WHEN I SAID I QUIT.
YOU DONE WITH PRACTICE?
YUP.
WHERE'S ŌTANI?
I DON'T KNOW. HE STOMPED OFF.
HE WAS IN A SUPER-BAD MOOD 'CUZ MIGHTY KEPT GETTING THE BALL AWAY FROM HIM.
BETCHA HE'S BUMMIN' BIG TIME.
GO FIND HIM, RISA. I THINK HE NEEDS SOME CHEERING UP.
WHY ME?!
WHAT IF HE DECIDES TO QUIT PLAYING BASKET-BALL?
YEAH, RIGHT. AS IF.

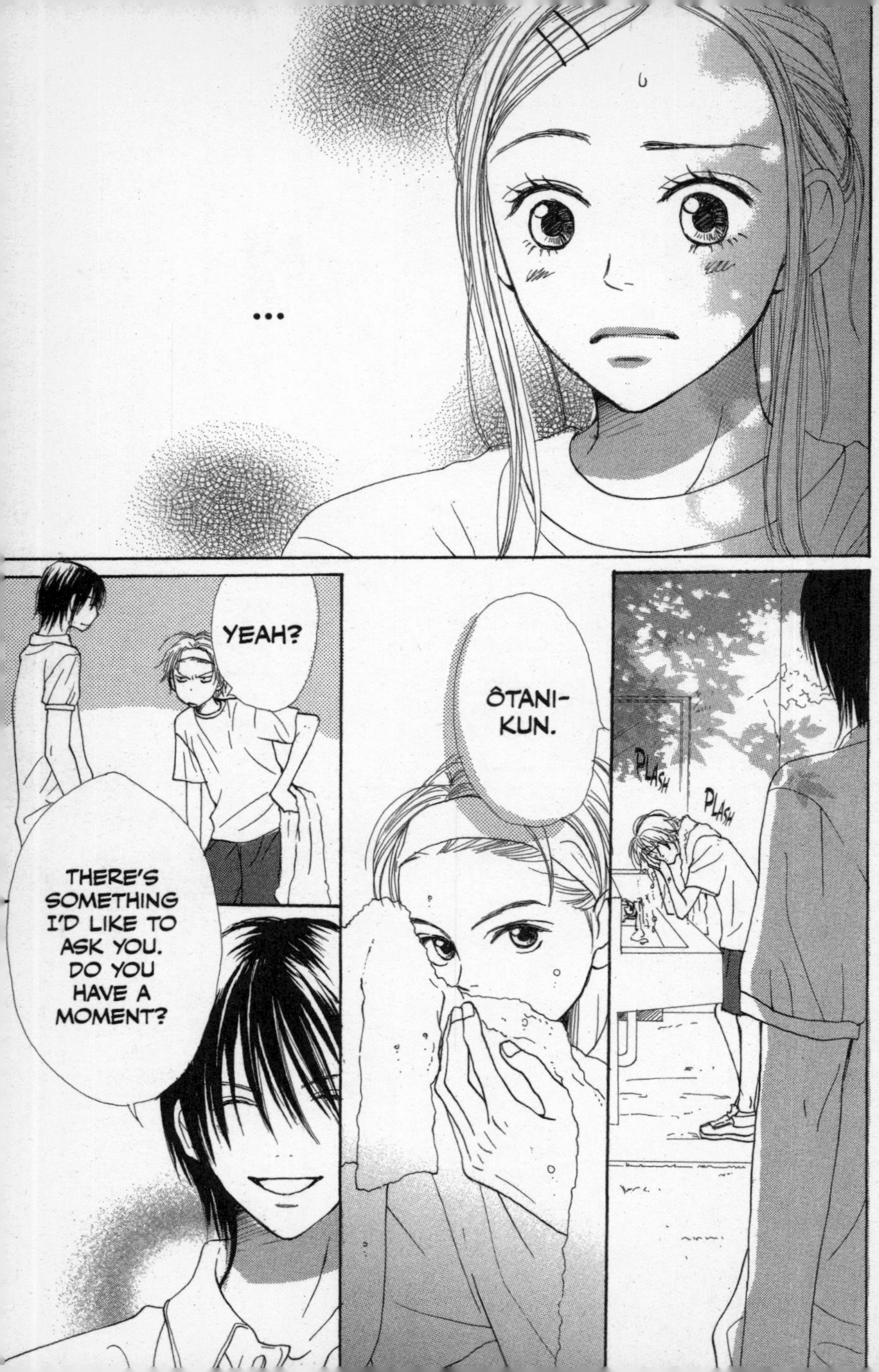
...
PLASH
PLASH
ÔTANI-KUN.
YEAH?
THERE'S SOMETHING I'D LIKE TO ASK YOU. DO YOU HAVE A MOMENT?

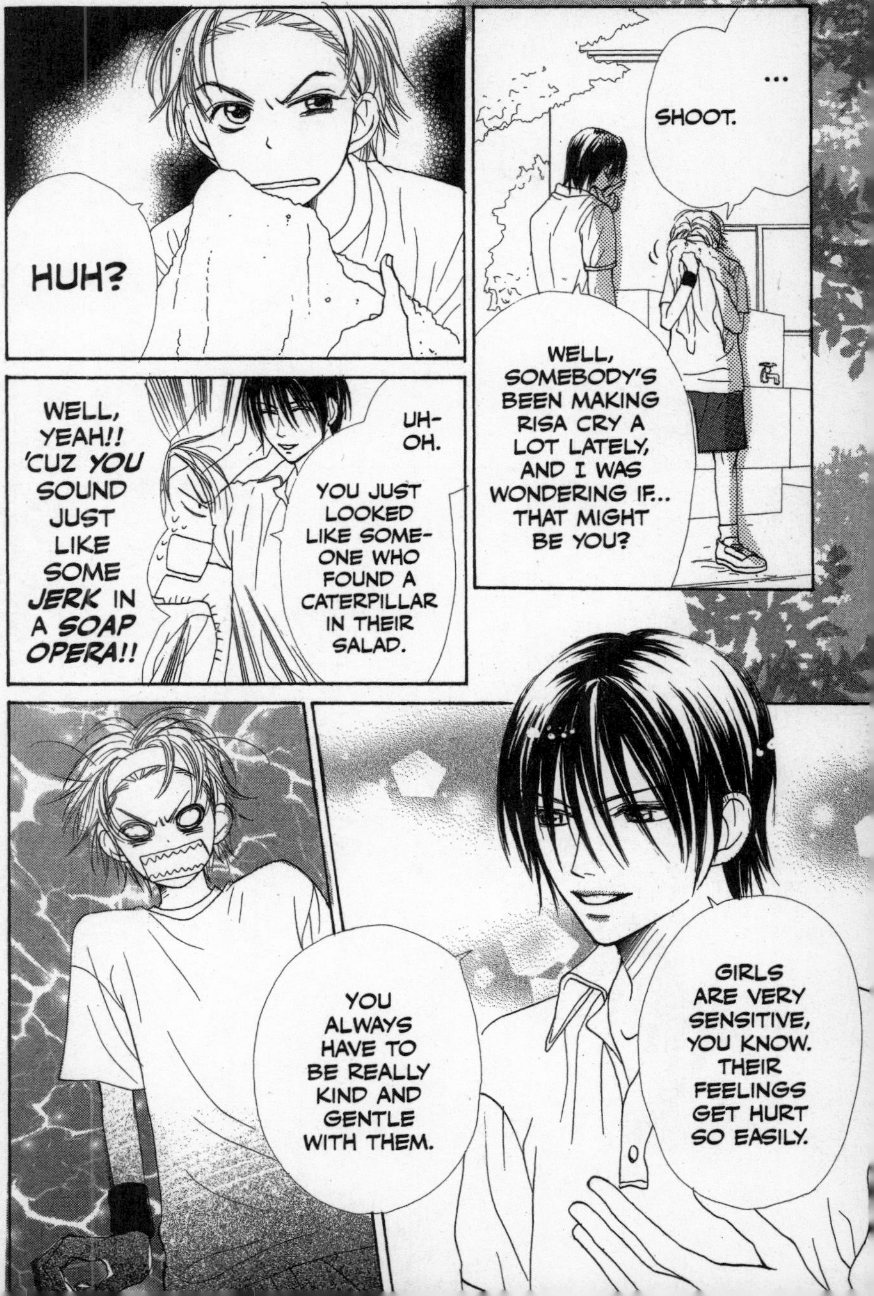
...
SHOOT.
WELL, SOMEBODY'S BEEN MAKING RISA CRY A LOT LATELY, AND I WAS WONDERING IF... THAT MIGHT BE YOU?
HUH?
UH-OH.
YOU JUST LOOKED LIKE SOME-ONE WHO FOUND A CATERPILLAR IN THEIR SALAD.
WELL, YEAH!! 'CUZ *YOU* SOUND JUST LIKE SOME *JERK* IN A *SOAP OPERA*!!
GIRLS ARE VERY SENSITIVE, YOU KNOW. THEIR FEELINGS GET HURT SO EASILY.
YOU ALWAYS HAVE TO BE REALLY KIND AND GENTLE WITH THEM.

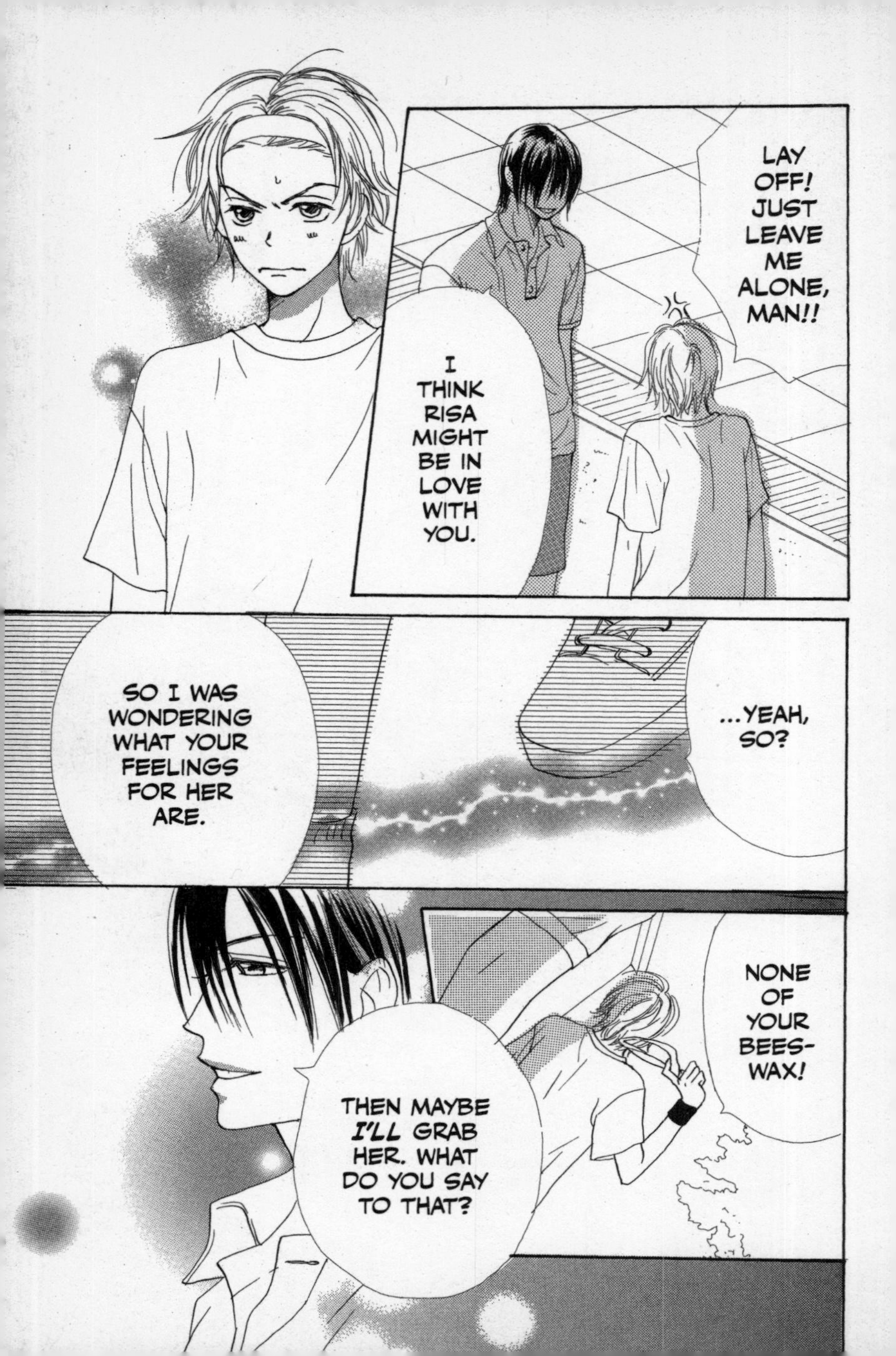
LAY OFF! JUST LEAVE ME ALONE, MAN!!
I THINK RISA MIGHT BE IN LOVE WITH YOU.
...YEAH, SO?
SO I WAS WONDERING WHAT YOUR FEELINGS FOR HER ARE.
NONE OF YOUR BEES-WAX!
THEN MAYBE *I'LL* GRAB HER. WHAT DO YOU SAY TO THAT?

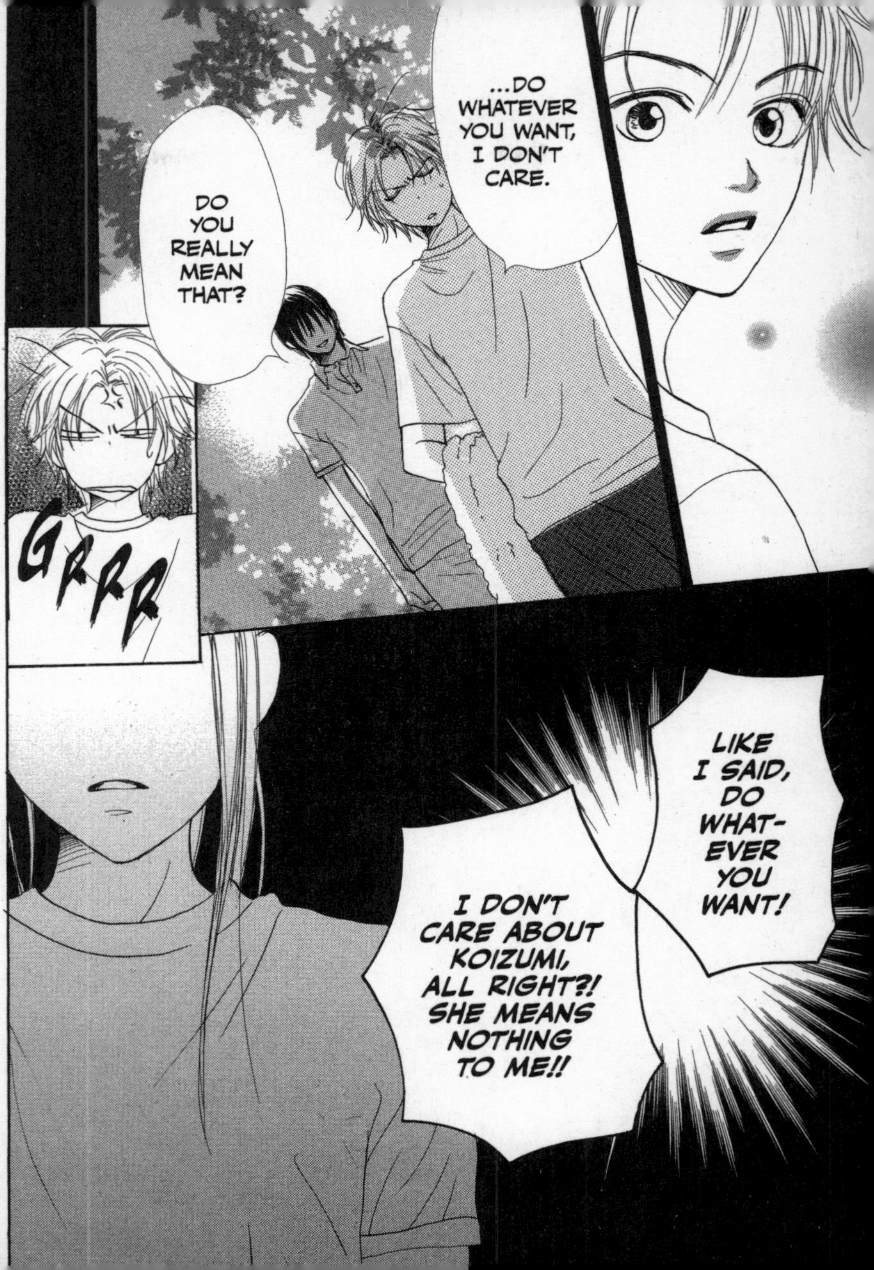
...DO WHATEVER YOU WANT, I DON'T CARE.
DO YOU REALLY MEAN THAT?
GRRR
LIKE I SAID, DO WHAT-EVER YOU WANT!
I DON'T CARE ABOUT KOIZUMI, ALL RIGHT?! SHE MEANS NOTHING TO ME!!

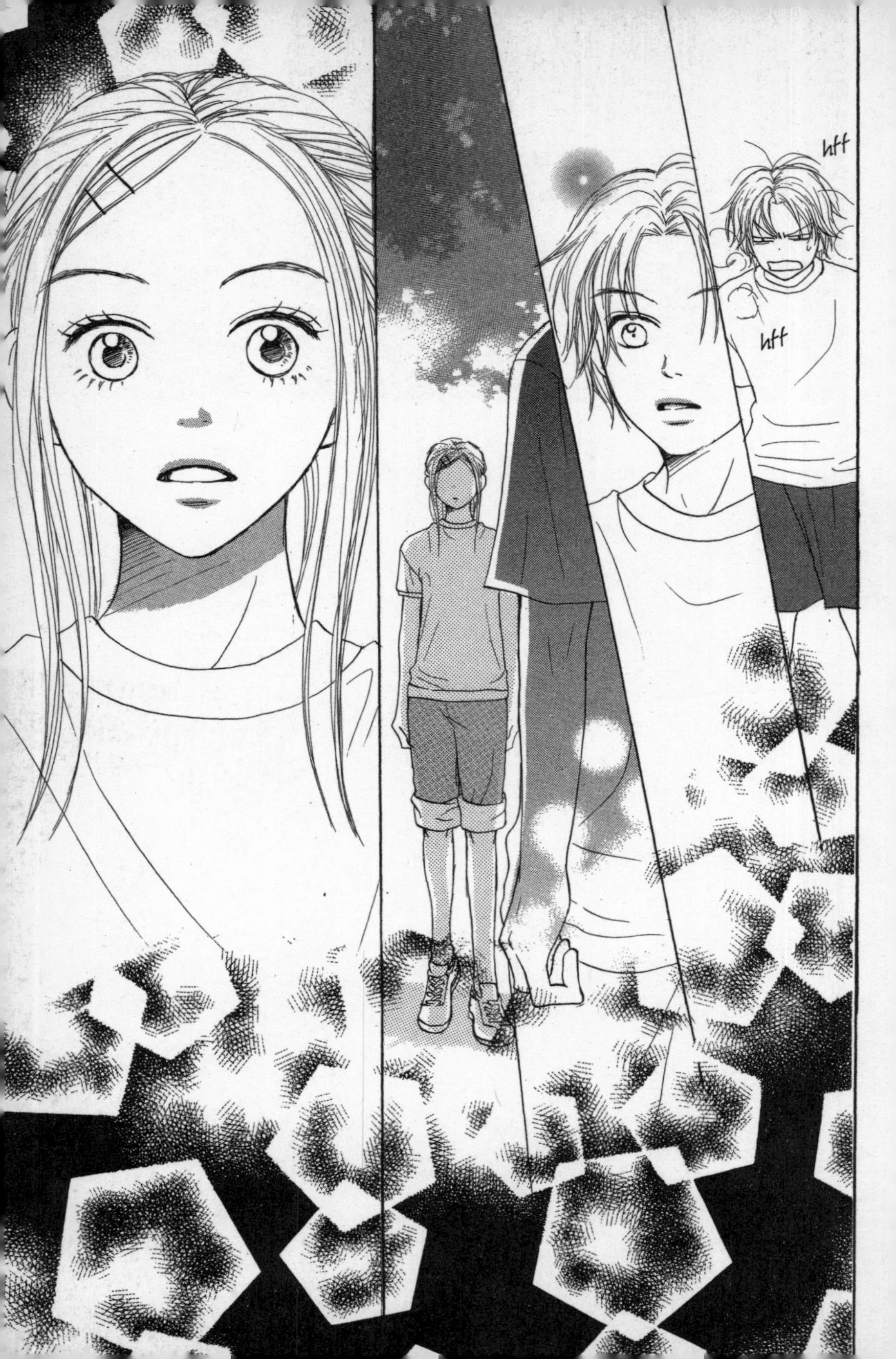
hff
hff

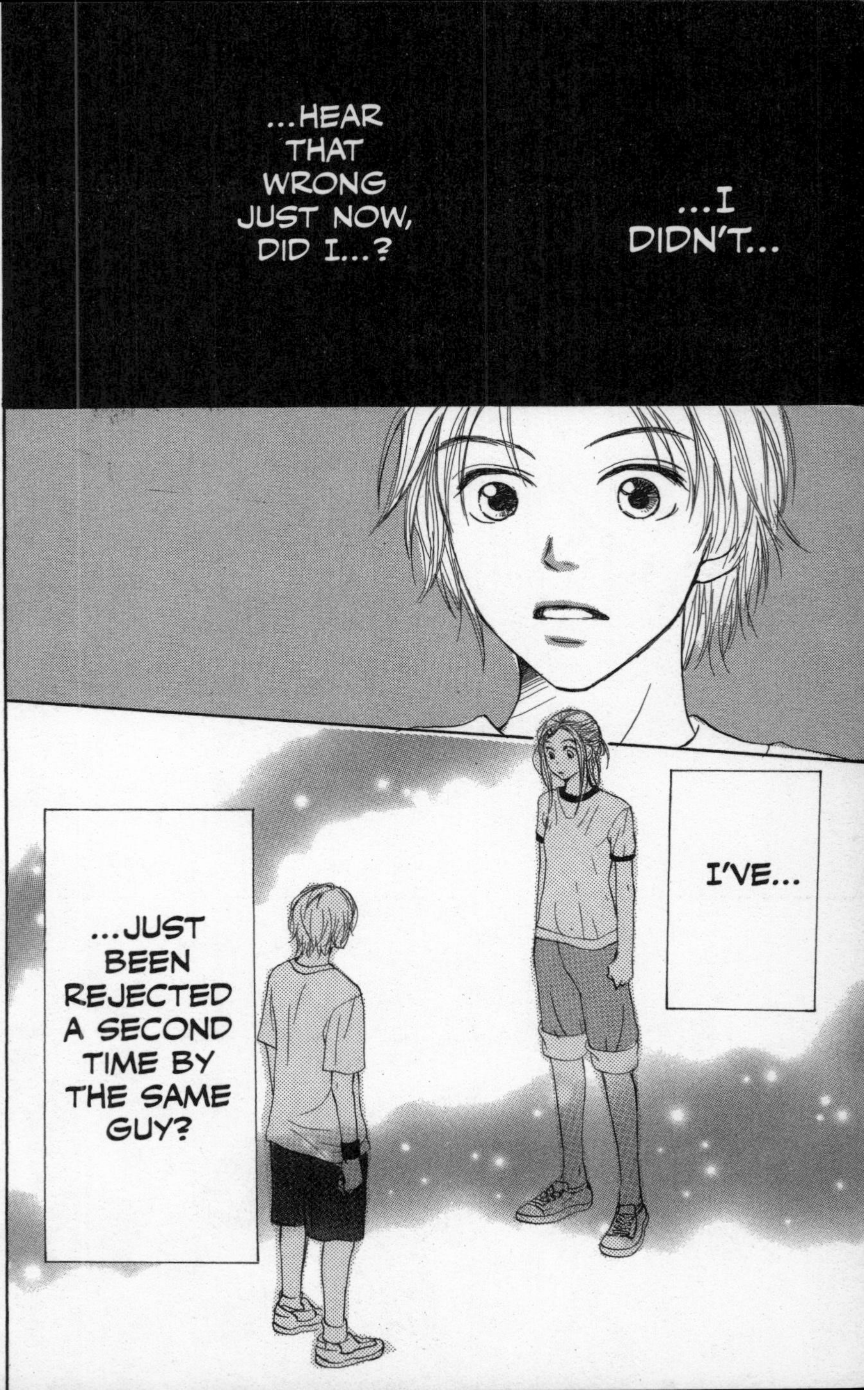
...I DIDN'T...
...HEAR THAT WRONG JUST NOW, DID I...?
I'VE...
...JUST BEEN REJECTED A SECOND TIME BY THE SAME GUY?

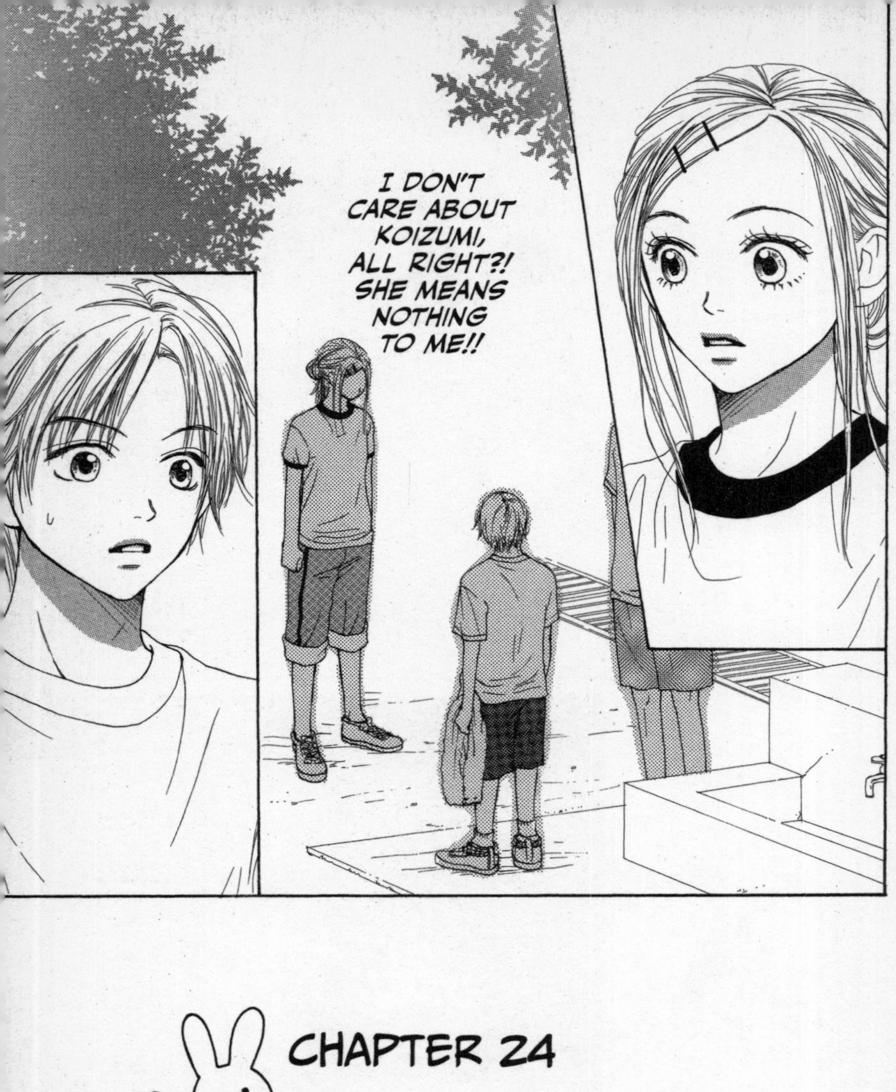
I DON'T CARE ABOUT KOIZUMI, ALL RIGHT?! SHE MEANS NOTHING TO ME!!

CHAPTER 24

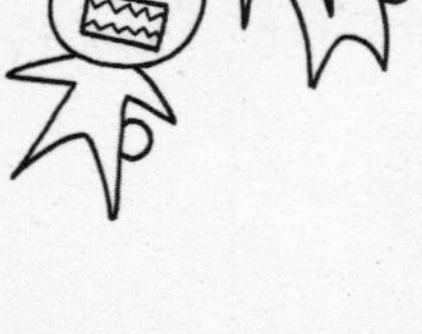

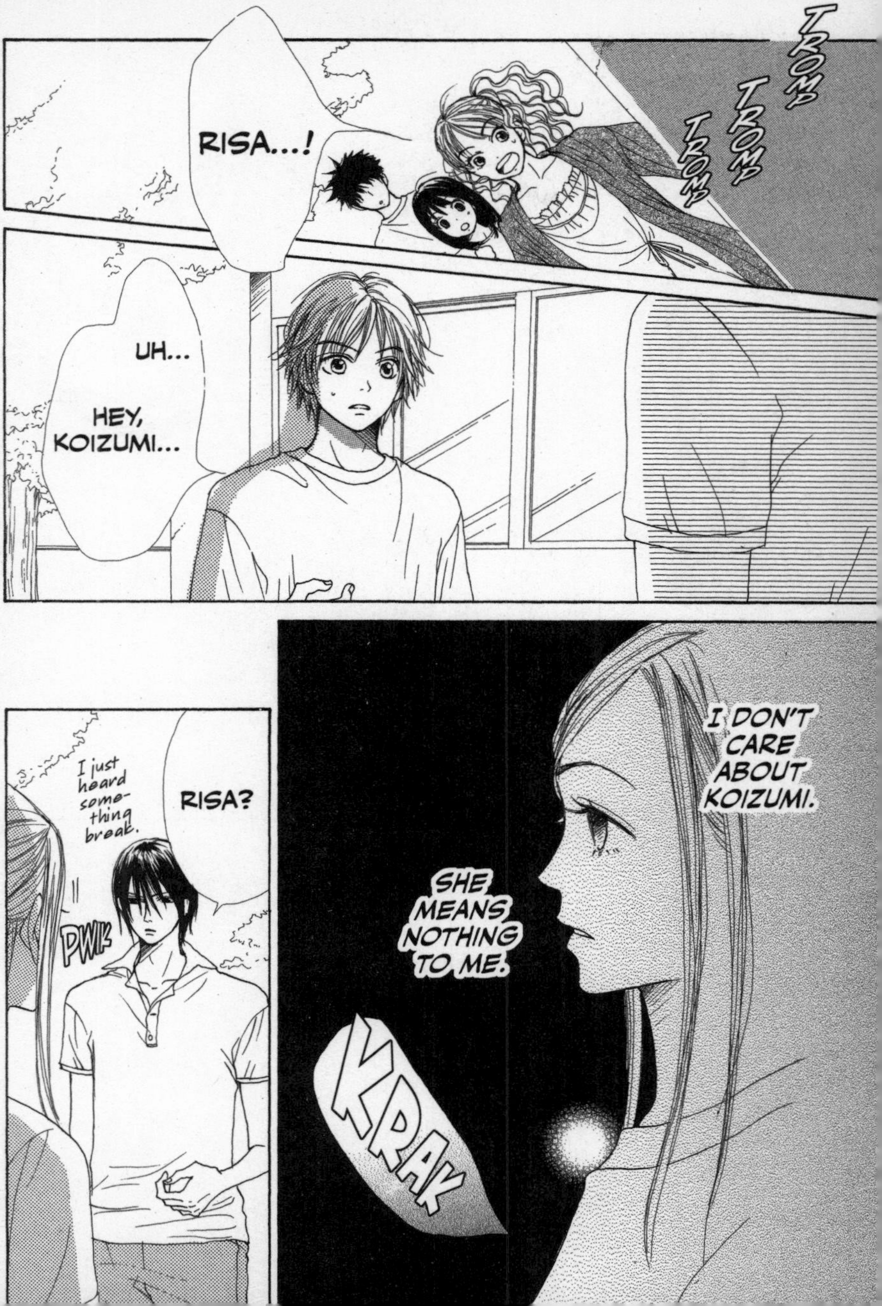
TROMP TROMP TROMP
RISA...!
UH...
HEY, KOIZUMI...
I DON'T CARE ABOUT KOIZUMI.
SHE MEANS NOTHING TO ME.
KRAK
RISA?
I just heard something break.
PWIK

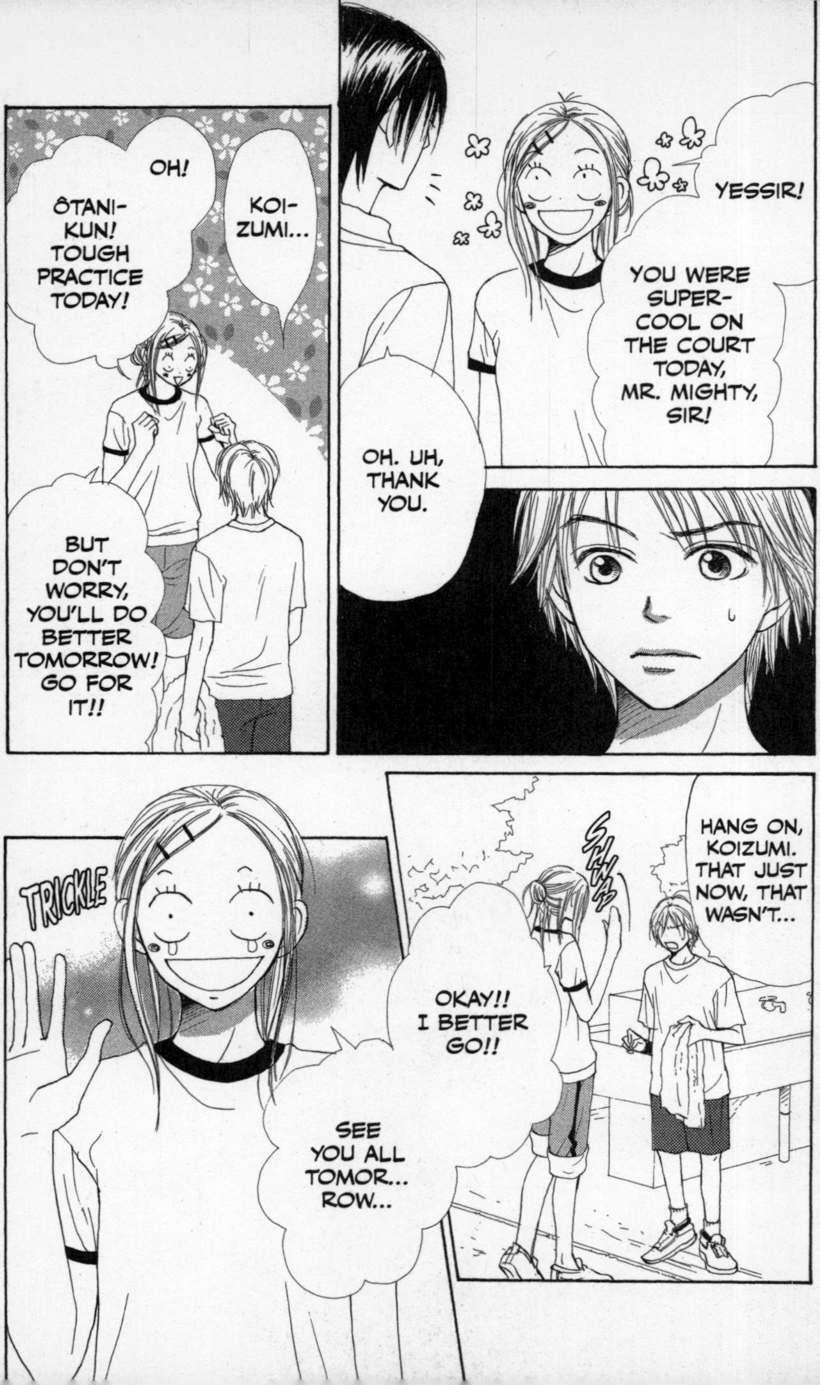
YESSIR!
YOU WERE SUPER-COOL ON THE COURT TODAY, MR. MIGHTY, SIR!
OH. UH, THANK YOU.
KOI-ZUMI...
OH! ÔTANI-KUN! TOUGH PRACTICE TODAY!
BUT DON'T WORRY, YOU'LL DO BETTER TOMORROW! GO FOR IT!!
HANG ON, KOIZUMI. THAT JUST NOW, THAT WASN'T...
OKAY!! I BETTER GO!!
TRICKLE
SEE YOU ALL TOMOR... ROW...

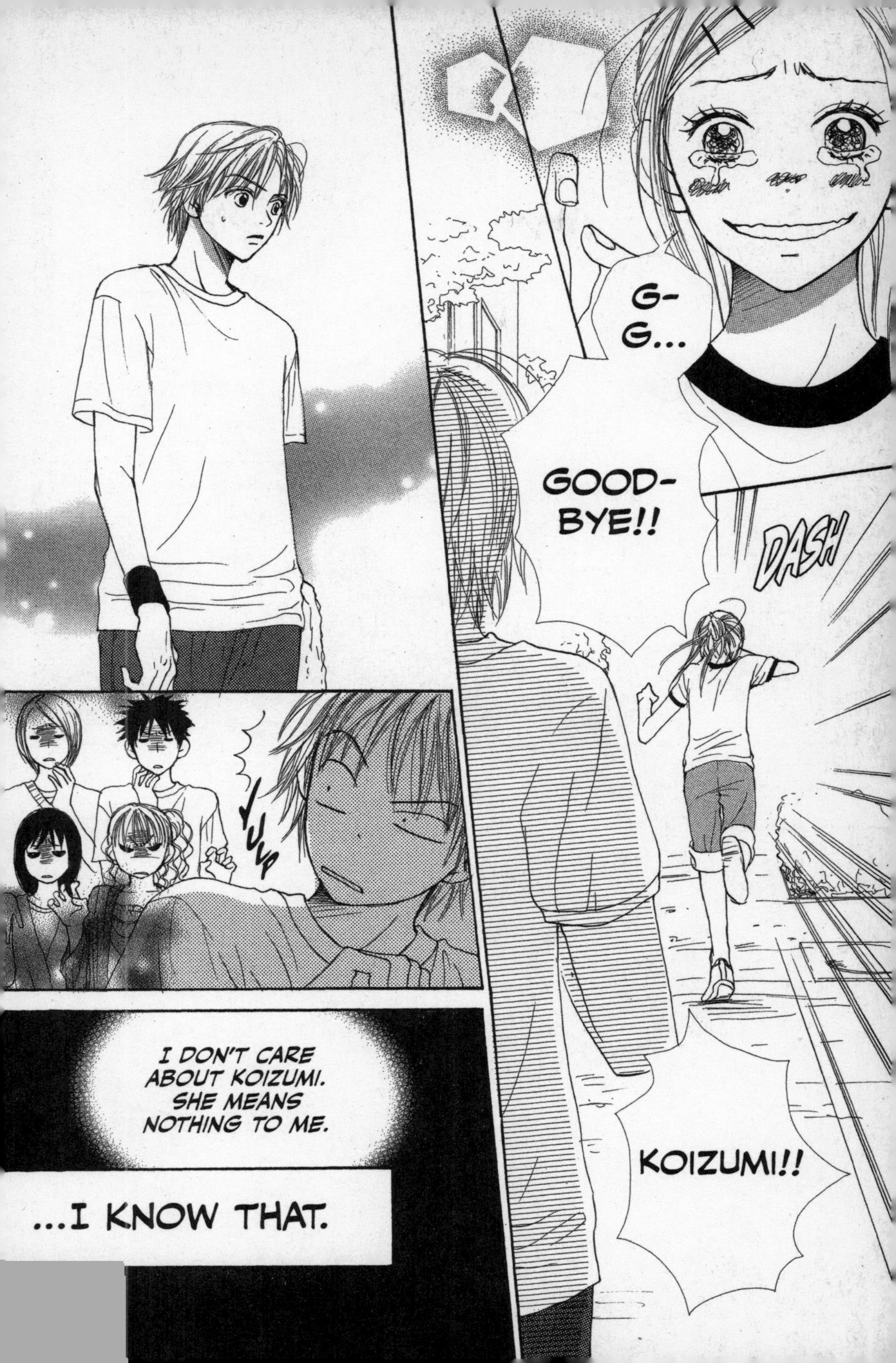
G-
G...
GOOD-
BYE!!
DASH
KOIZUMI!!
I DON'T CARE ABOUT KOIZUMI. SHE MEANS NOTHING TO ME.
...I KNOW THAT.

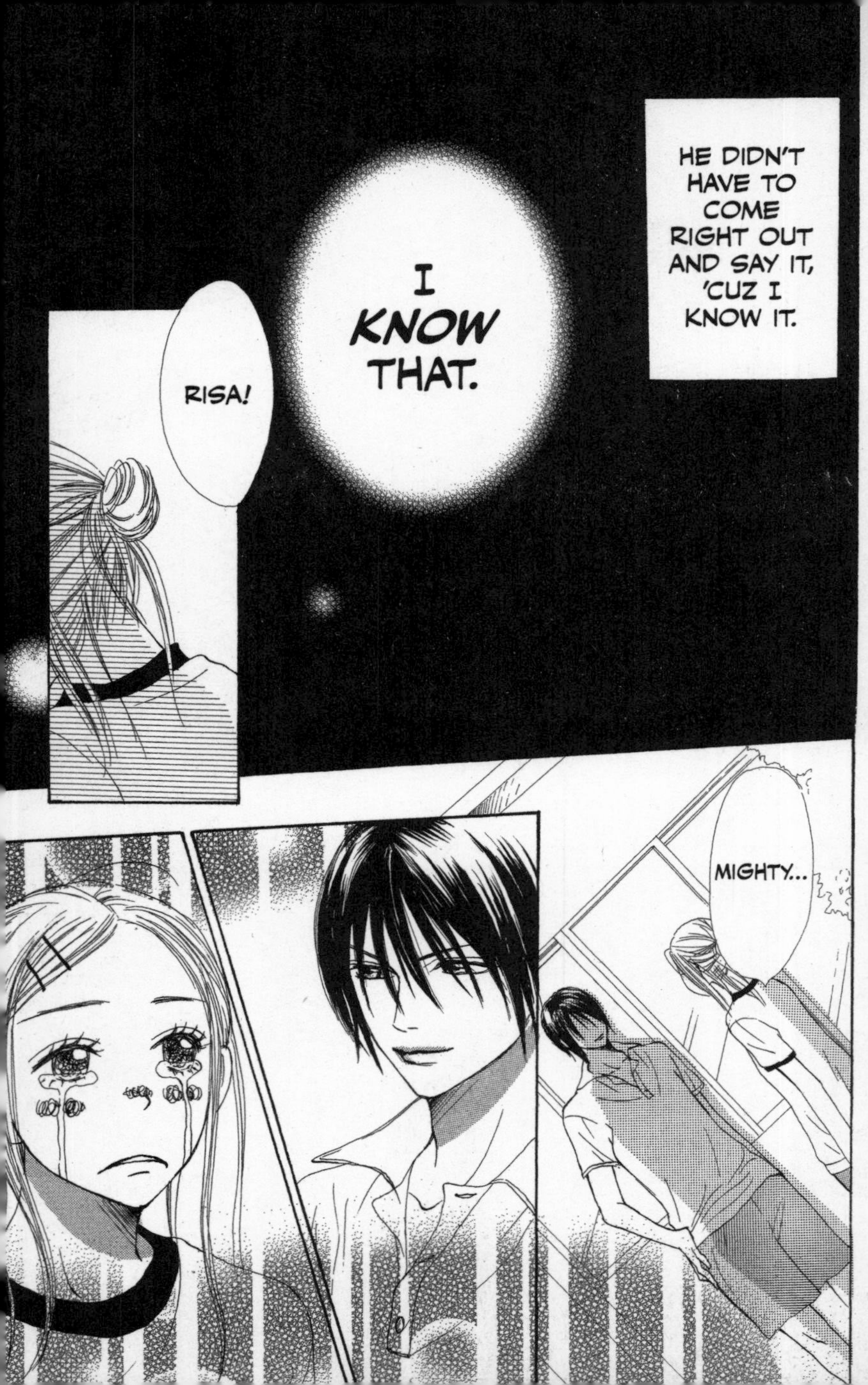
HE DIDN'T HAVE TO COME RIGHT OUT AND SAY IT, 'CUZ I KNOW IT.
I *KNOW* THAT.
RISA!
MIGHTY...

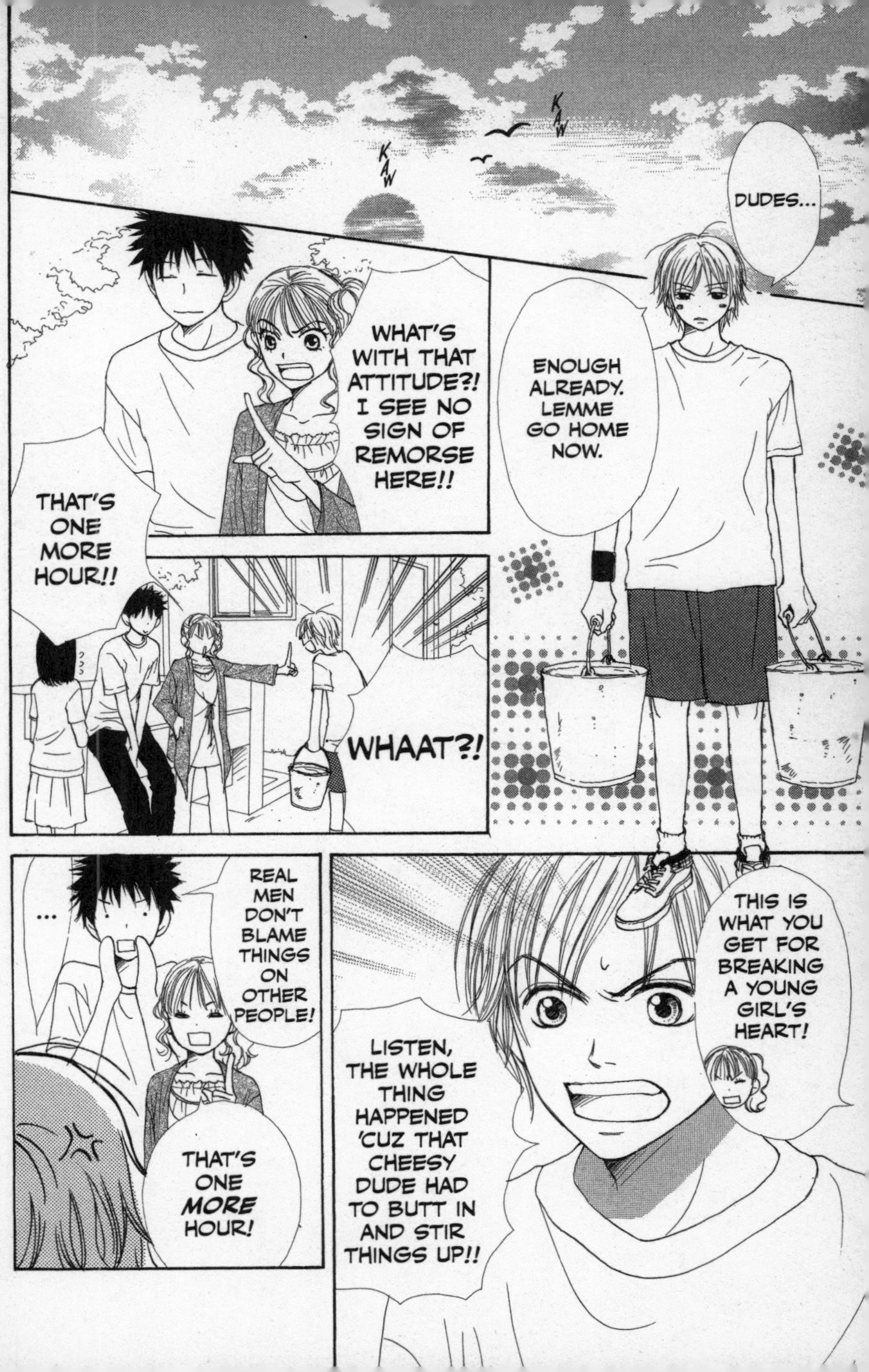
KAW
KAW
DUDES...
ENOUGH ALREADY. LEMME GO HOME NOW.
WHAT'S WITH THAT ATTITUDE?! I SEE NO SIGN OF REMORSE HERE!!
THAT'S ONE MORE HOUR!!
WHAAT?!
THIS IS WHAT YOU GET FOR BREAKING A YOUNG GIRL'S HEART!
LISTEN, THE WHOLE THING HAPPENED 'CUZ THAT CHEESY DUDE HAD TO BUTT IN AND STIR THINGS UP!!
REAL MEN DON'T BLAME THINGS ON OTHER PEOPLE!
...
THAT'S ONE *MORE* HOUR!

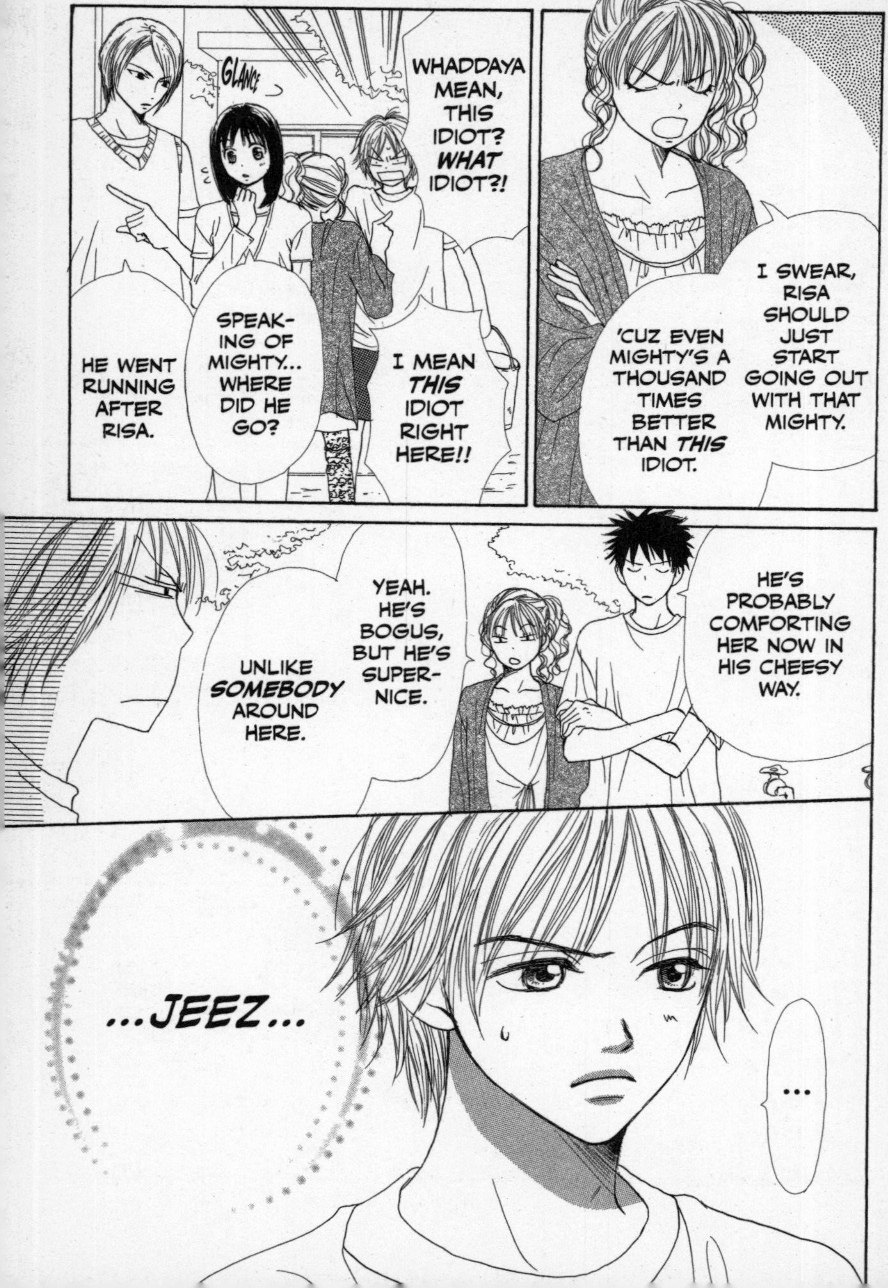
I SWEAR, RISA SHOULD JUST START GOING OUT WITH THAT MIGHTY.
'CUZ EVEN MIGHTY'S A THOUSAND TIMES BETTER THAN *THIS* IDIOT.
WHADDAYA MEAN, THIS IDIOT? *WHAT* IDIOT?!
I MEAN *THIS* IDIOT RIGHT HERE!!
GLANCE
SPEAK-ING OF MIGHTY... WHERE DID HE GO?
HE WENT RUNNING AFTER RISA.
HE'S PROBABLY COMFORTING HER NOW IN HIS CHEESY WAY.
YEAH. HE'S BOGUS, BUT HE'S SUPER-NICE.
UNLIKE *SOMEBODY* AROUND HERE.
...
...JEEZ...

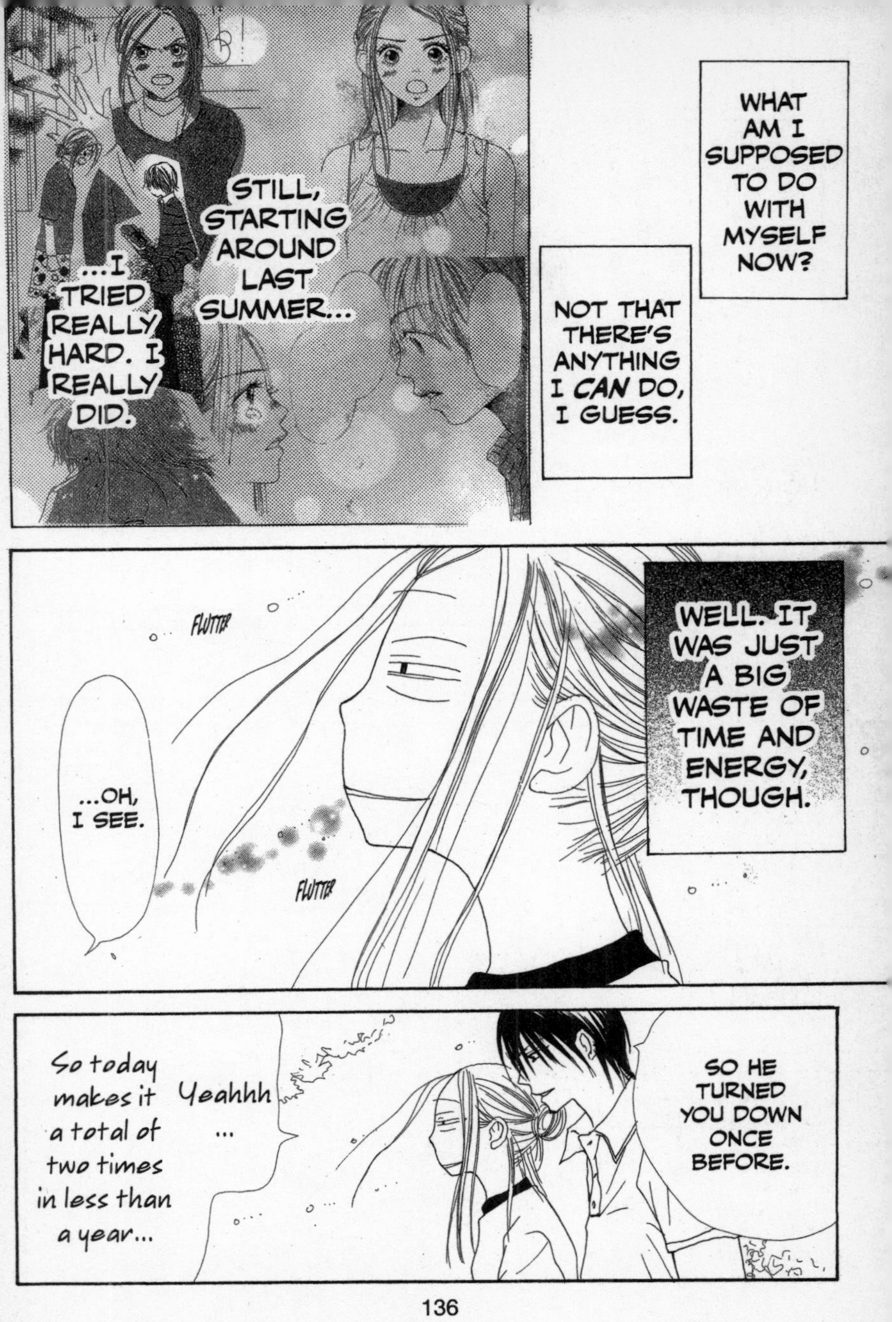
WHAT AM I SUPPOSED TO DO WITH MYSELF NOW?
NOT THAT THERE'S ANYTHING I *CAN* DO, I GUESS.
STILL, STARTING AROUND LAST SUMMER...
...I TRIED REALLY HARD. I REALLY DID.
WELL. IT WAS JUST A BIG WASTE OF TIME AND ENERGY, THOUGH.
FLUTTER
...OH, I SEE.
FLUTTER
SO HE TURNED YOU DOWN ONCE BEFORE.
Yeahhh...
So today makes it a total of two times in less than a year...

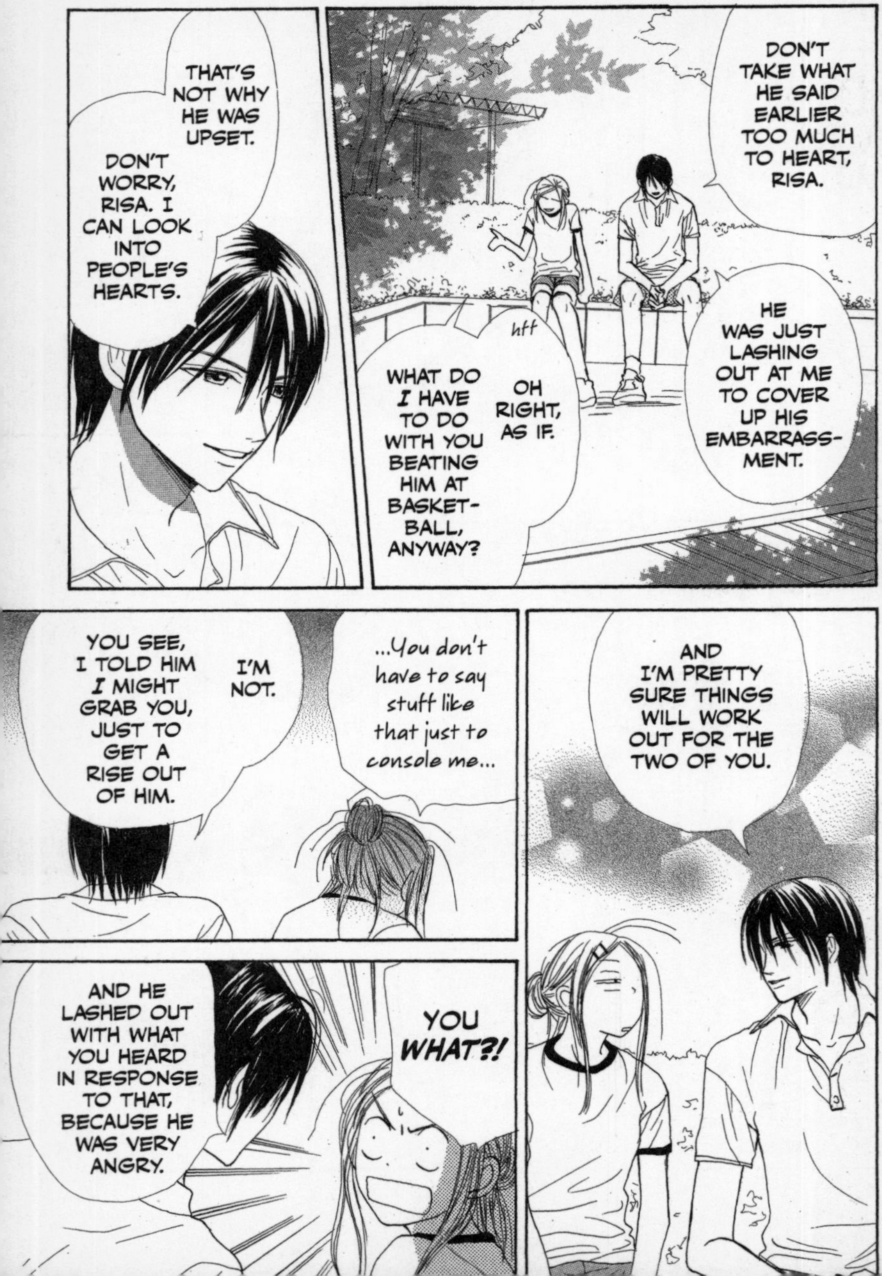
DON'T TAKE WHAT HE SAID EARLIER TOO MUCH TO HEART, RISA.
HE WAS JUST LASHING OUT AT ME TO COVER UP HIS EMBARRASSMENT.
hff
OH RIGHT, AS IF.
WHAT DO *I* HAVE TO DO WITH YOU BEATING HIM AT BASKETBALL, ANYWAY?
THAT'S NOT WHY HE WAS UPSET.
DON'T WORRY, RISA. I CAN LOOK INTO PEOPLE'S HEARTS.
AND I'M PRETTY SURE THINGS WILL WORK OUT FOR THE TWO OF YOU.
...You don't have to say stuff like that just to console me...
I'M NOT.
YOU SEE, I TOLD HIM *I* MIGHT GRAB YOU, JUST TO GET A RISE OUT OF HIM.
YOU *WHAT?!*
AND HE LASHED OUT WITH WHAT YOU HEARD IN RESPONSE TO THAT, BECAUSE HE WAS VERY ANGRY.

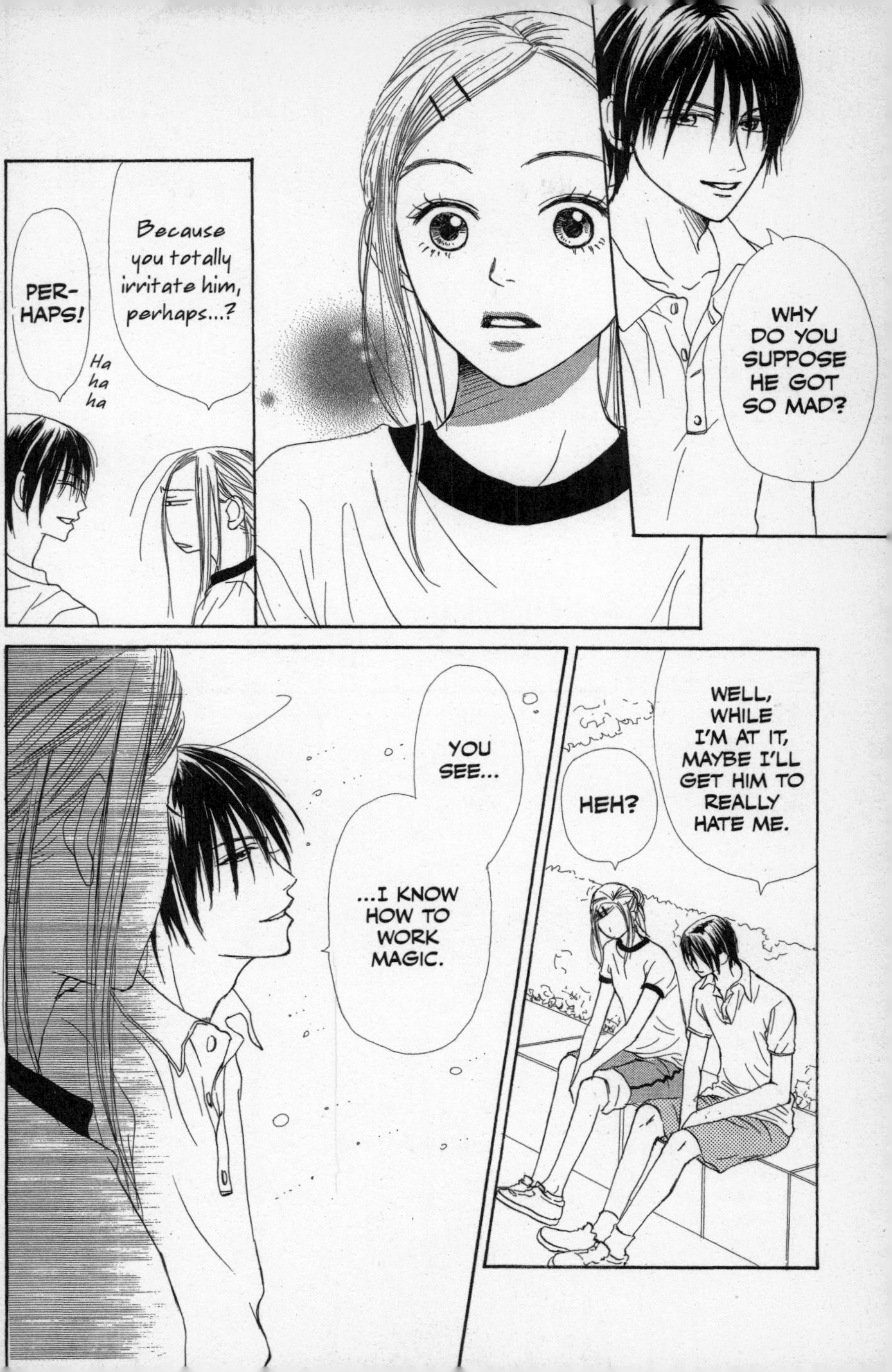
WHY DO YOU SUPPOSE HE GOT SO MAD?
Because you totally irritate him, perhaps...?
PER-HAPS!
Ha ha ha
WELL, WHILE I'M AT IT, MAYBE I'LL GET HIM TO REALLY HATE ME.
HEH?
YOU SEE...
...I KNOW HOW TO WORK MAGIC.

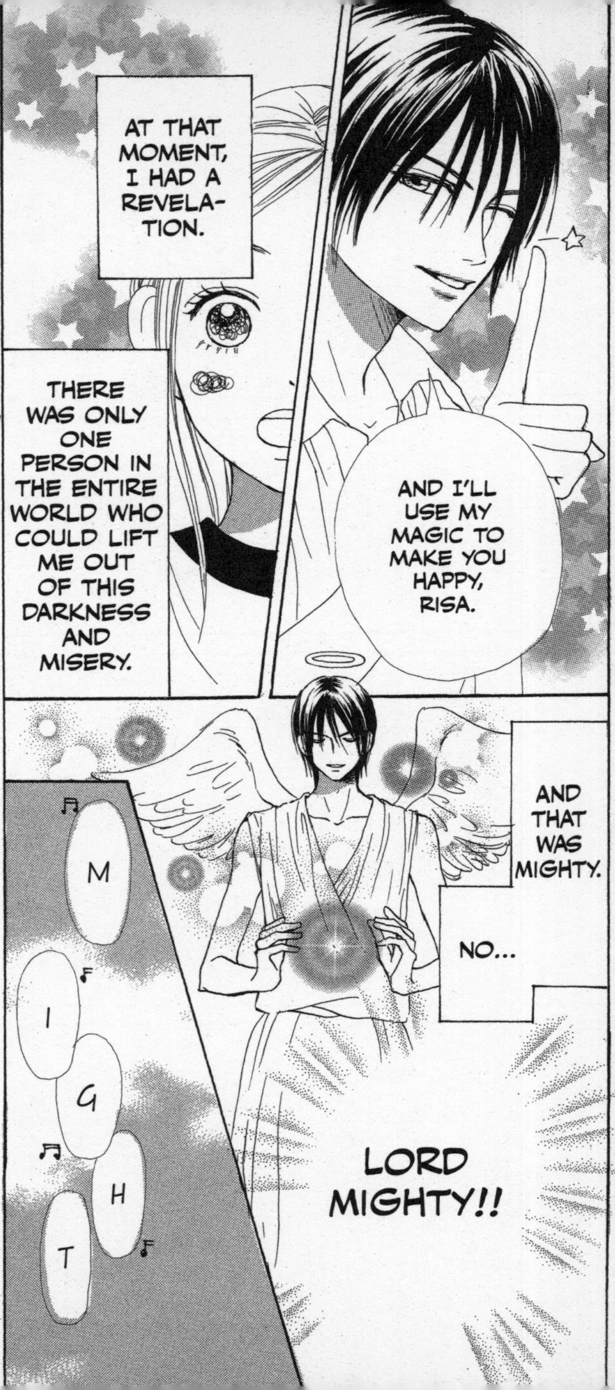
AT THAT MOMENT, I HAD A REVELATION.
AND I'LL USE MY MAGIC TO MAKE YOU HAPPY, RISA.
THERE WAS ONLY ONE PERSON IN THE ENTIRE WORLD WHO COULD LIFT ME OUT OF THIS DARKNESS AND MISERY.
AND THAT WAS MIGHTY.
NO...
LORD MIGHTY!!
M
I
G
H
T

4

This is something that is really ho-hum-who-cares, but I'm not too crazy about how the kanji for "like/love" (suki, 好き) looks, so I consciously avoid using it in my manga and write the word out in hiragana. I mean, it's a combination of "woman" and "child"!

I don't like the kanji for ore (a male form of I) either.

俺
↑
Don't you think this part is insect-like? Like a bug's tail.

俺

Eeeeeuwww!! Gross!!

And so, from pretty far back, I've been writing this word in katakana. I think it's cuter that way...

Oh gosh, who cares?! This really was a ho-hum-who-cares topic!! It's boring! You are so boring, Aya!

Wait, no, you see, I wanted people to know I'm not just some ignoramus who doesn't know her kanji. These are deliberate choices!!

So anyway...

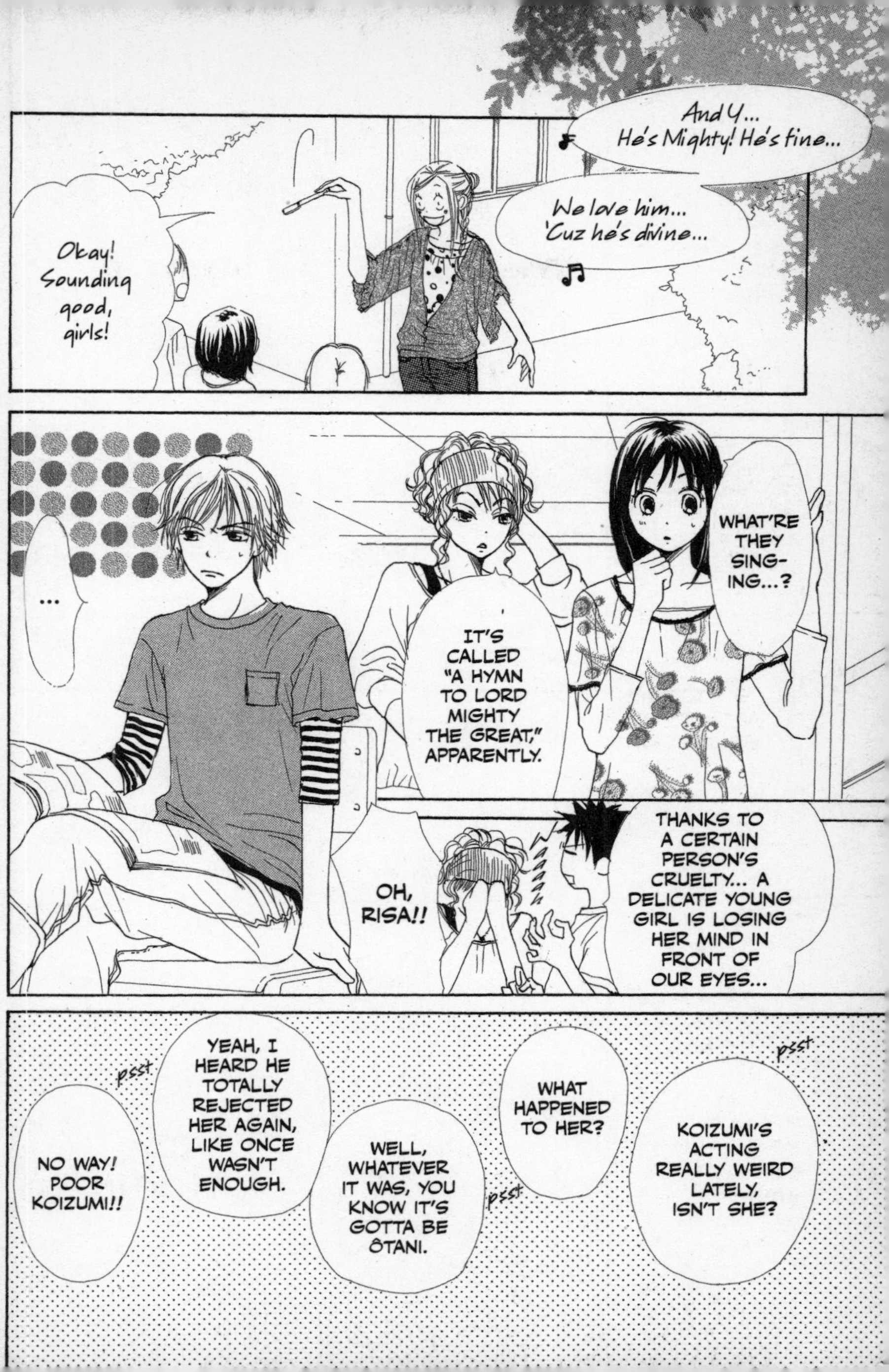
And Y... He's Mighty! He's fine...
We love him... 'Cuz he's divine...
Okay! Sounding good, girls!
WHAT'RE THEY SINGING...?
IT'S CALLED "A HYMN TO LORD MIGHTY THE GREAT," APPARENTLY.
THANKS TO A CERTAIN PERSON'S CRUELTY... A DELICATE YOUNG GIRL IS LOSING HER MIND IN FRONT OF OUR EYES...
OH, RISA!!
...
psst
KOIZUMI'S ACTING REALLY WEIRD LATELY, ISN'T SHE?
WHAT HAPPENED TO HER?
psst
WELL, WHATEVER IT WAS, YOU KNOW IT'S GOTTA BE ÔTANI.
YEAH, I HEARD HE TOTALLY REJECTED HER AGAIN, LIKE ONCE WASN'T ENOUGH.
psst
NO WAY! POOR KOIZUMI!!

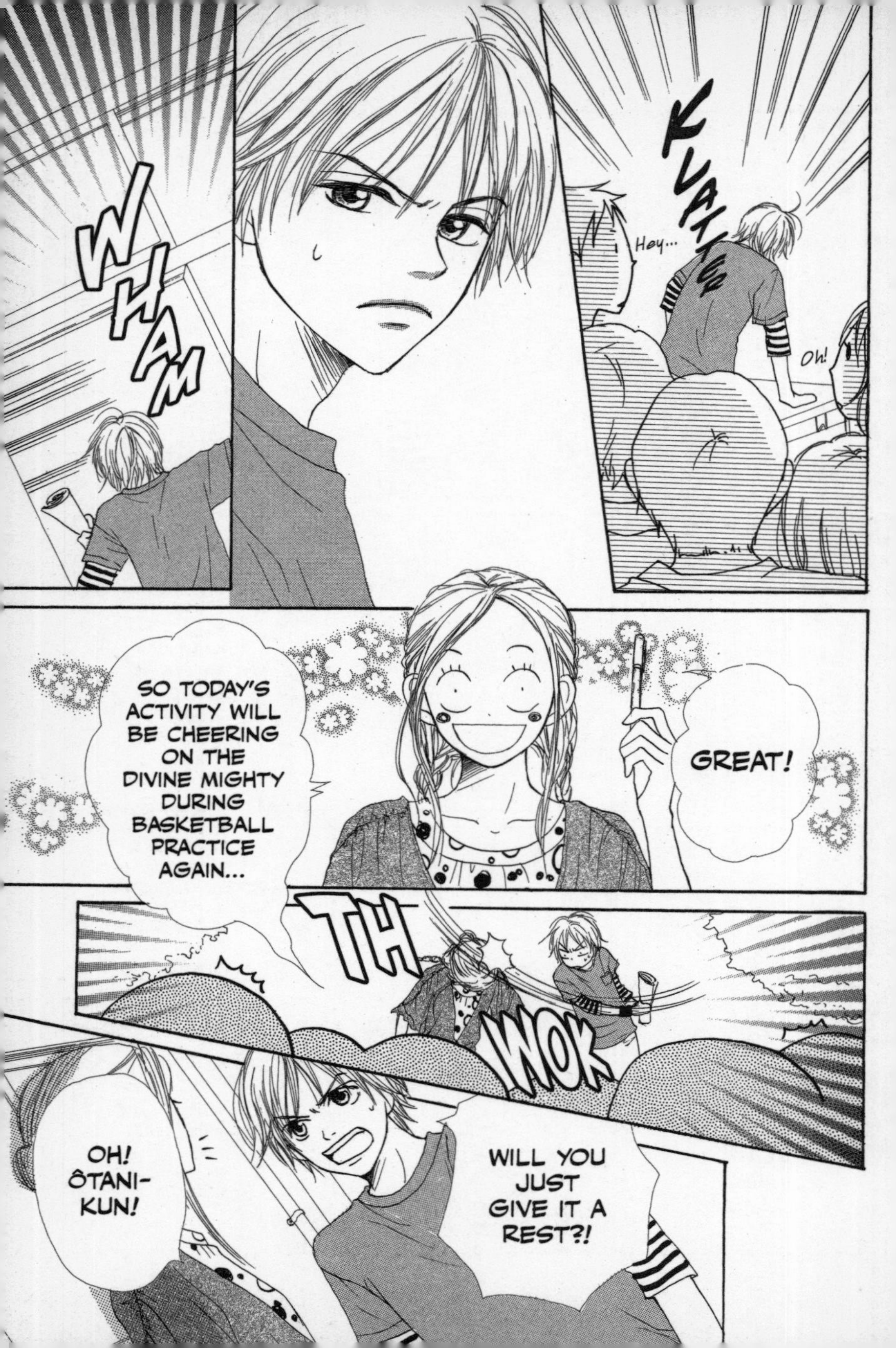
KLATTER
Hey...
Oh!
WHAM
SO TODAY'S ACTIVITY WILL BE CHEERING ON THE DIVINE MIGHTY DURING BASKETBALL PRACTICE AGAIN...
GREAT!
THWOK
WILL YOU JUST GIVE IT A REST?!
OH! ŌTANI-KUN!

KUN...?
BOW
HOPE YOU DO BETTER IN BASKET-BALL PRACTICE TODAY!
OKAY, SO LET'S ALL MEET IN THE GYM AT—
LISTEN TO ME, DOPE!!
THAT THING YOU HEARD ME SAY THE OTHER DAY—
YES?
When was that?
OH, GOOD.
JUST THE PEOPLE I WAS LOOKING FOR.
HAND THESE OUT BEFORE THE NEXT PERIOD STARTS, WILL YOU?
YESSIR! I'LL BE HAPPY TO!
BLINK BLINK
I DON'T GET IT. WHAT'S THE JOKE?
BLINK BLINK
DON'T ASK ME!!

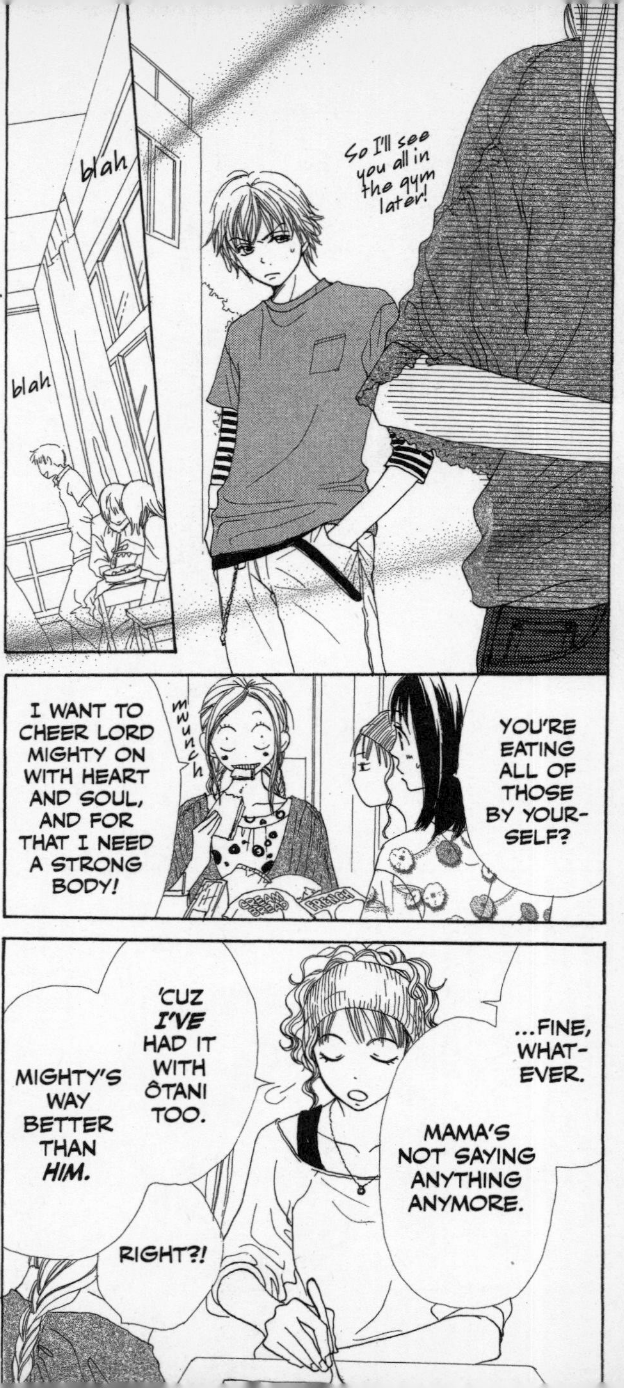
So I'll see you all in the gym later!
blah
blah
YOU'RE EATING ALL OF THOSE BY YOURSELF?
mwunch
I WANT TO CHEER LORD MIGHTY ON WITH HEART AND SOUL, AND FOR THAT I NEED A STRONG BODY!
CREAM BREAD
FRENCH
...FINE, WHATEVER.
MAMA'S NOT SAYING ANYTHING ANYMORE.
'CUZ *I'VE* HAD IT WITH ŌTANI TOO.
MIGHTY'S WAY BETTER THAN *HIM.*
RIGHT?!

5

Phooo...

This is the last one. But there are a couple bonus pages at the end. They're a report about the time I went on the radio.

What with one thing and another, I've been going quite a few times a month to Tokyo for work (I live in Osaka). I always take my unfinished manga installments with me... and work on them in dim hotel rooms...

Which makes me sound super-busy and kinda cool, but actually I'm just a very slow worker. hahahahaha

Well then, I hope to see you again. Next up is Volume 7. Time for the seventh-inning stretch! Want to release some balloons?

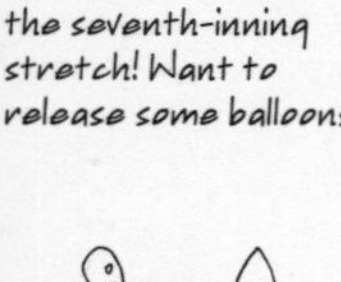
PWEE

Who'd believe a professional manga artist drew these balloons?

Bye!!

September 2003

Aya

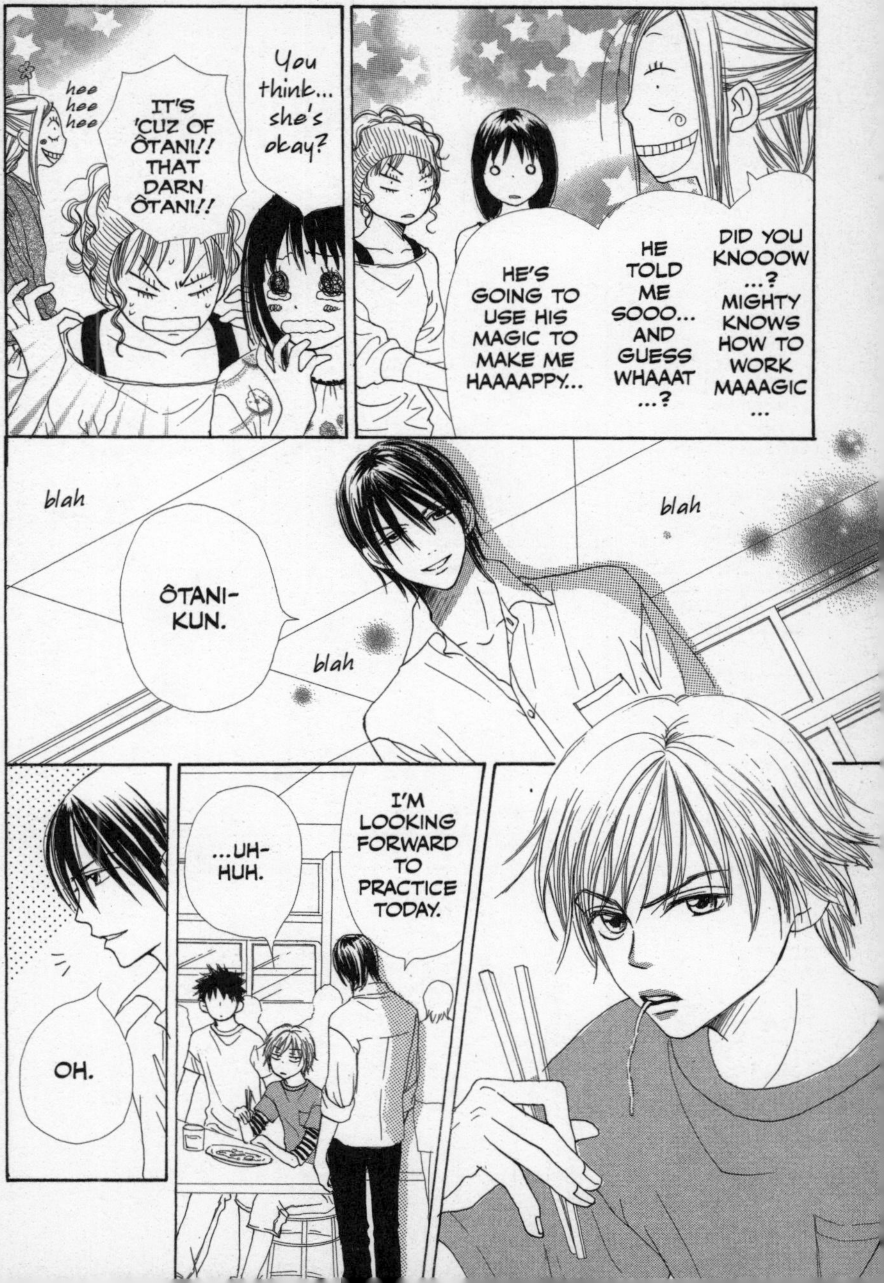
DID YOU KNOOOW...? MIGHTY KNOWS HOW TO WORK MAAAGIC...
HE TOLD ME SOOO... AND GUESS WHAAAT...?
HE'S GOING TO USE HIS MAGIC TO MAKE ME HAAAAPPY...
You think... she's okay?
IT'S 'CUZ OF ÔTANI!! THAT DARN ÔTANI!!
hee hee hee
blah
blah
ÔTANI-KUN.
blah
I'M LOOKING FORWARD TO PRACTICE TODAY.
...UH-HUH.
OH.

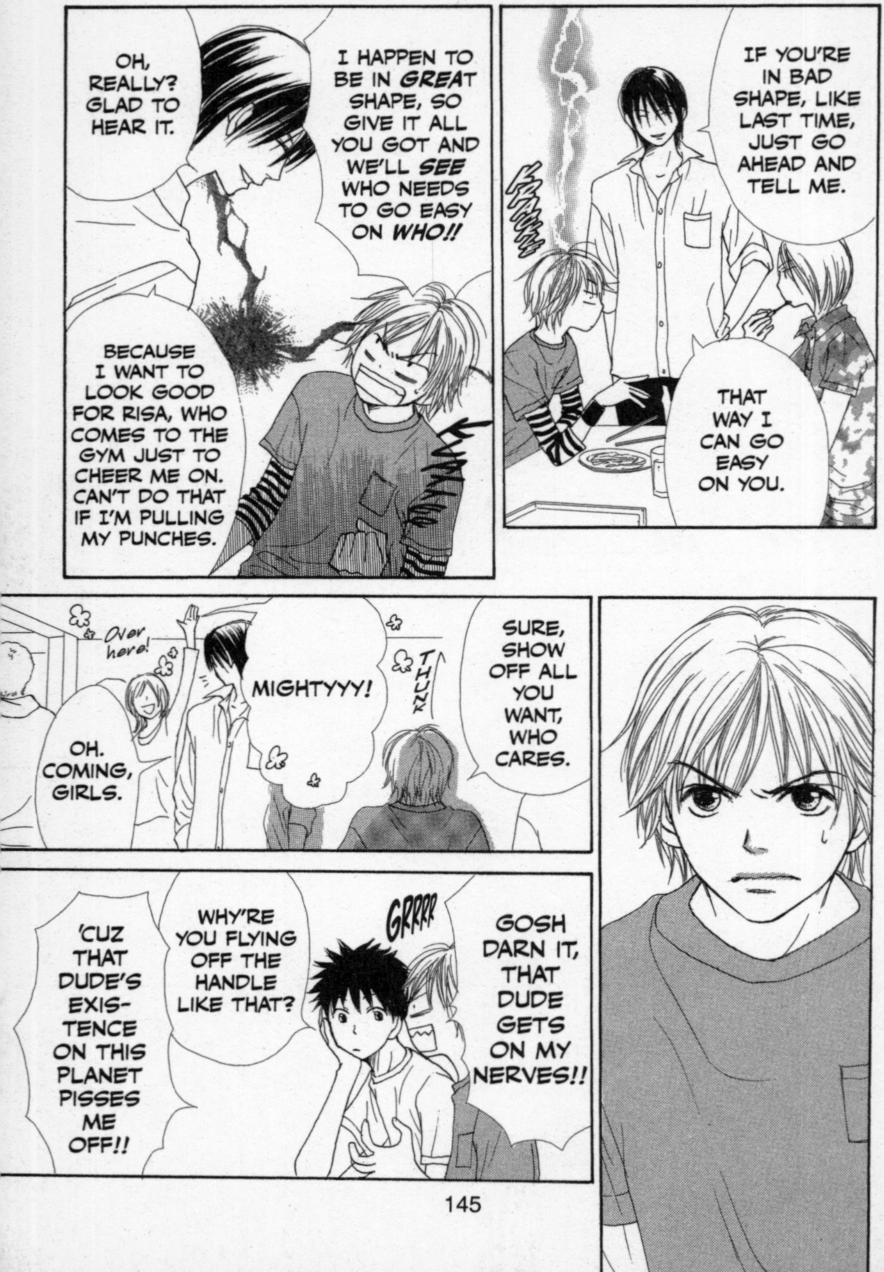
IF YOU'RE IN BAD SHAPE, LIKE LAST TIME, JUST GO AHEAD AND TELL ME.
THAT WAY I CAN GO EASY ON YOU.
I HAPPEN TO BE IN GREAT SHAPE, SO GIVE IT ALL YOU GOT AND WE'LL SEE WHO NEEDS TO GO EASY ON WHO!!
OH, REALLY? GLAD TO HEAR IT.
BECAUSE I WANT TO LOOK GOOD FOR RISA, WHO COMES TO THE GYM JUST TO CHEER ME ON. CAN'T DO THAT IF I'M PULLING MY PUNCHES.
SURE, SHOW OFF ALL YOU WANT, WHO CARES.
THUNK
MIGHTYYY!
Over here!
OH. COMING, GIRLS.
GOSH DARN IT, THAT DUDE GETS ON MY NERVES!!
GRRRR
WHY'RE YOU FLYING OFF THE HANDLE LIKE THAT?
'CUZ THAT DUDE'S EXIS- TENCE ON THIS PLANET PISSES ME OFF!!

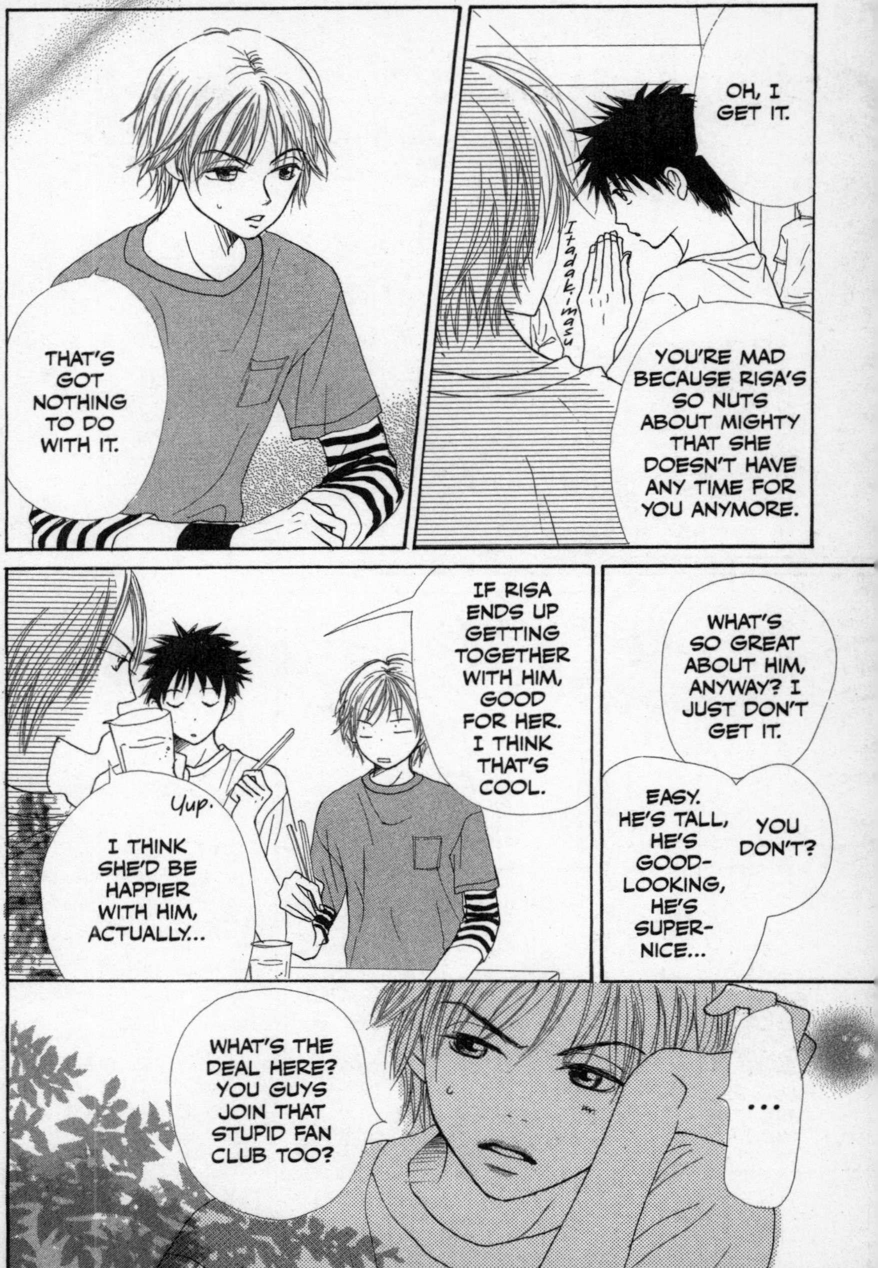
OH, I GET IT.
Itadakimasu
YOU'RE MAD BECAUSE RISA'S SO NUTS ABOUT MIGHTY THAT SHE DOESN'T HAVE ANY TIME FOR YOU ANYMORE.
THAT'S GOT NOTHING TO DO WITH IT.
WHAT'S SO GREAT ABOUT HIM, ANYWAY? I JUST DON'T GET IT.
YOU DON'T?
EASY. HE'S TALL, HE'S GOOD-LOOKING, HE'S SUPER-NICE...
IF RISA ENDS UP GETTING TOGETHER WITH HIM, GOOD FOR HER. I THINK THAT'S COOL.
Yup.
I THINK SHE'D BE HAPPIER WITH HIM, ACTUALLY...
...
WHAT'S THE DEAL HERE? YOU GUYS JOIN THAT STUPID FAN CLUB TOO?

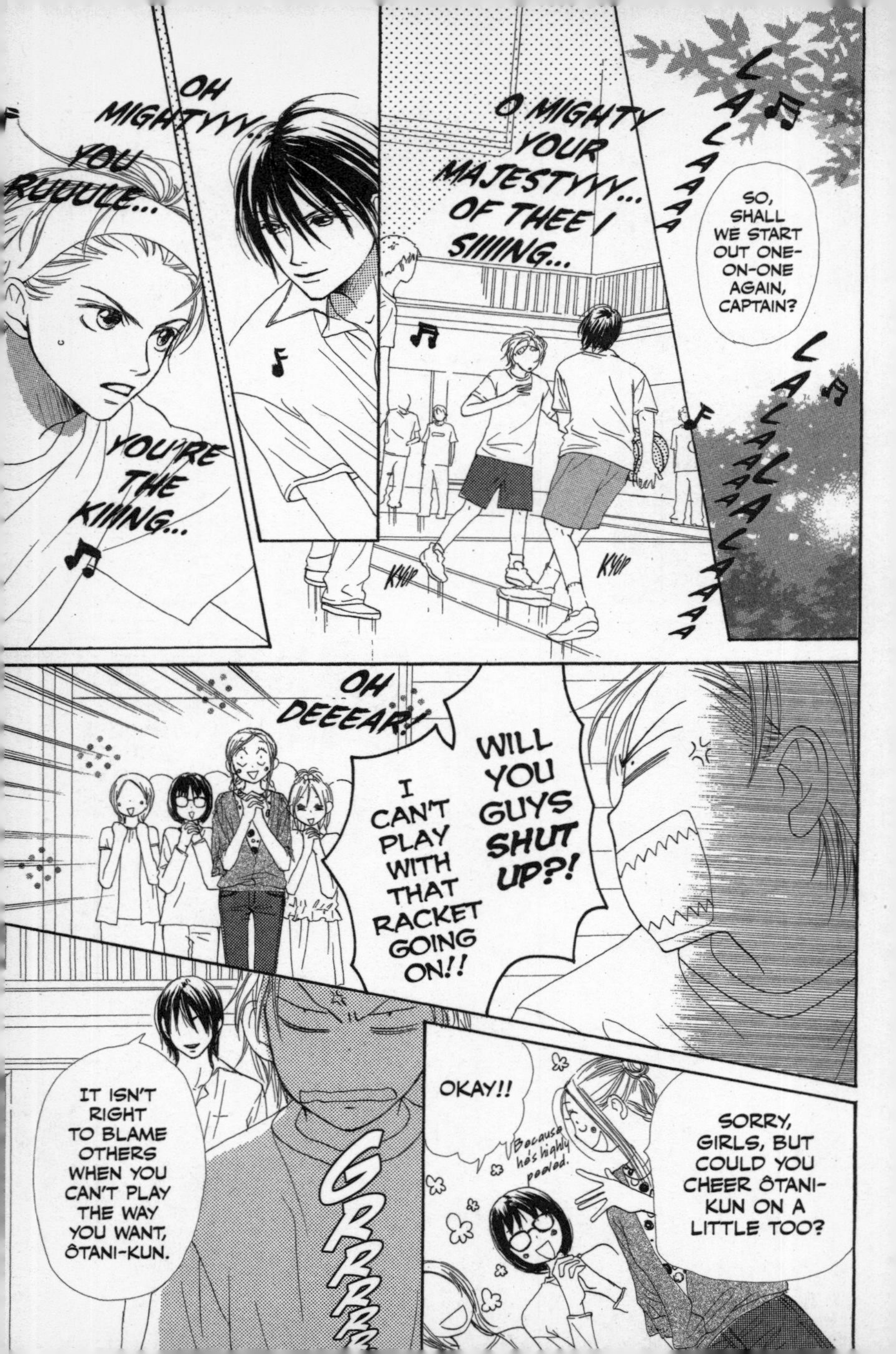

LALAAAAAA
SO, SHALL WE START OUT ONE-ON-ONE AGAIN, CAPTAIN?
LALALAAAAAAA
O MIGHTY YOUR MAJESTYYY... OF THEE I SIIIING...
KYUP
KYUP
OH MIGHTYYY...
YOU RUUULE...
YOU'RE THE KIIING...
WILL YOU GUYS SHUT UP?!
I CAN'T PLAY WITH THAT RACKET GOING ON!!
OH DEEEAR!
SORRY, GIRLS, BUT COULD YOU CHEER ŌTANI-KUN ON A LITTLE TOO?
OKAY!!
Because he's highly peeved.
IT ISN'T RIGHT TO BLAME OTHERS WHEN YOU CAN'T PLAY THE WAY YOU WANT, ŌTANI-KUN.
GRRRR

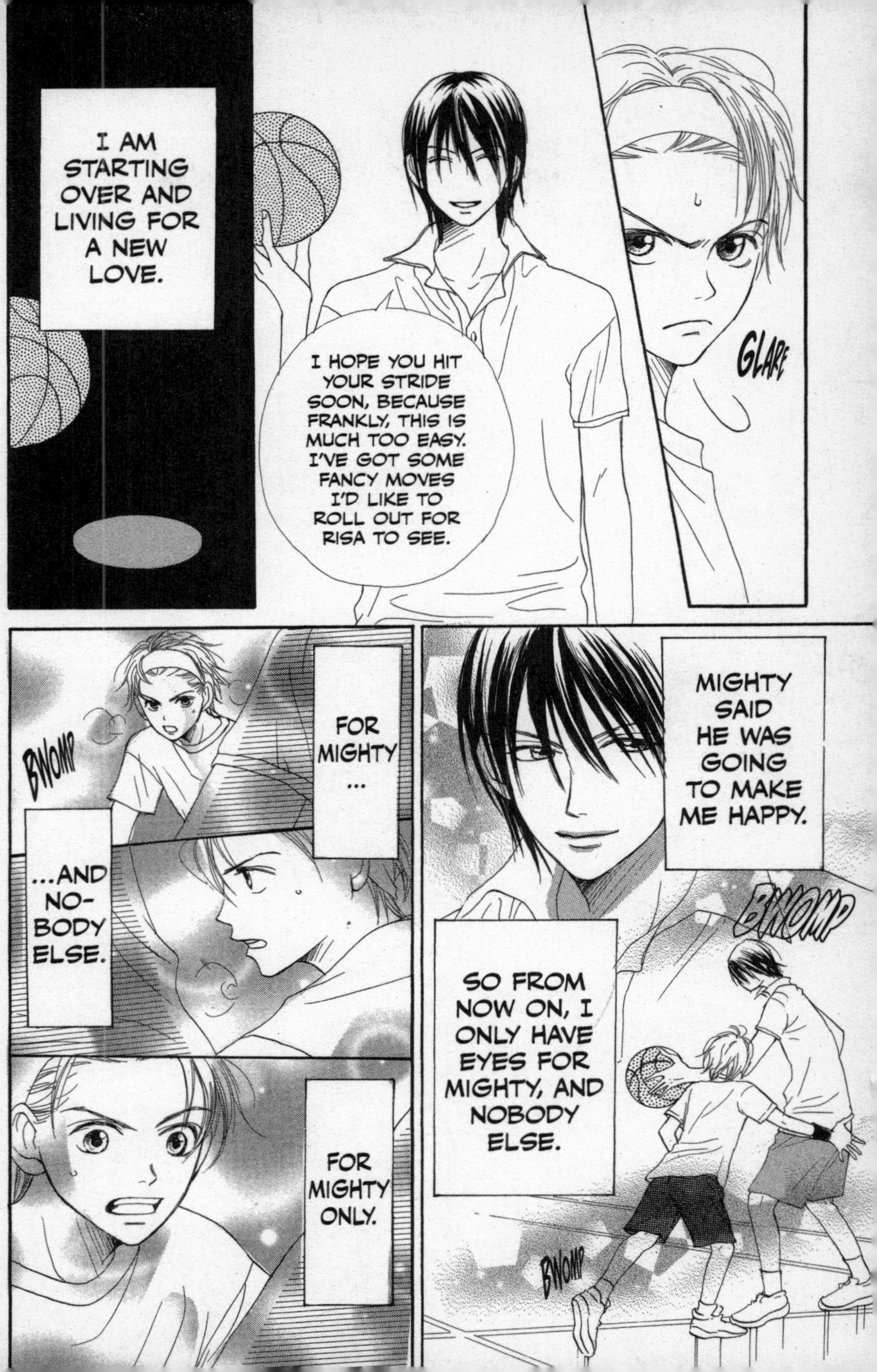
GLARE
I HOPE YOU HIT YOUR STRIDE SOON, BECAUSE FRANKLY, THIS IS MUCH TOO EASY. I'VE GOT SOME FANCY MOVES I'D LIKE TO ROLL OUT FOR RISA TO SEE.
I AM STARTING OVER AND LIVING FOR A NEW LOVE.
MIGHTY SAID HE WAS GOING TO MAKE ME HAPPY.
BWOMP
SO FROM NOW ON, I ONLY HAVE EYES FOR MIGHTY, AND NOBODY ELSE.
BWOMP
FOR MIGHTY ...
BWOMP
...AND NO-BODY ELSE.
FOR MIGHTY ONLY.

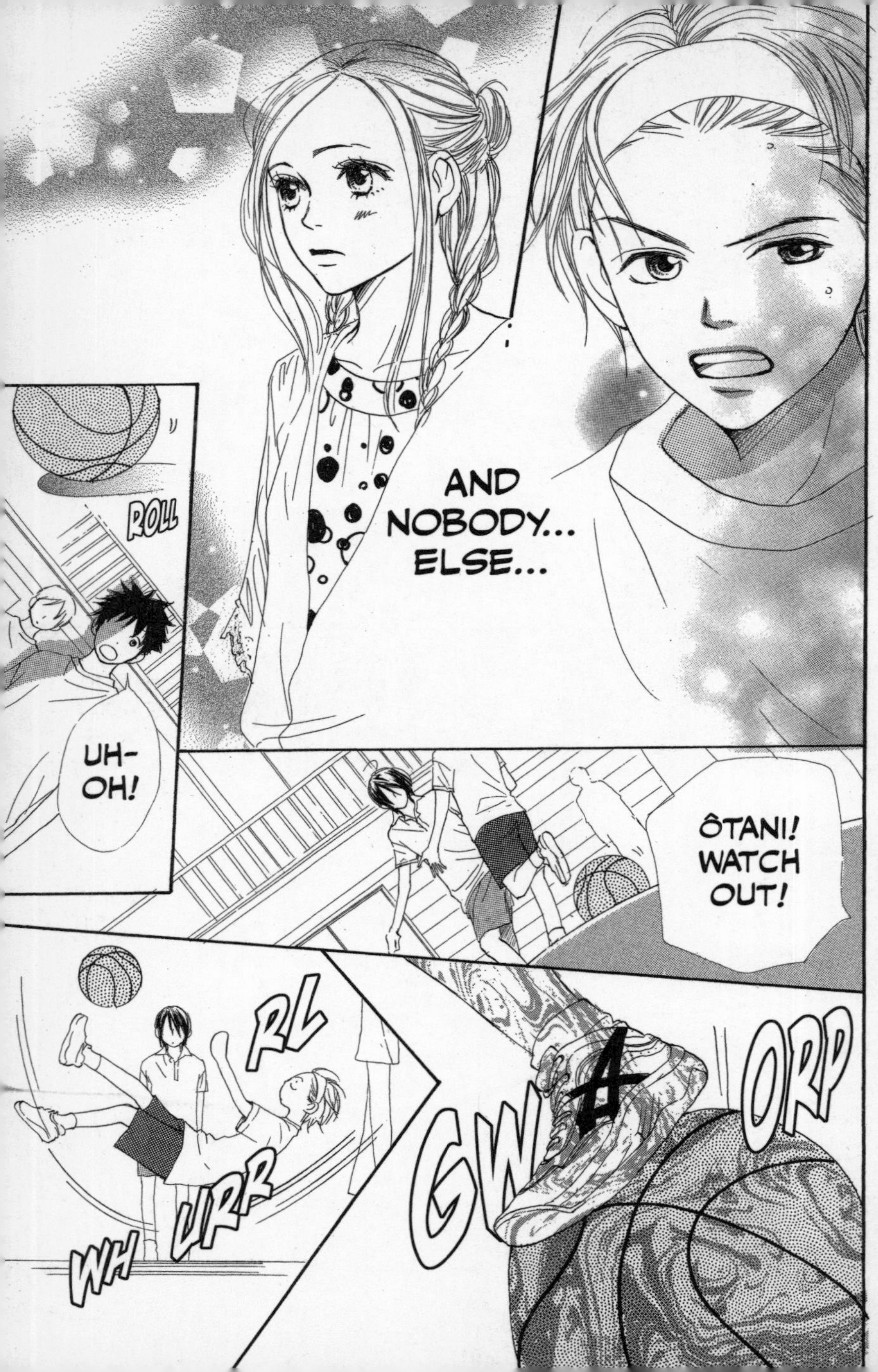
AND NOBODY... ELSE...
ROLL
UH-OH!
ÔTANI! WATCH OUT!
GW
A
ORP
WH
URR
RL

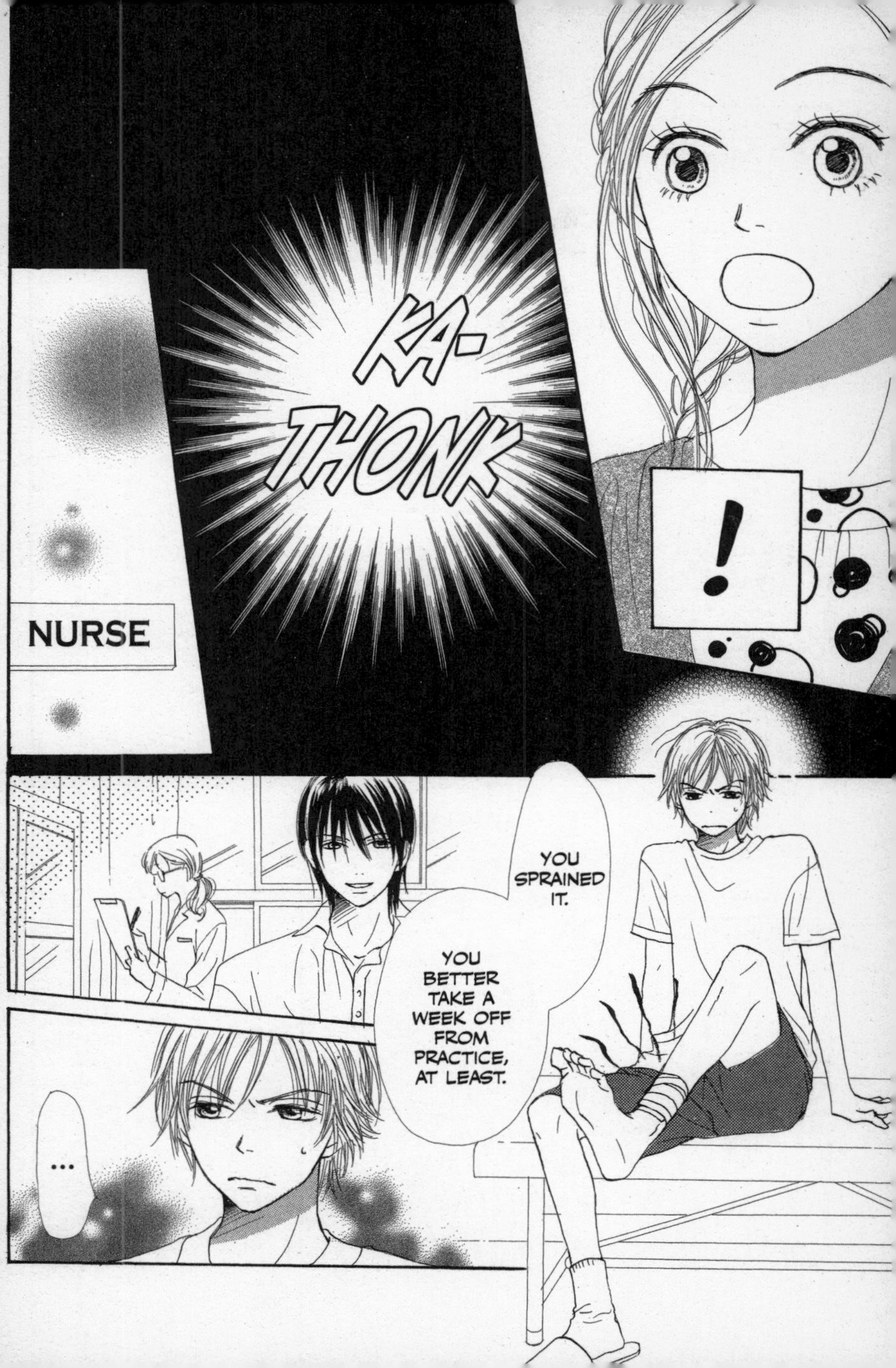
!
KA-THONK
NURSE
YOU SPRAINED IT.
YOU BETTER TAKE A WEEK OFF FROM PRACTICE, AT LEAST.
...

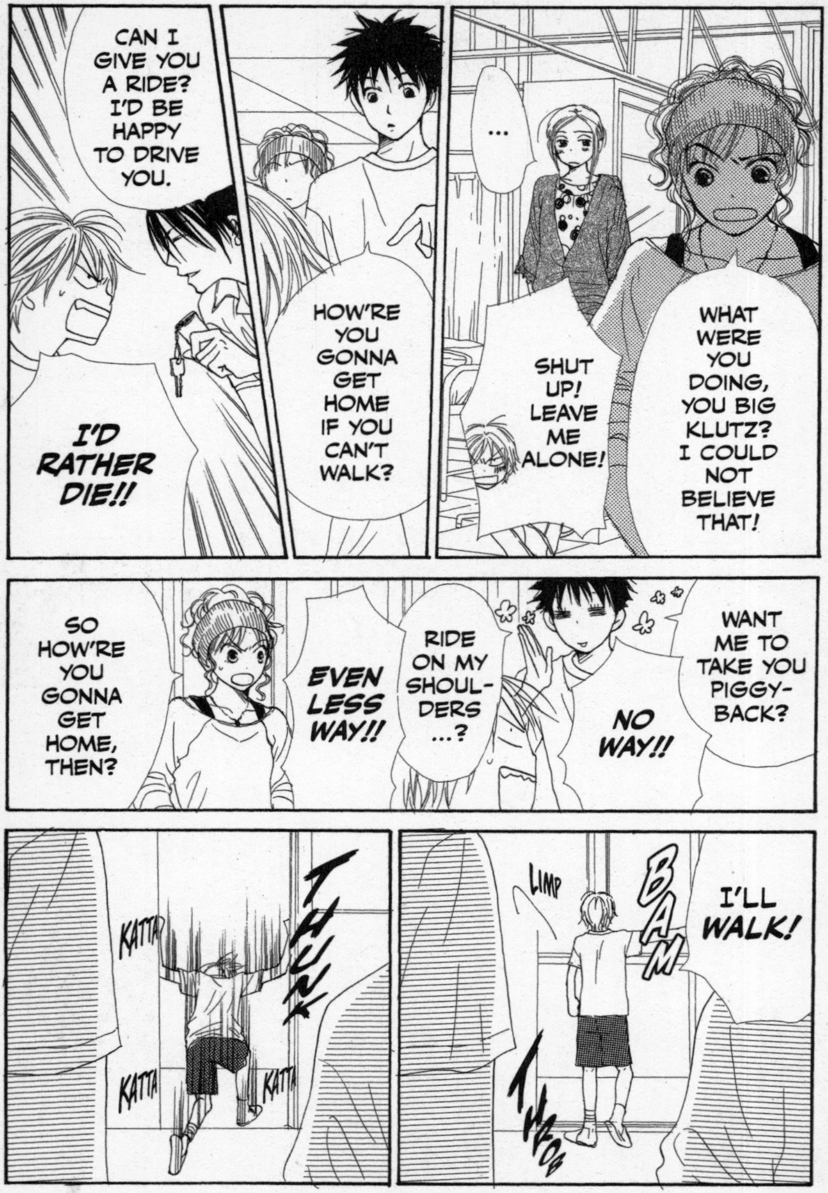

WHAT WERE YOU DOING, YOU BIG KLUTZ? I COULD NOT BELIEVE THAT!
SHUT UP! LEAVE ME ALONE!
...
HOW'RE YOU GONNA GET HOME IF YOU CAN'T WALK?
CAN I GIVE YOU A RIDE? I'D BE HAPPY TO DRIVE YOU.
I'D RATHER DIE!!
WANT ME TO TAKE YOU PIGGY-BACK?
NO WAY!!
RIDE ON MY SHOUL-DERS ...?
EVEN LESS WAY!!
SO HOW'RE YOU GONNA GET HOME, THEN?
I'LL WALK!
BAM
LIMP
THUNK
KATTA
KATTA
KATTA

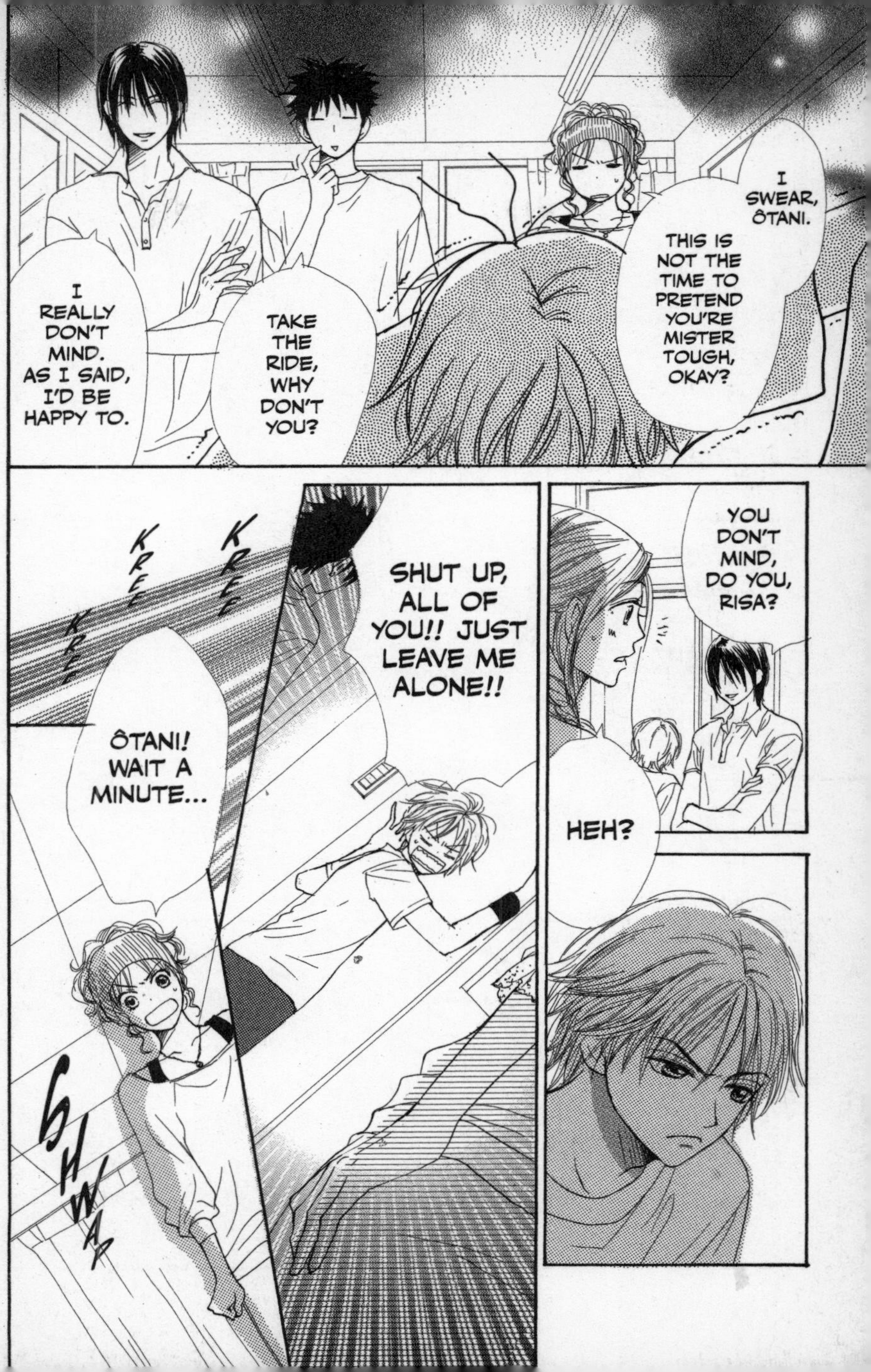
I SWEAR, ÔTANI.
THIS IS NOT THE TIME TO PRETEND YOU'RE MISTER TOUGH, OKAY?
TAKE THE RIDE, WHY DON'T YOU?
I REALLY DON'T MIND. AS I SAID, I'D BE HAPPY TO.
YOU DON'T MIND, DO YOU, RISA?
HEH?
SHUT UP, ALL OF YOU!! JUST LEAVE ME ALONE!!
KREE
KREE
KREE
ÔTANI! WAIT A MINUTE...
SHWAP

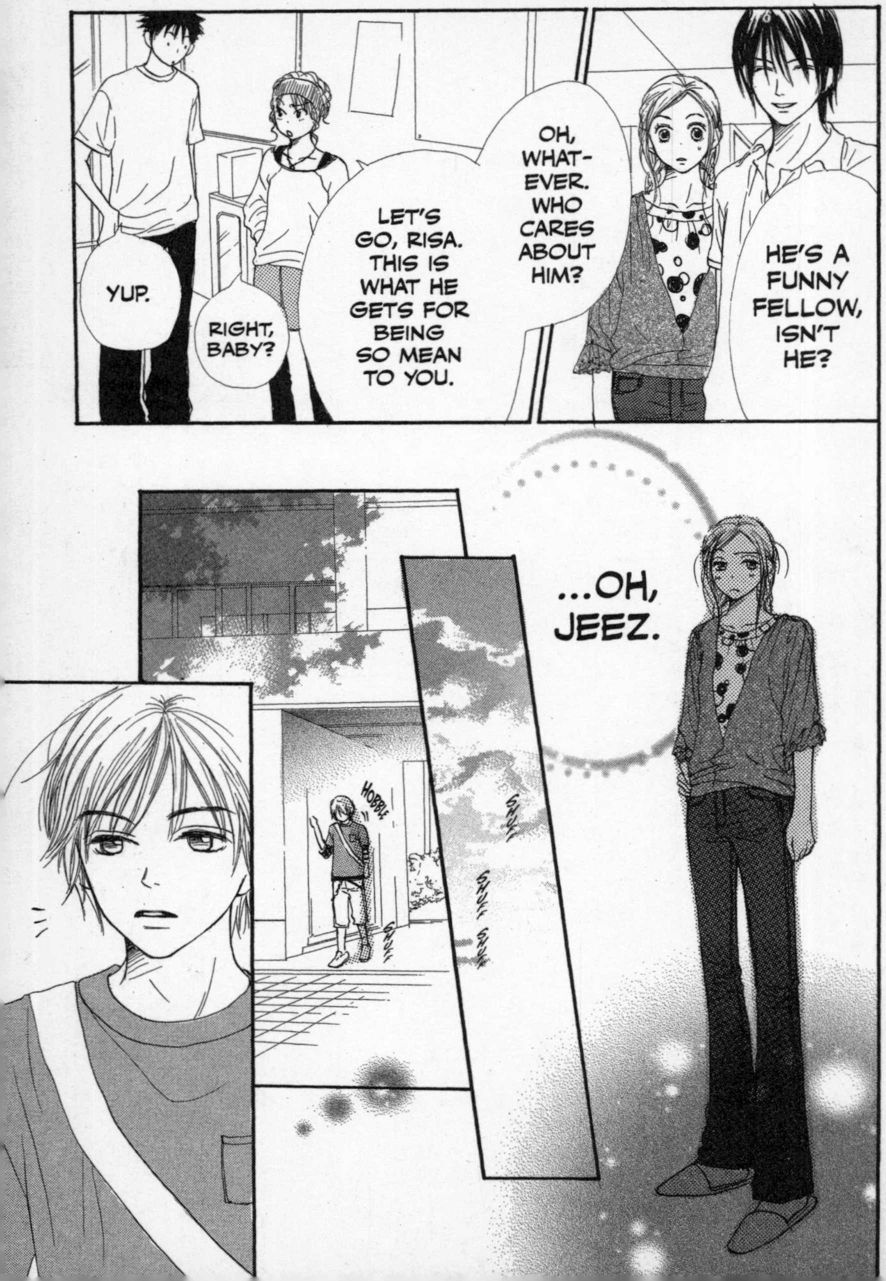
HE'S A FUNNY FELLOW, ISN'T HE?
OH, WHAT-EVER. WHO CARES ABOUT HIM?
LET'S GO, RISA. THIS IS WHAT HE GETS FOR BEING SO MEAN TO YOU.
RIGHT, BABY?
YUP.
...OH, JEEZ.
SHUFF
SHUFF
SHUFF
SHUFF
HOBBLE

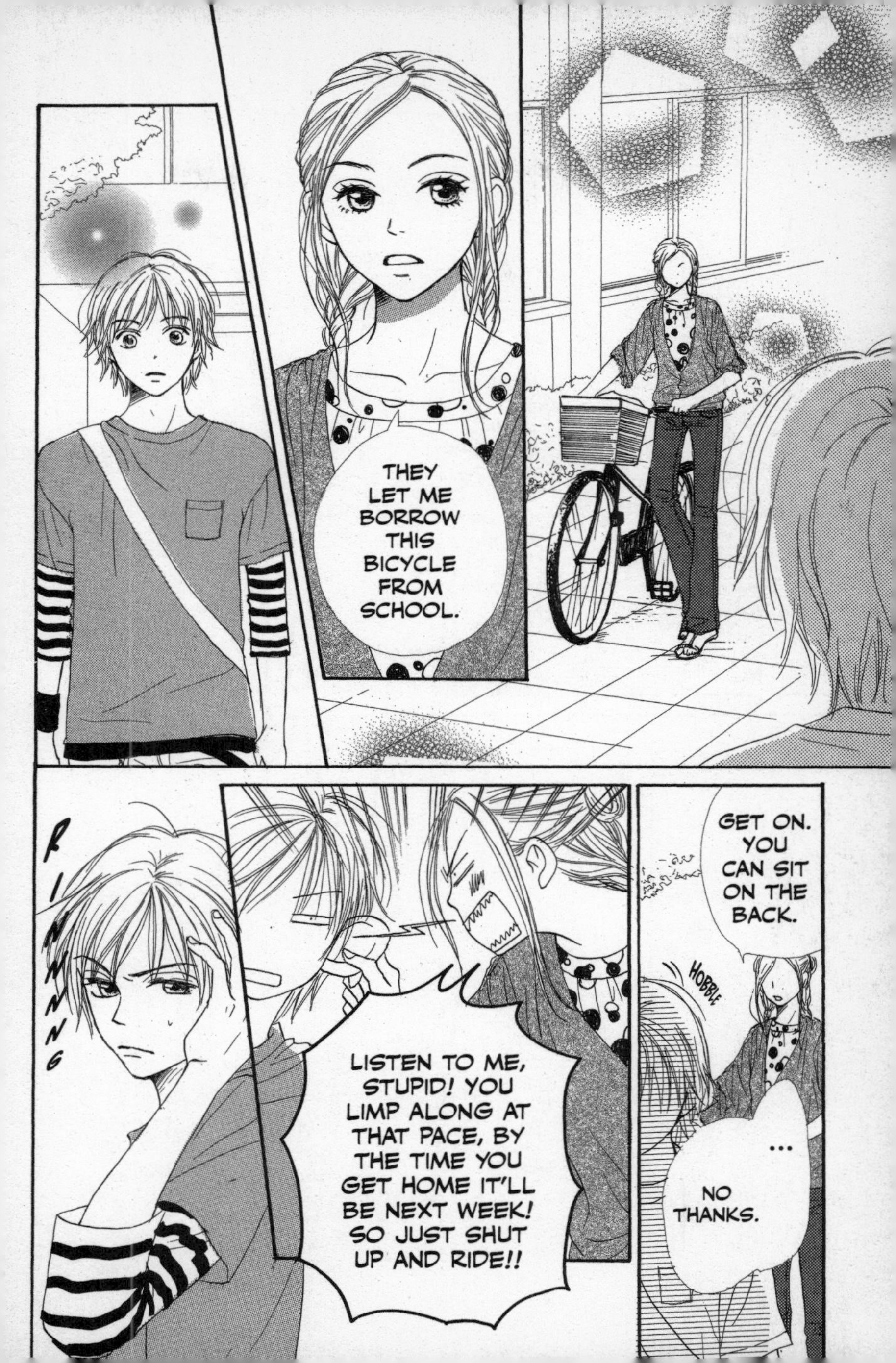
THEY LET ME BORROW THIS BICYCLE FROM SCHOOL.
GET ON. YOU CAN SIT ON THE BACK.
HOBBLE
...
NO THANKS.
LISTEN TO ME, STUPID! YOU LIMP ALONG AT THAT PACE, BY THE TIME YOU GET HOME IT'LL BE NEXT WEEK! SO JUST SHUT UP AND RIDE!!
RINNNNG

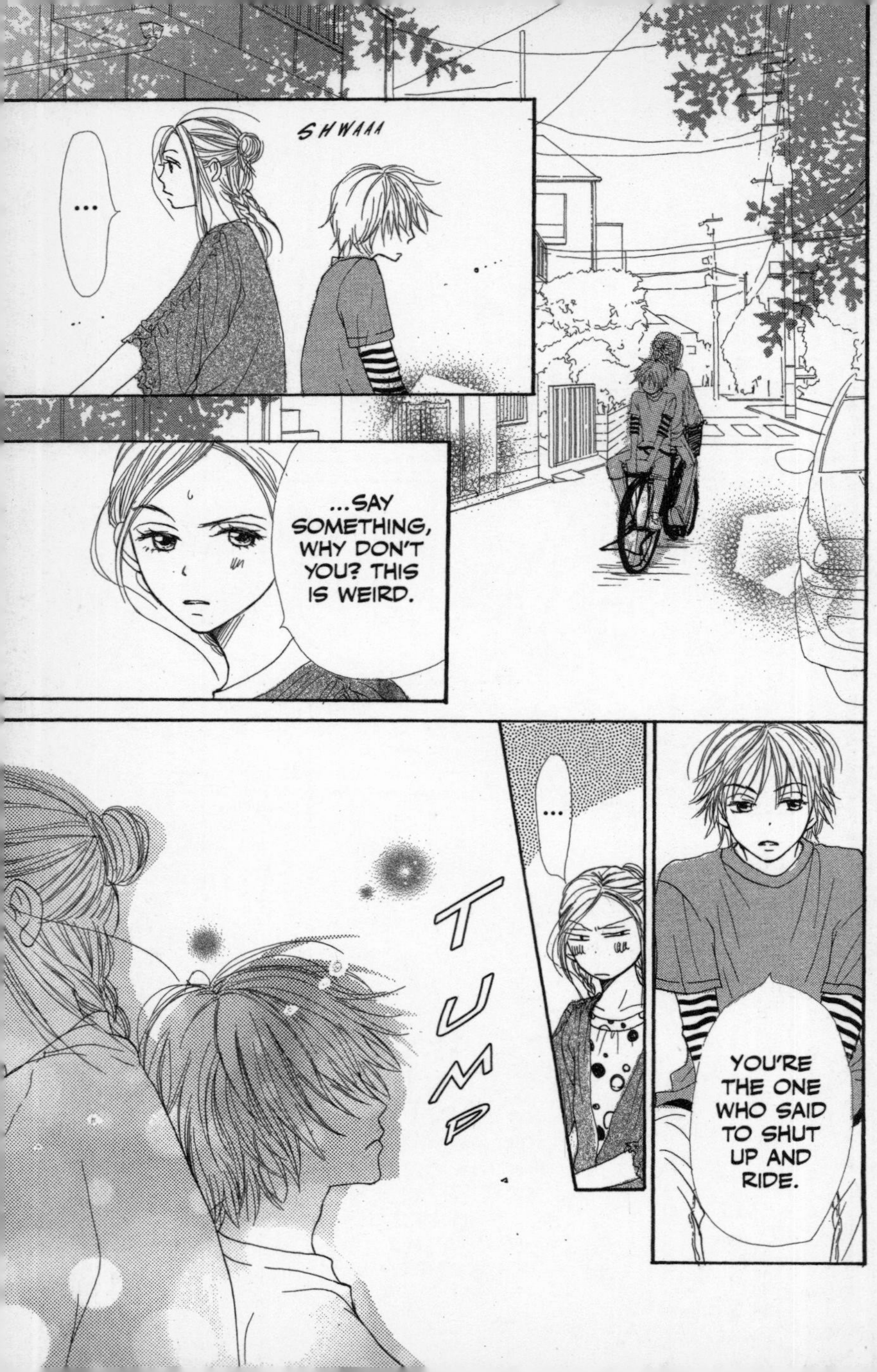
SHWAAA
...
...
...
...SAY SOMETHING, WHY DON'T YOU? THIS IS WEIRD.
YOU'RE THE ONE WHO SAID TO SHUT UP AND RIDE.
...
TUMP

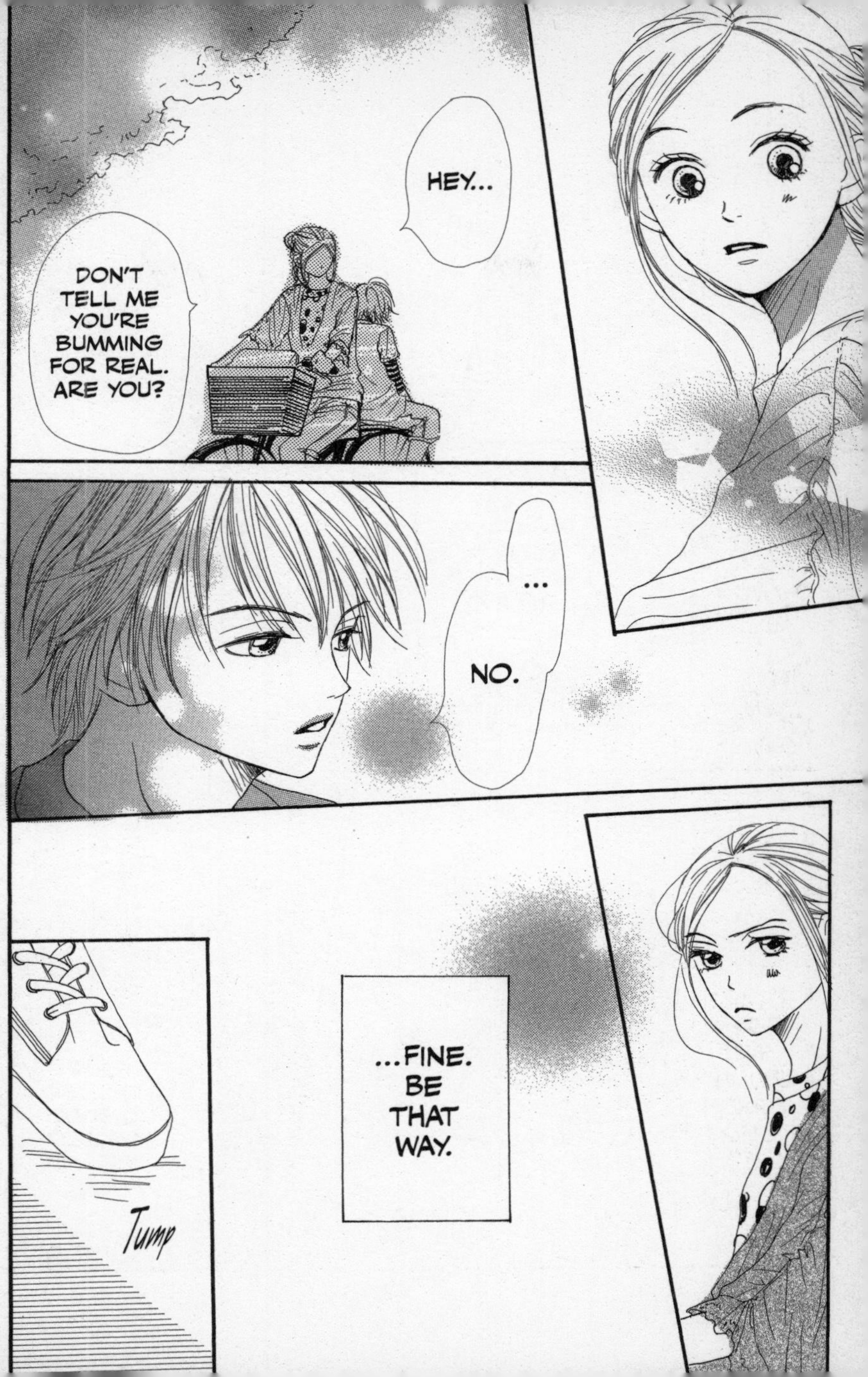
HEY...
DON'T TELL ME YOU'RE BUMMING FOR REAL. ARE YOU?
... NO.
...FINE. BE THAT WAY.
Tump

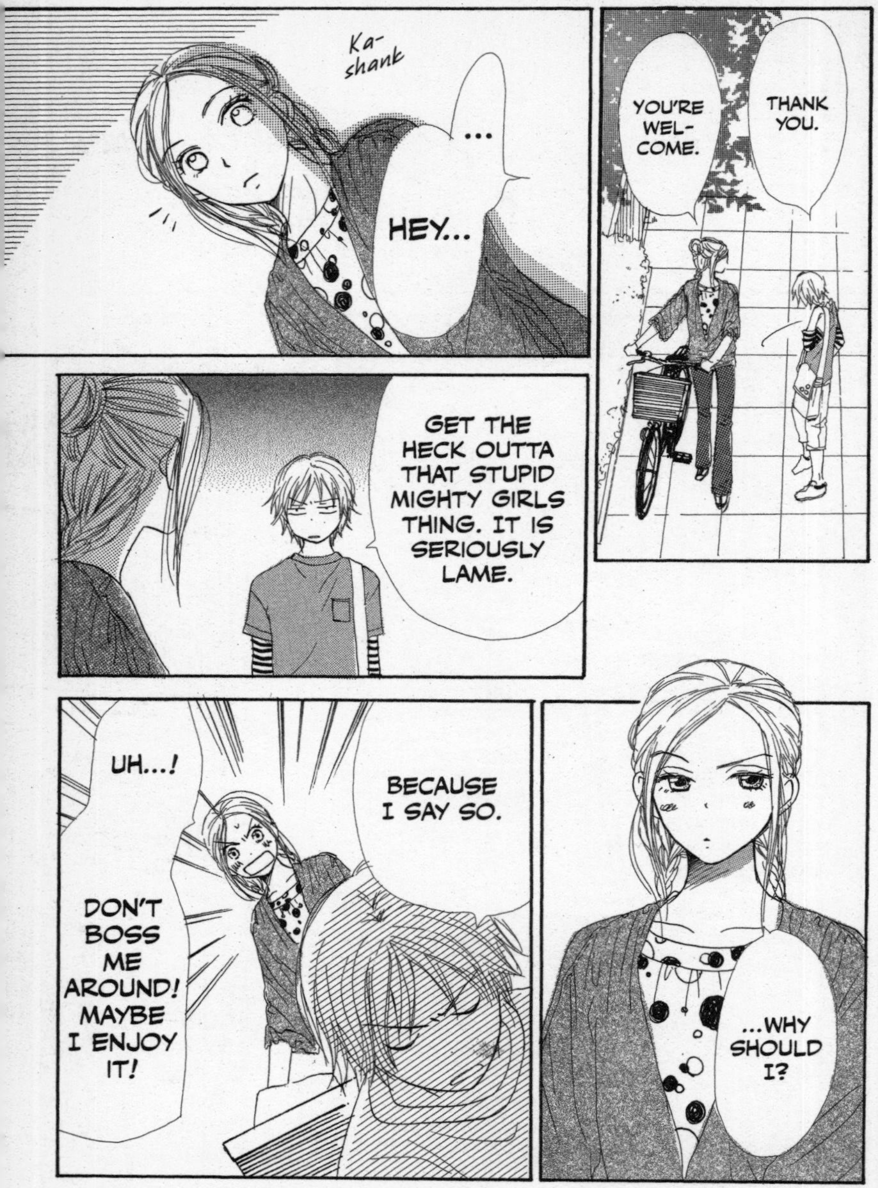
THANK YOU.
YOU'RE WEL-COME.
Ka-shank
...
HEY...
GET THE HECK OUTTA THAT STUPID MIGHTY GIRLS THING. IT IS SERIOUSLY LAME.
...WHY SHOULD I?
BECAUSE I SAY SO.
UH...!
DON'T BOSS ME AROUND! MAYBE I ENJOY IT!

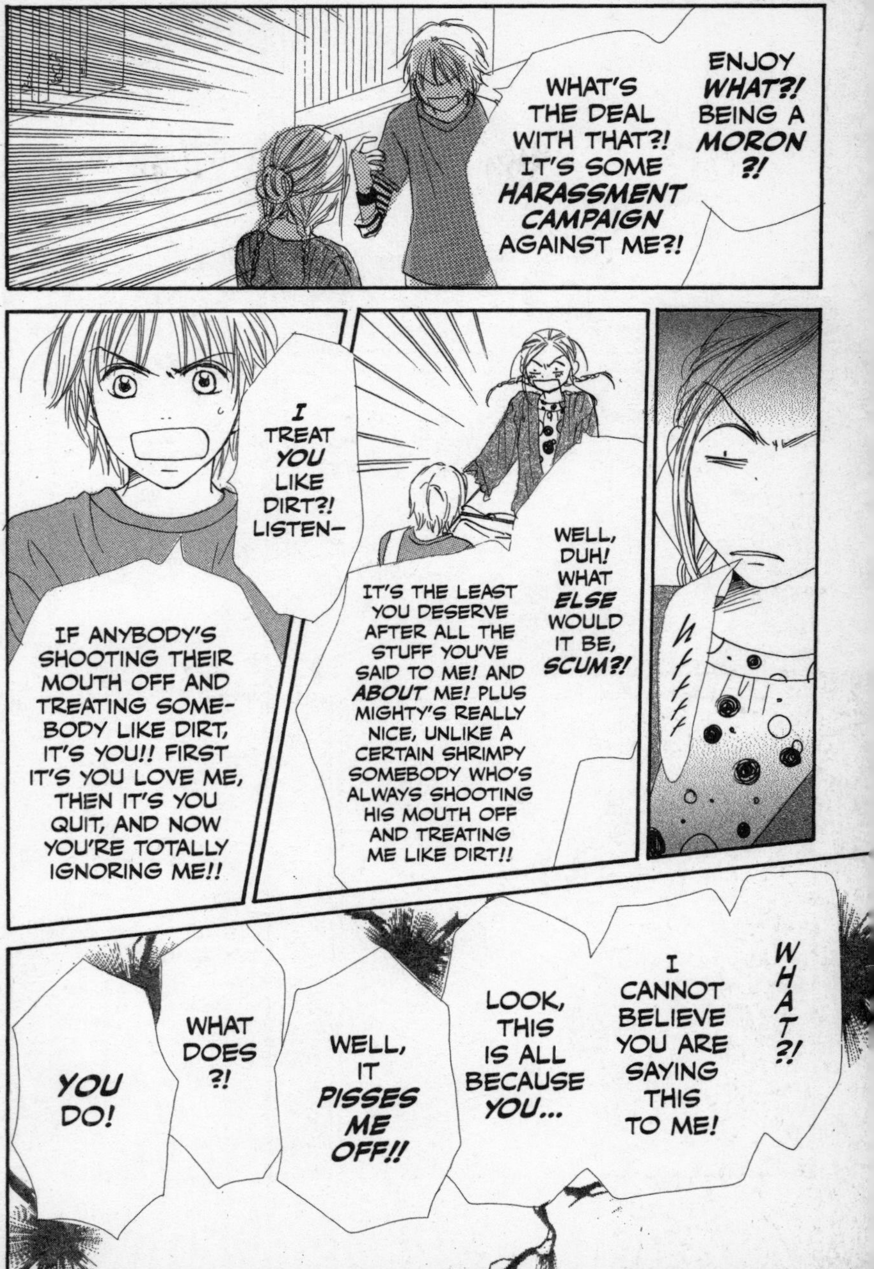
ENJOY *WHAT?!* BEING A *MORON* ?!
WHAT'S THE DEAL WITH THAT?! IT'S SOME *HARASSMENT CAMPAIGN* AGAINST ME?!
WELL, DUH! WHAT *ELSE* WOULD IT BE, *SCUM?!*
IT'S THE LEAST YOU DESERVE AFTER ALL THE STUFF YOU'VE SAID TO ME! AND *ABOUT* ME! PLUS MIGHTY'S REALLY NICE, UNLIKE A CERTAIN SHRIMPY SOMEBODY WHO'S ALWAYS SHOOTING HIS MOUTH OFF AND TREATING ME LIKE DIRT!!
I TREAT *YOU* LIKE DIRT?! LISTEN—
IF ANYBODY'S SHOOTING THEIR MOUTH OFF AND TREATING SOME-BODY LIKE DIRT, IT'S YOU!! FIRST IT'S YOU LOVE ME, THEN IT'S YOU QUIT, AND NOW YOU'RE TOTALLY IGNORING ME!!
WHAT?!
I CANNOT BELIEVE YOU ARE SAYING THIS TO ME!
LOOK, THIS IS ALL BECAUSE *YOU...*
WELL, IT *PISSES ME OFF!!*
WHAT DOES ?!
YOU DO!

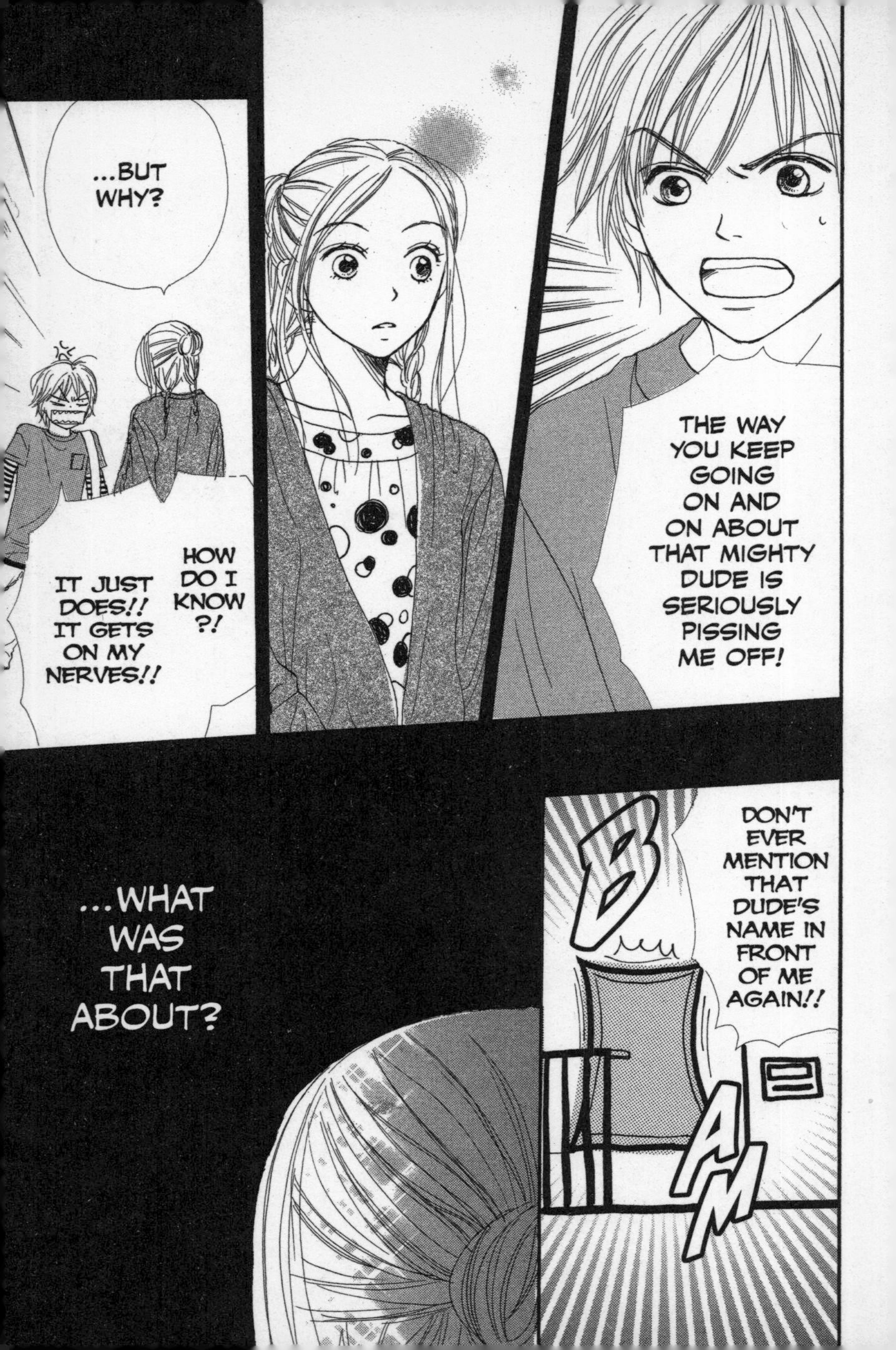
THE WAY YOU KEEP GOING ON AND ON ABOUT THAT MIGHTY DUDE IS SERIOUSLY PISSING ME OFF!
...BUT WHY?
HOW DO I KNOW?!
IT JUST DOES!! IT GETS ON MY NERVES!!
DON'T EVER MENTION THAT DUDE'S NAME IN FRONT OF ME AGAIN!!
BAM
...WHAT WAS THAT ABOUT?

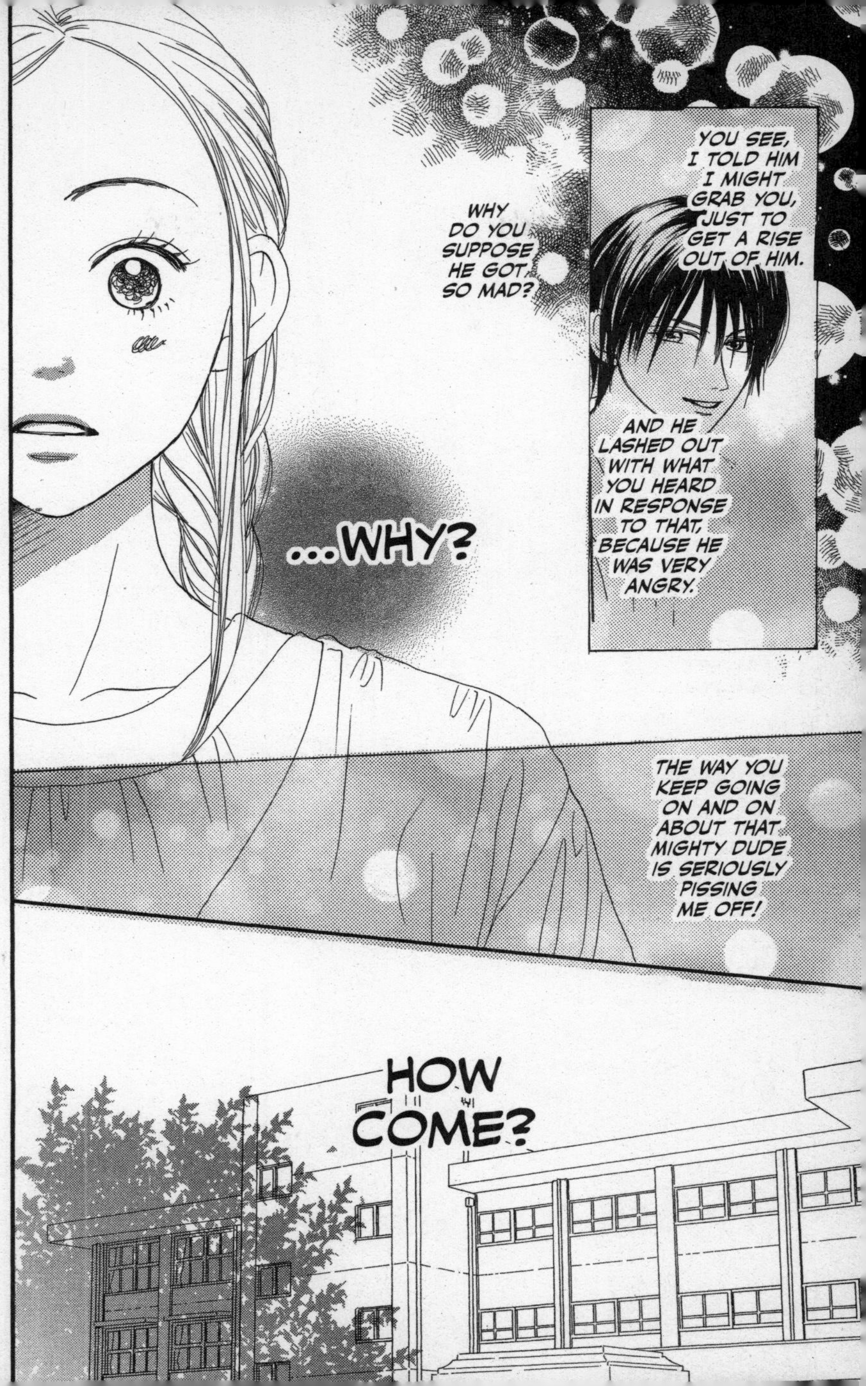
YOU SEE, I TOLD HIM I MIGHT GRAB YOU, JUST TO GET A RISE OUT OF HIM.
AND HE LASHED OUT WITH WHAT YOU HEARD IN RESPONSE TO THAT, BECAUSE HE WAS VERY ANGRY.
WHY DO YOU SUPPOSE HE GOT SO MAD?
...WHY?
THE WAY YOU KEEP GOING ON AND ON ABOUT THAT MIGHTY DUDE IS SERIOUSLY PISSING ME OFF!
HOW COME?

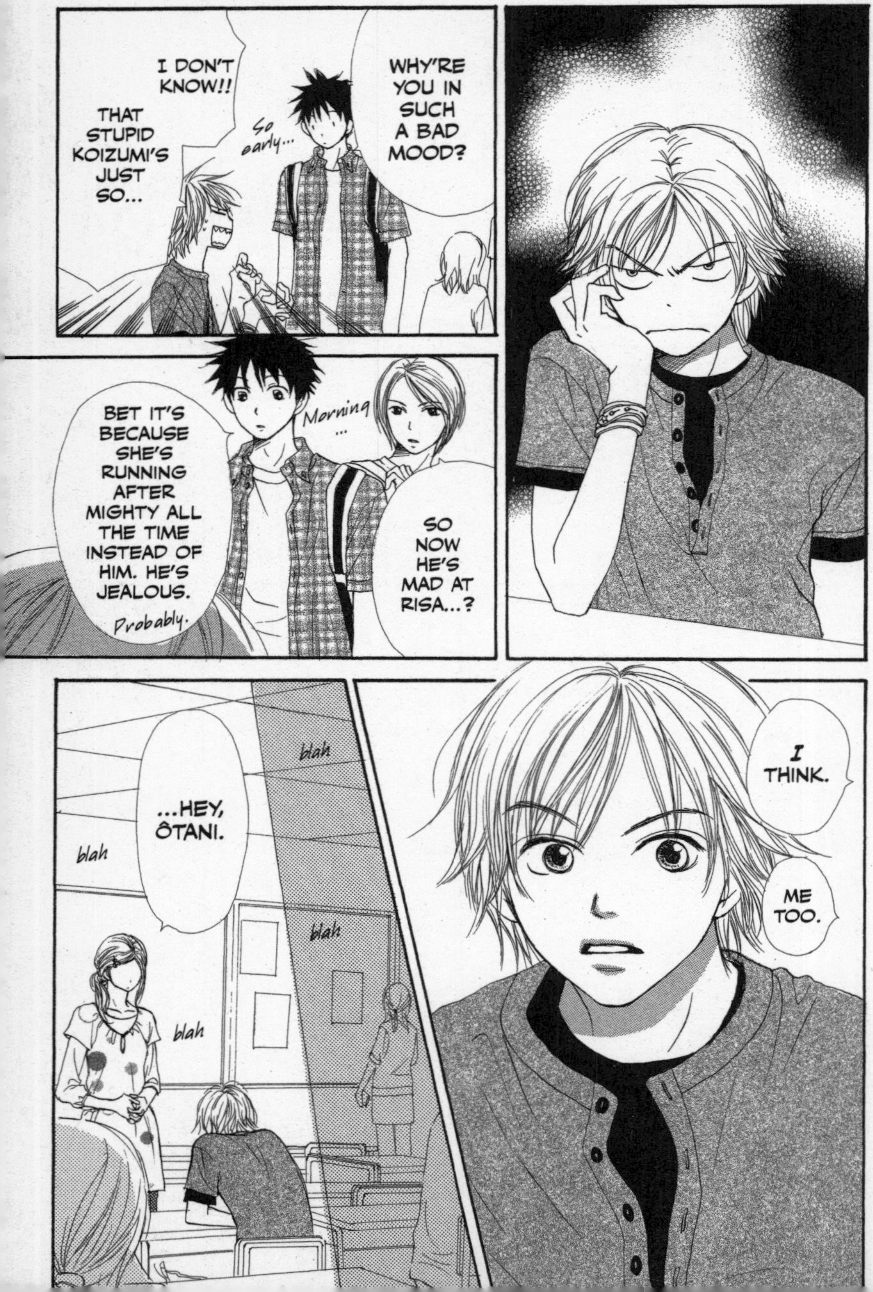
WHY'RE YOU IN SUCH A BAD MOOD?
I DON'T KNOW!!
So early...
THAT STUPID KOIZUMI'S JUST SO...
Morning...
SO NOW HE'S MAD AT RISA...?
BET IT'S BECAUSE SHE'S RUNNING AFTER MIGHTY ALL THE TIME INSTEAD OF HIM. HE'S JEALOUS.
Probably.
I THINK.
ME TOO.
blah
...HEY, ÔTANI.
blah
blah
blah

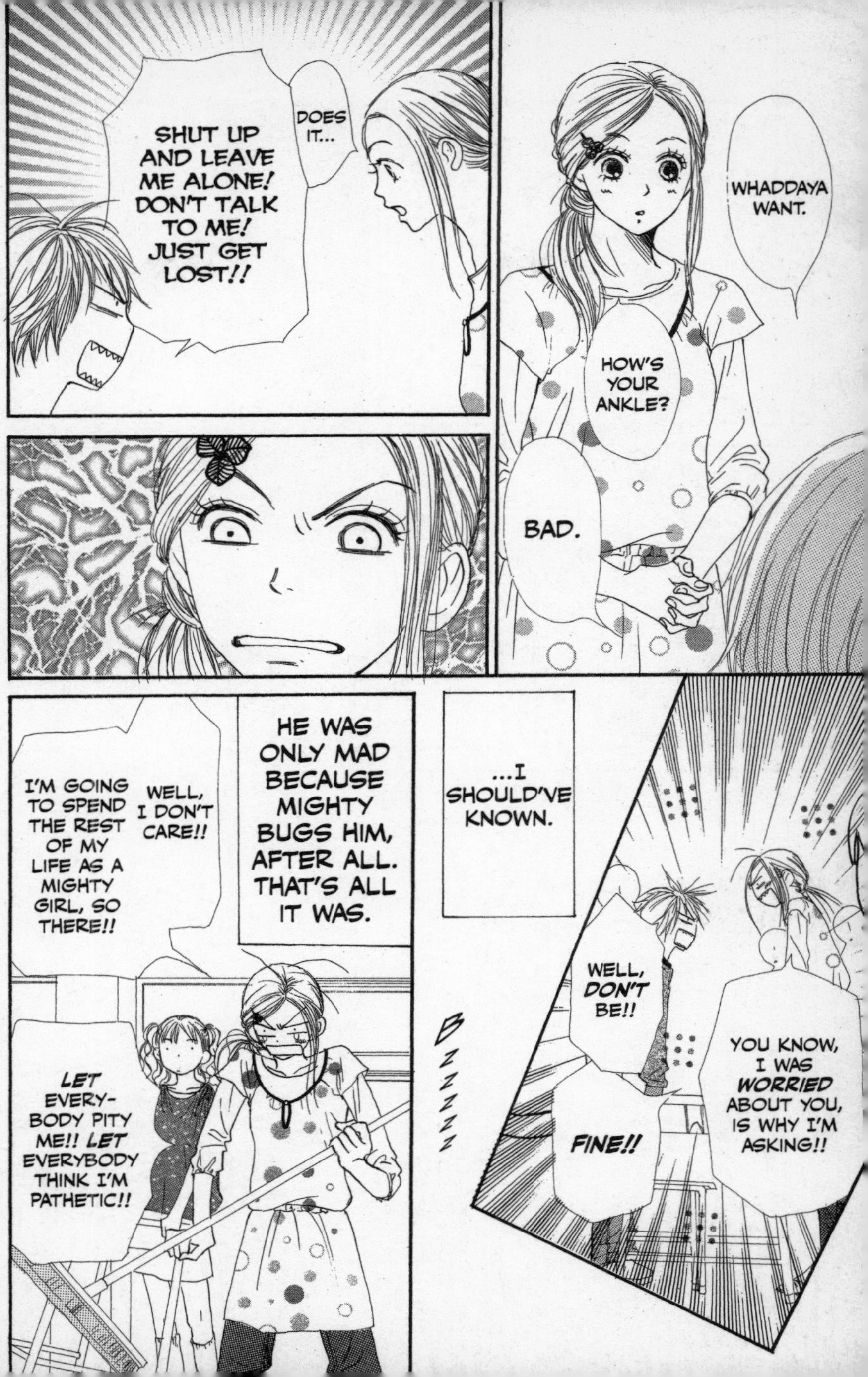
WHADDAYA WANT.
HOW'S YOUR ANKLE?
BAD.
DOES IT...
SHUT UP AND LEAVE ME ALONE! DON'T TALK TO ME! JUST GET LOST!!
YOU KNOW, I WAS *WORRIED* ABOUT YOU, IS WHY I'M ASKING!!
WELL, *DON'T* BE!!
FINE!!
...I SHOULD'VE KNOWN.
BZZZZZZ
HE WAS ONLY MAD BECAUSE MIGHTY BUGS HIM, AFTER ALL. THAT'S ALL IT WAS.
WELL, I DON'T CARE!!
I'M GOING TO SPEND THE REST OF MY LIFE AS A MIGHTY GIRL, SO THERE!!
LET EVERYBODY PITY ME!! *LET* EVERYBODY THINK I'M PATHETIC!!

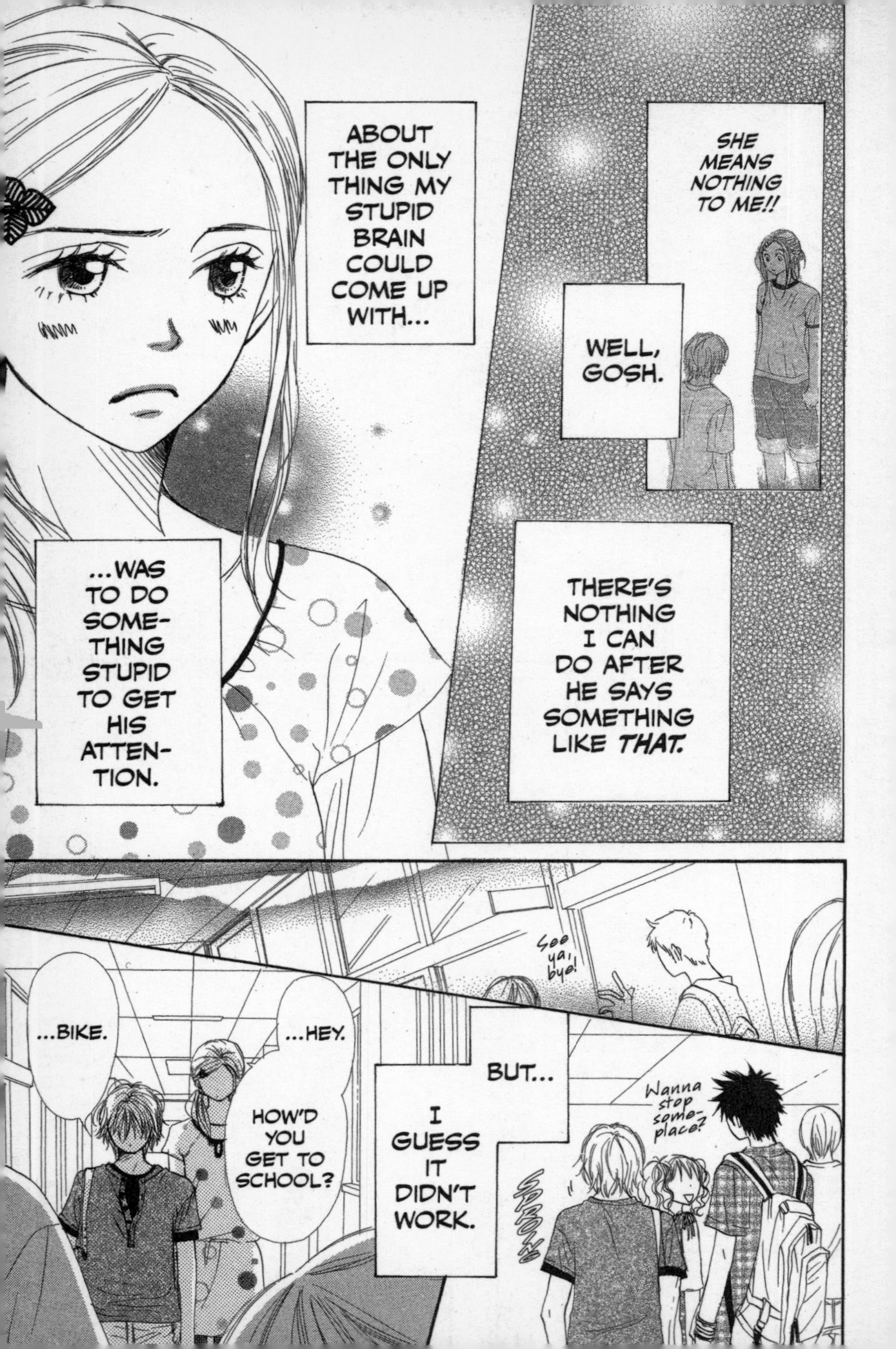
SHE MEANS NOTHING TO ME!!
WELL, GOSH.
THERE'S NOTHING I CAN DO AFTER HE SAYS SOMETHING LIKE *THAT.*
ABOUT THE ONLY THING MY STUPID BRAIN COULD COME UP WITH...
...WAS TO DO SOME-THING STUPID TO GET HIS ATTEN-TION.
See ya, bye!
Wanna stop some-place?
BUT...
I GUESS IT DIDN'T WORK.
...HEY.
HOW'D YOU GET TO SCHOOL?
...BIKE.

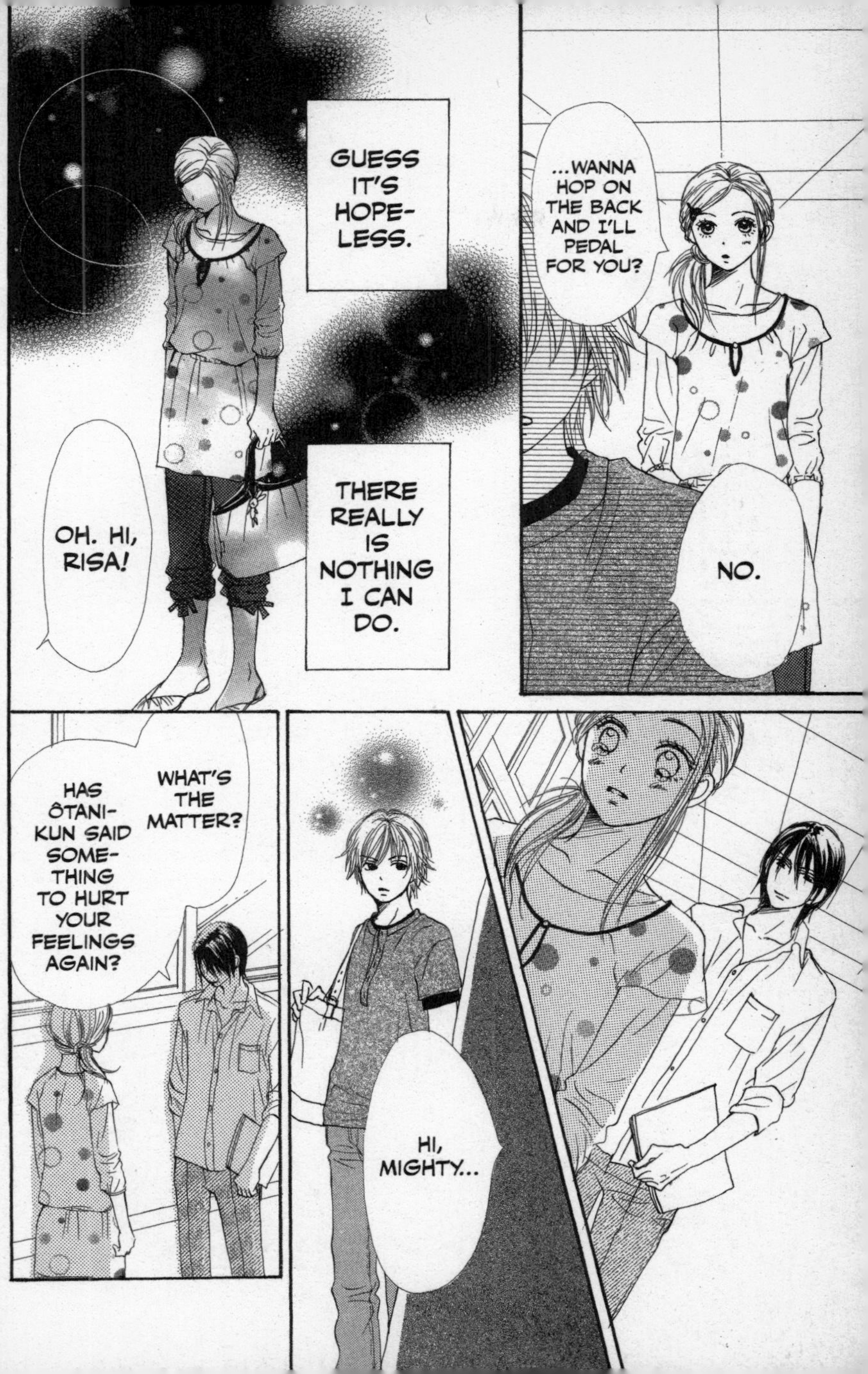
...WANNA HOP ON THE BACK AND I'LL PEDAL FOR YOU?
NO.
GUESS IT'S HOPE-LESS.
THERE REALLY IS NOTHING I CAN DO.
OH. HI, RISA!
HI, MIGHTY...
WHAT'S THE MATTER?
HAS ÔTANI-KUN SAID SOME-THING TO HURT YOUR FEELINGS AGAIN?

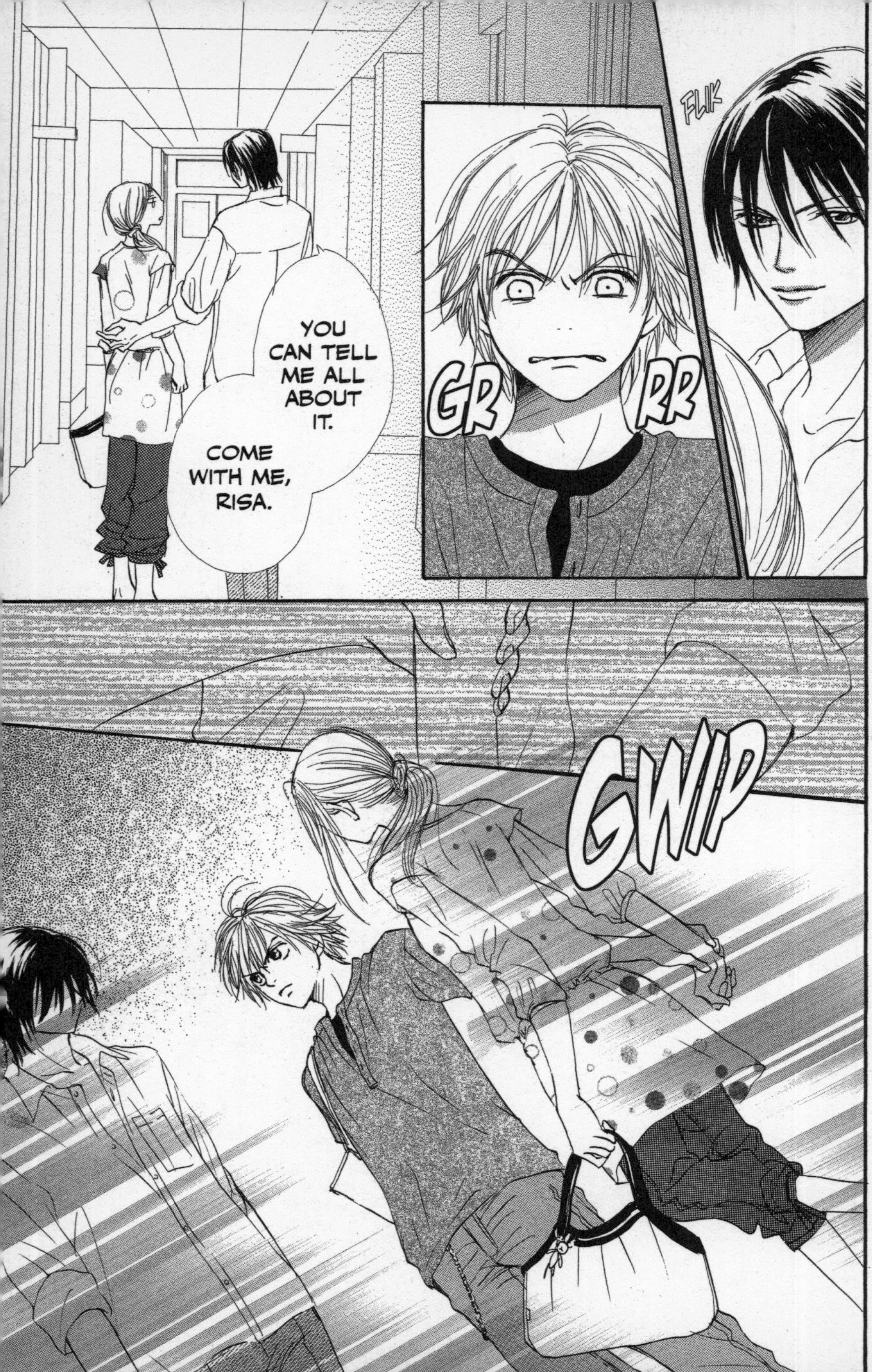
FLIK
GR RR
YOU CAN TELL ME ALL ABOUT IT.
COME WITH ME, RISA.
GWIP

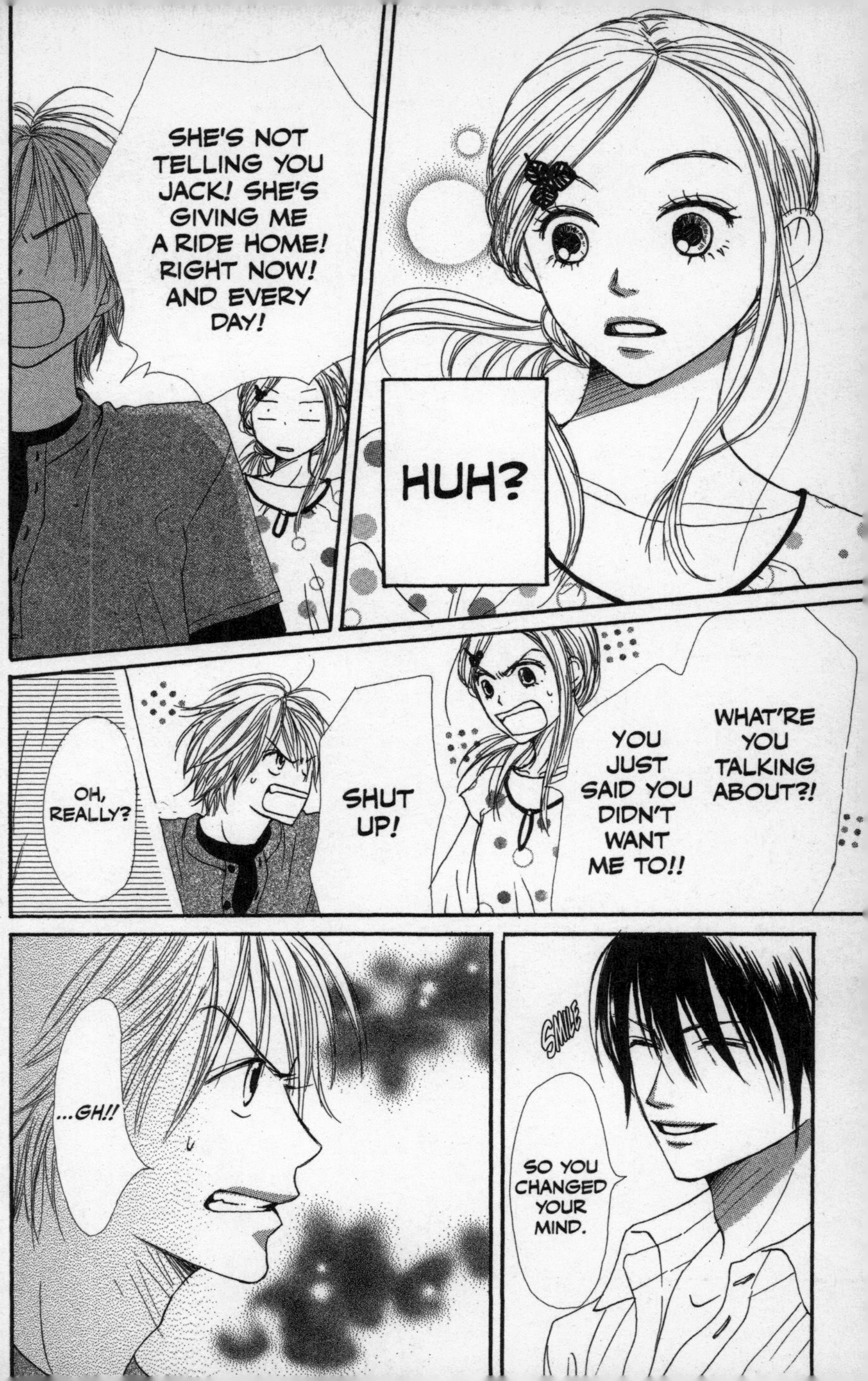
HUH?
SHE'S NOT TELLING YOU JACK! SHE'S GIVING ME A RIDE HOME! RIGHT NOW! AND EVERY DAY!
WHAT'RE YOU TALKING ABOUT?!
YOU JUST SAID YOU DIDN'T WANT ME TO!!
SHUT UP!
OH, REALLY?
SMILE
SO YOU CHANGED YOUR MIND.
...GH!!

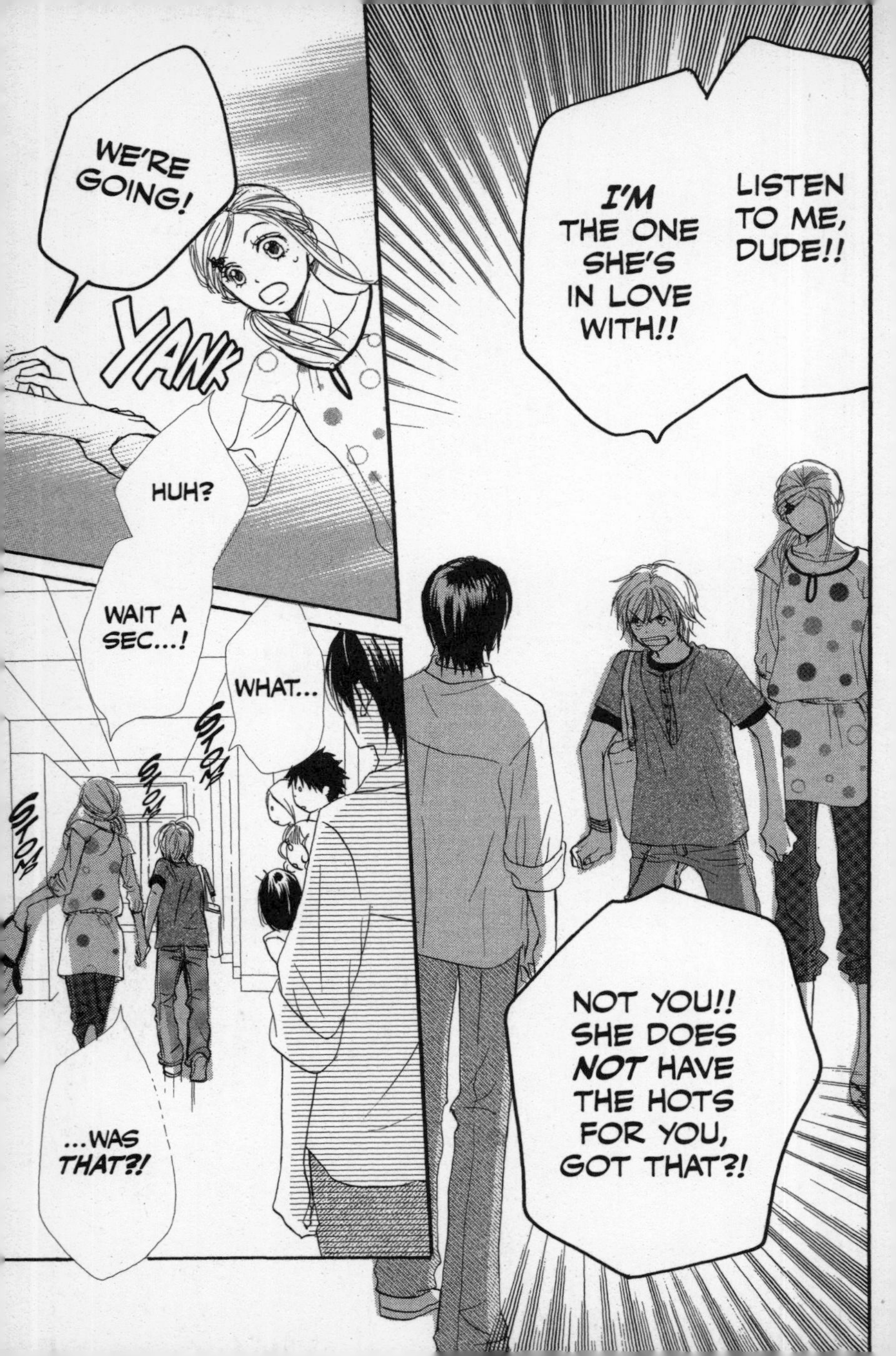

LISTEN TO ME, DUDE!!
I'M THE ONE SHE'S IN LOVE WITH!!
NOT YOU!! SHE DOES NOT HAVE THE HOTS FOR YOU, GOT THAT?!
WE'RE GOING!
YANK
HUH?
WAIT A SEC...!
WHAT...
STOMP STOMP STOMP
...WAS THAT?!

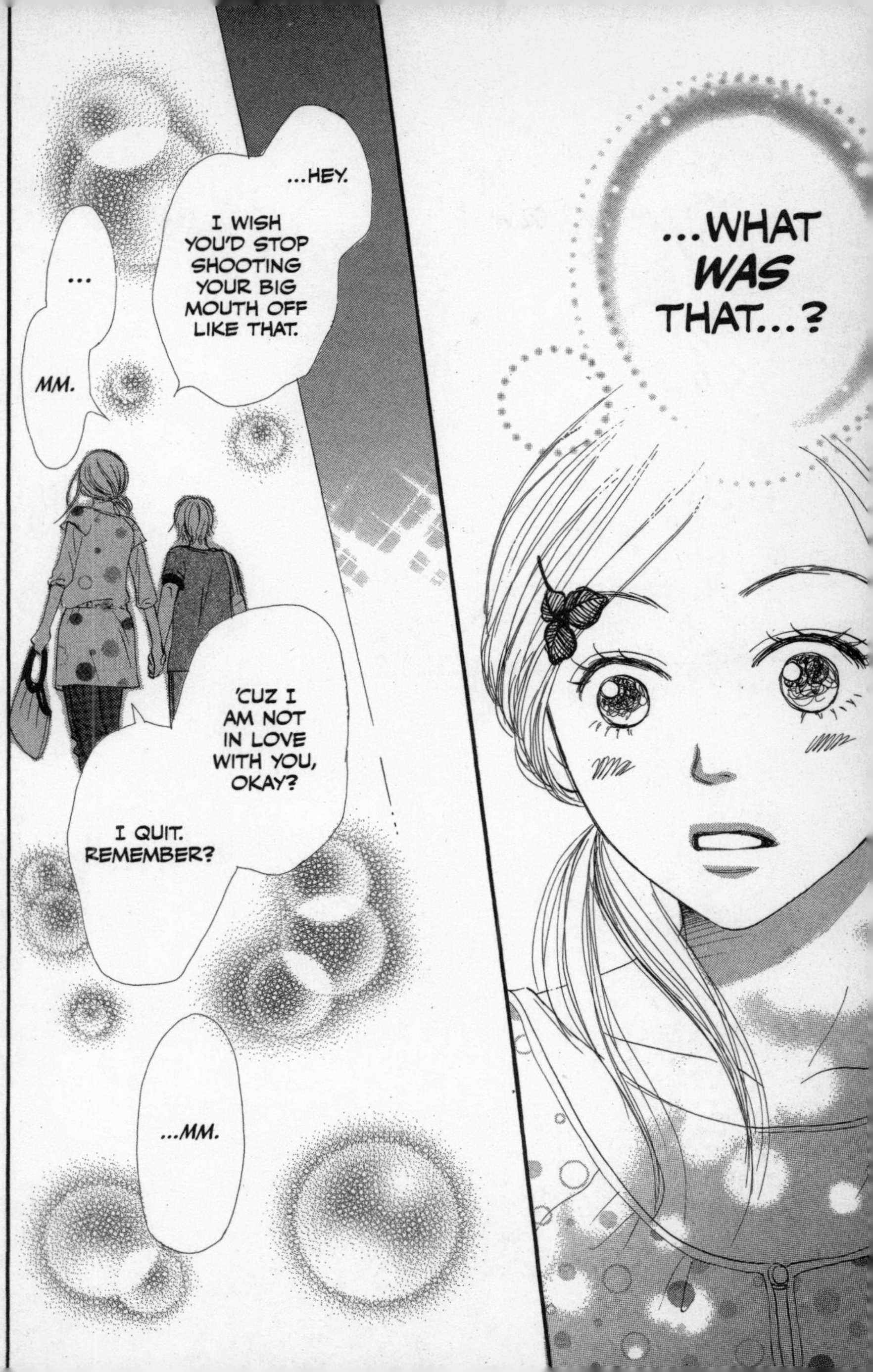
...WHAT *WAS* THAT...?
...HEY.
I WISH YOU'D STOP SHOOTING YOUR BIG MOUTH OFF LIKE THAT.
...
MM.
'CUZ I AM NOT IN LOVE WITH YOU, OKAY?
I QUIT. REMEMBER?
...MM.

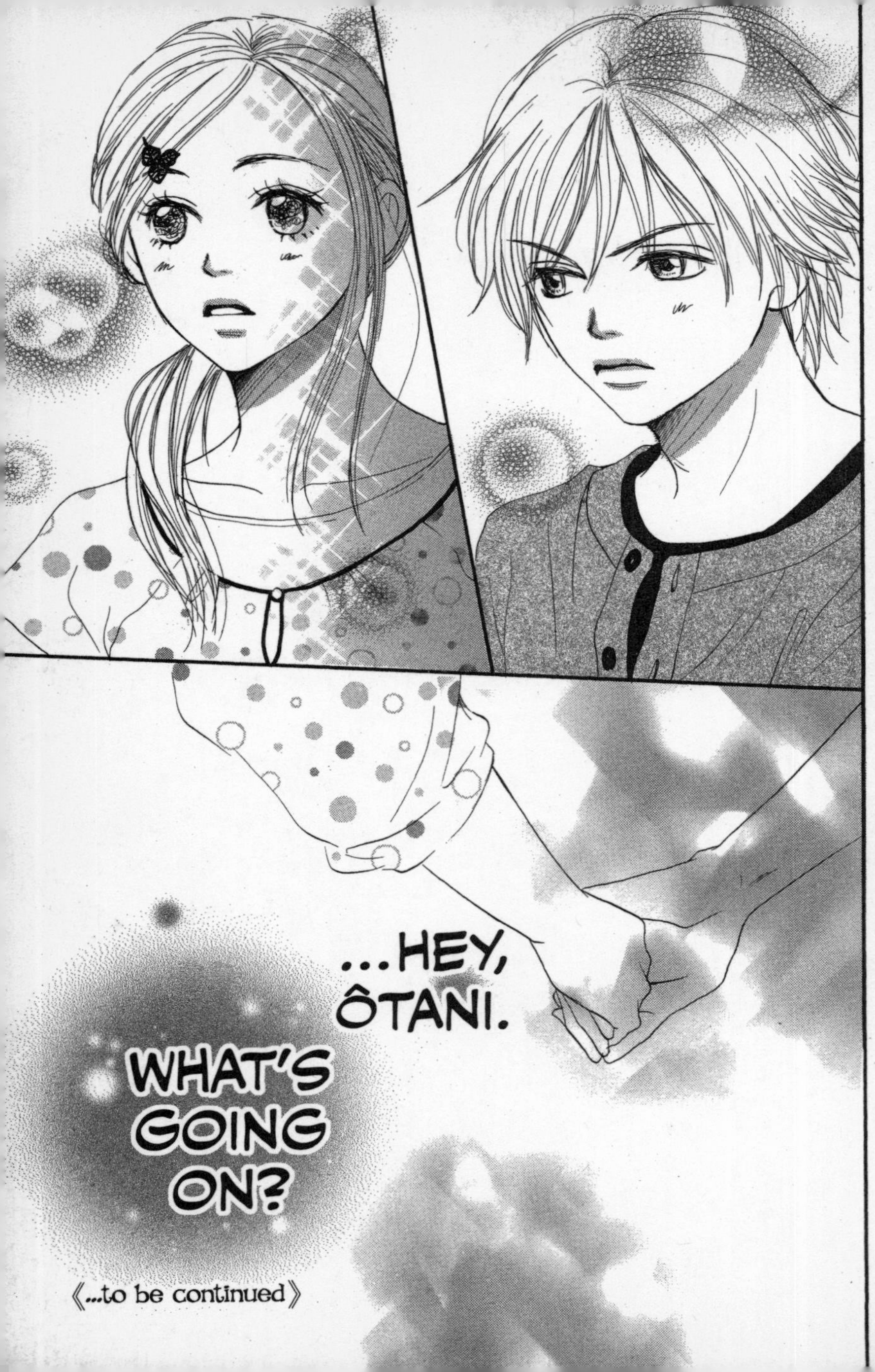
...HEY, ÔTANI.
WHAT'S GOING ON?
《...to be continued》

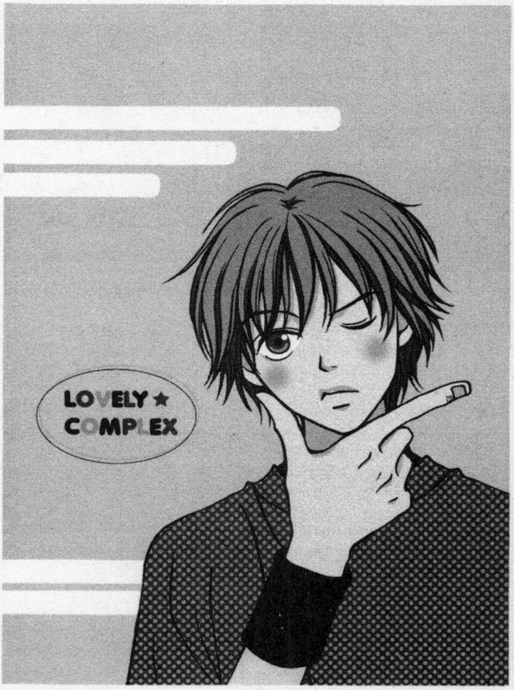
LOVELY★
COMPLEX

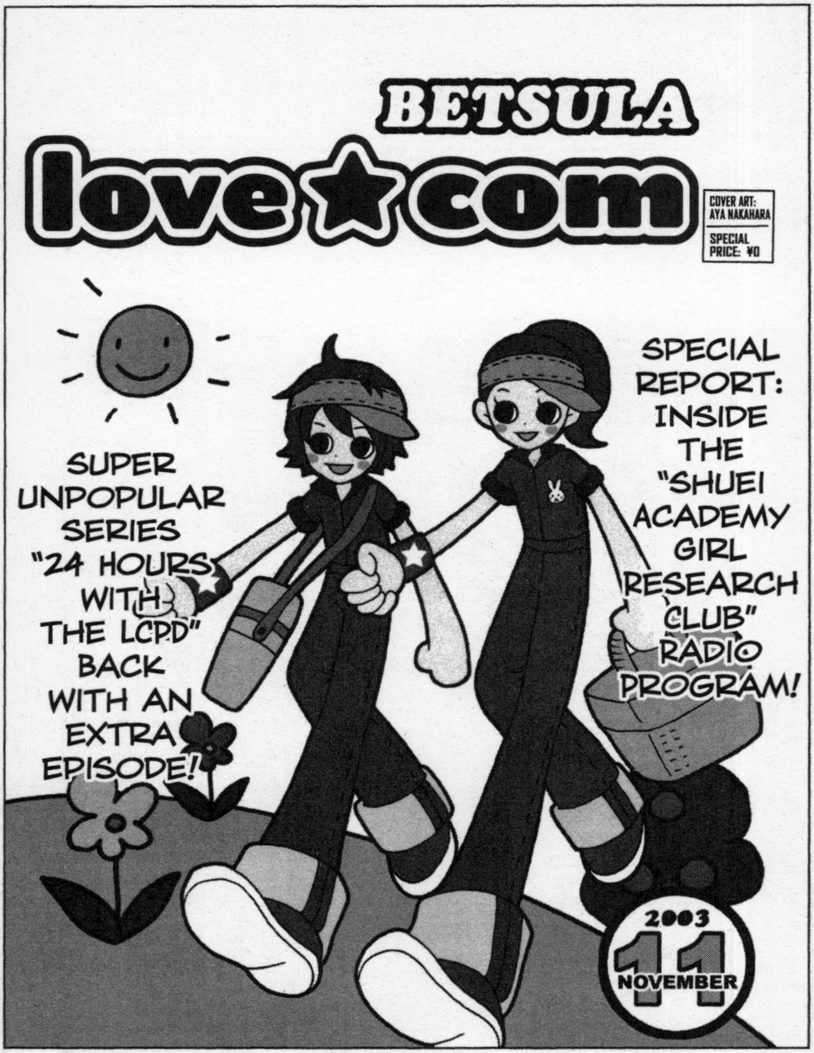
BETSULA
love★com
COVER ART: AYA NAKAHARA
SPECIAL PRICE: ¥0
SPECIAL REPORT: INSIDE THE "SHUEI ACADEMY GIRL RESEARCH CLUB" RADIO PROGRAM!
SUPER UNPOPULAR SERIES "24 HOURS WITH THE LCPD" BACK WITH AN EXTRA EPISODE!
2003
11
NOVEMBER

CHECK!

Special report:
Inside the "Shuei Academy Girl Research Club"
Radio Program!

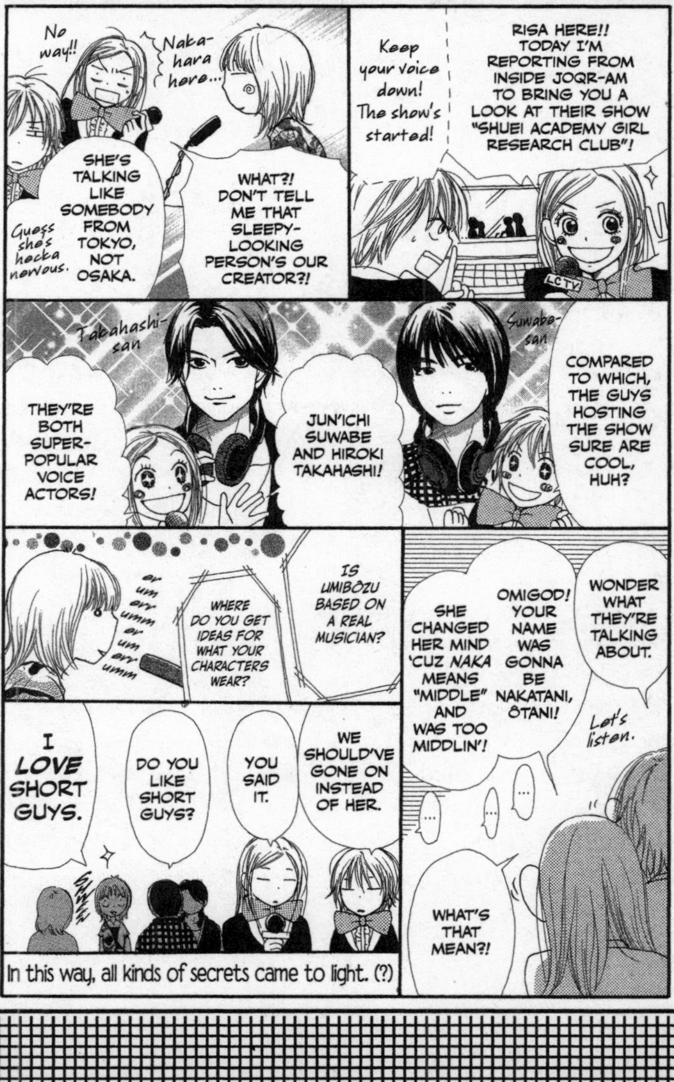
RISA HERE!! TODAY I'M REPORTING FROM INSIDE JOQR-AM TO BRING YOU A LOOK AT THEIR SHOW "SHUEI ACADEMY GIRL RESEARCH CLUB"!
Keep your voice down! The show's started!
LCTV
Naka-hara here...
No way!!
WHAT?! DON'T TELL ME THAT SLEEPY-LOOKING PERSON'S OUR CREATOR?!
SHE'S TALKING LIKE SOMEBODY FROM TOKYO, NOT OSAKA.
Guess she's hecka nervous.
Suwabe-san
COMPARED TO WHICH, THE GUYS HOSTING THE SHOW SURE ARE COOL, HUH?
JUN'ICHI SUWABE AND HIROKI TAKAHASHI!
Takahashi-san
THEY'RE BOTH SUPER-POPULAR VOICE ACTORS!
WONDER WHAT THEY'RE TALKING ABOUT.
Let's listen.
OMIGOD! YOUR NAME WAS GONNA BE NAKATANI, ŌTANI!
SHE CHANGED HER MIND 'CUZ *NAKA* MEANS "MIDDLE" AND WAS TOO MIDDLIN'!
...
...
...
WHAT'S THAT MEAN?!
IS UMIBŌZU BASED ON A REAL MUSICIAN?
WHERE DO YOU GET IDEAS FOR WHAT YOUR CHARACTERS WEAR?
er um err umm er um err umm
WE SHOULD'VE GONE ON INSTEAD OF HER.
YOU SAID IT.
DO YOU LIKE SHORT GUYS?
I *LOVE* SHORT GUYS.
In this way, all kinds of secrets came to light. (?)

Hello! Nakahara again. So anyway, I went on the radio. I wasn't on air for very long, but still, boy was I nervous. I'm not a very good talker. I'm boring! The stuff I talk about is so boring! But the two presenters came to my rescue by being funny and charming and I had a really good time. Both Suwabe-san and Takahashi-san were sooooooo nice! And even though they're probably super-busy, they took the time to read all my manga before the show, and actually remembered them all. swoooon I was so touched. And then, after the show, they were so concerned, asking me if I'd left out anything I'd wanted to say... swoooon They were both so wonderful that I thought, when I'm reborn I want to be just like them! They were so great... And, since they're voice actors, they both had such nice voices... Right now I am totally disgusted at my pathetic inability to put things into words. Those two were too wonderful for me to describe! Heh, heh! ← ?

   Suwabe-san, Takahashi-san and some other voice actors are in a group called STA MEN, which has a CD out. Check it out! ♡ 🐰 ♪

   Gotta say... When I think back to how I dragged myself to the studio muttering, "A radio show... I don't believe this...,"
I want to punch myself in the nose. 🐰💭

   All the program crew were so nice, too...and so great... And to think, all these wonderful people support my manga, even if it's for work, well... I am blessed. Just knowing this has made me a bigger person. Now I'm like, "Go, me! You can do it!" I am so glad I went. I tell you, you gotta be positive and experience everything. So come on, everybody, forward, march!! ...I was trying to end on an inspirational note, but it didn't happen. hahahahaha The End!!

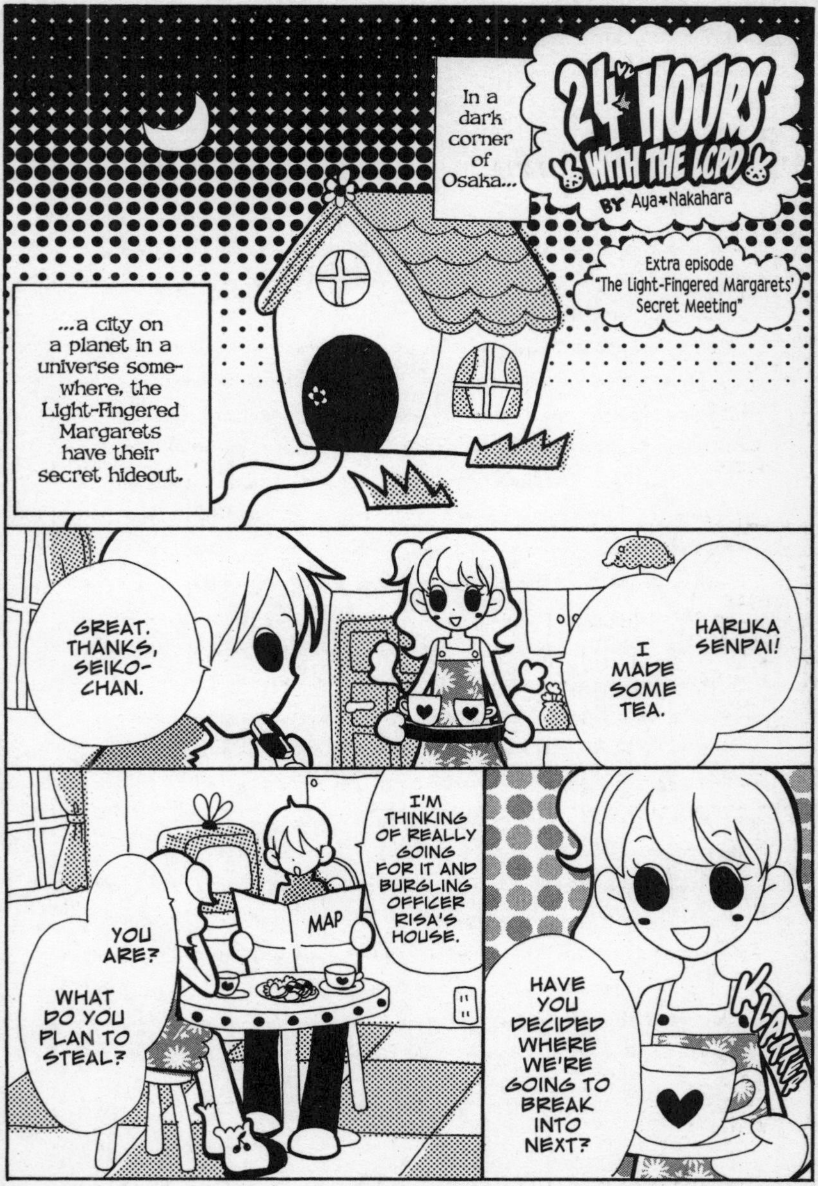
24 HOURS WITH THE LCPD
BY Aya*Nakahara
In a dark corner of Osaka...
Extra episode "The Light-Fingered Margarets' Secret Meeting"
...a city on a planet in a universe somewhere, the Light-Fingered Margarets have their secret hideout.
HARUKA SENPAI! I MADE SOME TEA.
GREAT. THANKS, SEIKO-CHAN.
HAVE YOU DECIDED WHERE WE'RE GOING TO BREAK INTO NEXT?
KLAKKK
I'M THINKING OF REALLY GOING FOR IT AND BURGLING OFFICER RISA'S HOUSE.
MAP
YOU ARE? WHAT DO YOU PLAN TO STEAL?

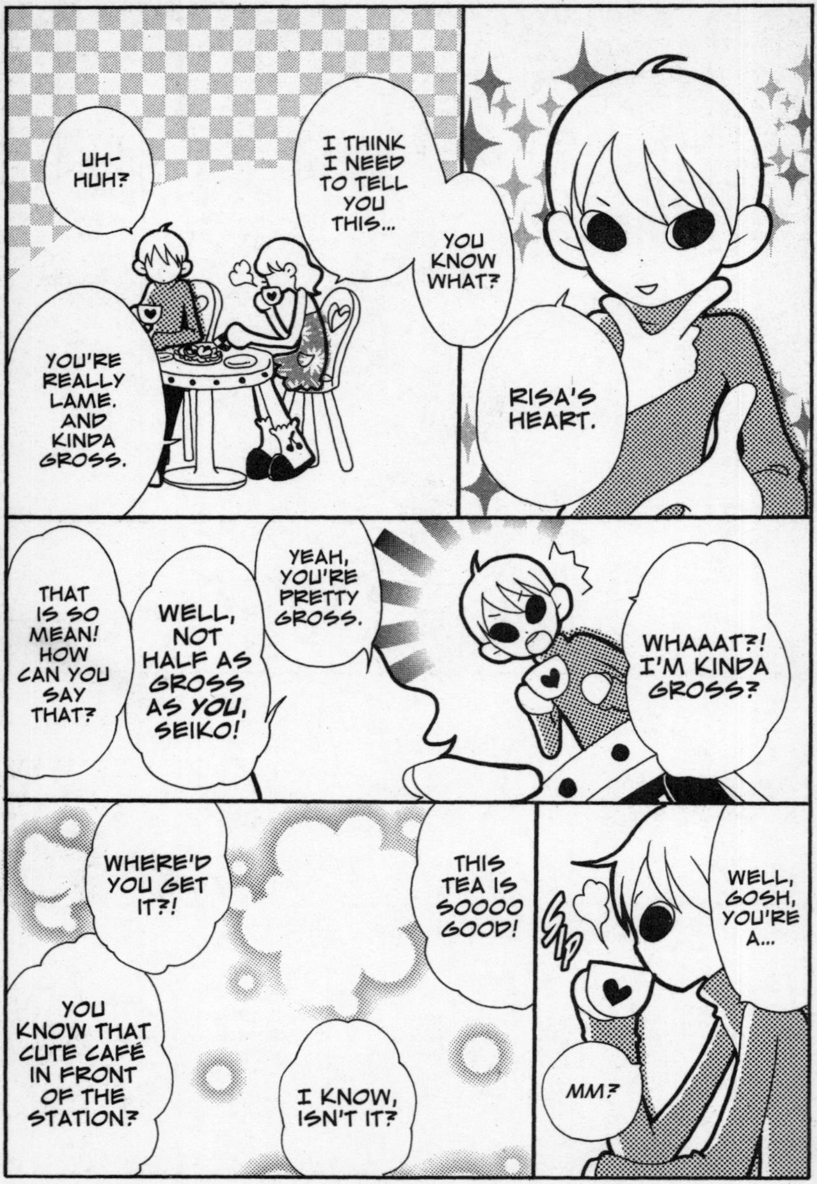
YOU KNOW WHAT?
RISA'S HEART.
I THINK I NEED TO TELL YOU THIS...
UH-HUH?
YOU'RE REALLY LAME. AND KINDA GROSS.
WHAAAT?! I'M KINDA GROSS?
YEAH, YOU'RE PRETTY GROSS.
WELL, NOT HALF AS GROSS AS *YOU*, SEIKO!
THAT IS SO MEAN! HOW CAN YOU SAY THAT?
WELL, GOSH, YOU'RE A...
SIP
MM?
THIS TEA IS SOOOO GOOD!
WHERE'D YOU GET IT?!
I KNOW, ISN'T IT?
YOU KNOW THAT CUTE CAFÉ IN FRONT OF THE STATION?

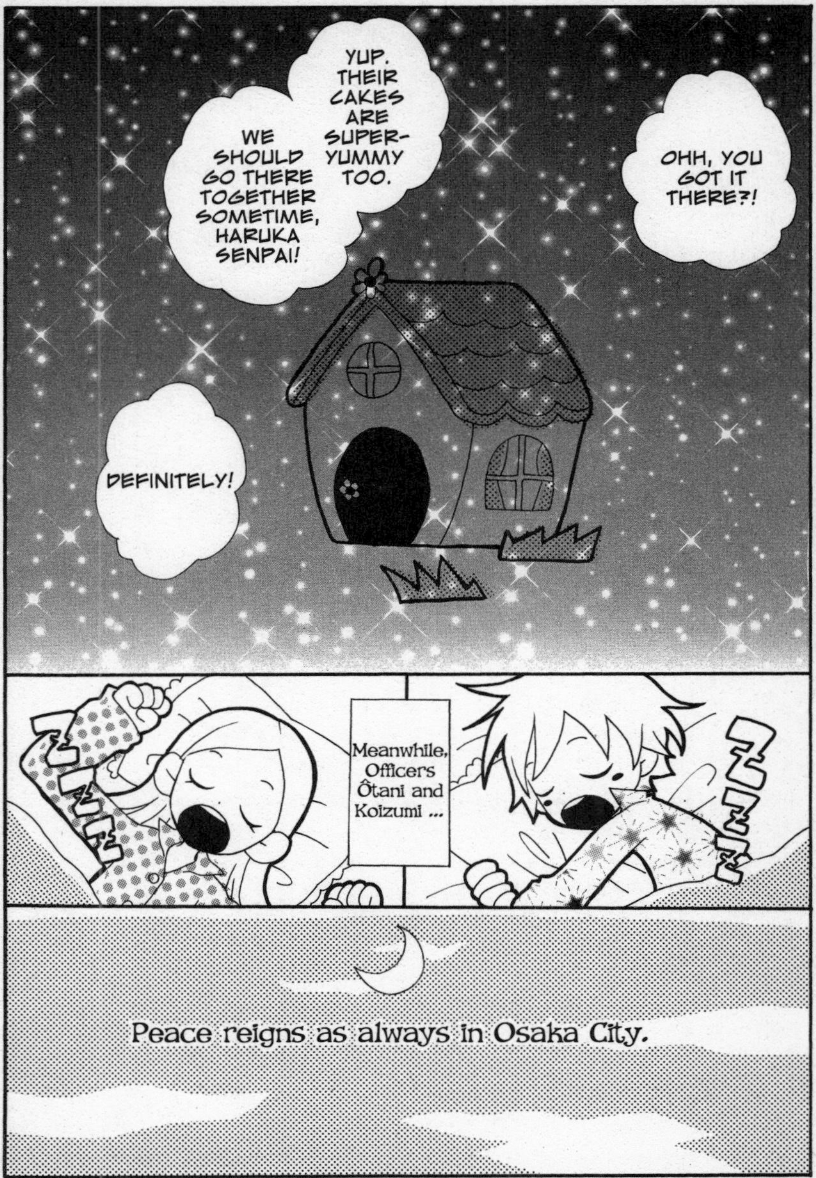
OHH, YOU GOT IT THERE?!
YUP. THEIR CAKES ARE SUPER-YUMMY TOO.
WE SHOULD GO THERE TOGETHER SOMETIME, HARUKA SENPAI!
DEFINITELY!
Meanwhile, Officers Ôtani and Koizumi ...
Peace reigns as always in Osaka City.
To be Continued?

glossary

Page 13, panel 2: Zopp Osaka
Named after the real venue, Zepp Osaka. There are also Zepp venues in others Japanese cities such as Tokyo, Sendai, and Fukuoka.

Page 13, panel 5: White Day
White Day is a Japanese holiday that occurs exactly one month after Valentine's Day, and is a chance for boys and men to give reciprocal presents to the ladies in their lives. Marshmallows and white chocolate are traditional, but not required.

Page 14, panel 3: Ôtani's long nose
In Japanese, someone who's very boastful or vain is described as being a tengu. A tengu is a mountain spirit who has wings and a long nose.

Page 17, panel 2: Chu and mouse
In Japanese, *chu* is the sound of a kiss and *chu chu* is the sound a mouse makes. All Nobu's talk of kissing makes her sound like a mouse.

Page 22, panel 2: Atchan
A nickname for Atsushi, Ôtani's given name. It is a common form of Japanese nickname, where *chan* is added after the first syllable of a name.

Page 43, panel 3: A new school year
In Japan, the school year is three terms and begins in spring rather than fall.

Page 50, panel 5: Call 119
119 is the Japanese emergency number to call in case of a fire. 110 is the number to call for the police.

Page 146, panel 1: Itadakimasu
What you say before you eat. Literally, it is the polite form for "I receive."

When I stop to think about it, it's already eight years since my debut as a manga artist. Whooo! Lately, through manga, I've been getting lots of opportunities to meet people who do other, non-manga work, and it's been a real learning experience. Although they don't draw manga, they do create things, so in that sense our work is the same, and hearing what they have to say is very interesting to me. Gotta say, boy am I glad I'm a manga artist! I'm so lucky! I'll keep working hard at it for years and years!

Aya Nakahara won the 2003 Shogakukan manga award for her breakthrough hit *Love★Com*, which was made into a major motion picture and a PS2 game in 2006. She debuted with *Haru to Kuuki Nichiyou-bi* in 1995, and her other works include *HANADA* and *Himitsu Kichi*.

LOVE★COM VOL 6
The Shojo Beat Manga Edition

STORY AND ART BY
AYA NAKAHARA

Translation & English Adaptation/Pookie Rolf
Touch-up Art & Lettering/Gia Cam Luc
Design/Yuki Ameda
Editor/Pancha Diaz

Editor in Chief, Books/Alvin Lu
Editor in Chief, Magazines/Marc Weidenbaum
VP of Publishing Licensing/Rika Inouye
VP of Sales/Gonzalo Ferreyra
Sr. VP of Marketing/Liza Coppola
Publisher/Hyoe Narita

Printed in Canada

Published by VIZ Media, LLC
P.O. Box 77010
San Francisco, CA 94107

Shojo Beat Manga Edition
10 9 8 7 6 5 4 3 2 1
First printing, May 2008

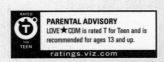

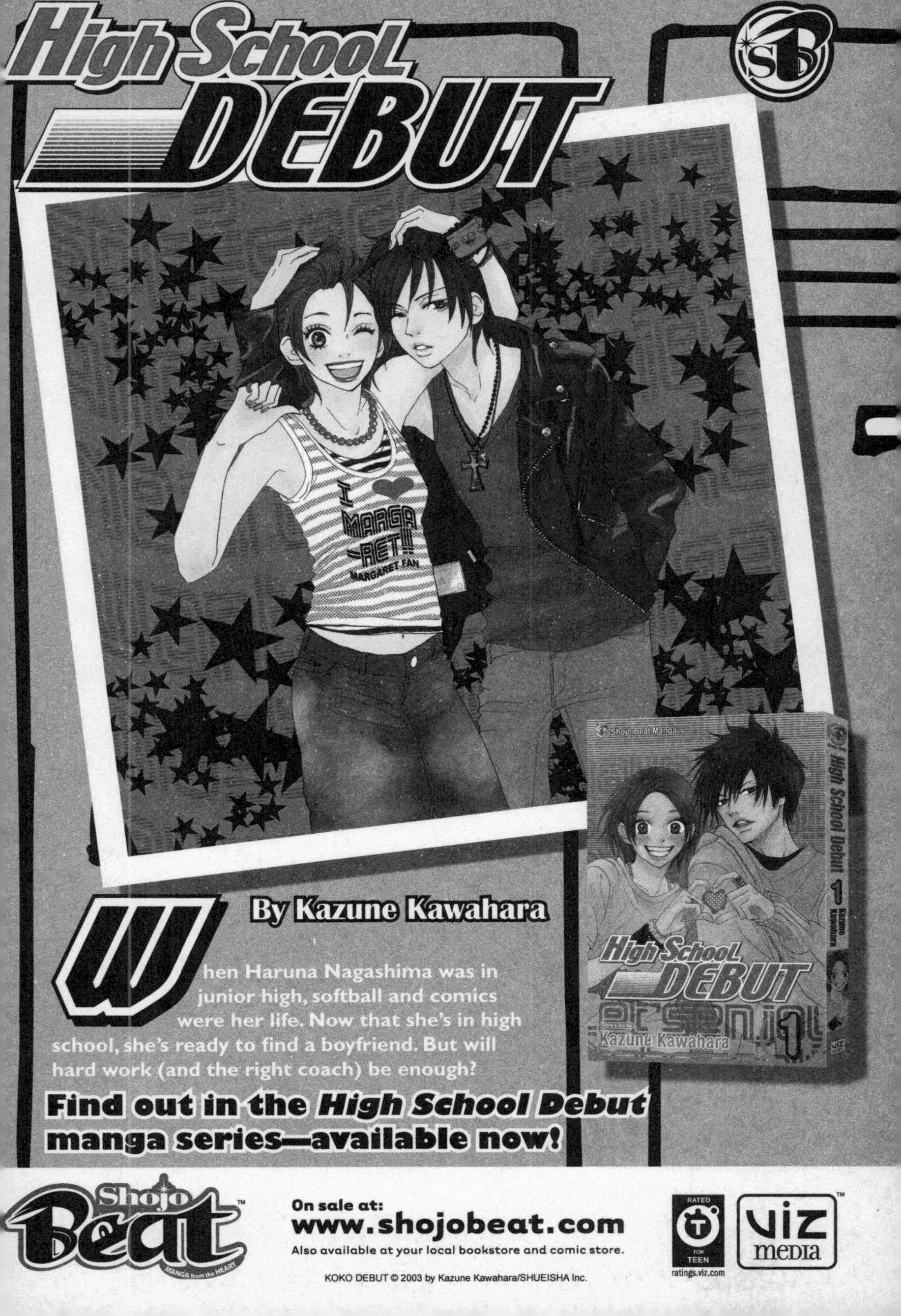
High School DEBUT
By Kazune Kawahara
When Haruna Nagashima was in junior high, softball and comics were her life. Now that she's in high school, she's ready to find a boyfriend. But will hard work (and the right coach) be enough?
Find out in the High School Debut manga series—available now!
Shojo Beat
MANGA from the HEART
On sale at:
www.shojobeat.com
Also available at your local bookstore and comic store.
RATED T FOR TEEN
ratings.viz.com
VIZ media
KOKO DEBUT © 2003 by Kazune Kawahara/SHUEISHA Inc.

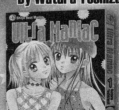
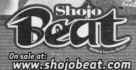

Tell us what you think about Shojo Beat Manga!

Our survey is now available online. Go to:

shojobeat.com/mangasurvey

Help us make our product offerings better!

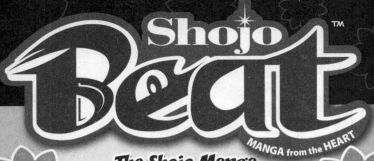

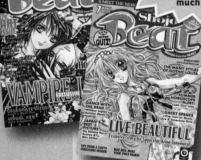
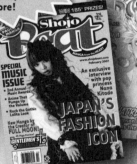
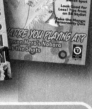

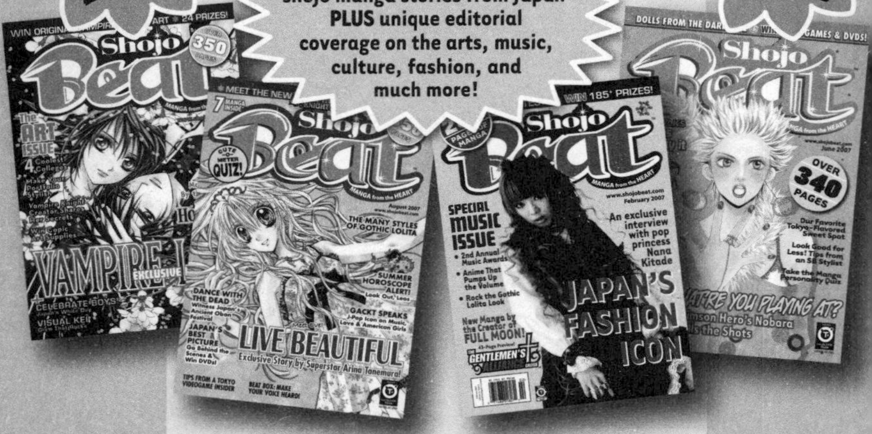

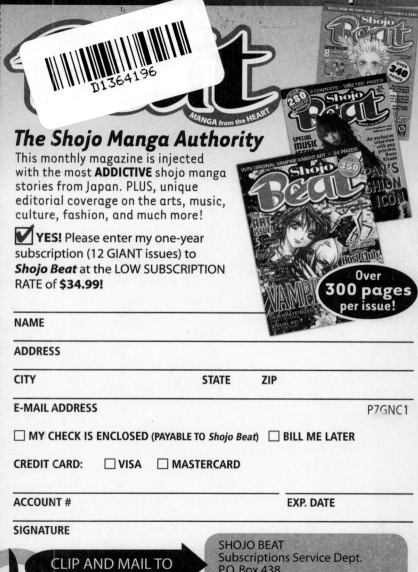